EARLY PRAISE FOR
PRETTY LITTLE WORLD

"When the literal walls come down among neighbors in adjoining Philadelphia row houses, three young families have the chance to create their own urban Utopia. But can they pull it off? Elizabeth LaBan and Melissa DePino pack *Pretty Little World* full of gourmet meals, marital scandal, inquisitive neighbors, and friendships whose bonds are sorely tested. The result is a skilled, funny, and highly engaging examination of family, love, and marriage in the City of Brotherly Love. This book is a win."

—Meg Mitchell Moore, author of *The Admissions*

PRAISE FOR *THE RESTAURANT CRITIC'S WIFE*

"A tender, charming, and deliciously diverting story about love, marriage, and how your restaurant-review sausage gets made. *The Restaurant Critic's Wife* is compulsively readable and richly detailed, a guilt-free treat that will have you devouring every word."

—Jennifer Weiner, #1 *New York Times* bestselling author of *Good in Bed*, *Best Friends Forever*, and *Who Do You Love*

"Elizabeth LaBan's novel *The Restaurant Critic's Wife* stirs in love and intrigue, making for a savory delight that pairs perfectly with your armchair. Prepare to be charmed!"

—Elin Hilderbrand, author of *The Rumor*

"A heartfelt and relatable look at a woman navigating the difficulties of marriage and motherhood—while struggling to maintain a sense of self. Written with charm, honesty, and an insider's eye into a usually hidden slice of the restaurant world, it's a winning recipe."

—Sarah Pekkanen, internationally bestselling author of *Things You Won't Say*

"In her debut novel for adults, Elizabeth LaBan cooks up a delectable buffet about motherhood, friendship, ambition, and romance (albeit one in need of a little more spice). She captures the essence of life with small children (smitten with a side of hysteria) and weaves a relatable, charming love story with the flair of an expert baker turning out a flawless lattice crust. LaBan's four-star story has the satisfying effect of a delicious meal shared with friends you can't wait to see again."

—Elisabeth Egan, author of *A Window Opens*

"Two things engage me when it comes to fiction—characters I want to spend more time with, and details, the juicier the better, from a world I'm curious about, but not likely to ever experience. Elizabeth LaBan's novel *The Restaurant Critic's Wife* has both . . . The best part? Ms. LaBan really is a restaurant critic's wife. Her husband writes for the *Philadelphia Inquirer*—which means that the wonderful details in the book both ring true and occasionally are."

—*New York Times, Motherlode*

"Author LaBan (*The Tragedy Paper*), who is married to a restaurant critic, excellently makes the joys and difficulties of young motherhood feel real on the page. Readers who are in the thick of raising a young family will enjoy, as will foodies looking for insight into the restaurant world."

—*Library Journal*

"The narrative flows effortlessly, and the dialogue is engaging and evocative. Lila and Sam's love and devotion, despite expected bumps along the way, provides a sensitive look at rediscovering yourself and your marriage."

—*Publishers Weekly*

"Thoroughly entertaining."

—*People*

"LaBan's writing . . . is like a dish of smooth custard—straightforward and a treat to take in. The detailed meal descriptions are likely to spark some hunger pangs, and the spicy and sympathetic Lila makes a perfect meal companion."

—Washington Independent Review of Books

"Readers will like LaBan's humor and breezy style, and many will relate to Lila's struggle to balance the demands of husband, kids, and job."

—Mary Ellen Quinn, *Booklist*

Pretty Little World

Pretty Little World

A Novel

*Elizabeth LaBan
and Melissa DePino*

LAKE UNION
PUBLISHING

Published by Lake Union Publishing, Seattle

www.apub.com

Amazon, the Amazon logo, and Lake Union Publishing are trademarks of Amazon.com, Inc., or its affiliates.

ISBN-13: 9781503941021
ISBN-10: 1503941027

Cover design by Ginger Design

Printed in the United States of America

For Auntie, Amanda, and Leah

CHAPTER ONE

If Celia had been paying attention, she might have noticed the signs—the pipes clanging much too loudly when she turned on the shower, the water pressure dropping off just enough to prevent her from completely rinsing the conditioner out of her long blond hair, the dirty water that had backed up into the utility sink in the laundry room. But Celia was never good at noticing things like that.

She had given herself twenty minutes to throw in the laundry, shower, blow-dry her hair, and get dressed before going downstairs to hurry the kids outside for some fresh air. It was tight, but in about half an hour she had the three of them—two boys and a girl all under the age of seven—dressed and out front to play. Two big orange cones blocked the end of the small tree-lined city street where she and her husband, Mark, had lived for the past eight years.

Celia dragged a card table through her narrow row house and onto the sidewalk and set up her laptop while the kids constructed an elaborate circus in the street using stuffed animals, Hula-Hoops, and a stool from the upstairs bathroom as a mini stage. As Celia opened her laptop, Hope, who lived two doors down, came outside with her daughter. Without a word, the little girl joined the circus by adding a trapeze, a jump rope she clumsily tied from one tree to another across the street. It occurred to Celia that it might be hard to untie the rope should a car come through, but she let it go. She'd let Hope worry about that.

"What are you doing?" Hope asked Celia, peering over her shoulder.

"Working out the details for Mark's birthday dinner tonight," Celia said, glancing up quickly to make sure that Ollie, her youngest, wasn't wandering toward the end of the street and into traffic.

"Really? What's there to work out? Leo's got everything ready. He's been awake since six o'clock cooking the whole meal. I think he's up to four courses, maybe five," Hope said.

"There's a lot more to a party than the meal," Celia said, not taking her eyes off the screen. "There's . . ."

"What the hell?" A scream came from directly behind them.

Celia and Hope turned to find Stephanie, who lived in the house in between theirs, standing on her stoop, her yoga pants soaked up to her ankles.

"What?" Celia asked. "What happened?"

"There's a flood in my house! I think the water's getting higher, and there's a strange noise coming from the wall between us," Stephanie said, hopping down her front steps in her bare feet.

Celia jumped up from her chair, causing it to tip and fall backward. "It better not have made it into my house," she said. "Not now."

"It's in my house," Stephanie said, taken aback. She pulled her wavy brown hair into a high ponytail, then bent down to squeeze the water from the hem of her pants. It made a small puddle on the sidewalk. "Didn't you hear me?"

"We're all connected, you know that," Celia said, taking another glance at the kids to make sure she had enough time to look inside her house without their getting into too much trouble.

"I have the kids," Hope said, glad not to be a part of the squabble or the water leak.

Stephanie reluctantly followed Celia inside, where Celia's husband, Mark, was already standing in a puddle of water, dressed for golf. He was crouched down in front of a huge water stain on their living room wall with a utility knife in his hand.

"I knew it," Celia said. "More damage."

Mark was an architect and was never good at leaving his work at the office. He had been working on their house since they moved in, and there was always some sort of construction project going on—exposed ceilings, old bricks missing their drywall covering, ripped-up tile.

"It's these goddamn hundred-year-old pipes," Mark said, jabbing his knife right into the wall.

"Did you turn off the water valve?" Celia asked.

Mark turned and glared.

"Well, I still hear something. Sorry. Keep cutting," she said.

Celia and Stephanie held their breath as Mark cut a rectangular hole in the wall. The soggy drywall yielded easily to the knife and the pressure of the water behind it, crumbling and falling away as the blade slid through. He pushed the drywall out of the way, and a rush of water ran over his hand and splashed to the floor, sending up a small geyser.

"Here's the culprit," Mark said, letting the water equalize before sticking his face into the hole as best he could. He moved back a little, reached up through the now trickling water, and grabbed a rusted and split pipe. Leaning in, he examined it. "Weird."

"What?" the women said in unison.

"There's a lot of space between us and the fire wall. That's strange," Mark said, leaning deeper into the hole. "Let me see."

They watched as he knocked around.

"Looks like there's a whole other layer of drywall behind this one," he said, using his knife to cut into it.

The drywall deep behind the pipes wasn't quite as wet as Mark's living room wall, so it took a minute to push the knife through and cut a small, jagged circle. Mark squinted through the hole to examine the brick behind it and realized suddenly that he was looking right into Stephanie and Chris's living room. Chris, who was mopping up the water, saw something poke through his wall and walked over to see what was going on. He leaned over and put his eye right next to the space, then jumped back, startled, to see another eye staring back at him.

"Oh my God," Chris called through the wall. "What just happened?"

"Is that Chris?" Stephanie said. "Why does he sound so close?"

"There's no fire wall here," Mark said.

"What do you mean, no fire wall?" Celia asked.

"There's supposed to be a brick fire wall between the houses."

"How the hell did they miss that during the inspection?" Chris asked. "No wonder you're always complaining about Stephanie's loud music."

"Looks like golf is out for today," Mark said, trying to calculate what he should do first.

"No way, man. We're going to make that tee time, come hell or high water," Chris said loudly. The women groaned.

Mark turned to Celia. "I should stay. We're going to need to fix this right away. We've only got. . ."

She shook her head and put her finger to her lips. "No, you need to go. It's your birthday. We can take care of this tomorrow."

Mark leaned toward Celia and whispered in her ear, "We need to tell them. This changes everything."

Celia shook her head vigorously. "Not now," she hissed. "It'll ruin their day. Just go play golf, and we'll tell them tomorrow."

"Caaarrrrrrr!"

Celia, Mark, Stephanie, and Chris hurried to their doors to find Hope, one hand aggressively in the air, shielding the kids from a small U-Haul that had lurched onto Emerson Street, run over the orange cones, and broken through the circus tightrope.

The driver's hands covered her face behind the tall windshield.

"What now?" Celia asked, exasperated.

"Will someone go talk to that person in the truck, please? They almost ran over Ollie. Couldn't they see the cones and the toys all over the street, not to mention the rope and the kids?" Hope ranted.

Hope's husband, Leo, came outside, car keys in hand.

"Is everything okay?" he asked, but didn't wait for an answer. "Some of the food is still on the stove. Please put it in the fridge when it's cool enough. I'm going to get the car. We're already late."

"Can you please give us a minute?" Hope said angrily. "We're in the middle of something here."

"Well, everybody better be ready when I get back. I don't want to miss our tee time," he said. Before he walked down the stoop, he turned to give Hope a kiss on her forehead. She let him. Then she raised her eyebrows and pointed to the truck, which hadn't moved at all.

"I'll take care of it," Mark said with a sigh, walking toward the U-Haul. The driver had her head down on the wheel, and Mark immediately noticed her long, silky dark hair.

"Hey," he said gently, knocking on the window. "Are you okay? Do you need some help?"

The driver looked up when she heard the tapping. Mark was surprised to see a familiar face.

"Nikki," he said, waiting as she rolled down the window. "What are you doing here?"

"Moving in," Nikki said. "I thought you knew my fiancé lives on this block?"

"Oh yeah, that's right," Mark said, flustered. What was his problem? She was just his hairdresser.

"As you can see, I'm having a little trouble with this truck," she said.

"Scoot over," Mark said, his hand on the door. He flashed his most charming smile, the one he usually saved for after his haircut was finished.

"Okay," Nikki said, sliding over to the passenger seat.

Mark pulled open the door and hoisted himself up. He started to adjust the seat, then realized he didn't have to. Nikki had long legs.

"Which house is it?" Mark asked, although he was pretty sure he knew. A single guy lived at the far end of the block. A lawyer, Mark thought. He had never had a conversation with him, but they waved whenever they walked by each other.

"The second to last one at the end, on the left." Nikki didn't say a word while Mark put the U-Haul in reverse and maneuvered it around the block. He backed in at the other end of the street and put it in park just as Will, Nikki's fiancé, his wet hair brushed perfectly back, dressed in a white T-shirt and dark jeans, came out the door.

"Thanks," Nikki said. "I couldn't have done that."

"Sure you could have," Mark said, getting out and nodding to Will.

"Hey, thanks for helping my girl," Will said, leaning in toward Mark. "I'm Will, by the way. I guess we haven't really met."

Mark smiled awkwardly as Nikki closed the passenger door and walked around the front of the truck.

"I'm Mark. Oh, and I almost forgot, we're having a dinner party on the street later. It happens to be my birthday today. You guys are welcome to join us." He gestured toward the group at the other end of the street staring in their direction.

Nikki looked at Will and raised her eyebrows expectantly. Will smiled but shook his head.

"Thanks, but maybe another time. I have something special planned for tonight," Will said, moving next to Nikki and putting his arm around her. "First night in the new house and all."

"Okay, but if you change your mind, the offer stands," Mark said.

Mark jogged back down the street, stepping over the makeshift circus rings, past Celia, Stephanie, Hope, and all the kids, toward Leo's waiting car. He took a bow, then waved as he opened the passenger door of the Subaru and got in.

Mark rolled down his window as Leo started to drive, and Chris waved from the back seat.

"Happy birthday to me," Mark called as they drove slowly away.

Celia, Stephanie, and Hope stood on the sidewalk and watched their husbands leave. The three women couldn't have been more different, but geography had brought them together, and after their children were born, they had become inseparable. Celia still looked like the lanky Midwestern cheerleader of her teenage years, while Hope was her opposite, dark-haired, East Coast, and sturdy. And Stephanie was tall and willowy, with long unruly hair and slow, fluid movements like someone who had dreamed of being a ballerina.

"He's lucky I let him go for the whole day," Hope said. "They better not be late tonight."

"Oh come on," Celia said. "You need to let boys be boys. Otherwise they'll get pent up and antsy, and that's not good for any of us."

"Hey, does anyone want a mimosa or something?" Stephanie asked, twisting her long ponytail above her head. "I want to do something fun while they're away, considering they left us to mop up the water."

"Not me," Celia said. "I need to clean up and get back to my list. I have a lot to do, and it'll be much easier with the guys out of our hair."

"Mimosa?" Stephanie asked Hope hopefully.

"Maybe later," Hope said, her eyebrows furrowed. "I should have written an end time on those free passes I gave Leo for his birthday. I'm worried they're going to get so caught up that we'll be left sitting here waiting for them all night."

"Oh my God, did you make Leo use one of those free passes for today?" Stephanie asked, dropping her ponytail and covering her mouth with her hand. "You mean, if he didn't have one to use he couldn't have gone?"

"No. I mean, I don't know. I guess he could have," Hope said, sorry she had mentioned the free passes she had gotten so much flack for. When Hope couldn't think of a single thing to buy for Leo's birthday last month—he certainly didn't need any more kitchen equipment—she came up with the idea for the free passes. With her daughter's construction paper she had made four colorful tickets, to be used whenever he wanted to do something away from the family.

"Well, I would have written him a free pass for today if you hadn't," Stephanie said, her brown eyes sparkling with the tiny threat. "Now I'm going to go mop up that water, and then I'm going to make a pitcher of mimosas—or maybe the other way around. I bet a yoga class's worth of babysitting that you both want one when you see it."

As much as the guys wanted off the block, the three women could spend days there, leaving only to get supplies for snacks and meals. They talked while the kids played, the cones blocking traffic on their tiny street. It wasn't quite as narrow as the famous Philadelphia alleys, but there was no parking allowed, and they took full advantage of that. In fact, the street was as much a part of their living space as their fifteen-foot-wide houses.

Emerson Street was nestled in the middle of four busy streets, just three and a half blocks from Walnut Street, the tony Center City Philadelphia shopping district. The block had a canopy of trees running all the way down. And every autumn, when the leaves had fallen, the men spent a day replacing the little white lights in the trees, so that every night it turned magical. Dog-walkers and shoppers went out of their way to walk down Emerson.

The houses themselves were charming, but small. The first floors mostly consisted of a combined living and dining room and a small kitchen, though Hope and Leo's kitchen was in their basement. Almost none of the houses had a bathroom on the first floor. And the majority of them had three bedrooms. But they all made the most of the space.

There was a tiny room off Stephanie and Chris's bedroom that started off as a closet, became a nursery when their son was born, and now served as Stephanie's office.

And they shared walls on both sides, which usually gave them great comfort, unless it meant sharing a flood or the occasional kitchen fire. If one of the women was alone at night, it was nice to know that someone was beside her, literally a few feet away.

Stephanie returned with a pitcher of mimosas and three cups and joined Hope, who was watching Celia already tapping away on her computer. Stephanie started to pour the drink into a plastic cup but stopped, distracted by the action at the end of the street.

"So check her out. I actually know her. She must be that cute lawyer's fiancée," Stephanie said, gesturing toward the far end of the block where a few guys were unpacking the U-Haul.

"You know her?" Celia asked.

"That's NikKAY," Stephanie said, tucking the pitcher and cups to the side of the stoop and standing up.

"Ohhh," Celia said, drawing out the word. "That explains why Mark helped her."

Stephanie had recognized Nikki right away. She had been cutting Chris's hair for years at a "just for men" salon that, when Chris first went there, seemed to Stephanie to be mildly threatening—like Hooters for haircuts. But one of Chris's fraternity brothers knew Nikki from his hometown, and he had vouched for her. Compared to how the other women working in the salon dressed, Nikki was tame, but still, no matter what she wore, she turned heads.

Nikki had recently started cutting Mark's hair, too, which provided an endless stream of innocent banter. When Chris and Mark joked about how hot Nikki was, saying her name with that extra emphasis on the last syllable—NikKAY—both Stephanie and Celia just rolled their eyes, but Hope still hadn't let Leo leave his male barber for her.

And after she overheard the other guys bragging about the way Nikki leaned into them when they were sitting in her chair, her large, perfect breasts gently pressing against the back of their heads while she smiled innocently at them in the mirror, she had ruled out any chance of it.

"But I have to say, she was very nice when I took Harvest in to have his hair cut," said Stephanie, distracted. "How do you think she can lift that huge box? She's so skinny."

"Beats me," Celia said. Catching herself staring, she abruptly turned her attention to Stephanie. "Wait—you brought your six-year-old to that salon?"

"Let's go down there and say hi," suggested Stephanie.

"I don't know," Hope said. "I should stay here with the kids, don't you think? And aren't you guys going to do anything about the holes in the walls?"

"Oh come on, the kids will be fine. We're right here. And I think we've all decided that the holes can wait until tomorrow. The water is turned off. What's a little flood and a missing wall between friends anyway?"

"Hi there!" shouted Stephanie as she bounded down the street, still in her wet yoga pants and barefoot, ponytail swinging, toward a startled Nikki, who had stopped in her tracks and stared while lifting a huge blue plastic bin from the U-Haul.

❧

By six, the kids were starving, and the husbands still weren't back from the golf course. Celia defrosted some meatballs, and Hope cooked up a pot of pasta. They let the kids eat outside on the stoops, since they were rushing in and out getting ready for Mark's birthday dinner. While the kids ate, Hope heated up the feast that Leo had spent all morning cooking. She tried not to get too angry about the guys' delayed return.

When the Subaru pulled up at 7:15 p.m., the white lights were twinkling in the trees, Ollie was asleep, and two card tables had been set for eleven—seven adults and four kids—including their across-the-street neighbor Mary, who lived alone and never refused an invitation.

Leo took over the food preparation and brought out each course one by one to show it off: homemade tomato and basil soup; chicken Milanese with baby greens tossed in fresh lemon juice and olive oil, topped with shaved Locatelli Romano; perfect rounds of eggplant parmesan with smoked mozzarella. For dessert, he had made a spectacular strawberry tart that looked even more professional than the one Celia had seen at the bakery the day before.

"So, Mark, how does it feel to be getting old?" barked Mary, by far the oldest at the table, after he had blown out the candles and the kids had disappeared into one of the houses, leaving half-eaten pieces of tart in their wake. "I remember when I turned forty," she said with a sigh. "That was right about the time I started losing control of my bladder."

"Mary, my dear, you always know just the right thing to say," Mark quipped. "But to answer your question . . . tired."

"Come on, Mark, you've got the life of leisure. That beautiful Midwestern wife of yours takes care of everything," Leo said, winking at Celia.

"I couldn't ask for anything more," Mark said, putting his arm around Celia's petite shoulders and giving her a squeeze. "Except maybe another five hundred square feet in that tiny house back there and, of course, control of my bladder until a ripe old age."

Celia laughed, flashing her dimples and straight white teeth.

"I did want to say something to everyone, though," Mark said, uncharacteristically sappy from all the beer and attention.

He stood up, leaning on the back of Celia's chair. "I want you all to know that I am really touched by this. When we moved to Philadelphia, we never imagined that we would be lucky enough to live in a place like this with all of you. You all mean so much to us—me, Celia, and the kids. Our family might be back in Kansas, but you're all family to us here."

"What the hell did you expect?" Mary snapped. "In my day—of course they're all dead or divorced now—our best friends lived right here on Emerson Street. We raised our families together, just like you people."

"Thanks for those encouraging words, Mary," Leo said, taking another bite of strawberry tart. "I'd like to think that we'll all be right here for a long time, having many more meals like this."

"Well, I wish you the best, Mark," said Mary, pushing herself up from her chair and bracing herself on the table. "Enjoy the last moments of your youth while you've still got them. It's all downhill after forty."

Mary ambled to her door, mumbling about her new knees and new hip. The door slammed behind her, and Mark, who was still standing, cleared his throat and ran his hand slowly through his hair. He looked around the table at everyone and knew he couldn't let this night go by without sharing their big secret, the one he and Celia both dreaded saying out loud. His eyes lost their sarcastic twinkle and suddenly looked serious.

"There's something that Celia and I have to come clean about. We haven't been completely honest with you lately."

Celia looked down. "Oh, sweets, do we have to do this right now?" she asked quietly.

"It's time, Ceil," he said. "They need to know."

"Well, what is it already?" Stephanie pressed. "You can tell us anything."

"Spill it, guys," Chris said.

Celia looked around the table. "We've decided to put the house up for sale."

"You've *what*?" Hope said, her words so forceful that a bit of crust came out with them. She looked at Leo, who was about to take another bite of the tart, but instead put his fork down and pushed his plate away.

Stephanie rolled her eyes. "Yeah, right," she said dismissively. "You've been talking about this for years, and you never follow through." She looked from Mark to Celia. "Or did you?"

"We've called the real estate agent," Mark said. "The sign goes up in a week."

"No wonder you were painting last weekend," Chris said. "Man, it sucks that you have that big hole in your wall now."

"No kidding," Mark said.

"I can't believe you waited so long to tell us," Stephanie said, looking directly at Mark.

"I'm sorry about that," Celia said. "We shouldn't have kept it from you. But it's hard for us, too, and we didn't want you to try to talk us out of it again. We've waited as long as we could, but now we just don't see any other choice. Our house is too small."

"This is crazy. We can figure this out. If you don't want to move, you don't have to. There are lots of things you can do with your house," Hope said, her voice a little panicked.

"I've done everything I can do with that house. There's not one more inch of usable space," Mark said.

"He's right, guys. Ever since Ollie was born, the four walls have just been closing in on Mark. On us," Celia said.

"But what will we do without you?" Stephanie asked. She shook her head, trying not to cry.

Hope leaned forward in her chair. "I've got it! Listen, really. You can move the kids to the upstairs bedroom, reconfigure the house. Or you could finish the basement, really finish it this time, not just throw a couch and television down there. Or build another floor on top. Something. There's got to be something you can do."

Celia shook her head. "It's different for you guys. We have three kids jammed in that small space, and Mark is all about space. It's what he does for a living. And besides, can you imagine having three teenagers in that house? It's just not feasible."

"But Ollie's not even two!" Stephanie cried.

"We're trying to think with our heads, Stephanie, not with our hearts. We're trying to actually plan for the future, not just live for today," Celia said calmly.

"Don't do that now," Hope said. "Plan for the future another time. We're not the only ones who think we're a family—Mark just said so himself. Don't we matter more than a few hundred square feet?"

"Please, we've been through it a hundred times. There is no other answer," Mark said quietly, avoiding their eyes. "We don't want to go any more than you don't want us to go."

"Then why do it? It just doesn't make sense," Hope said, standing up so suddenly that she almost knocked the white plastic chair over behind her.

"Things don't have to change," Celia said, turning to look up at her.

"I don't see how they won't," Stephanie said. "The kids are together every weekend, all weekend, and most weeknights they're either playing outside or in my basement. How will that not change if you're not right next door? Think about it. When was the last time we actually had to talk on the phone? Two weeks ago? If you move, that will probably be the only way we talk. Who will be there when you open your front door? And how will you be able to come play cards after the kids are asleep? Do you think your baby monitor is going to work in my house if you move off the block?"

"I just don't understand how you can do this," Hope said.

"I need to go in," Stephanie said, walking to her house and up her stoop.

"Me too," Hope said.

Hope and Stephanie closed their doors at the same time, creating a loud slamming noise that made Celia jump.

"You know, it's only because they love you guys," Chris said by way of an apology. "They'll get over it. We'll all be fine."

"Thanks, buddy," Mark said. "Thanks for saying that, even if you don't really think so."

"No, really, I get it. All good things have to come to an end. Just like your thirties," Chris said, standing and picking up a pile of dishes. "Let's get the kids to bed. I'll send yours out, okay?"

"Right behind you," said Leo, grabbing a few more dishes and heading in to get his daughter, Shoshanna. He looked back at Mark and Celia with a sideways smile. "Did you have to tell us tonight? Now this is what people are going to remember, not my luscious tart."

"Well, that went well," Mark whispered a few minutes later to Celia as they stood in front of the hole in the wall that led to Stephanie and Chris's. Celia had pushed a small bookshelf in front of it.

"What did you expect?" she asked. "This isn't going to be easy, but we've made the decision. What's done is done."

On the other side of the wall, Stephanie stood staring at the little hole.

"Chris!" she yelled, not bothering to lower her voice. "Chris! Come here. Hurry!"

"What is it?" Chris called as he made his way down the stairs.

"I know what we have to do," Stephanie said, not waiting for him to join her. She walked to the hole, which was big enough to put her hand into. She grabbed the drywall at the bottom of the circle and pulled. It was so soaked by now that it was easy. Once she started, she couldn't stop. She kept pulling, and the wall kept falling away, making the hole bigger and bigger.

"What are you doing?" Chris yelled when he reached her. "Have you lost your mind?"

Stephanie took a step back and looked at what she had done. Now the hole was almost as big on their side as it was on Mark and Celia's side. In fact, if she pushed the bookshelf back, Stephanie thought, she would actually be able to walk right into their house.

"I have not lost my mind. Just the opposite. I'm the only one who's thinking clearly around here," Stephanie said, pointing to the hole. "I have the answer. They want space? I'll give them space! We'll take down the wall."

CHAPTER TWO

Hope considered the pregnancy test in her sock drawer. It was the last one left in a three-pack she had bought more than a year ago. She fished around until she found the black plastic bag that concealed it, then went to the bathroom. Before she unwrapped it, she wanted to make sure she hadn't gotten her period, which was really just barely a day late anyway. It didn't take much detective work to find out she didn't need to use it. She sighed and stashed the pregnancy test back in the drawer.

When she got downstairs, Leo was in the kitchen with Shoshanna. He was standing at the counter eating Grape-Nuts with Greek yogurt and some sort of berries; Hope couldn't tell what they were. He was always going to random farmers' markets around the city and coming home with exotic fruits. Shoshanna, however, was munching on Captain Crunch.

"Hi, sweetie," she said to Shoshanna as she walked by, stopping to run her hand down her daughter's chin-length chestnut bob. Shoshanna had insisted on the same haircut as her mother, and Hope had relented, pained to see Shoshanna's long silky hair fall onto the salon floor and secretly proud at the same time.

"Good morning," she said to Leo, deciding that the fact that she wasn't pregnant wasn't worthy of notification.

"Ah! *Bonjour, mon petit chou-chou*," Leo said, leaning in for a kiss. Even though he was wearing the same frayed plaid robe that he'd had since college, and his light brown wavy hair was sticking up everywhere, Hope couldn't help but find him incredibly appealing. The same slow sexiness that he had exuded when they first met was still there, maybe even more so as he got older.

Hope leaned in distractedly to accept her husband's kiss, aware of his slightly overgrown mustache and goatee grazing the skin between her mouth and nose.

"Sorry, but I used the last of the milk on Shoshie's cereal," he said as he moved away, still chewing the same Grape-Nuts.

"Okay," Hope said, scrunching her mouth to the side while she decided what to do. For a second she thought about skipping breakfast altogether; she was supposed to play tennis in a little while. But she was hungry, and all the munching was making her even hungrier.

"I'll go to Celia's and get some," she said, wondering what Celia was cooking up for breakfast this morning. Besides, she was desperate to talk to her. She had been awake most of the night obsessing about ways they could reconfigure their house, real changes to give them the space they needed. Maybe if she could be more rational, she'd be able to change Celia's mind about moving. She'd done it before. The "For Sale" sign wasn't up yet. There was still time.

Hope slipped into her flip-flops and pulled open the door. It was a beautiful fall morning, cool but bright. She took a minute to admire the orange and yellow winter pansies that rose above the green-painted wood window box. For about a week she thought she'd killed them with too much Miracle-Gro. Leo always told her you could overdo it, but she hadn't believed him. This time, though, she'd put way too much in—triple the recommended amount. And sure enough, all the flowers had disappeared. But now they were coming back brighter than ever.

Hope fingered one of the soft petals, walked past Stephanie's to Celia's, climbed up the steps, and knocked.

She could hear people moving around inside. In fact, it sounded unusually busy. Celia was always organized with the three kids, and at this time of morning Hope would have expected her to have them all sitting at the table, Ollie strapped into his wooden restaurant high chair while Celia cooked. She rarely gave them cold cereal, even though she was by herself most weekend mornings. Mark was usually long gone— already deep into one house project or another.

Hope waited, but nobody answered. She knocked again.

"Hello?" Hope called. "I can hear you in there."

She moved to the far side of the stoop and, holding onto the railing, pushed her body over so she could look in the window. Nobody was sitting at the big round table in the kitchen at the back of the house, and Celia was not in her usual morning position in front of the stove. Hope moved her eyes to the room just in front of the door. The bookshelf had been pushed away from the hole in the wall, the hole on the other side was now much bigger, and the kids were running back and forth between the houses.

"Hey," Hope called, moving back to the door. "Let me in!" She banged hard three times.

Hope was just about to get down on her knees to open the mail slot and yell through it when Celia pulled open the door, Ollie in her arms.

"Hi," she said, like there was nothing unusual going on. "Sorry that took so long."

Celia took a step back and held the door open. Hope hesitated for a second and then walked in, joining everybody on Celia's side of the wall.

"How did the other hole get so big?" Hope asked, a little annoyed that something had changed and she was the last to find out about it.

"Stephanie said it was so wet it just fell away," Celia said. "I didn't realize until this morning because we had that bookshelf there. But

I made some biscuits and gravy, and Stephanie smelled them, and Harvest started knocking on the back of the bookshelf. The next thing we knew, it was like this."

"Yeah, it's actually kind of cool if you think about it. We always joked about digging a tunnel between the houses. Now we have one," Stephanie said.

"I guess," Hope said, starting to feel more left out. She had completely forgotten about the milk, the house plans, and her need to move things along so she wouldn't be late for the tennis clinic.

"Yep, enjoy it while it lasts. Mark's at Home Depot getting the drywall right now. He thinks he fixed it, and the water's back on, but we have a plumber coming sometime this week to make sure it won't happen again. Once that's done, he's expecting your husbands to help put this wall back up."

Stephanie stopped fidgeting with her hair and looked at Celia. "Yeah, about that," she said. "There's something I wanted to, um, suggest. I have an amazing idea. At least I think it's an amazing idea. It could be the solution to our problem. But you've got to have an open mind, okay?"

Hope and Celia both looked at Stephanie for a minute. Then Hope turned to Celia.

"Anyway, I needed some milk," Hope said.

"Just go on in and get it," Celia said, pointing over her shoulder toward the kitchen.

"No, wait, guys, don't you want to hear my idea?" Stephanie asked, eyes wide and head nodding.

Celia sighed. "Well, I guess I should be grateful that you're speaking to me at all. Let's have it. What's your idea?"

"Picture this," Stephanie said, waving her hands along the damaged living room wall like Vanna White. "Space beyond your wildest dreams. The house that you always imagined, 24/7 child care, gourmet meals, and tennis partners on call. Friends to watch movies with and play cards with at any time of day. Six hands to clean."

"Sounds like a dream to me," Celia said.

"No, that's just it. It doesn't have to be a dream. We can make it happen. It can be a reality right here on Emerson Street."

"What are you talking about?" Hope asked, milk in hand, ready to get back to her day.

"A commune."

"A commune?" Celia and Hope said together.

"That's right," Stephanie said. "A commune or a co-op or a multiple-family dwelling, whatever you want to call it."

"You've gone off your rocker," Celia said.

"Please, Stephanie, this is no time for jokes. Our best friends are abandoning us. It's crisis time," Hope said.

"Exactly. And a crisis calls for action, right? This," Stephanie said, sweeping her arms along the wall, "is the ultimate in taking action. The way I see it, Mark wants more space. We all want the company, and who doesn't want extra hands around to pick up the slack with the kids and the housework? I propose taking down this wall and then taking down the wall between my house and Hope's. We can leave our upstairs rooms the way they are. We would have one huge living area. Mark could do the plans."

"Have you been reading your hippie books and listening to the Grateful Dead again?" Hope asked.

"Maybe," Stephanie said, smiling.

"Is something like that even possible?" Hope asked. "I mean, wouldn't the whole place collapse?"

"Not if you installed the right steel beams. Mark told me that he thinks these houses might have been joined at one time because of the missing fire wall."

"Stephanie, I love that you want us to stay so much you would be willing to demolish part of your house, but I think you know as well as I do that there is no way we would go ahead and even think about something like that," Celia said. "I'm sorry to say this, guys, but I can't imagine anything that would keep us here at this point."

❧

Later that day word spread that a burglar had broken into Mary's house. Apparently someone put a brick into her garden glove and threw it through her back window, climbed in, and stole her jewelry and silver. She had lived there for thirty-one years without any problems and rarely left her house now, but the person broke in during the short time she was out. Mary's house was on the other side of the street from Stephanie, Celia, and Hope, and backed onto a tiny alley that seemed a little creepy to them.

"I've always been grateful that we live on this side of the street," Hope whispered to Stephanie as they sat on Hope's stoop watching the repair people go in and out with new locks and windowpanes.

"Me too," Stephanie whispered back.

The day had gotten away from them, and now all the dads and kids were at Mark and Celia's—the men watching the Eagles game and the kids casting and directing a Harry Potter play. It was up to Hope and Stephanie to get food for the kids' lunches tomorrow, and Celia had given Hope her list.

"Come on, if we're going to go shopping, we should get it over with," Stephanie said, lightly tapping Hope's thigh as she got up.

They fell into a quiet rhythm as they walked to the small, overpriced grocery store two blocks away.

"I think I'm just going to get those prepackaged organic smoothie drinks," Stephanie said. "I'm tired of making lunches."

"Me too. I think I'll get the Lunchables. The kids like the make-your-own-pizza version," Hope said. She took out Celia's list and read it. "Listen to this: bananas, apples, whole-grain bread, with a note to make sure the fiber count is at least three grams, sliced turkey, and sliced ham."

"You know, Celia could make all the kids' lunches."

"What are you talking about? She's too busy to do that."

Stephanie turned slowly to face Hope. "She wouldn't be if we lived in a commune."

"Do you hear yourself talking?" Hope asked. "People do not break walls down between their homes no matter how much they like each other. It just isn't done."

"It could be," Stephanie said. "Mark can figure it out—whatever support it needs, he can do that, come up with some plans."

"You know it's never going to happen. Besides, who in the world would live in a commune?"

"We would! We practically do now! Can't you picture it? It would be so great, Hope."

"I'm not saying that it wouldn't be fun. I'm just saying that you need to be realistic. Besides, what would Chris say about it?"

"He's totally in. He thinks it's a great idea. He loves having all the kids around, and it'll make it even easier for him to hang out with the guys and watch games and stuff."

They stopped at the corner across from the supermarket.

"And what about the break-in at Mary's? Wouldn't you feel safer if we were together? Who's going to break into a house where six adults live?" asked Stephanie.

"Let's just say that you could talk me into it—and I'm not saying that you can, because I don't think it's logistically possible—but I know you would never be able to talk Celia and Mark into it. Celia would worry about what people think. And if the walls are closing in on Mark now, would he really want two more kids in his household? Besides, it's just not normal. Everyone would make fun of us—of the kids."

"Normal," Stephanie said. "I hate that word. What's normal anyway? How many people eat dinner out on their city street with two other families most nights of the week? And how many other people are lucky enough to live next to the two families they like best in the world?"

~

That night in bed, after the barbecue was all cleaned up and everyone was in their own house, Hope wondered if anyone was using the hole. Even though she hadn't let on to Stephanie, Hope imagined what it could be like. In the morning there would be nothing separating them. They could all come down in their pajamas. With the walls down, they could have a huge kitchen and living area. It would be like the times they went to Stephanie's sister's house at the Jersey shore and they all lounged around eating pancakes. The kids could play all day, and there would always be someone to watch Shoshanna if a chance to play tennis came up. And Shoshanna would never be lonely—even if she turned out to be an only child. She would have four built-in brothers and sisters.

"What do you think it would be like to live with everyone in one big house?" Hope asked Leo. They were lying side by side in bed reading, but Hope hadn't actually read a word of the book she was holding, a collection of Raymond Carver short stories. Leo was deep into the seventh Harry Potter book.

"Nice," he mumbled, keeping his eyes on his book. A second later he turned the page.

"You do? Think it would be nice?" Hope asked, sitting up a little and turning to face him.

"What are you talking about?" he asked, clearly annoyed at the interruption.

"Well, since I'm not pregnant, and since everyone is talking about living together . . ."

"Wait a minute, did you think you were pregnant?" Leo said, reluctantly marking his place in the book and closing it. He looked at her.

"No, not really. I guess it was just wishful thinking. My period wasn't even really late," Hope said, then stopped. She rolled her eyes to the side in anticipation of the tears that usually came when they talked about this, but there were none.

"You know Mary's house was broken into. Someone stole her dead husband's wedding ring. It's just that if we lived with everyone, I would feel safer." She looked at Leo.

"Are you serious?" he asked. "Is this something you're really talking about? Like what? Move to a bigger house together?"

"No, break down the walls between our houses. It's Stephanie's idea. A way to keep us all together. A way that Mark and Celia could get the space they need and not have to leave us."

Leo was quiet for so long she thought for a few minutes that he was feeling the same way she did.

"It doesn't make any sense," he said. "You can't knock down the walls. And even if you could, what if we want to move one day? How would we sell our portion of the house? And what about privacy? How would we ever have sex if we were all living together?"

Hope had to admit that Leo had a few good points. But the truth was she didn't care about any of them right now. She even thought that she might be able to deal with the guys trying to get Leo to join them at the bar on the corner a few nights a week. Maybe she wouldn't even make him use his free passes for that.

"Don't you like things the way they are?" Leo asked. "I love being with everyone out there as much as you do, but I also like coming home and closing the door behind us."

"I like things the way they are, too, but if we don't do something, everything is going to change anyway," Hope insisted. "When Stephanie mentioned it this morning, I thought it was just another one of her crazy ideas, but now I'm not so sure. It isn't like we haven't joked about this sort of thing a million times."

"Is this about not wanting to be left out?" Leo asked.

"Partly, I guess," Hope answered honestly. "But I think it's more than that. I don't know."

Hope paused and thought back to the scene that morning, to their standing on either side of the hole, no walls between them. "I have to go downstairs. I have all the kids here first thing tomorrow. Stephanie has a yoga class, and Celia has an important interview for that promotion she's after. I'll have to get everyone to school. I thought I'd make some Pillsbury cinnamon buns tonight so everyone can eat fast." Hope pushed the quilt off and got up. She went over to Leo's side and kissed him.

"I'll be back soon," she said.

Leo picked up the heavy book again, but he couldn't focus. He knew they had something special on the street, something unusual. But to live with everyone? It was an insane idea, but for some reason it did sound intriguing. It could mean more time with the guys without having to come up with one excuse or another. More important, it would mean more people to cook for, and more people to appreciate what he cooked, just like when he lived in that great Paris apartment with his cooking school friends. They were five adults living together—why would this be much different?

And although Leo unsuccessfully tried to stop the thought from forming, he wondered if it might be nice to have Stephanie around more. There was just something about her that made him feel relaxed and free. He knew that there was an undeniable, and of course innocent, connection between them. Instead of pretending he found a fabulous wine that he thought only she would appreciate, or that he needed a lemon or an egg, or help with his mountain pose, they could be living together.

All right, he told himself, *it's worth entertaining. If this is what Hope really wants, why fight it?* He rarely won once she set her mind to things anyway.

～

Leo wrinkled his nose. The smell of Hope's reheated processed cinnamon buns was interfering with his cappuccino making. It was all about smelling and listening. Listening to the milk sizzle, just enough but not too much, in the nonstick pan. Listening to the coffee bubble up and smelling the exact moment when it was ready, when it got a little creamy on top. He turned off both burners, one after the other, and poured the milk into a metal pitcher as Hope reached around him for forks and cups. All the kids were sitting at their kitchen table gobbling up the buns. Leo watched for a second then shook his head. It wouldn't have taken much longer for Hope to make the buns from scratch, using yeast, flour, brown sugar, and the special cinnamon he bought recently at Fante's in the Italian Market.

"Want one?" Hope asked, thrusting the trans-fat-and-preservative-laden confection in front of him as he gently whipped the milk with his tiny electric whisk.

"No thanks," he said, putting down the pitcher and pouring the dark coffee into two mugs that had raw sugar waiting in the bottom. He stirred until it dissolved, then lifted the milk and scooped the heaviest off with a spoon, dropping it into the cups. He took his time adding the rest of the milk, then stood back to admire his perfect creations. He loved that first sip when the stiffer milk got caught in his mustache.

"Here it is," Leo said, lifting a cup toward Hope. Hope shook her head.

"No thanks," she said, getting Shoshanna another bun. "It's a good thing I made three batches of these. The kids love them."

"You don't want any? Look at this, it's beautiful," Leo said.

"No, it's too heavy and sweet for me at this time of day," Hope said.

"This is the exact time of day when it isn't too heavy and sweet," Leo protested.

Hope smirked and shook her head as she eased the last bun out of the pan and plopped it on Shoshanna's plate.

"Hey, you know what the rabbi said—if you don't indulge your spouse, he or she will go elsewhere," Leo said, throwing out their usual line when one disappointed the other.

"Yeah, well, he was talking about sex," Hope said quietly, leaning in toward Leo and changing her smirk to a smile. "And I would rather do that than drink the cappuccino. We have to go anyway."

While Hope worked to get the kids up the stairs and out the door, Leo stood on the stoop hoping Mark or Chris might emerge so that he could offer one of them the other cappuccino. He couldn't stand that the beautiful cup might go to waste.

"Bye, see you, Daddy," Shoshanna called.

"Bye, Daddy Leo," the other kids echoed.

"Bye, sweetie," Hope said, waving.

Leo tried Chris's door first, then Mark's, but there was no answer at either house. He was just deciding that having two cappuccinos for himself this morning wouldn't be the worst thing in the world when Stephanie turned the corner holding her yoga mat and looking as relaxed and spacey as ever.

"Hi," she called to him.

Without a word he handed her the still-steaming mug. She raised her eyebrows, then took a sip. She didn't bother to wipe the perfect foam from her upper lip as she leaned in to smell the hot drink.

"That is the best cappuccino I have ever had," Stephanie said dreamily. "Can you make this for me every morning?"

CHAPTER THREE

Mark wandered through the dark, cool, and immensely quiet aisles of the Old City Lighting Emporium, navigating around the collection of disembodied chandeliers, cast-off bronze pole lamps, and piles of tarnished sconces ripped from colonial Philadelphia row homes that had been, inevitably, sold to some developer and filled with generic Home Depot fixtures. Ever since Ollie was born, Mark found himself escaping to places like this, trying to ignore that nagging feeling of coming unglued. It's not that he didn't love Ollie—of course he did— but his arrival had put Mark firmly over the edge in a life that had already stretched him in unexpected ways.

Celia had pushed hard for Ollie, but Mark had been hesitant. Ted and Lu were already in school, and he had just gotten his bearings. Even so, she had wanted another baby desperately, and he had always had a hard time disappointing her, especially after the sacrifices she had made. They had moved east and away from her family because of his job, and she had left Kansas without a complaint. In fact, she had been so blindly proud of him that he still felt guilty about it all these years later.

"Hey, you."

Mark turned and stared at the woman standing behind him. It was Nikki, the hairdresser, again.

"Shopping for a client, or just hiding?" she asked.

"Oh, hey, you startled me. You can't go sneaking up on people like that."

"So, which one?" she persisted, leaning against a cluttered metal shelf, arms crossed, waiting.

"Which what?" he asked, turning to face her but leaning back against the wall behind him, putting a little extra distance between them, not at all sure what the question had been or how he should answer.

"Shopping or hiding?"

To his own surprise, he quickly recovered. "Always hiding. Even when I'm shopping," he said. "Are you getting settled into your new house?"

"Yep. I'm becoming domesticated," she teased, "just like the rest of you old married people." She took a step closer to him, just close enough that he could smell her shampoo—was it lemon? No doubt one of those expensive salon products that she always insisted he needed. He fingered his coarse dark hair, remembering suddenly that she had told him he needed conditioner, which he never bought, for what she called his "Dago fro." He'd been taken aback the first time she teased him about it, but that was Nikki. She was sweet and naive, even to the point of seeming a bit ditzy, but then she'd say something so brutally honest or perceptive that you felt uncomfortable. He was convinced that she had no idea how incredibly sexy that was.

"You know what they say, you're not complete until you're married . . . then you're finished," he said.

"Ha, ha, you're hysterical. I happen to be very excited about my wedding, and my marriage, too," she said. "Thanks for helping me. The U-Haul really threw me off."

How old was she? He had never been good at judging women's ages. She looked to be in her twenties, but something in her eyes told him she was at least thirty.

"So I guess I'll see you back in the neighborhood?"

Mark didn't know if that meant he should be the one to leave or if Nikki would go first.

"Okay then, see you there," he said, and too abruptly he turned, waved, and jogged down the wide staircase and out the double glass doors. He stood squinting in the midafternoon sun on the corner of Second and Arch, feeling silly. He was forty years old, a grown man, for God's sake, and he had just regressed into an awkward fifteen-year-old who didn't know how to hold a conversation with a good-looking woman. He stood for a moment marveling at the fact that he still felt like the guy who was everyone's best friend but nobody's boyfriend. Propelled by something he couldn't name, instead of going home, he turned around and went back in.

When he reached the second floor again, she was still in the same spot, squatting down examining what looked like a miniature antique flashlight, turning it over, trying unsuccessfully to unscrew the bulb.

"Let me take a look at that," he said, standing behind her. "You know, I *am* a professional."

She glanced up, not quite sure who he was for a moment, his face obscured because of the light pouring in through the high arched window behind him.

"Mark? You're back." Was that a note of relief he detected in her voice? He couldn't be sure.

"So I was on my way over to Homegrown to look at some doorknobs and drawer pulls, very exciting, I know. You interested in coming along?"

Nikki stood up, tugging at her short skirt and tucking a few loose strands of long dark hair behind her ears. She smiled warmly, like she had been waiting all day for an invitation. "Sure, why not?"

Mark couldn't get it out of his head. All week, he kept replaying the scene in his mind, trying to figure out what had happened, what it had meant, if anything. He hadn't done anything wrong. Celia never asked about his day anymore, so he didn't have to lie—not that he would, necessarily. By the time he got home, she was asleep, a *Sex and the City* rerun playing on the television in their bedroom. To his relief, the next morning was so hectic getting the kids off to school that the events of the previous day never came up. This was what their life was like now. Entire days and nights passed without their even knowing what had filled the other's time.

It was the car ride home that got him in the end. He and Nikki had spent the whole afternoon in and out of the shops in Old City, doing what he loved most—perfecting the details of his latest project, finding the small accents that would make his clients' home on Twenty-First Street an authentic representation of their personal style. Sometime between the handwoven dish towels and 1950s coffee table, perfectly restored, they had fallen into an oddly comfortable rhythm, like they were old high school friends who had hung out in each other's basements, listening to music and sneaking beer when their parents weren't home. He had completely forgotten who he was or what he was supposed to be doing during those few short hours. For what felt like the first time in a really long time, he was just living in the moments as they unfolded.

"So what made you want to be an architect?" she'd asked over a devil's food cupcake with cream cheese frosting in the tiniest of bakeries.

"A well-intentioned but misinformed guidance counselor. How else do we end up being what we are?" Mark had told this story before, and it was always good for a laugh, but this time he stopped, wondering why all of a sudden it seemed more sad than funny.

"Tell me about it," she said.

"So I'm seventeen years old, a shy, skinny Italian kid in a suburban Kansas high school filled with strapping Midwestern jocks. I've got two older brothers who both lettered in varsity sports and dated at least one cheerleader; maybe it was the same one, I can't be sure. Then there's me. My favorite after-school activity is the drama club."

"Ah-ha. I can see where this might be going. An athletic underachiever."

"Precisely."

"Go on."

"This may surprise you after witnessing my starlike qualities, but I'm not the lead in the play, which may have been somewhat acceptable to Dad and the strapping peers, but I am the best, the foremost, set designer that ever set foot on the eastern edge of Kansas."

"Wow, the chicks must have dug you."

"Right again. So I go to my guidance counselor to discuss college applications. But, of course, I'm seventeen, no clue what I want to do but get out of Kansas."

"But you were so talented! Kansas needed you," she teased, smiling, wondering why she had never noticed how funny he was.

"I tell the guy—now mind you, he's wearing those thick black-rimmed glasses, not the hip kind, either, and something like a pale blue short-sleeved dress shirt with one of those eighties knitted square ties—I don't really like any of my classes except art. And I'm really good at making the sets for the plays. Do you know what he decides in that fateful moment?"

"I can only guess," she said, lips pursed, slowly shaking her head in mock sympathy.

"He tells me that I should be an architect, that the only career for someone who likes making sets for a play is architecture. Four years of undergrad, then three and a half more grueling years at Cornell. So here I am. An architect."

"Wow, but you ended up liking it, right?"

"I guess that's the million-dollar question. Do I like it? I don't know. Do you like cutting people's hair?"

She sat for a moment, chin propped in the palm of her hand, thinking.

"Some days."

Mark reached across the table and gave her free hand a quick pat.

"Well, there you have it. Jobs are all the same. Some days you like them, and some days you don't."

He hadn't anticipated it when he asked if Nikki needed a ride home, but once they were alone inside the old Mercedes station wagon, the entire mood changed. Doors and windows closed, sitting inches apart with nowhere to look but straight ahead or at each other, the tension between them was palpable for the fifteen minutes or so it took to get from Old City back to Emerson Street. Mark sat silently, awkwardly, almost embarrassed by the three car seats behind them, with nothing at all to say after an afternoon of easy conversation, staring at the traffic on Market Street ahead of him, leaning over to change the radio station every few minutes. When they finally parked the car, Nikki made an excuse about needing milk before going home. Mark walked away feeling disoriented, hands shaking, with a tiny voice telling him it was a good thing he knew right from wrong. Another man could be headed for trouble after an encounter like that.

❧

Celia did her usual speed walk home, her iPhone blasting the soundtrack from *O Brother, Where Art Thou?* She was always running late, carrying too many bags. She turned the corner to Emerson Street, hoping that there would be a clear path to her door. Today had not been a good day, and all she wanted to do was get the kids settled and go back to her computer.

"Well hello, Celia," Leo bellowed, a half-full glass of wine in one thick hand, the other waving high in the air like he was hailing a cab. *Nearly made it,* she thought. The last thing she wanted was to have another conversation now about their moving.

Celia jiggled her key into its hole. *Damn lock. Nothing ever works right in this house,* she thought. Mark had recently replaced the doorknob with a fancy antique piece in preparation for showing the house. He said he thought it looked more authentic, but the lock hadn't worked smoothly since. He always needed a project, she got it, but why did it have to be the house that they were living in? Couldn't he just concentrate on his clients' renovation projects? For once, she just wanted to live somewhere where there was no construction going on. No drywall dust, no half-painted walls, no exposed ceilings or hanging wires. Just a nice, clean, finished house.

"Oh, hey, Leo," she said, wishing that she could just open the door and let her babysitter go for the night. She glanced at Leo over her shoulder, never straying from her assault on the lock.

"Here, let me help you with that," Leo said, handing her his stemless wine glass and taking the keys. "Go ahead, drink it. It looks like you need it more than I do."

"Thanks," she said, holding the glass but not drinking as Leo pushed open her front door. "Got to go. Thanks again."

Celia shut the door behind her, relieved not to have to get into it with Leo. Inside, it was unbelievably quiet. Where were the kids and the babysitter? Usually the house was chaos this time of night, with Lu throwing a fit because Ted wouldn't let her have a turn on the Wii and Ollie melting down from a long day in the park, throwing mashed blueberries at anyone who happened to be sitting across the table from him.

Celia opened the basement door and climbed down the narrow steps, her right hand holding the white stucco wall for balance. Nope—not on the video games. She headed back up to the first floor, promptly dismissing the idea of throwing in a load of wash while she was downstairs. She could take care of that in the morning as usual.

As the human resources director for a local consulting firm, she was pretty sure she had devised a foolproof system for keeping her house in order: laundry before work on weekdays, vacuuming at night, and shopping and cleaning on Saturday mornings. Growing up the youngest of seven children could also have had something to do with it. Never getting any attention, she had always said, made her self-sufficient, and self-sufficiency was the key to an organized—and happy—life.

"Hello," she called. "Anybody home?"

"Over here," replied Stephanie's muffled voice. That's when Celia noticed Ollie. He was perched on all fours, smiling at her through the hole in the wall.

"Maaaaaaaaaa," he called, and crawled back out of sight into Stephanie and Chris's.

"Come on over," Stephanie called. "The kids are eating. I finished work early and sent your babysitter home. They wanted those chicken nuggets; you know, the ones in the yellow box?"

Celia sighed and grabbed her keys. She started toward the front door and then stopped and reconsidered. *Well, darn, why not,* she thought, turning around and ducking to walk through the hole, her black pants picking up some dust along the way. There, seated around Stephanie's oblong teak table, were Ted and Lu and Stephanie's son, Harvest, eating chicken nuggets—the healthy kind—with organic ketchup and cut-up strawberries. Celia stood up, unsuccessfully brushing the dust from her clothes, then went straight for Ollie, who, babbling in his foreign baby language, was furiously pushing the buttons on the DVD player and stomping his little feet.

"Chris isn't home yet," Stephanie said. "Sit down. I made some pasta—the kind you like with sausage and cherry tomatoes."

"Thanks for this," Celia said, nodding toward the kids and taking the bowl of herb-scented penne. What was she thinking, wanting to do this alone tonight after the day she'd had? What a relief to have everyone already eating their dinner.

Stephanie sat down next to Celia, taking Ollie onto her lap.

"How was your day?" Stephanie asked seriously.

"Bad. I had to fire someone, some poor guy I had gotten to know a little lately," Celia said, relaxing into the chair. "It turns out his wife started a relationship with some old boyfriend and just happened to tell him last week that she was leaving him for this old flame."

"No way!" Stephanie said.

"Yeah, so you can imagine how hard it was for me to go ahead and fire him on top of that." Celia sighed, stabbing her fork into the pasta. "And it makes me so mad that I have to do the firing. I mean, each manager should take responsibility for his or her own people. If I get the promotion, that will be the first thing I change."

"Good," Stephanie said. "Are you still working on that application?"

"Yeah, I need to finish it tonight," Celia said, letting out another long sigh. "Five years is long enough to be director. It's about time I move up before I get stuck spending my life firing people."

"You go," Stephanie said, letting Ollie down and taking Celia's empty plate to the sink. "I'll get them ready here and read to them, and then I'll bring them over in a little while."

"Really?" Celia asked.

"Go, do your work," Stephanie said, opening her bottom drawer of Tupperware so Ollie would be entertained while she loaded the dishwasher. "I'm happy to do it."

∽

Nikki sat at the bar at Tempt, feeling both at home and awkward in the dark, upscale strip club on Columbus Boulevard. Ever since she started taking pole dancing classes at Flirt Fitness, she had made lots of great friends, some of whom actually danced at clubs. Before, she would have judged them—Catholic school could do that to you—but everyone she met at pole class was so genuine that she found herself spending more time with them than she did with her friends from home in New Jersey. Pole had become her escape and had given her confidence. She had been a gymnast when she was little and found that she was good at pole; so good, in fact, that she had begun filling in for some of the teachers at the studio.

She sipped her ginger ale and watched her friend Kat dance on the stage in the center of the long oval bar that filled the room. Kat was wearing a supershort cheerleader skirt and pasties that looked like mini sparkly pom-poms. The place was empty since it was early on a Tuesday, and Nikki was waiting for the amateur competition to start because Kat had recruited a few girls from the studio to show off what they had learned. Nikki wasn't up for it—she liked to keep her dancing confined to home or the studio—but she was happy to come out and support her girlfriends.

Kat finished her routine and made her way to the barstool next to Nikki.

"You are so awesome," said Nikki.

"Thanks," said Kat, pushing the glass toward the bartender for a refill. Kat was tall and thin with the most beautiful olive skin and silky brown hair. Her makeup was artfully and tastefully done. It looked like she was an actual cheerleader, except, of course, for the nakedness and the pasties. "But when can I get you up there? You're so good. You deserve to be seen in public! Come on, all your friends are doing it," she teased.

Nikki shook her head. "Honestly, Kat, I love you, but I am not getting up there ever, no way. You know I love to dance, but my grandma would roll over in her grave." She put her hand up in the air, stopping Kat before she could reply. "Nope. Don't even try it."

"Fine, fine, I get it," said Kat, reaching past Nikki to group-hug the three girls from the studio who had just come in the double doors. "Are you guys excited? Come with me. I'll bring you backstage!"

The foursome left Nikki sitting alone at the bar with a recently filled ginger ale, replaying in her head the last time she'd been here. It was last year sometime, maybe around the holidays? She had come to drop Kat off for work one night and had to pee really badly. She remembered some sort of Christmas decorations around the bar . . . some garland with little lights. When she came out of the bathroom, she saw him, Mark, her client-turned-neighbor, sitting at the bar eating a hamburger by himself. She wasn't sure if he saw her; she hoped not. After she spotted him, she got out of there quickly. She didn't want him to wonder why she was there. It was one thing to act a little trashy at the salon, another thing entirely to be seen at a gentlemen's club. No matter how much she had changed her attitude about Kat's line of work, Nikki knew she never wanted to be thought of as a stripper.

And now she knew Mark better. She still couldn't get over that afternoon they had spent together. Something was so easy, so comfortable, so safe that day. It was the strangest feeling. Not exactly like she wanted to cheat on Will or was really attracted to the guy, but more like something that felt like a puzzle piece actually matched up just right when she was with him. She couldn't stop thinking about him, about how he smiled with his lips shut while his eyes lit up, or how he had strong but delicate hands.

She was startled out of her daydream by the girls parading from the dressing room in skimpy-looking Village People costumes. No, she could never do this, she thought. That would be crossing a line that she couldn't cross back. She vowed to herself in that moment to always stay on this side of it.

Mark started to walk down Emerson, then thought better of it. Instead, he continued to the back parking lot, looking in the windows of his neighbors' houses as he went. When he got to his own, he took a few steps back and watched. He could see Celia clearly through the second-floor window. She was bustling around, Ollie in her arms all ready for bed, pushing Lu and Ted toward the stairs. In minutes she was back down, vacuuming aggressively, turning every few seconds to refresh the e-mail box on the computer.

She had moved the exact same way when they were in high school. The tasks were different, but the energy level was the same. Back then, when she was president of the student council and the lead in the school musical, and he was leading the stage crew and waiting to win her love, he couldn't get enough. He used to think of her as his western meadowlark—the state bird of Kansas. He was so grateful for her, of course, but somewhere along the way, everything she was, everything that she did so well, just made him feel worse about himself. He had never imagined his life the way it had turned out. Maybe he was so busy trying to impress her and everyone else that he had stopped thinking about what he actually wanted.

While he was looking in the window, Celia stopped moving for a rare few seconds and stared off into the distance. He almost ducked, getting the feeling that she was looking right at him. But she wasn't. The look on her face . . . Mark wasn't sure, but it made him feel . . . responsible. She deserved so much better than him. He couldn't stand it. He turned and walked to the end of the block and into Dante's, hitting the speed dial for Chris's cell. Chris picked up on the first ring.

"Yo."

"Around the corner. Barstool near the window waiting for you."

"Have you even been home yet?" Chris asked.

"As far as you know, I'm still at a client meeting. I just can't deal with it yet. She'd have me in there vacuuming and putting the kids to bed. I need a drink before I can face it."

"Okay, see you in ten." Chris picked up the Harry Potter book again, trying to find his place while cuddling up next to Harvest on top of his Hulk sheets. Harvest hated blankets. Every night when he snuck into their bed, he would lie between Chris and Stephanie, kicking off the blankets from the middle so that both parents were left shivering. But both of them always ended up snuggling up to his warm little body. Harvest would sprawl out between them, arms stretched above his head, mouth wide open. He was just perfect, even when he wasn't.

"Come on, Dad, read," Harvest said sweetly. For a second Chris thought about calling Mark back and canceling, but he had sounded so unhappy. He quickly finished the chapter and was out the door.

Mark was taking the first sip of his second beer when Chris, his thick blond hair still matted from lying with Harvest, slid onto the barstool next to him at Dante's.

"Long client meeting?"

"Yeah, they're a royal pain in the ass. Can't they ever get their schedules together? I got there late, and the wife still hadn't shown up. When she got there, they spent at least an hour debating the tile that they chose in the first place."

"In my next job, there will be no clients," Chris said, waving down Terri behind the bar and miming taking a drink. "Or bosses, for that matter. Did you even call Celia?"

"Nope. Why rock the boat?"

Two more beers and a greasy pile of wings later, Mark still hadn't told Chris about his encounter with Nikki. Maybe there was nothing to tell. Maybe that's why he couldn't bring himself to do it.

"So I'm sure by now you've heard about Stephanie's commune idea," Chris said.

"Leave it to your wife to come up with something like that," Mark said.

"What do you think about it?" Chris asked.

"I think it's the silliest idea I've ever heard, and I assume you do, too," Mark said.

"Well, actually . . ." Chris started.

"Don't even go there," Mark said. "There is no way I'm going to further the damage in my home, which, I want to point out, I am hoping to sell within the month." Mark's eyes went to the TV above the bar. He was quiet for a minute. Then he looked at Chris, the only friend who ever really got him, the one who he was afraid could see through him. "You know I love you, man, and I love what we have on Emerson, but at this point I feel a little too much like a fish at the end of a rod. I need a bigger pond, and I need to get rid of that hook—which right now I think must be that damn house. You know what they say: if you love a fish, then set him free."

"I think it's a bird, or a butterfly. I don't think a fish has anything to do with it," Chris said, grinning. "But really, don't you think you might be able to get that if we took down the walls? I mean, you would have the living space—it would be more than forty feet wide, close to fifty, even. And talk about a bigger pond. There would be so many people around that Celia wouldn't even miss you. Really, pal, give it some thought. It's possible that the thing you're looking for is just a few steel beams away."

~

After everyone was in bed and Mark still hadn't come home, Celia sat in her upstairs office, which doubled as a playroom and den, and continued to work.

Today's termination had her so distracted that she had forgotten her laptop at work and had to borrow Stephanie's Mac. Now she leaned forward and stared at the computer screen. How the heck did she get back to the web browser on this thing?

She slid the wireless mouse. Windows kept opening, but not one of them a web browser. Finally a page ballooned open, immediately filling the screen with three smiling fiftysomethings dressed in L.L. Bean garb, arms draped over each other's shoulders, posed in front of what looked like the rustic cafeteria at the KU family camp where she, Mark, and the kids spent a week every summer.

Rethinking the Commune, it announced in big blue letters. *Intentional Communities Reinvent a Cooperative Way of Living.*

Celia glanced over her shoulder, then quickly scanned the page.

Welcome to the website dedicated to modern communal living!

All across America, baby boomers are reinventing the commune of the '60s and '70s in myriad ways. In the last few decades, our society has become increasingly fragmented, leaving us isolated from our neighbors and without the support network of an extended family. This site will connect you with America's new pioneers in cooperative living, from intentional communities based on religious calling or lifestyle to a flexible model called "cohousing" and more.

Celia tiptoed over to the door and slid it closed. Then she continued reading. First she read about the family in New Hampshire that wanted to buy only local food. They had gotten together with like-minded environmentalists who looked, from the online photo album, like they had been separated from each other at birth: women with long braided hair, Birkenstocks, and those gauzy shirts, men with more facial hair than she had ever seen. Then there were the schoolteachers in Texas who had recruited nearly eighty others, from retirees to young families, to collectively buy a ranch.

Hadn't she and Mark always talked about doing something crazy like packing up and moving to Italy for a few years, homeschooling the kids while Mark worked in the local village? He'd get a job where he used his hands. He could be a carpenter or a gardener . . . anything to just simplify their existence. Maybe Stephanie wasn't so off base. Breaking down the walls and living with their friends in a commune might not be moving to a foreign country exactly, but it could be a kind of change of scenery, a new adventure, a way to simplify their lives. Maybe it would be like the KU sorority house, or a better version of her huge family growing up. Or, on second thought, maybe it would be like those crazy people who'd lived in that commune everybody called a cult down the road from her parents' house.

Celia shook off the last thought as quickly as it came, remembering how it had felt to come home to a house that was settled and orderly tonight. Mark always joked with her that with their busy schedules they needed another wife, the old-fashioned kind, like a June Cleaver. And if they did this, she'd have much more time to focus on work and getting where she needed to be. More than that, though, it could be a way to avoid moving. The thought of starting over with so much going on in her life was exhausting, even to her. She could see Mark's point about needing more space, and she agreed with him. But this would give him that space, not to mention a new project to tackle.

She heard Mark's footsteps on the stairs, then a tiny knock and the squeak of the door.

"Hi," he said, leaning on the doorframe.

"Hi," Celia said, quickly closing the laptop. She turned around. "Late meeting?"

"Yeah, they drive me crazy. I'm going to hit the hay," Mark said.

"When I got home tonight, Stephanie had all the kids over there. They'd gone through the hole. She fed them and got them ready for bed. Then she sent them back over here through the hole."

"The plumber comes the day after tomorrow. As soon as that's all set, I want to get that drywall back up. We'll probably lose at least a week before it's all ready and the agent can put the sign up," Mark said, coming over to Celia and leaning on her desk.

"I know," Celia said. "But there's something about Stephanie's idea that makes sense to me. Maybe we should consider it, give it a chance. Is it even possible to do something like that? Take down the walls?"

"Anything is possible if you have the money and the wherewithal," Mark said. "Is it practical or smart? No. We're moving, Ceil. We've been through this over and over this last year, and that's the plan."

"I know," she said again, surprised by his stubbornness. Usually she could get him to pretty much consider anything. "But can you at least think about what it would take, make a few calls? I'm curious myself, and that way they'll think we did everything we could before we move. Can we at least do that?"

"Sure," Mark said, too tired to argue anymore and nice and buzzed from one too many beers. "We can do that."

CHAPTER FOUR

"Stephanie!" Chris yelled down the stairs, wearing only a white under-shirt and black dress socks.

He leaned on the iron railing that led to his third-floor bedroom and waited. When he didn't get an answer, he turned to root through one of three plastic laundry baskets overflowing with unfolded clothes. There were lavender yoga pants, all colors and kinds of socks, and Harvest's red-and-orange-striped pajamas, but no underwear.

"Stephaneeeeee!" he yelled, but again there was no reply, only the sound of the Red Hot Chili Peppers playing loudly on the downstairs computer. He grabbed a damp towel from the bathroom floor, wrapped it around his waist, and skillfully bounded down the spiral steps, two at a time. When he got to the first floor, he found Stephanie and Harvest dancing furiously in the living room to "Dani California." Harvest played air guitar, and Stephanie shook her head to the beat, her long hair flying, covering her face with every dramatic nod. She picked up Harvest and spun him in a circle as she sang along loudly.

"Stephanie!" he yelled again, this time standing only three feet away. She stopped midspin to stare at Chris in his towel.

"Hey, hot stuff—where are your pants?" Stephanie asked Chris breathlessly, gently dropping Harvest to his feet then turning down the volume.

"Well, in order to wear pants, I would need some clean underwear. Is this basket clean?" he asked, pointing to yet another laundry basket filled with unfolded clothes.

"Why don't you smell it? Ooh! The waffles! Harvest, sit down. Breakfast is coming right up!"

Stephanie ran to the toaster, extracted two almost burnt organic waffles, and plopped them onto Harvest's plate.

"Can I have that good syrup, please, Mom?" Harvest asked, taking a seat. "The kind we have at Mommy Hope's house?"

Stephanie opened the refrigerator and peered inside. "Absolutely not, Harvest. That stuff will glue your insides together. It's filled with high fructose corn syrup and cellulose gum. And look! I have the real stuff—from the actual maple tree." She held up a glass bottle filled with amber-colored syrup, a proud smile on her face. "Trust me, you'll love it."

"Yuck," Harvest said, sticking out his tongue.

"You better watch it, or I'll make you come maple sugaring with me like my parents used to do on our spring breaks. Then you'll really appreciate that syrup on your plate."

"Come on, Stephanie," Chris said, exasperated. "You promised that when you started working from home you'd have more time to straighten up. Remember? Since you'd be around more? I don't ask for much—just some clean underwear and maybe to finally see the floor of our bedroom once you go through all that stuff you just moved from your parents' house."

Stephanie poured syrup onto Harvest's waffles, making no effort to prevent it from dripping onto the table. She replaced the cap and put the syrup back in the refrigerator, ignoring the sticky mess moving slowly down the bottle.

"Well, it's hard, Chris. I never have any concentrated time to get things organized around here. I get to it when I can. I'm busy, too, you know," she said, turning up the music a few notches and shaking her hips.

"But you're a professional organizer! Am I the only one who sees the irony in this? That your own husband can never find a pair of underwear, and when he does, he can't tell if it's clean or dirty?" Chris asked.

"My business is just that—my business," Stephanie replied. "Must I be constantly working? I need to be free of responsibility sometimes, too, you know, have a little fun."

Even though she pretended to be irritated by her workload, Stephanie loved the business she had started a year ago. She also loved its name—Clear. Basically she helped other people organize their lives, whatever that might mean. She assisted people while they got their houses ready to sell, she helped people erase all traces of an ex-spouse from their homes after a divorce, and she offered encouragement to people to get rid of baggage that was weighing them down. If she ever found it boring or tedious, which was rare, she just reminded herself that she was making $100 an hour and getting a look into people's secret lives. And every time, after the love letters and the diplomas and the huge, unwanted stamp collections had been disposed of, she looked forward to the next cluttered den or overrun office.

"Is there a party going on over there?" a voice called from the other side of the gaping hole in the living room wall.

"Always," Stephanie replied. "Do you guys have any coffee? Our machine's still broken. I'm starting to crash."

Mark stuck his head through the hole. "Nope, sorry. Just drank the last of it. Nice outfit, Chris."

"My wife—*the personal organizer*—can't seem to keep our own household organized. I'll bet you can always find clean underwear in your house," Chris said to Mark.

"As a matter of fact, I can. My wife always has the laundry done. She wakes up at five thirty every morning to do it. She can fold the laundry, feed the kids breakfast, and brush her teeth all at the same time." Mark looked at Stephanie and raised his eyebrows and shrugged. "Just saying, Stephanie . . ."

"Whatever, Mark," she said, pretending to sound mad. "Go back through your delusional rabbit hole; you know, where it's still the 1950s?"

"Touché, my dear. Hey, Chris, why don't you just go commando today? It might make you more relaxed at work," Mark called, ducking back through the hole.

"Ha ha, Mark," Stephanie said as he disappeared into his house. "Not a bad idea, though, hon. Sounds like a way to spice up your day."

She turned to face Chris, taking in his all-American good looks—the classic jawline and boyish blond hair. Back at her private Quaker high school, where she'd spent her senior year, she had dated mostly grungy antiestablishment types—many who had big dreams of feeding the hungry. She never would have imagined ending up with a guy like Chris. He was someone who might have gone to the more conservative prep school down the road, someone who, in the immaturity of her youth, she might have looked upon with disdain.

"Seriously, Stephanie. Can you help a guy out? Think hard—is this basket clean or dirty?"

"Hmm," Stephanie said, pursing her lips. "Dirty. Yeah. It's dirty. I brought it downstairs so I could throw it in today while I catch up on my e-mails. Sorry."

Chris sighed and turned to go upstairs.

"Hon, I really am trying," Stephanie pouted as she dropped another waffle onto Harvest's plate.

"I know you are," Chris said, grabbing her around the waist and hugging her tightly. "I'm going to get ready for work now, but you can make it up to me tonight." He snatched a used pair of underwear from the basket and headed up the stairs.

❧

The lack of clean underwear pretty much set the tone for Chris's whole day. He never stopped feeling ungrounded and exposed, and now he couldn't wait to climb into bed. He had been notified about the accounting error first thing, and then he'd spent the rest of the day trying to find what had gone wrong. For months he had been working day and night so that his company could be sold to a private equity firm, and when the analysts had found the discrepancy in the books that morning, he had felt sick to his stomach. This could ruin his chances to get out. If all went well and the company actually sold, maybe he'd consider cashing in his stock options and spending some time figuring out what he really wanted to do with his professional life.

By the time he got home that night, Harvest was already sleeping. Chris hated to miss bedtime. He had loved being a father from the moment Stephanie told him she was pregnant. He was excited about every ultrasound, every piece of baby gear they bought, and every single kick that made her huge belly look like there was someone playing soccer inside.

On the day their son was born—a perfect summer morning—Stephanie had proclaimed it Harvest Day. All throughout her pregnancy, she had rubbed her belly and told their unborn child that she was growing him on a vine like a tomato. So in that first amazing moment when they saw their son and Stephanie decided that there could be no other name for him than Harvest, Chris couldn't help but agree.

He went up to the second floor, stepped over the picture books, piles of clothes, and plastic toys, and stood in front of Harvest's bed. For a minute he considered climbing into bed with him, but he knew that with all Harvest's tossing and turning he would never get a good night's sleep.

He continued his ascent to the third floor, where Stephanie was sorting through a pile of clothes on the bed. She looked up and smiled.

"Wow. You're not usually this late. Hard day?"

"It was okay," Chris said, undoing his tie and hanging up his suit jacket. He knew Stephanie well enough to know that when he really wanted to talk he had to take it slow and build up to it; throw too much at her and she'd lose interest. "How was your day?"

"Great, but as you can see, I haven't gotten too far with the cleaning up."

Chris looked around the room and nodded slowly. The bed was unmade, the nightstands were still covered with junk, and the same baskets of laundry held the same unfolded clothes.

"But I did practice my yoga today," she said. "Want me to tell you about it?"

Chris struggled to find a clear spot on the dresser for his watch—the one his father gave him when he finished his MBA—and turned to face her. She was sitting on the edge of the bed, looking at him expectantly.

"Okay, first tell me about your yoga. Then I'll tell you about my day," Chris said, joining Stephanie on the bed.

"You know, my serious, buttoned-up businessman," she said, pulling off her shirt and flinging it across the room, "I could show you instead." As usual, she wasn't wearing a bra.

"This is getting more interesting by the second," he said, moving closer to her.

"Did you know that yoga positions are good for other things besides plain old exercise?"

"They are, are they?"

"Mm hmm," she said, wriggling out of her pants to reveal a tiny thong. She reached for his belt buckle. "They say that when a couple lines up their chakras, they can get an amazing amount of pleasure."

"I'm up for some chakra alignment," he said, closing his eyes as she unzipped his pants.

He let them drop to the floor and started to climb on top of her. She gently pushed him away, then got onto all fours. "Now this position," she said, arching her back slowly, "is called cat."

"Meow," he said appreciatively.

She sat back on her heels and slowly spread her feet underneath her, keeping her knees touching. "And this one," she said, lowering her shoulders toward the bed behind her until her back was arched, "is called the reclining hero."

She reached for his hands and pulled him on top of her now, spreading her knees apart.

"You can come to my rescue anytime," he whispered.

"Did I ever tell you how much I have come to love yoga?" Chris said a little later, picking up his suit pants from the floor and smoothing out the wrinkles.

"You liked that, did you?" Stephanie said, clicking the buttons on the television remote. "Have I seen this one?" She was watching the opening scene of an old *Law & Order* episode.

"You know I don't watch that junk." Chris gathered the laundry baskets and piled them on top of each other next to the stairs. Then he started to collect the glasses and coffee mugs that were on the dresser and night tables. "So things aren't going so well at work," he started. "Bowman has been on my back, and the accountants found this major—"

"Oh, hon, it'll pass. Things always have a way of working themselves out," she said, clicking back to the menu on the TV. "I definitely saw that one. Ooh! Here's an episode of *Lost* I haven't seen yet!"

He looked over at his wife of almost ten years, sitting cross-legged on the bed, eyes fixed on the TV, blankets tangled into a pile and pillows falling on the floor. When they met, all he had wanted to do was take care of her, give her a little stability. She had grown up moving every few years—her parents thought nothing of picking up and leaving to find a new adventure, a new learning experience. Her dad was a teacher, and a great one at that, so he always managed to find a job, while her mom was a freelance writer who did everything from ghostwriting to magazine articles to advertising copy—whatever kept the money coming in. Stephanie had told Chris many times that she felt like a nomad for most of her childhood. What she needed from him, what he imagined she saw in him, was a home where the space inside actually meant something. He understood where her crazy idea for the commune came from—it was a way to make sure nobody could ever leave, a way to build a home where people would want to stay put. Leave it to her, though, to want to have a traditional family in such an untraditional way.

"You're probably right," Chris muttered. "And there's something else I wanted to talk about, now that I have your full attention," he said sarcastically. He waited a minute, and when she didn't look away from the television, he continued anyway. "Harvest is getting to be so old, Stephanie, I can't believe it. Don't you think it's time we thought about that second baby we've been putting off?"

Stephanie moved her eyes away from the screen.

"Hon, I just started my own business. How am I going to have a baby now? Not to mention getting through an actual pregnancy. I thank my lucky stars that Harvest is a little older and easier now," she said dismissively. "And anyway, if we really do make this place a commune, you'll have plenty of kids around."

"But," Chris said just as the phone rang. He sighed and leaned over to answer it.

"Hey, Celia," he said. "Yeah, we were just talking. Well, I was talking, she's watching *Lost*. Hold on. Stephanie, Celia's on the phone. She wants you to go downstairs for a minute."

Stephanie paused the TV and reluctantly climbed out of bed. He watched as she tried to untangle herself from the twisted sheets that hadn't been straightened in days.

"Tell her I'll be right down," Stephanie said as she pulled a white terry cloth robe from the bedpost and wrapped it around herself, then went down to the first floor where Celia was waiting on her own side of the hole between the houses.

"Can I come in?" Celia asked.

"Of course. What's up?"

Celia sat down at the table, and Stephanie took the seat next to her.

"So, that commune you've been talking about," Celia said. "I've been giving it some thought, and I want you to know that I see your rationale."

"You do?" Stephanie yelped. "Yay!"

"I want to tell you this because it means so much to me that you would want to share your home with us. But, Stephanie, I don't see how we could ever really go ahead and implement it. There are so many roadblocks, and Mark won't budge," Celia said. "I've talked to him, but he is adamant, which in itself is kind of strange. I mean, he isn't usually so stubborn. Normally I could at least engage him in a dialogue."

"What do you mean? You can always get him to see your side," Stephanie said.

"Not this time, apparently, and besides, I'm not sure what my side is. Maybe that's the problem. But here's the good news. I did get him to agree to look into the logistics of it," Celia said.

"I can totally do it," Stephanie said quickly. "I'll talk him into it. Let's have a meeting tomorrow night. Here. No—at Hope and Leo's. Leo can cook. Quick, call her and see if that's okay."

"I'm willing to open the lines of communication," Celia said seriously. "But I don't see us coming to an agreement."

"Just call her!" Stephanie squealed.

Celia took out her cell phone and called Hope, and a minute later the meeting was set.

CHAPTER FIVE

One package of cookies would have been plenty. But Hope had made every sort of slice-and-bake cookie she could find—chocolate chip, oatmeal chocolate chip, sugar, peanut butter. She also baked Pillsbury crescent rolls, which she stuffed with chocolate chips then sprinkled with powdered sugar. She was about to make the open-and-spread brownies when the doorbell rang. She looked at her watch. She had half an hour before she had to pick up Shoshanna and Harvest at school, so she should have just enough time to bake the brownies. She put down the unopened yellow tube and walked up the stairs and to the door, wondering if it could be Nikki. She had left a note on her door earlier saying she had a welcome package for her, something Hope did for every new neighbor.

Suddenly Hope was sorry she'd done it. She didn't want to get to know a new person, especially that Nikki. She pulled open the door, putting on an unnatural smile, and almost laughed with relief when she saw Chris standing there. He was wearing his work clothes, a suit with a classic navy-and-green-striped tie. His tie was loosened, and he had dark circles under his eyes.

"Hi," Hope said warmly, dipping her head a little so her hair covered the right side of her face. She ran her hand through her chin-length bob, starting at her forehead, revealing her high cheekbones and perfect dimples. As usual, she wasn't wearing any makeup. Leo always said that she didn't need it.

"Are you coming to tell me not to get Harvest? Your wife just called to ask me to pick him up."

"Oh, no," Chris said, distracted. "I didn't know she'd called. But I'm glad you're home. Can I come in?"

"Sure," she said, holding the door and moving out of the way. Chris walked through the living room and right downstairs toward the kitchen, normally the epicenter of indoor action on the block, probably because of all of Leo's home cooking and Hope's not-so-homemade baking. Hope pushed the front door shut, locked it, and followed him.

"Wow," he said, looking around. "Are you opening a bakery or something?"

"No," she said, giggling. "Just trying to welcome that new neighbor of ours, and then of course there's the meeting tonight. I want to have plenty of dessert for that."

"Can I have one?" he asked, pointing to the chocolate-filled crescent rolls.

"Sure. Help yourself," she said.

He reached for one, powdered sugar landing on his tie. He didn't notice.

"Pillsbury?" he asked, chewing. "It doesn't get any better than this."

"That's what I always say," Hope said, waiting for the usual ribbing about why she, the wife of a gourmet, chose to use all these premade doughs. But it didn't come. Chris finished his crescent roll in three bites, found a napkin in the third drawer without asking, and sat down at the kitchen table.

"So do you still want me to get Harvest?" she asked when he didn't say anything. Shoshanna and Harvest were both in first grade at a very progressive, and very expensive, private school seven blocks away. Leo had insisted on sending Shoshanna there, and Hope hadn't fought hard. She had known it was a battle she couldn't win.

"I guess. If that's okay," Chris said.

"Yeah, fine," Hope said, checking her watch and deciding that at this point there wasn't enough time to bake the brownies. She turned off the oven and sat down across from Chris.

"So what's going on?" she asked.

"I just had a brutal meeting with our potential buyers," he said, stretching out his long legs so that they almost touched Hope's under the table. She shifted in her seat. "You know how I've been trying to prep the company for sale. I mean, I've been working on this for months, and today I was supposed to present our plan to them. My CEO said he wanted me to lead the presentation since I wrote it—I am the CFO, after all. It's *supposed* to be my job. I have to admit after yesterday's debacle I wasn't sure what was going to happen, but I pulled out a total miracle, or I thought I had. Once the meeting started, though, Bowman took over and completely undermined me."

"That's terrible," Hope said, furrowing her eyebrows and looking right at him. "I know how hard you've been working on that. When you told me about that mistake in the books, I worried about how it would go today."

"You did?" Chris asked. "That's nice of you."

"But it's worth sticking it out for the money, right?" Hope asked. "I know Bowman's a jerk, but this is what you've been working for."

"That's the problem," Chris said. "I just don't know if the sale will actually go through based on today's meeting. We may have to start over with another buyer. It's a total mess."

"I'm really sorry to hear that," Hope said.

"Thanks," Chris said. "I'm just so unhappy there. I have to tell you, I'm not sure I can stand it much longer."

"Does Stephanie know you feel this way? What did she say?"

"Well, you know, she's a little distracted. I haven't even had a chance to tell her about the meeting today," he said. "She's at a client's house—*organizing.*"

At that moment his phone rang. He stopped talking and looked at the number.

"Speak of the devil," he said, answering the phone. "Hi. How's the organizing going?"

Hope rarely heard Chris be sarcastic about Stephanie's work. In fact, he had been the one to encourage her to leave her job at the Philadelphia Museum of Art to start her own business.

"I'm sitting with my other wife," he said, smiling at Hope. Hope smiled back but quickly looked away. "Oh, I'm just telling her about my tough day at work." He waited. "Not so great." He waited again. "Yeah, Bowman was a prick." He waited again, and Hope glanced at her watch. She had to go. She stood up, but Chris made no move to do the same. She re-tied her shoes, got her bag.

"I have to go get the kids," she mouthed to Chris.

"Hold on, Stephanie . . . okay, mind if I just hang out here until you get back, Hope?" he asked. "On second thought, I'll come with you. Stephanie, I'm going with Hope to get the kids. I'll meet you here when you get home. Hope has baked enough to feed an army."

~

Mark wasn't feeling well. He sat at his desk, and the dizziness that he had at first thought was his imagination got worse and worse. He put his head down on his folded arms. He was supposed to pick up Ted and Lu. How was he going to do that? He could feel pressure in his sinuses. It must be some sort of infection. He forced himself up and walked to the water cooler. The cold drink made him feel a little better, but still, going to that crowded playground at that run-down public school was the last thing he wanted to do. He despised that place. It was nothing like the sprawling, pristine public schools that he and Celia had attended back in Kansas. But when he had mentioned the possibility of sending their kids to private school, Celia had vehemently disagreed. They were both products of public education, she had argued, and they had turned out just fine. It was a matter of principle, she had insisted, to support and actually use the available public schools. Mark went back to his desk, reached into his pocket for his phone, and speed-dialed Hope.

"Hey, Mark," she said. There was the sound of a bus or truck moving behind her.

"Hi, Hope," he said, relieved that she'd answered. "I need a favor. I just got a call from a client who needs me to come over immediately. Some crisis with the stone floor he chose. Could you pick up my kids on your way back? And then grab Ollie, too? The sitter has to leave early for a doctor's appointment." The school was really just four blocks out of her way and, luckily for everyone involved, got out fifteen minutes later.

"No problem. The kids will be happy to see each other," Hope said.

Chris grabbed the phone away from her.

"Shirking the parenting duties again?" he joked into the phone. "What is that, the fifth time this month? I might call the authorities on you."

He listened to what Mark said, laughed, then handed the phone back to Hope.

"Oh, tell him to come over after his meeting," Chris said to Hope.

"I'm sure Celia has informed you about the meeting at my house tonight, Mark," Hope said. "I'll take care of the kids, and you and Celia can come over when you get home. Leo made some great soup."

Mark was quiet for a minute. He had a hard time admitting he didn't feel well to anyone, but now he wished he had.

"Sounds good," he forced himself to say.

~

"I'd like to call this meeting to order," Stephanie said, raising her glass of Albariño. It was one of the five wines Leo had brought home tonight, including her favorite Gewürztraminer. They had all just sat down to steaming bowls of butternut squash soup with lemongrass and scotch bonnet chiles that Leo had whipped up. The kids were fed and had gone upstairs to watch *Shrek* in the den.

"Oh phooey," Celia said. "I forgot the agenda I printed up."

Stephanie took a lipstick from the pocket of her sweater and wrote "COMMUNE" in capital letters on her napkin. She handed it to Celia. "Here's your agenda."

Celia crumpled it up and threw it across the table at Stephanie, sending them both into a fit of the giggles. Stephanie kept trying to talk, but broke down laughing each time.

"On behalf of my wife, I would like to open our official discussion about her proposed commune," Chris said. "We're going to have to do something about that gaping hole in our living rooms sooner or later. Now, we can just cover it up—and go back to the way it used to be minus one third of us—or we can actually try living together, which, I want to point out, we pretty much do anyway. What are your thoughts? Hope?"

"Why do I have to go first?" Hope asked.

"Well, you already know where we stand, so think of it as going third," Chris said gently.

"There are so many things about this that seem crazy and impossible, but there are more things, I think, that sound unbelievably great. I say we do it," Hope blurted. "At least I vote for trying it. I would be happy to take care of the kids, get them to school, pick them up. I can be with Ollie during the day. I like the idea of being with all of you at night."

As soon as she said it, though, Hope felt a moment of panic, a feeling she remembered having only twice in her life: on her wedding day and when Shoshanna was born. Both times, mingled with the euphoria that had poured out of everyone around her, she was struck with a feeling of terror. She couldn't shake the idea that she had now created something that she absolutely couldn't live without, something that would cost her everything to lose.

Trying to banish the feeling, she put a large spoonful of hot soup in her mouth and waved, indicating she was finished talking. Chris nodded. "Celia?"

"I'd like to go ahead and look into what it would take to turn this into one big floor," Celia said slowly. "I have to admit that Stephanie makes a good argument. It's been great to come home and find my kids happy and fed at her table, especially with all the pressure I'm feeling at work these days. But we would have to set some serious ground rules, of course, including payment for services rendered." She paused and looked at Hope pointedly before continuing. "And we'd have to figure out how we'd present it to the outside world . . ." She paused again, wondering if she should stop there.

"And?" said Stephanie, bouncing up and down a little on her chair.

"Well, I grew up down the road from a seventies commune. Do you remember those people, Mark? Everyone always called it a cult," Celia continued without waiting for Mark's reply. "I know that's not our reality, but the whole town was always gossiping about them, and no one would talk to their kids at school. I don't want people gossiping about us or being mean to our kids. We all know that we live in the biggest small town in America."

Hope looked at Celia. "I understand," she said. "I'm not naive enough to think people won't gossip. In fact, I'm sure they already do. But I just love the thought of finding a way for us to still be together."

"I know," said Celia. "So do I. But to be perfectly honest, neither Mark nor I is convinced this is a feasible idea. Even so, Mark has agreed to look into what it would take. Mark, your thoughts?"

But Mark could barely think at all. His dizziness had come back full tilt, and while at first he thought the soup would taste good, now it was too sweet and the consistency too thick for him. He wanted chicken broth. But he didn't want to offend Leo, who always paid close attention to how much people ate of his food.

"I'm still trying to figure a few things out," he said as clearly as he could.

"Let me just say something for a minute," Stephanie said. "Mark, you are as much a part of my life as anyone is. I ask that you please consider this idea, at least give it a try. What do you have to lose? You said before that you thought the walls between our houses might have been down once. We never would have known it if there hadn't been that flood. It's like the universe has put this right in front of us. We can't just ignore the signs."

"I'll make a few calls tomorrow," Mark said. It didn't seem worth his energy to argue about the craziness of the idea. There was no way in the world it could actually happen. He would have to be the one to figure out the supporting walls and the steel beams, and he had no intention of doing any of that. Maybe he would make one call to his contractor, and then he'd be able to tell Celia and the rest of them that he'd looked into it. That he'd done his best.

"In addition to the other concerns," he added, "there's a legal side to all of this. These houses are not zoned for multifamily use. They just aren't. They are strictly single-family homes. I know, because people try to break up houses all the time and rent out parts of them, and they get themselves into trouble. What you guys are talking about is the same thing in reverse."

There, he'd said his piece. Now he wanted to go to bed, but he didn't want to push his luck. He'd been out at night so much lately that he knew tonight it would be better to persevere and go to bed with a clear conscience. Though at this point, he seriously doubted that he could make it through the rest of the meal.

Stephanie sat up and pushed her hands toward the center of the table.

"Okay then, we'll keep it a secret," she said. "That makes sense to me anyway. We don't need people knowing our business. Right? Does anyone else have anything to say? Leo, you don't mind cooking like this for us every night, right?"

"As long as everyone is eating, I'm cooking," Leo said, studying the color of the wine in his glass. "Nothing would please me more. That is, if this is what my wife really wants."

At that moment the doorbell rang. It took Hope a minute to realize that she should get up to answer it. They were, after all, at her house. She pushed her chair back and opened the door. It was Nikki.

"Hi," Hope said, feeling far away from the moment she'd left that note for Nikki. "Come in."

The room was silent. Mark felt even dizzier at the sight of her. Nobody said anything.

"Is it someone's birthday or something?" Nikki asked.

All six of them had the same thought—*no, just a typical night*—but no one said it.

"I have treats for you," said Hope, remembering why Nikki was here and happy to have a reason to go downstairs. She filled a paper plate with a variety of baked goods and came back to the dining room. Stephanie was asking Nikki if she had settled on a yoga instructor yet.

"Thanks so much," Nikki said, taking the plate.

"Do you want to join us?" Leo said finally. "We have plenty of wine."

"Oh, no thank you," Nikki said, inching toward the door. "Will should be home any minute. But thanks for this."

"How did she know you baked for her?" Celia asked when Hope returned to the table.

"I left her a note," Hope said. "I stopped by earlier."

"Excuse me for stating the obvious and pointing out a possibly major complication, but what would we have done if the walls had been down and the doorbell rang?" Celia asked.

"Not answer it, I think," said Hope.

"Yes, I agree, but that's not a long-term solution," Celia said. "At some point everyone has to answer his or her front door."

"You guys are so uptight," said Stephanie, rolling her eyes. "Loosen up a little. No one is going to care about our little commune."

"I agree that people wouldn't quite understand," Leo said, turning toward Stephanie. "But, correct me if I'm wrong, wouldn't that be *their* problem?"

"Totally," agreed Stephanie.

"Where were we?" Chris said, trying to get back to official business.

"Well, the two of us are in, Celia admits to seeing some merit in the idea, Mark is going to look into the logistics, Hope wants to try it, and Leo is happy to cook for us," Stephanie said.

"You're not going to sing 'Kumbaya' every night, are you, Stephanie?" Leo asked, putting his wineglass to his mouth and draining it.

Stephanie smirked at him. They were all quiet for a minute. Chris was the first one to speak again.

"Sounds like we might have ourselves a commune."

CHAPTER SIX

Chris rounded the corner to Emerson Street, adjusting the black laptop bag on his shoulder and fishing for his keys in his suit jacket pocket. The block was deserted—everyone had gone in for dinner, and the orange cone was back in its spot at the far end of the street. Even though he had probably missed eating with Stephanie and Harvest, he was certain he had not missed bedtime again. He had been working all weekend, so he hadn't felt guilty about ducking out at 7:00 p.m.—early by company standards. Maybe he would even try to make it over to Dante's for a beer if Mark felt better.

He picked up the pace and had just approached the middle of the block when Mark's door slammed open and Celia ran in the opposite direction. She climbed up their neighbor's stoop and banged on the door.

Chris broke into a jog, dropping his briefcase on his top step. Their neighbor Colin was an emergency room nurse at Pennsylvania Hospital and the block's go-to guy for strange rashes and croupy coughs, but Celia rarely imposed on him.

"Celia, what's wrong? Is it one of the kids?"

She didn't turn around. "I need help. Mark is so sick. He said he felt a little better today, so I went to work, but when I got home, I don't know, he was worse. I shouldn't have stayed so late, but I was prepping for an interview and . . . darn it, where is Colin? I saw him go in a few minutes ago."

Celia rang Colin's doorbell again, but when he didn't answer, she turned away.

"I have to get back home," she said, moving down the stoop.

"You go, I'll get him," Chris said.

Chris knocked again, yelling Colin's name up at the open window. The dead bolt clicked, and Colin opened the door wearing his green scrubs. "What's happening?" he asked, snapping into professional mode. "Is one of the kids sick?"

"No, it's Mark. He wasn't feeling well all weekend, but Celia said he's much worse now. I don't really know what she meant, but it must be pretty bad if she came looking for you," Chris said, jogging to keep up as Colin sprinted to Celia and Mark's stoop.

The door was open, and they climbed the two flights of stairs to the third floor. They found Mark sitting on the edge of his bed and Celia holding his hand, talking to him quietly. Mark looked up at Colin and Chris, confused.

"Dad? Why are you here?" he mumbled. "Can somebody turn off the lights?"

Then Mark turned to Celia. "I need to go to work. The plumber's coming this morning, and he won't take no for an answer," he muttered, shaking his head. "I've got to go now. The train is going to leave without me."

Celia turned to Colin. "He's been sick all weekend with the flu," she said, her voice low. "But when I got home from work, I heard him talking up here. I thought he was with one of the kids, but he was just sitting here talking to himself. I asked him what was going on, and he looked right at me and kept talking. Half of it sounds like gibberish and the other half doesn't make any sense."

"Chris, I need you to call 911 and then go downstairs and wait for the ambulance. Celia, what are his symptoms?" Colin said, stooping to look into Mark's eyes.

"Fever, headache, nothing really out of the ordinary," Celia said. "Until now."

"Mark, do you know who I am?"

"Huh?"

Colin stood up. "Mark, can you tell me what year it is?"

Mark stared back at Colin. "I'm so tired," he said, slurring his words.

Within minutes they could hear the siren outside, and soon the EMTs were upstairs checking Mark's vital signs, then lifting him onto a stretcher and securing the orange straps. Celia followed them downstairs, stopping at the second floor where Ted and Lu were huddled on the bottom bunk and Ollie was standing in his crib.

"Everything is going to be okay. Daddy is sick, and we're taking him to the doctor," she said, using all her might to steady her shaking voice. "Chris, can you get the kids? I need to go." She bolted down the narrow stairs, stopping at the bottom for a few seconds to wipe away the hot tears she didn't want anyone to see. Crying would mean there was something really wrong, and in order to keep moving, she had to believe that wasn't the case. When she felt she had it under control, she headed out the door. Hope and Stephanie were waiting for her.

"I'm coming with you," Hope said to Celia. "Stephanie, call Leo at work. Tell him what's happening."

"Got it," Stephanie said, taking Ollie from Chris's arms. "Chris, you go, too. I've got the kids. Find out what's going on and call me right away."

"I'll be right behind you," Chris said to Celia. "I'll take a cab."

Celia turned and grabbed Stephanie's hands. "Please, can you move the bookshelf and close up the hole? I don't know who is going to be in and out of the house, and I don't know when I'll be back."

Stephanie nodded and watched as Celia and Hope hopped into the ambulance. Colin slammed the double doors shut, tapping twice on the back of the truck to signal the driver to go. The siren sounded, and the ambulance pulled away.

Stephanie grabbed Shoshanna's hand and climbed Mark and Celia's steps.

"Shoshanna, can you please hold Ollie for a minute?" she said, putting the toddler in the little girl's lap on the stoop.

Stephanie forced the bookshelf in front of the hole, then locked the door behind her, lifted Ollie, and herded all the kids into her house. Chris was inside getting his wallet and keys.

"God, I just can't believe it. He didn't seem that sick, did he?" Chris asked, his voice shaking.

"He'll be okay. He's got to be. Now get out of here, and call me as soon as you know anything," Stephanie said, pushing him out the door.

When Chris had gone, Stephanie turned to the five little dumbstruck faces staring in her direction. This was the quietest she'd ever seen them.

She took a deep breath and smiled brightly. "Okay, kids. Things are going to be just fine. Mommy Stephanie will take care of everything."

～

Leo was ready to go home. It had been a fine night, but now the last table of two wouldn't leave, and he was tired of talking to the guy about wine—usually his favorite subject. The man was so clearly trying to impress his date that he had become combative, vehemently disputing all of Leo's suggestions.

"You can call it a night," he told Samantha, Vega's manager. "I'm sure they'll leave soon. If they don't, I'll start to turn out the lights. It's a Monday, for heaven's sake!"

"That would be great," Samantha said, rubbing her six-months-pregnant belly.

"Do you want me to call you a cab?"

"No, my hubby said he'd meet me halfway. Walking is better than sitting. And I'm off tomorrow."

"Oh, right, enjoy it," Leo said, glancing back at the couple. The woman looked drunk and bored. The man kept talking, waving his arms as he spoke. Leo was hoping to catch up with the guys at Dante's tonight. But at this rate it didn't look like that would happen.

Leo put his hands in the pockets of his khaki pants and walked to the big, glassed-in wine tower that spanned two floors of the Vega Tapas Bar in Old City, where he had been sommelier for more than three years. When he first started at Vega, he had invited his parents in from New York to visit. But as always, his father had been only mildly impressed, making a pointed comment about all the money spent on that expensive Manhattan private school and Ivy League education. Served him right, Leo had thought at the time, for taking me to all those fancy restaurants as a kid.

He knew he should check on the couple; the man probably wanted to order something else, but he didn't want to. Almost all the tables were cleared and reset for tomorrow. He watched as one of the waiters held glasses up to the light to check for spots before placing them on the tables.

Leo stepped into the small external elevator that only he was allowed to use and pressed "up." He could adjust the speed so he slowly moved toward the high ceiling. Then, when it could go no higher, he had the option of moving left or right. He moved to the dessert wines, thinking that if worse came to worst, he could suggest a sweet wine to end the annoying couple's evening. Maybe that would do it. He was just choosing between a Canadian ice wine and a late-harvest sauvignon blanc from Chile when he saw the woman start to doze off. Was that possible? He must be imagining it. But then the woman shook her head a bit and sat up straighter, fidgeting with her expensive silk scarf. The man was finally quiet for a few seconds while he stared at her, then he signaled the waiter to bring him the check. *What a relief.*

Leo pushed the button to make the cart move to the right, stopping at the red wine bin. He chose a Gaja Barbaresco to take home and moved back to the middle and then down, where he locked the elevator for the night. He put the Barbaresco on the bar and walked over to the table as the man was signing the credit card slip.

"Thanks for coming in tonight," he said, all smiles and energy. Leo was good at this when he wanted to be.

"Hey, I still don't think that Portuguese white paired well with the octopus salad," the man said, though clearly he had lost his steam. Leo actually felt sorry for him. He stood for a minute facing the table, nodding as though he were in deep thought. The man fiddled with his tie, which was covered with corkscrews. The woman looked completely bored.

"You know what? Now that I think about it, you are absolutely right. A chardonnay from California would have been much better. Why don't you try that next time?"

The man looked dumbstruck. Leo smiled and walked away from the table. He watched as the couple made their way through the empty loft restaurant toward Market Street. Then he moved to the window and saw the woman get quickly into a cab. So much energy for nothing. If he were a betting man, he would guess that they would never see each other again.

"Are you all set to lock up?" Leo called to the last waiter, grabbing the Barbaresco.

"All set. See you tomorrow."

Normally Leo would walk home on a night like this. Hope and Shoshanna were probably already asleep, and he loved walking through the quiet streets toward the glowing yellow face of the city hall clock that marked the intersection of Broad and Market Streets. It always helped to clear his head, put his day in perspective.

He had just started the long walk west on Market Street when his phone vibrated in his coat pocket.

"Well hello, Stephanie. You're calling mighty late on a school night," he said.

"Oh my God, Leo. I'm so sorry. I was supposed to call you hours ago. Have you heard from Hope yet?" Stephanie asked.

"No, why? What's going on? Is she okay?" he asked. "Is Shoshanna okay?"

"They're fine. But Mark's not. They took him away in an ambulance a few hours ago. I promised Hope I'd call you, but I was so flustered I totally forgot. Can you come over after work? The kids are all still up, and I just can't get myself together. I haven't been able to get anyone on their cell phones for the last hour, and no one at the hospital will give me any information."

"Hang tight. I'm on my way," he said.

Nikki knew that she shouldn't be walking alone this late at night. There had been that break-in at the old lady's house—Nikki tried to remember her name. She was so loud and crude that it was hard to absorb anything she said. Then Nikki remembered that when the old lady had introduced herself, she'd done it to the tune of "Miss Mary Mack" in that raspy, grating voice. Her name was Mary. Now she'd remember that. But even scarier than the break-in was that two days ago a woman had been raped in an alley just three blocks from here. Sure, it had been almost dawn when it happened, but still. People didn't expect things like that in this neighborhood.

Nikki took her cell phone out of her pocket and gripped it tightly, then tucked her hair deep into her collar. She had heard once that when walking alone you should never leave your long hair out for an attacker to grab. She wanted to be ready to dial 911, because the truth was that if something did really happen, who would be there for her? Will was never around. He probably wasn't even home from work yet, although he was supposed to be.

Nikki had gotten so tired of waiting for him that she had decided to go out and get their favorite: the makings of an ice cream sundae. At first she thought the bigger store on the corner of Spruce would be open, but it closed at nine. So she wandered a little, ending up at a dingy store on South Street. She found chocolate ice cream, Cool Whip, Hershey's syrup in the can, and even a small jar of maraschino cherries. The jar was dusty on top, but she bought it anyway.

Nikki took a deep breath and started to relax as she crossed the street at Dante's. Just then a cab screeched to a halt at the intersection behind her. One of her new neighbors—the guy with the goatee that Mark and Chris always hung around—jumped out and slammed the door.

"Hi!" she called cheerily, although he seemed to be in a huge hurry.

"Oh, hey. Sorry to be rude, but I've got to run. My friend is in the hospital," Leo said, picking up the pace. "But I guess you didn't need to know that. Sorry, I'm a little out of it."

Nikki stopped. "Which friend?"

"Oh, that's right, you know him. Mark. It's Mark."

"Wait!" she said, and Leo stopped and turned around. "What's wrong with him? Is he okay?"

Leo wondered briefly why she cared. He didn't have time for this; he wished he'd never mentioned it. "I don't know," he said testily. "That's why I'm in a hurry. I'll let him know you were asking."

"But . . ." Nikki started to say, but Leo was already unlocking the door, which he promptly slammed behind him.

Nikki stood in the middle of Emerson Street, under the little white lights in the trees, trying to make sense of her life here with Will in this strange place that appeared so warm and welcoming. She knew, of course, that looks could be deceiving. Despite the introductions and the baked goods, she wondered if she would ever really feel she belonged.

She had imagined her new life so many times—what it would be like when she finally left New Jersey. When she moved away from her mother and all the high school friends who still remembered what her hair looked like in eighth grade, that she had worn that awful bright yellow dress to the senior prom, and that she was dumped by her date halfway through the night. There had to come a time when those things stopped mattering, she always told herself. This was supposed to be that time.

She finally moved toward her front door. As she turned the key, she held her breath. *Please let him be home. Please let him be home.* She pushed the door open, a hopeful smile on her face, but the house was empty.

Why had she thought that getting engaged and moving in together would change things? If anything, it was worse now. They didn't have to arrange anything anymore. Will never asked what she wanted to do. He just knew that when he got home from work—whatever time that might be—she would be there waiting for him. Now he was even pressing her to quit her job—too many men lusting after her, he said, and besides, he made plenty of money to support them. And he said he was more than okay with her knowing how to pole dance, but he was always asking a lot of accusatory-sounding questions about Kat and her friends from the studio. He would never forgive her if he knew that she had been to Tempt, no matter what the reason. Nikki hadn't even told him that Kat worked there. It was important that he knew that she was strictly all his, and having a friend who was a professional pole dancer would put her too close to danger.

Nikki considered making the sundaes and leaving them to melt all over their new Crate & Barrel table—just to rub in how late he was. Will hated when things were messy or out of place. Then she considered leaving, continuing her walk around the city. What would he think if he got home and the house was empty? That would teach him a lesson.

Instead, she pulled a spoon out of their neatly arranged kitchen drawer, sat on the recently sanded pine floor, and started eating. Why should she care so much about how she looked when Will was never around to notice her anyway? What was the point of having a perfect body if there was no one to see her naked, no one to appreciate that she was still the exact same weight that she had been in high school?

Then she thought again about Mark and the day they had spent together and how he had listened to her, really looked at her. She thought about the car ride home and how she knew that he wanted to kiss her, but he was so awkward and shy, though charming and funny at the same time. She wondered what was wrong with him now and hoped it wasn't anything too bad. If only his friend had told her more. But why would he? She was practically a stranger.

Nikki thought about what might have happened if they had kissed and wondered what it would be like, kissing a man who wasn't Will, a man who seemed to be the polar opposite of Will. She had replayed this scene over and over since that day, each time adding a little more, going a little further in her fantasy.

Will still wasn't there when she took her last bite of cheap chocolate ice cream from the bottom of the carton. She slowly walked up the stairs to the empty bedroom, deciding that next time she wouldn't soothe herself with ice cream. She needed company. She needed friends. If this ever happened again, she would go to Tempt.

∽

By the time Stephanie heard the beep-beep-beep of the alarm down-stairs alerting her that the front door had been opened, she had all five kids on her third floor and the water filling the deep Jacuzzi tub in her master bathroom.

"Leo, is that you?" she called.

"It's me. Can I come up?"

"Yes, please. I'm all the way on the third floor."

Leo, noticeably winded, arrived in her bedroom, which had no door except for a wooden baby gate left over from when Harvest was too small to navigate the steep, twisting staircase.

"No news?" he asked, wrestling with the latch to the gate.

"No," she said. "I'm totally panicked. I wish they would call."

"I tried Hope from the cab, but there was no answer. Maybe they had to turn off their phones," he said. "I'm sure they'll call as soon as they know something."

Stephanie wrangled Ollie free of his clothes, leaving him to toddle around in only an Elmo diaper.

"Can I help?" he asked.

"Can you get the boys dressed, and I'll bathe the girls? I'm going down to set up the Pack 'N Play," she said, tucking Ollie in the crook of her arm and unhooking the gate again.

With Ollie settled into his makeshift bedroom across from Harvest's room, Stephanie trudged back upstairs. Leo already had the older boys in the striped pajamas Stephanie had put out. They were sitting on her bed, looking at books.

"Come on, girls, you're up," she said to Shoshanna and Lu, trying hard to keep a smile on her face. The little girls giggled in the deep tub, the bubbles threatening to take over the room.

"Just a few more minutes," she said, eager to get them into bed. "I'll be right back with your pajamas."

Stephanie got the girls dressed and then released them to jump onto her bed on either side of the boys, all of them snuggled together with

Leo, their hair freshly washed, smelling of watermelon. Her cell phone rang. She froze for a second before grabbing it off the night table.

"It's Chris," she said to Leo, pushing the button to answer it. "Oh my God, Chris. We've been waiting. What's going on?"

She stopped and listened, glancing sideways at Leo. Then she went into the bathroom and closed the door behind her. Leo could hear her voice as he read softly to the kids, but he couldn't make out what she was saying. He rushed through the last few pages of the chapter and hustled them down to Harvest's room and to bed.

As soon as they were all tucked in, he climbed back up to find Stephanie sitting on the edge of the bed, staring at the bathroom door.

"Stephanie . . . what is it? What did he say?" Leo asked, sitting down next to her.

"He's, um, really bad, I guess. They say he has swelling on his brain. A virus that caused encephalitis, I think. He's in a coma."

"A coma?"

She nodded, covering her face with her hands. "He's been having seizures, and now he's on a ventilator. They, uh, they don't know if he's going to make it."

Leo didn't say a word. He sat, mouth open, eyes fixed on a spot on the wall in front of him, breathing heavily in and out of his mouth.

"This is just crazy. How can he be in a coma?" Stephanie said, leaning her head on Leo's chest.

"They have to know more. Maybe I should call my dad, see if he can recommend a doctor down here. To make sure Mark's really being taken care of," Leo said, thinking that his father, a prominent New York surgeon, always knew the right strings to pull in an emergency.

"I need to lie down," Stephanie said, walking around to the other side of the bed. She lay down with her back to Leo, knees curled up to her elbows. He could hear her crying quietly. "Chris and Hope are going to stay there with Celia. You can go home if you want. The kids are fine."

Leo got up slowly and looked at her. For one second he thought about how Chris slept next to her every night. Then he pushed that thought away. He stood at the top of the stairs for a minute before turning back and shutting off the overhead lights. He walked to the bed, over to Stephanie's side. She was crying hard. He wanted to lie down with her, wanted to hug her and tell her everything would be okay. Instead, he reached down and squeezed her heaving shoulder.

"I'll be on the couch right downstairs," he said. No way he was going to leave her here alone with five kids, especially when he knew Lu and Ted would be asking about their dad and where he was when they woke up. He hoped they would have a better answer in the morning than they did now.

"Thank you," she whispered.

~

Mark made it through the next six days. Over and over Celia was warned that this could be it and she should prepare herself, whatever that meant, and over and over Mark lived through that hour or afternoon or day. Each time she had to talk to one of the doctors or Mark's family or their friends, she felt like she was playing a role, like she wasn't actually in her own body. She began to imagine herself as Jackie O during those conversations, poised and composed, looking people in the eyes and nodding solemnly, holding her left hand in her right and tilting her head just so. More times than she could count, though, she had to excuse herself to go to the bathroom, just to lock herself in a stall, where she would try desperately to breathe, talking herself down from the panic that was vibrating inside her.

She was grateful that they all took turns sitting with her, forcing her to eat, staying with Mark while she ran to the bathroom or gave the kids a quick call, using all her energy to sound more confident than she actually felt, just in case he woke up in the three minutes that she was gone. He had been intubated for the entire week, unable to breathe on his own, and in a coma until yesterday, when he started to show small signs of improvement.

Now Chris and Leo walked down the long corridor to the double doors marked "Restricted Access," where Celia was leaning against the wall. They each gave her a hug and stared awkwardly at the door to the ICU, needing to be near Mark, although as the days went by, they had grown to dread it, too.

"Is there anything else we can do right now?" Chris asked.

"No, no, there's nothing. You all have done so much taking care of the kids, just being here with me. I'll never be able to repay you for that."

"Come on, Celia. We couldn't be anywhere else right now," Leo said, putting his arm around her.

"They're in there trying to remove the breathing tube. After yesterday's fever, they wanted to wait another day. But it's down now, thank God. And the doctor says that the sooner they get him breathing on his own, the better. The nurse said she'd be out to get me as soon as they finish. I'm just so glad you guys are here."

They stood in silence next to each other, alternating between staring at the floor and taking turns peeking through the tiny square windows in the double doors as they waited for Tanya, Mark's nurse, to give them news. Tanya had been with Mark since the beginning, and it already seemed like they had known her forever, that she was someone who would figure importantly in their lives from now on. When Tanya finally emerged from the ICU in her hot pink scrubs and royal blue Crocs, she was not her usual upbeat self.

"Celia, honey, let me give you the good news first. We were able to remove the tube. He's breathing on his own again."

"Oh, thank God," Celia said. "Can we go in now?"

"I can take you all in, but I want you to know that he has suffered some major trauma, and he's not himself yet. The doctor will give you more details."

"But he will be himself again, right?" Celia asked.

"What you have to keep in mind is that bringing him in when you did saved his life," Tanya said gently.

They were all quiet for a minute.

"I'm ready. The guys will be with me," Celia said finally, taking a deep breath.

Tanya pressed the square button on the wall. The double doors opened slowly inward. The unit was always bustling with activity, and now was no exception. Celia and Tanya, followed by Chris and Leo, walked down the brightly lit hallway almost to the end, where Mark's room was on the right. They stopped to don their required blue paper masks and found Mark strapped to the bed in the tiny glass-enclosed room, his chin still marked from the tape that had held the tube keeping him alive all week. He was tugging at the black Velcro wrist restraints; he had been ever since he woke up yesterday, and by now he had dark purple bruises on both wrists.

"Mark, we're all here. You're going to be okay," Chris said.

Mark tilted his head, motioning Chris to come closer. Chris bent down, his face next to Mark's.

"Be a pal, man," Mark whispered, his voice low and raspy.

"What can I do for you?"

"Be a pal. Come on. Give me some scissors." He lifted both bruised wrists a few inches—as far as they would go in the restraints—and dropped them back down on the bed.

Chris stood up. "I can't do that, man. Hey, buddy, do you know who we are?"

Mark blinked heavily, looking from Chris to Leo and back to Chris again.

"No," he mouthed, and closed his eyes.

CHAPTER SEVEN

Leo and Chris let out a collective sigh of relief when the elevator doors closed and they felt themselves being moved down, away from the intensive care unit where Mark had been since he arrived. He was finally being transferred to a regular room.

"I hope I never have to go to that floor again," Chris said, watching as the red light descended with the floor numbers. He dropped Mark's black nylon overnight bag and turned to look at Leo, who was holding a flower arrangement in the crook of one arm and pulling the dead flowers out with his other hand.

"Do you think we have time for a quick cup of coffee?" Leo asked.

"Sure," Chris said. "Should we drop these off first?"

"No. In fact, I think I'm going to throw this one away," Leo said, lifting the arrangement that was now missing most of the flowers. He opened his hand to show a mash of dried yellow and orange mums.

"Good idea," Chris said as the elevator doors opened. He led the way to the hospital cafeteria, where he put the bag on a table and joined the now empty-handed Leo in line. Chris thought about ordering a milkshake but decided that was too indulgent considering the situation, and instead followed Leo to the coffee station.

Once they paid and sat down, Leo was sorry he had made the suggestion. The others were probably wondering where they were, and he couldn't seem to find the words he had thought he wanted to say when they were in the elevator. They sat quietly for a few minutes.

"That could have been really bad," Chris finally said. Leo nodded and stared down at the table. He had told himself since that first day that God or the universe or whatever higher power there might be would not take one of his best friends away from him so suddenly and inexplicably. He felt in his bones that Mark would be okay. Until today, until Mark was finally moved to his new room, free of tubes and restraints and everything else, he had not really let himself think about what could have been. Not only had Mark survived, but the doctors said that he had managed to escape without any apparent damage to his brain, which was nothing short of a miracle.

Chris got up, threw out his coffee, and put his hand on Leo's shoulder as they walked down the long hallway.

~

Celia stood in the doorway watching Mark try to socialize with the people who had not been allowed to come see him until today. He was still so weak, but so much better. Even so, if she let herself, she kept returning to the images forever burned in her mind of Mark lying with a tube down his throat, completely unavailable to her or the children, and with no way of letting her know if he would ever be back.

"I've been thinking about our living arrangements," Mark said when they were finally alone at the end of visiting hours. His voice was still raspy from the breathing tube.

Celia stopped staring out the window and turned to face him. "And?"

"I think we should do it. I think this commune thing is worth a shot," Mark said.

She shook her head. "Oh, sweets, after what we've just been through, I think we should stay put for a while and give you time to recover. We don't have to jump into anything just yet."

"But that's just it, Ceil. We need to do it *because* of what we've been through. Maybe I was wrong about the walls closing in. Maybe this will be just the thing I need," Mark said.

"But you said yourself that it would be chaos, that it would make our lives more complicated."

"I was wrong about the chaos. It's all chaos anyway," he said quietly, trying to push away the thought that maybe if he had been more grateful for his life, he wouldn't have gotten sick.

"I guess we found that out," Celia said. "The hard way."

"We never would have made it through this without them. And in some strange way, with all of us together, the holes in our lives seem to get filled in."

"You sound like Stephanie," Celia said, shaking her head.

Mark tried to smile. "I guess there's nothing like a near-death experience to bring out your inner hippie."

"You need to get some rest," she said, standing up and spreading out the blanket that had been folded at the bottom of his bed.

"You know I'm right, Celia," he said. "The question is do you agree?"

She took a long time to answer. Mark was having trouble keeping his eyes open.

"I agree," she finally said.

～

Nikki pulled the door shut and, like she had done every single day since she had found out that Mark was in the hospital, turned right instead of left. She had no real reason to go that way. The salon was in the opposite direction and so was the coffee shop, but she figured that maybe someone would come out of one of the houses at just the right time and she could ask how Mark was doing. She even considered knocking on Chris's door since she knew him the best, but then he might wonder why she was asking. She barely even knew Mark as far as he was concerned.

Just as she was about to turn the corner, ready to give up again, she heard a door open behind her. It was Mark's wife, the pretty blonde. Nikki had never really looked right at her before, but now she was transfixed, watching as she put her key in the lock and fought to turn it, throwing her whole body into it, jiggling the key, and pulling hard on the doorknob. She really seemed to be struggling. Without thinking it through, Nikki walked over to her.

"Can I help?" she asked Celia, who turned to face her and froze. Nikki noticed that her eyes were red and she wasn't wearing any makeup, but she was still so classically beautiful, with high cheekbones and perfectly straight white teeth.

"I'm just trying to get this darn thing to stop fighting me," said Celia.

"I'm Nikki. I don't know if you remember me. I'm Will's fiancée. Let me try."

Celia finally released her grip on the doorknob, leaving the key inside the lock with the keychain, a small plastic-framed photo of kids, dangling. She turned to Nikki. "Thanks, but I've got it," she said. "My husband is in the hospital, and I'm just not myself these days."

"Oh, I didn't know! Your husband is Mark, right? Is he okay?" said Nikki, immediately feeling a pang of guilt about the lie that jumped out of her mouth unplanned.

"He is, finally. He had a terrible infection, but he's recovering. He's supposed to come home today or tomorrow."

Nikki looked down at Celia's hands and noticed they were shaking.

"Please let me help," said Nikki. "I'm good with my hands." Nikki reached past Celia and grabbed the doorknob and key. Celia moved out of the way.

In an instant, Nikki had the door locked and was holding out the keys to Celia.

"Thanks so much," said Celia, shoving them in her purse. "I have to go," she said and took off down the street without glancing behind her.

"Bye!" called Nikki, watching Celia jog away, her own feet still glued to Mark and Celia's top step. She waited until Celia turned the corner and then headed back home. She had lost interest in getting her nails done as she had planned. She suddenly felt the need to be alone.

The house was finally quiet. Mark closed the front door and returned to the dark, cool living room. It seemed like a completely new place to him, foreign in its sounds and light patterns, the clock ticking almost too loudly and the morning sun streaming through the first-floor windows. He had been home from the hospital for three days, and finally Celia had agreed to let him be alone, without someone to wait on him or be there in case of a relapse.

Their latest babysitter, a serious redheaded nursing student from Penn, had been the last one to leave, out to Taney Park with Ollie tucked safely in the stroller. She had left reluctantly, telling Mark that he should drink lots of liquids and that he should call her on her cell if he needed anything, anything at all. She was studying to be a nurse, she reminded him, and could maybe be helpful. But he was fine, he said, and assured her that he would drink lots of tea and water and that he just needed to rest.

Mark wasn't supposed to go back to work, even part time, for another few weeks, and he relished the days ahead of him—no responsibilities, just blissful time to himself. He moved to the kitchen table and picked up the drawings he had been tinkering with last night. *Not bad for an invalid,* he thought, admiring his handiwork. *This will be a challenge. Supporting walls, stairs in odd places, three kitchens.* He picked up the phone and dialed Yogi's number, which he knew by heart.

Yogi answered on the first ring. "Yah, hallo!" he shouted in his high-pitched, overexcited voice. Mark imagined him smiling through the phone. Yogi, a fiftysomething Israeli man with bright blue eyes and an infectious laugh, was in a perpetually good mood. He was the contractor of choice for the neighborhood, always ready for a last-minute job thanks to the endless stream of twenty-year-olds he brought to the US from Israel and parented just like they were his own.

"Who's this?"

"It's Mark at 1816 Emerson Street. Do you have a few minutes to stop by today to look at a new job?" he shouted back. He couldn't help himself.

"You bet. I come right over," Yogi said, and the phone went dead.

Mark knew what "come right over" meant to Yogi, though, so he settled back onto the couch with Sunday's *New York Times*, a guilty and infrequent pleasure since the birth of his kids, figuring he had at least an hour to himself. But as he turned to the real estate section, the doorbell rang. He got up slowly and moved toward the door, pulling his dark blue flannel robe closed over his faded KU T-shirt and plaid pajama bottoms. He ran his fingers through his unruly hair.

He turned the dead bolt and then the doorknob. It wasn't Yogi.

"Hey," Nikki said.

"Hey, yourself."

She was carrying a casserole covered with aluminum foil. Dressed in jeans and a short-sleeved white sweater, her long dark hair pulled back into a high, tight ponytail, she looked at him through extra-large sunglasses.

"So I heard . . ." She stopped and looked down at the casserole. "And I wanted to bring you something." He could see that her hands were shaking.

Mark stood motionless in the doorway for a moment then opened the door wide, hoping she wouldn't notice that his hands were shaking, too. "I'm sorry, do you want to come in? I was just going to have some coffee."

Nikki glanced up and down the street. "I guess," she said, stepping out of the bright October day and into the house, looking for a place to put the meal she'd brought, a lasagna that had taken her nearly a full day to make, with homemade meatballs and gravy, not just ground beef and tomato sauce from a jar. She walked to the refrigerator.

"Do you mind?" she asked, then opened it after he nodded, rearranging until she was finally able to squeeze her addition on top of a Tupperware container of leftover spaghetti. She closed the refrigerator and wandered into the living room, then took off her sunglasses and put them on the window ledge. She didn't know what to do with her hands.

"Sugar? Cream?" Mark asked, catching her as she took a quick glimpse of herself in the full-length mirror by the front door. She smoothed her hair and rubbed some blush from her cheeks.

"Just black," she said, sitting down on the couch. He was proud of that couch—it was in mint condition, a midcentury modern piece with slate-blue wool cushions. He'd found it at an auction in New York a few years after he finished graduate school, and he'd been desperate to have it. He had scraped together every dollar he could at the time, knowing it would be worth it. There were two kinds of things you buy for your house, he always told clients, the pieces you put on the curb when you're finished with them and the pieces that you keep forever. This was the ultimate keeper.

He handed her the mug and sat down, leaving a full cushion length between them, sliding back as she leaned forward, her elbows propped on her knees.

She turned and looked at him over her right shoulder. "You didn't say how you are," she said.

Mark looked straight back at her. "I'm doing fine. Much better, thanks." He took a sip of coffee, then looked down into his cup. "I've been thinking about you," he said. "And that day."

She kept looking at him, even though he wasn't looking back. "When your friend told me you were sick, and then I didn't see you around for a while, well, I was, you know, worried."

"Don't you go and worry about me. I'm pretty tough," he said, puffing out his chest and making a muscle, then letting out a deep breath and slouching back onto the couch.

"Oh yeah, you look it," she said. "Real tough."

"Yeah, I'm just an old married person, isn't that what you called me that day?"

Nikki laughed. "Married, yes. Old, well, that's relative."

"You could say that."

"So what's it like having kids?" she asked, looking at the photo on the wall of Ted, Lu, and Ollie in their Halloween costumes. "Me and Will, we're engaged and all, but I don't think we're kid people. I've never really been that interested in being pregnant, and Will, you know, he is so into his job. He really gets off on the thrill of being a lawyer."

"Kids. Well, they're great, but it's a challenge. I used to be able to deal with them better than I can now, I guess, but I couldn't live without them either."

She put her coffee cup on the floor. "Yeah, I guess you're never lonely," she said, looking over her shoulder at him.

"That's not exactly true."

She slid over and back until their legs were touching. Her face was close to his, just inches away, and he was afraid to breathe. They sat staring straight ahead while the clock ticked loudly behind them.

She turned quickly and kissed him, her lips soft and wet and new, like something he hadn't ever felt before, but familiar at the same time. Her hand had moved. Now it was on his thigh, close to his crotch. Or at least it seemed to him that it was close to his crotch; he didn't want to look. He felt himself begin to swell. He groaned softly and contemplated moving her hand away, though it seemed like it might be an impossible thing to do. He was surprised to find himself beginning to kiss her back, moving his tongue into her mouth slowly and gently. He couldn't do this. He was married. Celia had just seen him through what he hoped would go down in the history books as the worst week of his life. He thought these things, but he didn't move away, didn't stop kissing Nikki. He had almost died, for heaven's sake. Did he always have to follow all the rules exactly?

Three loud knocks at the door made him jump from his seat and knock over his coffee. He ran to the kitchen for a towel, hurrying to scrub the brown stain from the rug. That's when he heard Hope's voice. "Mark, open up! It's me and Yogi."

"Nikki, I . . ." he said as he looked from her to the door, slowly moving toward it.

"Mark! I know you're in there. Come on, open up," Hope called.

Mark tightened his robe and opened the door.

"What took you so long?" Hope asked. "Are you feeling okay?"

"Hi, yeah, I'm fine," he said, turning to Yogi. "I see Hope's found you. Thanks for coming over. Let me introduce you to a new Emerson Street resident," he said as he opened the door wide to reveal Nikki, now standing directly behind him, sunglasses on again. "Nikki, this is Yogi. He does a lot of work around the neighborhood. And you know Hope—she's the baker extraordinaire. Nikki here just stopped by to bring us a meal."

Yogi smiled. He was wearing his trademark white pants and matching T-shirt, which advertised his company, Sun Builders, on the back.

Hope stepped past Mark into the house.

"So," Hope said slowly. "Nice to see you again, Nikki. Checking in on our guy here?"

"Oh, just dropping off some food," said Nikki, pushing her sunglasses on top of her head, revealing her big dark eyes. "Nice to see you, too. I was just leaving, though."

She had to squeeze by Hope, then Yogi, to get down the narrow steps.

"Thanks again. See you later," Mark said, interrupting Yogi's stare by shutting the door. "Why don't you come over to the kitchen table? Hope, come see the drawings I did for our little project."

~

Hope stared at the piece of paper on the table in front of her. "What's that?" she asked, pointing to a shaded area at the back of the middle house.

"That's where the kitchen will be. Same place, only bigger. Wait until Leo sees all the space he's going to have. Take a look here," Mark said to Yogi. "How big of a beam do you think we'll need to secure the openings?"

"I don't know. I got to take a look at the walls. This is some big plans. Tell me again what you trying to do here?" said Yogi, who had taken the pencil from behind his ear and started to write on a little spiral notepad he pulled from his back pocket. "Start from beginning. You buying the house next door and putting them together?"

"Nope. What we actually want to do is combine the three houses on the first floor—mine, Hope's, and the one in between us—into one house."

"So where you put the front door?" Yogi wondered aloud, running his fingers through his curly gray hair and scratching his head.

"I think for the time being we're going to keep using our own front doors and just open it up on the inside. We'd like to be discreet, if you know what I mean." Mark glanced at Hope. The three front doors were her idea, and both he and Celia had agreed that it was a necessity. "So we'll share the first floor, but keep the rest of the houses intact."

Yogi hit himself on the forehead with his palm. "Oh!" he exclaimed. "Now I know. Like kibbutz, back in Tiberius, near the Sea of Galilee. You know, how Marx say, 'from each to his ability, to each to his needs' or something like that." He shook his head, trying to remember the right words.

"Did you live on a kibbutz?" Hope asked, eyes wide.

"No, no, not me, but my cousin, he lived on Kibbutz Yasur. Great! Great! Now tell me when you want kibbutz."

Mark and Hope looked at each other. It was all moving so fast. "When can you get your guys in here?" Mark asked Yogi.

"Ahhh, I got a couple guys can do demo. How about later this week, I get a few of my guys in here for you. Special price just for you and your kibbutz. Let me think about it. I call you. Got to go now. My son Nadav over there on Pine Street doing painting. You will like what we do here," Yogi said, flipping shut his notebook and sliding it into his back pocket. Hope and Mark walked him out, and he climbed into his white van with the red Sun Builders logo on the side. He slammed the door shut, leaned out of his window, and shook Mark's hand. "Mazel tov," he said. "I make this good for you." Hope and Mark watched as Yogi drove to the end of Emerson and made a left, still waving at them from the open window.

"So . . . you've been busy, I see," Hope said to Mark, who was already walking slowly back up the steps. He needed some time to think. What was that with Nikki? Just a crazy moment, he told himself, something that would never happen again. He knew one thing: he was not a cheating man.

"I have no idea what you mean by that," he said, looking at her over his shoulder. "*L'chaim!*" he called in his best Yogi accent, lifting an imaginary glass to Hope.

"Mark," Hope said, catching him right before he disappeared into the house. "Everything okay? You haven't had much time to process the whole illness with our, you know, construction project starting up so quickly . . ." Hope's voice lowered to a whisper.

"I've got it all under control here, Hope. Don't you worry one little bit."

But when he got to the top of his stairs, Mark wasn't so sure. He stood in front of the framed picture of him and Celia on their wedding day. They were sitting on a bench in his parents' backyard, and Celia was wearing a crown made of flowers that he had carefully handpicked that morning. Her eyes were captured halfway between looking at the flowers in her hand and looking at him, and the expression on her face was open and joyful and, he forced himself to whisper the word out loud, *trusting*. The words *forsaking all others* ran through his mind. The guy in that picture was never, ever going to kiss anyone but the woman sitting with him on that bench. He couldn't help but wonder, who was this guy standing here now?

❧

The following morning, Yogi pulled up in front of 1816 Emerson Street at 8:00 a.m. sharp. The door of the white van slid open and out hopped four of the most strikingly handsome olive-skinned twenty-something Israeli men the three women had ever seen, all dressed in the Sun Builders uniform, white on white. They bantered in a mixture of Hebrew and English as they unloaded their tools, while Hope, Celia, and Stephanie gaped at them from the sidewalk.

"Where does he *get* these guys?" Stephanie said, taking particular notice of the tallest of the group as he lifted a sledgehammer from the truck, his muscular arm bulging.

"He ships them in from Israel," Hope said. "They're all nephews and cousins who want to come here after the army. He puts them to work for a few years, and then they mostly go back. He takes care of them, though. He told me once that he normally has five guys living with him at a time until they get on their feet. When they go, the next shift comes in. Yogi's just such a good guy."

"All I know is seeing them makes me wish for a minute that I was twenty and single again. Although I guess I wasn't even single when I was twenty. You know I've been with Mark for twenty-two years? Doesn't that sound absolutely crazy?" Celia asked.

". . . yeah, yeah, we know. You finally realized that you loved him when he carried your drunken butt home from the party after the prom and you weren't even his date," Stephanie said.

"Well, he did," Celia said. "It was a two-mile walk, and if you want to be accurate, I realized I loved him the moment he told me that he counted every step because he didn't want it to ever end."

"Speaking of being single, how was that lasagna our girlfriend Nikki brought?" Hope asked, rolling her eyes. Celia told that prom story at least twice a year, and Hope wanted to cut her off before she made them guess the number of steps, which they all knew was four thousand and eight.

"Oh, come on now, don't be catty. That was very thoughtful of her," Celia said, climbing her stoop and yelling for the kids.

Lu and Ted dawdled down the steps, followed by Mark, who handed them their backpacks. Normally he would have just let them walk away, but today he grabbed them, one at a time, leaning his face into their hair and inhaling their scent. He could have died and never had a chance to do this again. He held on to Ted a few seconds longer, telling himself he was being silly. He hadn't died. He was right here.

"I'll see you kids after school," he said. "And I'll see if the sitter can stay after work tonight to chat," Mark said to Celia, who was already running down the street after them. "You know, since you are the pro at letting people go, I thought I'd leave it up to you."

"Not this one," Celia said. "This time I'm delegating. I'll call you later. Try to get some rest if you can."

"See you later tonight," Hope called to Celia. "And don't worry— we'll be great. I really want to do this."

"Are you absolutely sure?" Stephanie said to Hope after Celia turned the corner. "It's a lot of responsibility, taking care of all five kids every afternoon and Ollie all day. It would make us all feel better if we could pay you."

"Absolutely not. You know I would never let you pay me. Besides, you'll be with me two of those afternoons," Hope reminded Stephanie as they started down the street toward school with Shoshanna and Harvest. "There's no reason for them to hire babysitters if we're all living together. I want to do this. I need to do this."

They waved to Mark as they turned the corner, and it couldn't have been better timing, because Mark now saw that the tall one, whom Yogi alternated between calling Yaakov and Sammy, had climbed Hope's steps and was trying to turn the doorknob. They had instructed Yogi to enter and exit the construction site only through Mark and Celia's front door and then do all the work from the inside.

"No! No!" Yogi shouted, pointing to Mark's door. "You only go in this door! This one! Discreet, they said!"

Yaakov looked from Yogi to the other workers and shrugged. "Okay. Okay," he said and followed them into Mark's. There was so much commotion outside that Mark knew it was inevitable that he would have to deal with Mary. So when he heard her upstairs window slide open, he braced himself.

"Mark! Hey, Mark!" she screamed from her third-floor window. "What the hell are you doing down there? Sounds like a goddamn party."

Yogi's guys looked up, and Mary stared back at them, indignant.

"What? What the hell do you think you're looking at?" she asked.

Mark hustled them into the house, whispering his apologies.

"I've got this, Mary," he called to her when they were safely inside. "Don't you worry. I'll ask them to keep it down."

"You better," she yelled, slamming the window shut.

It took six days for four guys to finish demolition of the two walls and secure the area around the holes between the houses. They had brought a Dumpster to the parking lot behind Emerson Street so they could haul away the massive amount of drywall and, in between Stephanie's and Hope's houses, the bricks that had separated them. They made sure that the Dumpster sat right behind Mark and Celia's house, and if anyone asked, they simply said Mark was redoing his kitchen again.

The process was painstaking, removing old drywall and layers of brick as they secured the upper floors with steel beams, which made two large openings that joined the three first floors. They went from Mark and Celia's through to Stephanie and Chris's, then finally to Leo and Hope's, where their former living room would be turned into a carpeted playroom filled with shelves for all the toys they had collectively accumulated. Stephanie and Chris's first floor, which sat in the middle, would become their common kitchen and dining room. The adult living room would be in Mark and Celia's house, complete with a wet bar transformed from their kitchen at the back of the house. That's where they would put Chris's big-screen TV and, of course, Mark's couch.

On the seventh day, Yogi and his crew got right to work patching and finishing the areas around the holes.

Mark handed Yogi an envelope with a check to pay for the construction. It was the three families' first official financial transaction together. They had decided to open a joint house account, where each family would deposit an equal amount of money for the renovations and to buy groceries and house supplies every month, though there was still some talk about having Hope and Leo opt out of the grocery payments since they planned to do so much of the child care and cooking. Hope kept saying that's not how it was done in a family; would a mother get paid for taking care of her own kids?

"Come, come, I have something for you," Yogi said to Mark, motioning toward the van.

"Look," said Yogi. "I get this for you. Another job, they getting rid of it. For you and your friends, for kibbutz."

"That's too much," Mark said. "We can't accept that. At least let us pay for it."

"No, no," Yogi said, waving him away. "My pleasure. You give me a gift, too. Your little kibbutz reminds me of home."

Mark smiled and took another look.

Inside the van sat the perfect addition to their new home: a handmade Nakashima-style dining table carved from a heavy slab of walnut, just the right size for their new family of eleven.

CHAPTER EIGHT

"Are you with me?" Leo whispered to Celia and Hope. They were sitting around the table Yogi had given them, eating breakfast.

"I can't," Hope whispered back, folding a napkin and using it to wipe maple syrup off Lu's place mat. "I have the kids today."

"They have school, don't they?" Leo asked.

"Not Ollie," Hope said.

"And I can't," Celia whispered, looking up the stairs closest to the table for signs of Stephanie. "I have a huge meeting. Plus, I'm still working on the house rules. We have to go ahead and get them approved so they can be implemented."

"Approved? Implemented? Can the first rule be to treat this like a home and not like a corporation?" Leo teased. "It's a good thing we didn't let you write the rules before we moved in together. We'd be well into amendments by now." Celia gave him a sterner look than usual, so he decided not to bring up the time they had rented a moon bounce for one of the block parties and Celia wanted to chart, by age and first letter of each child's last name, which children should jump at what time.

"Well, it looks like I'm on my own then," Leo said, forgetting to whisper, just as Stephanie came down the stairs, dressed in lavender yoga pants and a gray tank top.

"On your own for what?" Stephanie asked, choosing an empty seat.

"We have waffles and cereal," Celia said. "And some orange juice."

"Great," Stephanie said. "But I'm not hungry. On your own for what?"

"For deciding what color to paint the playroom. Nobody seems to care. I'm thinking orange, or maybe black," Leo said, proud of his quick thinking.

"Oh," Stephanie said, twirling her long hair over her head absentmindedly.

"So you don't have an opinion?"

"Not really," Stephanie said, getting up and grabbing her yoga mat, which was still stashed near the stairs from yesterday. "I have yoga. I just couldn't get up for the early class today."

She slowly walked to the door and, without even saying good-bye to Harvest, left the house.

"What's wrong with her?" Celia asked, getting up from the table and moving clockwise to kiss each of the kids on the top of the head.

"I don't know," Hope said. "Maybe she's bummed about turning forty today. Or maybe she's worried that with all the craziness we forgot her birthday. I should have wished her a happy birthday. What was I thinking?"

"Not to worry. It'll be even better this way because she'll be pleasantly surprised later," Leo said. "I have today off. I'm thinking Jamaican. What do you guys think?"

"Sure," Hope and Celia mumbled at the same time.

"I'm going to head to West Philly to check out one of those Caribbean stores. I'll make jerk chicken, which I better have marinating by noon or it won't have any flavor. Maybe some coconut rice and peas. Um, grilled plantains. What else? Some good rum punch. Hope, can you at least help me with the cake? I'm thinking coconut will fit in well with the theme."

"I assume you have a recipe in mind?" Hope asked.

"There's a great one in the *Barefoot Contessa*," Leo said. "I'll get it for you."

For a minute Leo couldn't think of where to look for his cookbooks. They had all been taken down from the grand bookshelf to make room for the toys on his side of the house. Then he remembered that they were in a box in the grown-up living room. He still felt a little like he was walking into someone else's house when he walked through to what used to be Mark and Celia's first floor. Mark was sitting on the bottom step, fully dressed for the first time in a long time.

Mark had felt pretty good as he showered and dressed, but as soon as he came down the stairs and saw that stupid couch, he could feel himself starting to get an erection. No matter how hard he tried to forget, the couch still reminded him of Nikki, which always resulted in the same panic from that day—dread and excitement, followed by an overwhelming wave of regret.

"Hey," Leo said quietly. "You okay?"

"Oh, yeah, just a little tired still, I guess," Mark said, leaning his elbows on his knees and trying to think of the least sexy thing.

"Are you worried about going back?"

"Maybe a little," Mark lied.

"Come on, have some breakfast, and I'll walk you to work. You can do it," Leo said, offering his big, warm hand.

"Sweets?" Celia called from the next room. "I have waffles and OJ. Come on in."

Mark slowly pushed himself up, brushed the front of his pants just to make sure he was okay, and followed Leo into the dining room.

"Oh, hold on," Leo said, stooping to look at a box of books. Luckily the one he was looking for was near the top. He grabbed it and took it back to the dining room, finding the right page and handing it to Hope.

"This looks complicated," she said.

"I don't think it will be," Leo said. "It should be pretty simple, actually."

Hope glared at Leo, feeling the sting of his tone. She was usually pretty good at ignoring it, knowing he didn't mean to sound the way he did sometimes. But now that there were other adults around to witness it, it was harder to take. With her face still set in an annoyed expression, she looked at Mark. He was too distracted to give her the reaction she wanted; it was taking all his energy not to look down at his crotch.

Leo didn't notice any of it; he was busy planning the party. He was secretly happy that the opening of the walls coincided with Stephanie's birthday. It seemed natural now that he would help with the celebration. In years past he had held back, letting the others deal with most of the details. Last year was particularly hard for him. Chris didn't do anything until the last minute, and then they ended up having pizza and beer on the street. Stephanie had seemed happy enough with it, but Leo would have done something more, something spectacular like she deserved. Besides, this was the first elaborate meal he would cook in their new kitchen, which they had outfitted mostly with his extensive collection of high-end kitchen gear, supplemented with special items like Stephanie's ice cream maker and Celia's deep fryer. The rest they packed away in their basements, except for the silverware, glasses, and dishes that made up their eclectic new collection.

Mark took a seat next to Ollie. He was fine now. The sight of his family had completely eliminated his arousal. He tried to catch Hope's eye, tried to smile at her to make sure she was okay, but she was looking over the cake recipe.

Chris came quietly down the stairs, glancing around the table.

"Is she gone?" he asked.

"We thought *you* were gone," Celia said, taking a pile of dishes to the sink.

"Leave those, I'll take care of them," Hope said. "Yes, she's gone. And she seemed a little out of it, I think."

"Huh, I can't believe I missed her," Chris said. "She spent an unusually long time in the bathroom while I hid in the closet, thinking I'd surprise her with a little gift first thing in the morning. But she never came back." Chris put a small bronze box on the table.

"Do you mean to tell me that you didn't wish her a happy birthday either? And that you've been hiding in the closet this whole time?" Hope asked.

"I kept thinking she'd come back in," Chris said. "Damn. I wanted her birthday to start off right."

"It's an awfully pretty box," Celia said, putting on her jacket. "What is it?"

"Some necklace she told me she wanted," Chris said. "I couldn't think of anything else. I was hoping she'd wear it today."

"Oh, did you get that necklace from the place on Twentieth Street? She really wanted that," Hope said.

"Well, see you guys later," Celia said, interrupting Hope and coming back to kiss Mark on his head. "Have a good first day back, sweets. Don't work too hard, please." She walked to the door and turned back. "Hey, this is nice," she said. "Not having to worry about the dishes before going to work, knowing Ollie is with family. Okay, I'm really going now."

"Shoes, coats, you don't want to miss the whistles," Hope said to the kids as she made a few trips from the table to the sink with dirty dishes.

"I guess I blew the first part of the day. I hope that doesn't interfere with her chakras or good energy, or whatever it is that it might interfere with. But there's still time to make it up to her. I'm going to go in late, or maybe I'll take the whole day off," Chris said, helping himself to some orange juice. "Should we have a party tonight?"

"Yeah, that's a good idea," Leo said after what was a slightly awkward silence.

"Should we do pizza again? I found a new place that delivers," Chris said.

"If you want to," Leo said slowly. "But I don't have to go in today either, and I'd be happy to cook something. I thought Jamaican food might be festive."

"That sounds great," Chris said, running his hand through his thick blond hair and flashing a satisfied smile. "Then I can concentrate on the gifts. I don't think this necklace is quite enough—and maybe I'll get some decorations, lights or lanterns or something. Thanks, Leo. Hey, Hope, I'll help you get the kids to school."

Chris stood up, grabbed his coat, and joined Hope, who was standing with the kids in a bunch by his front door.

"Do you think?" Chris said, pointing over his shoulder at Hope's door a few feet away.

"Actually, yes," Hope said, gently pushing Shoshanna in that direction. Then, after she made Lu and Ted stand by their own front door, she pushed the stroller over and put the brake on, unlocked Celia and Mark's door from the inside, and went back to her own. This was the first day Hope was taking all the kids at once, and they hadn't even discussed how they would exit the doors to keep suspicion down. She was glad Chris was thinking about it.

"I'll go first," she said. She grabbed Shoshanna's hand, walked out, and pulled the door closed behind them then locked it. She went right to Celia and Mark's door and knocked. She waited one second, noticing that there was absolutely nobody out on the street anyway, and then she pushed open the door.

"Hello?" she called. The kids looked at her like she was crazy. "I'm here. I'll take them to school for you. See you later."

And with that Chris and Harvest came out of their door.

"Good morning," Chris said as he always did. "It's a beautiful day in the neighborhood."

"Hi there," Hope said, dropping the charade. "Can you get Ollie down? We're already late."

Once everyone was on the street, Hope glanced back to make sure all the doors were closed.

"That was a little tiring," Chris said when they were off the block. "Maybe it isn't really necessary?"

"No, I think it is. It would look weird if we all came out the same door every morning," Hope said. "It wasn't that hard. Maybe sometimes we'll just pretend that everyone stopped by at the same time. We used to have mornings like that, right? Like if you ran out of Benadryl and Celia left her umbrella at work—you could both end up at my house at eight o'clock."

"Sure, of course," Chris said, standing in the middle of Nineteenth Street like a crossing guard as the group crossed. "We can mix it up."

"Who picks us up today?" Ted asked, poking Lu in the back with the hard part of his baseball cap.

"I will," Hope said.

"Oh good," Lu said, not noticing her brother's torture techniques. Hope smiled to herself.

"So I'm thinking we need a word of the day," Chris said. "Something we can learn and talk about. Each morning we'll pick one."

"Sure," Hope said, taking one hand off the stroller and brushing it down the back of Shoshanna's shiny hair. "Like what?"

"I'm thinking like respect or responsibility, something like that," Chris said.

"Okay," Hope said. "Not so much a word we've never heard of, more a word that means a lot."

"Well, we can do both," Chris said. "But, yeah, like an everyday word that has lots of meaning."

"Expelliarmus!" offered Shoshanna, who didn't even seem to be paying attention to the conversation. This started a small riot among the kids, who circled around each other pointing and waving imaginary Harry Potter wands.

"How about *togetherness* for today's word," Hope offered when they finally settled down.

"*Togetherness*," said Harvest. "That's dumb. Spells are cooler! Yeah!" That set them off on another bout of jumping around yelling whatever spells they could think of and periodically falling to the ground in mock defeat.

"Okay, okay," Chris said. "We can switch off. Today's word can be *whateverarmus* and tomorrow's word can be *togetherness*."

"Okay, but after that I'm going to come up with something much more obscure than *togetherness*, and I can promise you it won't be a made-up magical word," Hope said playfully. "I'm going to stump you."

"I welcome the challenge," Chris said, smiling, already trying to think of a word that might stump Hope. "In fact, I look forward to it."

~

Chris talked Hope into having a cup of coffee together after drop-off, but when he followed her and Ollie out and up Twenty-Third Street, she started to worry that he wanted to spend the morning with them.

"I'm going to cut off here," he finally said at the corner of Twenty-Second and Chestnut. "I think I'll hit the dollar store first, then head to Anthropologie to find Stephanie some new clothes. I think that's my best bet."

"Wave good-bye, Ollie," Hope said as Chris left them. Then she breathed a sigh of relief. She was looking forward to being alone with Ollie—the walk to school had been fun, but chaotic. Maybe it would be okay if she never had another baby. Maybe Ollie would be enough. In a way, it was the perfect setup. She could love him and play with him and have a hand in raising him, and then give him back at night. She was surprised by her own thoughts. She and Leo had been trying to get pregnant again, unsuccessfully, for over two years. It was the one big goal in front of her right now, the thing she had to have. But lately, it hadn't seemed quite as important.

"It's just you and me," she said. "What should we do now?"

"Gagee," Ollie said.

"Oh, I have an idea," Hope said.

She steered them across Chestnut Street and into Di Bruno Bros. market, where she could get most of the ingredients for that difficult cake Leo expected her to make. But there, on one of the packed shelves, right next to the Swiss chocolate, was the genuine Barefoot Contessa coconut cake mix, with a photograph on the front that looked just like the one in Leo's cookbook. The box had almost everything she needed. Hope would just have to mix up the batter and then add butter and cream cheese to the frosting mix.

"Brrr," Ollie said.

Hope saw that he was pointing at a bin of long baguettes.

"Brrr for bread, right, Ollie," Hope said, leaning down to choose a good one. She broke off a piece and handed it to Ollie, who grabbed it out of her hand and stuck it in his mouth in one motion. Hope laughed.

An older woman stopped to witness the exchange and smiled, looking down at Ollie.

"You are the cutest little baby!" the woman said. "How old is he?"

"A year and a half," Hope said proudly, reaching down to touch his blond curls.

"Well, enjoy him," the woman said. "It goes by so fast. He certainly has your eyes."

For a split second Hope contemplated saying that he wasn't actually hers, that she was just taking care of him. But what would the point be? She'd never see this woman again, and besides, she kind of liked it.

"Thanks," Hope said and walked away.

Stephanie lay on the floor, feeling the wood beneath her mat. This was the longest yoga class in history. Usually it flew by and she left wishing she could do more. Not today. She moved her arms so her wrists and palms faced up and tried to tuck her shoulder blades underneath her. She moved each foot one at a time so her legs were completely stretched out, with the backs of her heels on the floor. Savasana—corpse pose. The room was silent.

She tried not to think, or at least she tried to block out the thought she kept having: that it might be a relief to be a corpse and not have to worry about things. She didn't know what to do with any of it. She couldn't believe she was forty today. She was mad that Chris hadn't said happy birthday first thing, while they were in bed. Then he had gone off to work without a word while she was still in the bathroom. And, to make it even worse, nobody mentioned her birthday at breakfast. She wasn't sure what she had expected, but something. She could explain all that away if she wanted to, though. They were busy, Chris was preoccupied at work. What she couldn't explain away was the fact that she was pretty sure she was pregnant.

How could she have another child now? She was so far away from the baby stage, much further away than she thought she'd ever be if she had a second child. Harvest was already six!

Without realizing what she was doing, she found herself on her feet. Harvest! She hadn't said good-bye to Harvest.

"Are you okay, Stephanie?" her teacher, Chloe, asked, startled.

"Fine, sorry," she said, feeling dizzy. "I'm so sorry. I have to go."

"But we're almost through," Chloe said. "Why don't you finish out the class?"

"No, I can't," Stephanie said, moving toward the door and trying not to step on hands or heads. Not a single person even looked up. Were they all asleep, Stephanie wondered, or just being polite?

"Namaste!" Stephanie yelled as she sprinted down the stairs and out the front door. She stood in the bright sunshine wishing she could go back and do that over. Talk about bad karma. Plus, Harvest was already in school, so there was nothing she could do about him right now anyway.

Stephanie started to walk in the general direction of home, making rights and lefts onto the smaller, tree-lined streets. Maybe she should buy a pregnancy test. Or she could just swipe one from Hope who, she knew, had a stash of them. My God, what would Hope think if she knew Stephanie was pregnant? She shook off the thought. She couldn't worry about that right now. Right now she had to be sure, but she was almost certain without taking a test. This is exactly what it had felt like. She had felt crampy right around the time she should have gotten her period, and then it never came, and the cramps went away. And then—she hated the thought of this—she got that awful nausea in the afternoon. Did she feel slightly nauseated now?

Her phone vibrated in her jacket pocket. Shit. She had a client at 9:30 a.m. on the other side of town. She picked up the pace and looked up Susie's number.

"Susie," Stephanie said into the phone in her most professional voice. "I'm on my way. I'll get us some coffee."

By the time she arrived at her client's house, she felt better. Honestly, with the renovations and deciding to all move in together, it was enough to make her period late. Also, maybe living so close to Hope and Celia was throwing her cycle off. Why hadn't she thought of that before? Stephanie got busy helping Susie clean out two huge, packed file cabinets. She was completely present while she advised Susie to throw away the birthday cards her mother had kept for her from her eighth birthday. She helped her organize her report cards from elementary school in a file. And she actually enjoyed listening to the poems Susie got from her boyfriend during her senior year of college. They reminded her of the poems her own college boyfriend used to write for her. The one with the surfer haircut. The one who had a trust fund but pretended he didn't. Each morning he would see what Stephanie was wearing and then write a poem trying to guess her mood. She had loved it at first, but after a while it somehow took the fun out of getting dressed in the morning, knowing that "shirt pink" might be rhymed with "together linked" or "skirt long" with "forever song." She finally started to try to pick things that she couldn't, for the life of her, rhyme with anything, but he always managed to think of something. Stephanie didn't mind sharing some of this with Susie, and she was more than happy to be able to tell her honestly that she hadn't kept a single one of those poems.

∽

Celia couldn't concentrate. There was nothing she hated more than seeing people in the office surfing the web or doing something that so obviously had nothing to do with the job at hand, and yet she couldn't help herself. She had restrained herself from writing the rules before and during construction—heck, she'd wanted to write them before they even hired Yogi. But everyone had teased her so mercilessly that she'd decided to use it as an opportunity for personal growth. Wasn't she always telling her employees to see challenges as opportunities to learn about yourself and grow?

First she wanted to figure out how many house rules there should be. She googled rules for communal living, rules for a kibbutz, rules for cohousing. Most of what she found was convoluted and, in the case of a few of the kibbutzim, way too religious. Obviously religion was not an issue for these rules. She was Baptist and Mark was Catholic, Hope and Leo were Jewish, and Stephanie and Chris were Catholics-turned-pseudo-Buddhists. At least Stephanie was. Ever since Celia could remember, that had been a good thing, with everyone learning about each other's beliefs and traditions and having more to celebrate with the different holidays.

Thinking of religion led her to the number of rules. Ten, obviously. There were ten commandments, and so there should be ten "Emerson Street House Rules." On the other hand, of all the rules a doctor abided by, there was just one that people remembered: first, do no harm. And since she had grown up learning in Sunday school that the Golden Rule was the only one you ever really needed, was one simple rule the way to go? She wasn't sure.

Celia quickly checked her e-mail and voice mail to assuage her guilt. Then she opened a new file on the computer and wrote the first rule, but after that one she was stumped. She wanted to write something about each child being first and foremost the responsibility of his or her parents, but what did that even mean? And she considered stating that all house members had to clean up after themselves, but already today Hope had waved everyone away and done the dishes herself.

Celia looked again at her computer screen. Then she had an idea. She went into the supply room, found cardboard and markers, and brought them back to her desk. She didn't even care at this point if anyone was wondering what she was doing. She started to write bubble letters, neatly coloring them in with different colors—red, yellow, blue, orange. When she was finished, she sat back and smiled. Then she leaned forward and added two words in parentheses below what she had already written.

"That should do it," she said to herself, then picked up the phone and dialed Mark's number. She wanted to hear his voice.

"This is Mark," he answered, and Celia had to close her eyes for a minute. There was a time not too long ago when Celia thought this normalcy might be gone forever.

"Hello?" Mark called into the phone.

"Oh, hey, sweets, it's me," Celia said, fiddling with a pen. "I just wanted to see how you're doing. Are you tired?"

"Not so bad," Mark said. "They're giving me a break today, letting me settle back in."

"You haven't told anyone about, you know, the arrangements, right?" Celia asked.

"You sound like you're talking about a funeral," Mark said. "But no, I haven't. I'm assuming that you haven't either?"

"Correct," Celia said. "And I don't plan on it. In fact, I think we might need to go ahead and come to an official agreement about keeping it quiet. I have no idea how it might affect my promotion."

"Leave it to my wife to think the whole world is watching her," Mark chided. "Does anyone there even know where you live, or care, for that matter?"

"They care about personal conduct," Celia said defensively. This wasn't the conversation she'd meant to have when she called him.

"I can vouch for your personal conduct," Mark said. "But I get it. I don't want people knowing our business either."

"Do you feel strange about Hope being with the kids? Do you think it's too much to ask of her? I wish she would at least agree to let the rest of us pay for her share of the groceries," Celia said after a minute. Hope, of course, had refused to be paid, which Celia both understood and worried about.

"No, she wants to do it," Mark said quickly, suddenly aware that he had been rushing to hang up and go back to sitting at his desk quietly daydreaming about what might have happened if he and Nikki hadn't been interrupted. A daydream never hurt anyone.

"Hey, I have an idea. Do you want to see if we can go out to dinner tonight, just the two of us?" Celia said, sorry the conversation had gotten so serious.

"Are you kidding? It's Stephanie's big birthday bash," Mark said, happy to have the excuse.

"Oh yeah, what was I thinking?" Celia said, surprised by her disappointment. "Maybe another time."

"Sure," Mark said, his mind already wandering back to Nikki's long hair and slim waist. He closed his eyes and saw her slowly undressing him. As soon as he hung up, he felt a welcome wave of relief. When he got home, they would all be there, picking up his slack while he figured out where the old Mark had gone, while he got control of himself. Hope and Stephanie would give Celia the attention she needed, and he wouldn't have to feel like he owed her more of himself than he could give right now.

Leo enjoyed the drive to the market and took his time walking up and down the aisles full of coconuts and plantains and pigeon peas. When he got home, the house was empty. It smelled of fresh coconut. He looked around the kitchen for the source of the aroma and found a beautiful cake, iced with white frosting and covered with flakes of coconut, on what used to be their dinner table. They had hauled it upstairs so it could serve as a makeshift island in the big unfinished kitchen. Leo was truly surprised; he hadn't really thought Hope would be able to do it.

At that moment the door opened and Hope walked in holding Ollie in her arms. She had taken the bag with the Barefoot Contessa box and anything else that might have given her away to the garbage can on the corner.

"Hi," she called, putting Ollie down on the carpet of the playroom and surrounding him with toys. "Did you see the cake?"

"Yeah, it's beautiful," Leo said coming over to her. "I'm impressed."

For a split second Hope thought about telling him the truth, but then Chris came in his door with bags, and Mark came in his. Leo got to marinating, Chris got to wrapping and decorating, and Mark took a seat in the living room where he put his feet up and closed his eyes.

"So you were there for almost four hours," Hope said to Mark. "Was everyone happy to see you?"

"Are you kidding? I was the life of the party," Mark said, opening his eyes. "But now, my dear, I think I might go take a nap before everyone else gets home and the next party begins."

"Good idea," Hope said.

At a little before three, Hope started to get Ollie ready to pick up the other kids. She was putting on his second shoe when Chris came down the middle stairs.

"Hey, I'll go get them," Chris said. "You stay here with Ollie."

"That would be great," Hope said.

Once the kids got home, they were put to work coloring a big banner for the party. It read, in the Jamaican theme: "Happy 40th Birthday, Mon!" Chris wrote the words for them, and they spent the rest of the afternoon coloring it in and drawing tropical pictures.

At five thirty, when Celia came in from work, the house looked and smelled like the Jamaican Jerk Hut just down the street. The chicken had been marinated, and Leo was slow-cooking it on a barbecue grill out back. The rice was ready and mounded into big bowls. Celia took a minute to admire her blue-and-green ceramic bowl next to Stephanie's yellow one. They looked just like they belonged together.

"Smells great," Celia said, putting her bag down on the floor. Then, thinking that somehow she must be breaking a rule, she picked it up and moved it into the living room. At least now it was in her house. "I tried to call Stephanie a few times today. Has anyone heard from her? Is she here?"

~

Stephanie's client Susie was reading something about a hot pink ribbon that Sammy, her long-lost college sweetheart, had vowed to keep forever when the unmistakable nausea hit. Stephanie shifted in her chair, thinking maybe it was the smell of all those pressed, mildewed flowers that kept falling out of the yellowing folded letters. Or maybe it was the cup of cold coffee Susie had left on the table.

"Long, billowy, like you," Susie read. "The satin slips through my—"

"Susie, I'm sorry to interrupt, but I'm suddenly not feeling well. Can we call it a day?"

"Oh, yes, of course," Susie said, folding up the old piece of paper. "I got carried away today. Sorry to have kept you here so long."

"No, it was great. You got rid of a lot of things," Stephanie said, trying not to gag. Oh how she hated this. She had a huge fear of vomiting. "But listen, don't throw anything out yet that has to do with Sammy. We'll start there next time."

"Thanks, Stephanie," Susie said, smiling. "And at some point I'd love to get to that coat closet."

"No problem," Stephanie said, getting up and walking to the door. She considered stopping at the bathroom first but decided fresh air would be better. And she was right: as soon as she breathed in the cold October air, she didn't necessarily feel better, but her nausea was not as bad.

She waved down a cab, got in, and tried not to breathe. The smells were so strong everywhere today.

"Eighteen fourteen Emerson Street, please," she said, putting her head back against the seat. "Actually, just drop me at Eighteenth."

She knew she had to lie down. That was the only thing that would make her feel better. The cab came to a stop just below Emerson Street. Stephanie paid and went around the back. She looked into what used to be her own private kitchen. They were all there. Leo, the kids, everyone except Celia and Mark, as far as she could tell. She waited. When she saw them all following Leo out of the kitchen, Stephanie snuck in the back door and turned sharply up her flight of stairs without even looking into the playroom. She felt a pull toward Harvest's voice, but the need to lie down was stronger. And the kitchen smelled so awful!

She waited on the second-floor landing to see if anyone had heard her, but there was no indication that anyone had. She continued up, stopping in the bathroom to splash some cold water on her face. She pulled down the Sea-Bands from the top shelf that she hadn't used in years and put them on, took a piece of hard candy from her nightstand drawer, and lay down on the bed. She propped herself up with three pillows and closed her eyes, tasting the sugary sweet of the candy and breathing slowly in and out of her nose. She put one hand above her navel and the other below it, feeling her abdomen rise and fall. She lay as still as a stone. In the past, whenever she felt like she was going to throw up, this had been her ritual, and somehow the feeling always passed. If she was right about this, she should feel better in about forty-five minutes anyway. That's the way it had happened when she was pregnant with Harvest.

Forty-five minutes and she would know for sure.

CHAPTER NINE

Stephanie grabbed one of the large white shopping bags and started stuffing. The clothes that Chris had bought her were strewn all around their bedroom, tags still on, half of them inside out. First she had tried on the wide-legged pants, but she couldn't even get the zipper up. She had checked the tag three times, and each time it said the same thing—size four—which meant that she was either bloated or already showing. How could that be possible? If she had calculated right, she was only six weeks pregnant. The pants had to be a fluke. Next she slipped on the wispy T-shirt printed with delicate pale yellow birds. *Damn,* she thought as she turned sideways and looked into the full-length mirror. *This is just not going to work.* Even though she knew she wasn't going to like any of it, she tried on every last item again, getting more and more frustrated by the minute.

By the time she had picked everything up and filled the two bags, she had worked herself into a frenzy. She stomped down the two flights of steps, pushing her wavy hair over her shoulder, put on her jacket, and started up Eighteenth Street toward Anthropologie. Luckily her favorite salesperson, Kendra, was behind the counter on the first floor of the sprawling turn-of-the-century-mansion-turned-trendy-retail-establishment.

Impossibly tall and thin, with flawless caramel-colored skin and impeccable taste in clothes, Kendra always helped Stephanie when she needed an outfit for something or an opinion on what went with the one item that she just had to have.

"What happened?" Kendra asked, pulling the crumpled clothes from the bags one by one. "I picked it all out myself."

"No, Kendra, I really love everything. I'm just a little pissed at him. First of all, he waits until the day of my birthday and expects you to bail him out, and second of all, I just don't need this stuff right now . . ."

"Are you sure you want to return it all?"

"Yes, absolutely. I'll be back in, though, soon. I promise. Maybe when I'm feeling a little more rational."

"No worries. It's just a shame that you don't have a great birthday present to enjoy," Kendra said as she scanned each item. "Do you have your card? I can credit all of this back."

Stephanie handed her American Express card to Kendra, who ran it through the machine. They both waited what seemed like an inordinately long time for the receipt to print out. Kendra folded the long slip of paper and handed it to Stephanie with her card.

Stephanie turned over the receipt and looked at the amount. "Oh my God, he spent $758? Well, I guess I deserve it, right?"

"Of course you deserve it. Come back when you're ready, and I'll help you with the winter line. A new jacket just came in that I know you'll love."

Stephanie thanked Kendra, exited through the massive double wooden doors, and walked down the high flight of steps onto Eighteenth Street. *I do deserve it,* she thought, *especially if I'm going to be fat and miserable for eight more months.* She stood on the corner and looked up and down the street. She had been so sure that returning the clothes would make her feel better, but she just felt empty. So instead of turning right and heading home, she turned left toward her favorite shoe store. But before she got there, in the window of a small boutique, the most amazing bag caught her eye. It was large enough to fit all the stuff she always carried around, but was incredibly sleek. It was made of a slick eggplant-colored patent leather—the "in" color for the season—with chunky silver buckles that secured the short shoulder strap to the deep, rounded bottom. She walked past the security guard directly to the inside of the front window and picked it up.

"This is an incredible bag," said the slim blond woman behind the counter. "There's only one of them, and I want it so badly, but even with my discount, it's a little out of my range. I'm so jealous!"

Stephanie turned over the price tag. She narrowed her eyes and looked closer, sure that she had read wrong, but she hadn't: $950. The salesperson stopped typing into her computer and looked at Stephanie, who was still staring at the tag.

"Is everything okay? Do you still want it?"

Stephanie snapped open her wallet, determined to do whatever it took to make herself feel better today. "Of course I do," she said and handed over her credit card.

She walked down Eighteenth Street back toward Emerson, feeling the pleasant weight of the bag on her shoulder. The salesperson had put her new purse inside a black velvet bag, then into a shopping bag. Even so, Stephanie felt lighter now, strangely euphoric. *Why the hell not,* she thought. *I never treat myself. I just turned forty, and this is something that will fit no matter what size I am.*

As she passed the sidewalk cafés that bordered Rittenhouse Square, a notion crept into her head, first slowly, then it gained momentum. *No one knew that she was pregnant. No one knew!* She started to jog, moving faster and faster as the thought grew and developed. When she got to her door, she fumbled with her keys, her hands shaking. She took her phone from her jacket pocket. Twelve fifteen. Chris would be home any minute. He was meeting her here for lunch today. There was a lot of leftover Jamaican food, and since she had been so out of it last night, he had pressed her to have lunch with him, and she had agreed, even though he was the last person she wanted to see right now.

She dropped her bag inside the door and ran up her stairs, two at a time, into the third-floor bathroom. There, just where she had left it in the trash can this morning, was the pregnancy test and its wrappers. She grabbed a brown plastic grocery bag from under the sink and stuffed it all in and tied it tight, still shaking and listening for Chris's footsteps. When she got downstairs, everything was quiet, so she bolted out the door without locking it and headed to the public trash can on the corner. At exactly 12:22 p.m., she was back in the house. She plopped herself on the couch, took a deep breath, and leaned her head against the wall. She had gotten rid of all evidence of her pregnancy, so now she had some time to figure out how she felt about it. At the very least, she had a little time to think.

~

That night, when they went to bed, the sheet of paper hanging below Celia's poster was still blank.

Celia had unveiled the rules after dinner, and she had been really proud of herself. One simple rule: take care of each other (and yourself) was all that they would ever need, she'd said. Besides, Stephanie and Hope were always talking about the rules of their kids' school—take care of each other and get smarter—so she had known that they would be happy with it. But just in case, Celia had decided that in the spirit of consensus, she would solicit input from anyone who wanted to provide it. So she'd hung up a sheet of paper where, anonymously or not, they could add any additional rules that they thought were necessary. It would be an ongoing process, she told them, and they would revisit and discuss them at their weekly meetings, presided over by, of course, Celia. She had been elected unanimously as the person in charge, or, as Leo liked to call her, the first wife.

Hope felt good about everything—the house, the rules—until later, when she was getting ready for bed. Opening her sock drawer to retrieve those comfy cotton socks that kept her feet toasty when the nights got cool, she immediately saw the empty black plastic bag, the one where the last of her pregnancy tests had been. She pulled it out and opened it wide with both hands. Nothing. She crumpled it angrily and threw it in the trash. It wasn't like she needed it anyway, but to invade her privacy like that? What had Stephanie been thinking? *It just had to be her,* Hope thought. *No one else knows but her.*

Hope was already in a foul mood since she was starting to feel a little crampy. Her period was due in a few days, and she always got terrible PMS . . . that is, every month of her life except the nine when she was pregnant with Shoshanna. *How dare she go into my stuff and take something?* Hope thought. *And was Stephanie pregnant? She didn't even want to be! Now that would just be the icing on the cake.* Hope lay awake in bed, her mind racing. If Stephanie were pregnant, what would she do? Even if she wasn't sure that she wanted another baby anymore, Hope didn't know if she could handle watching it come so easily to Stephanie. She imagined how hard it would be to be around her, seeing her belly grow round, watching her prepare for a new brother or sister for Harvest. She looked at the clock—2:20 a.m. She had to do something.

Hope got out of bed, careful not to disturb Leo, and padded down the stairs to the kitchen, stopping by the playroom to grab a marker from the blue plastic bin. She stood in front of the refrigerator and used the thick black marker to scrawl one cryptic line.

When she was satisfied with what she had written, she returned the marker to the bin and tiptoed back upstairs.

∾

"Huh," Celia said at breakfast, standing in front of the refrigerator with her hand on her hip, staring at the sheet of paper. Scrawled in marker it read: "Don't take things that aren't yours!"

"Is someone going to own up to this?" she asked. "I think it's really important that we keep the lines of communication open between us and give feedback when necessary."

Everyone just stared at her from around the table, then went back to eating breakfast.

"Looks like somebody's being a little passive-aggressive," Leo said, taking his last bite of a buttered baguette, then bringing his empty plate to the sink. "I would venture a guess that it's not one of us guys," he said as he passed Hope and Shoshanna, bending down to kiss each of them good-bye. "I'll see you all tonight," he said as he walked into the playroom and out through his own front door.

"Hate to say it, ladies, but I am not touching this one with a ten-foot pole," said Chris, grabbing his briefcase and starting toward the middle door. He threw Stephanie and Harvest a kiss, then mimed catching one. "Love you!" he called, leaving through the door at the front of the dining room.

"Well, it certainly wasn't me, so that leaves the two of you," Celia said. "I'm going to work now, but if you need me to mediate, I can help tonight. In the meantime, I suggest you start acting like adults and figure whatever this is out." She gave each of the kids a kiss on the head on her way into the living room, grabbed her suit jacket, and exited through the farthest door on the left. She locked the dead bolt behind her, bent down, and lifted the mail slot. "Talk it out, guys!" she called into the house.

"I'm sorry," Stephanie said to Hope, looking down at the table. "I was panicked, and I shouldn't have gone into your room. I just knew that you had one."

"Well, are you?" Hope hissed, unable to contain her anger. She knew that she shouldn't do this in front of the kids.

"I can't talk about this right now, Hope," Stephanie said, wishing she had never stolen the test.

"Well, I guess that's a yes then," Hope said.

"Not necessarily," Stephanie said back, standing and gathering the breakfast plates with the intention of ending the conversation. "Come on, kids, you need to go."

Hope turned and rolled her eyes at Stephanie. "Can you at least help me get them out the doors?"

Stephanie nodded without looking at Hope. "Sure," she said.

～

Stephanie was back at the dining table staring into her coffee cup when Mark came down the stairs dressed in jeans and a T-shirt.

"Not going in today?" she said to him as he sat down across from her, pouring a bowl of cereal and helping himself to strawberries.

"Nah. The doctor said to stick to part time for two more weeks, but to tell you the truth, it's starting to drive me nuts. I feel so much better, and I don't know what the hell to do with myself anymore. I want to get out there."

"So what's on the schedule for today?"

"I don't know. Maybe I'll hit the driving range or something. And I have to get to work on our kitchen. You?"

"I have a client this morning," Stephanie said. "I'll be back here in the afternoon."

She sat for a minute, listening to him crunch his cereal, watching as he turned the pages of the *Philadelphia Inquirer*. "Mark?"

"Yeah?"

"I need to talk to someone about something, and not that you're my last choice or anything, but I don't know who else . . ."

He looked up at her, suddenly aware of how drawn and tired she appeared.

"I'm pregnant," she blurted.

Mark stopped chewing, confused. "That's, uh, a good thing?"

"Well, I guess that's the big question."

"I see," he said, folding the newspaper and sliding it away from him.

"So, the thing is, I think I want to . . . um . . . *not* be pregnant. I haven't told Chris yet. You know how much he would want the baby. I can't tell Hope or Celia I feel this way. Celia has no idea this is going on, but Hope guesses. I don't know what they'd think of me. I don't know what *I* think of me right now, except that I know that I just don't want to go through this again. I keep trying, but I can't find a part of me that does."

Mark let out a deep breath. "I think you have to talk to Chris about this, tell him how you really feel. I agree he would want a baby, but he wants you more."

Stephanie shook her head. "I'm afraid to. Once I tell him, that's it, there's no taking it back. Every once in a while he asks me if I want to try to get pregnant again. He would see this as the best news ever. I'll eventually tell him, I promise, but in a little while, after I have all my options figured out and can make a better case for what I want to do," she said. "And, God, I love Harvest more than anything in the world, but that was enough of a surprise. Don't get me wrong. Once the shock wore off and Chris and I decided to get married, I never considered another option. And now I am totally in this: me and Chris and Harvest."

"Any chance that if you let this sit, the shock would wear off again and you could be in it like before?" Mark asked.

"I don't think so. Not this time. It's different. I believe without a doubt that I was meant to have Harvest," Stephanie said. "And I just don't think this is meant to be."

Mark sat quietly for a moment. "I get it, Stephanie. I do. No one understands that more than me. I know what it feels like to be trapped in a life you feel you don't quite belong in any longer, to be a person you don't quite recognize. A few months ago I would have told you that we accept it and live with it and make the best of what we have. That we have no choice but to learn to love what is given to us or what we chose because we thought we would love those things no matter what, even when we start to wonder if that's true anymore. But you're getting me on a different day, and I think there is the chance for change, the chance to have more control over the shape of our lives." Mark leaned back. Did he really just say that? And a better question might be, did he believe it?

"You do?" Stephanie said. "You don't think I'm an awful person?"

"Stephanie, you act like you haven't been one of my wife's best friends for years, like you haven't been one of my best friends. You act like I didn't brush death a few weeks ago. I don't think we have to be stuck—not anymore, anyway. I'll support you in whatever you do."

They sat across the table from each other, both wondering what it would take to go back once a line was crossed, if you could go back at all.

Stephanie was the first to speak. "You won't tell anyone, right? Not even Hope if she presses you? Promise me."

"My lips are sealed," he said, raising his fingers to his mouth and turning an imaginary key.

~

Nikki stood naked in front of the full-length mirror. First she curled her eyelashes with the new lash curler that she had picked up at the fancy new cosmetics store on Walnut Street, then she carefully applied black mascara to her upper and lower lashes. She finished with a touch of under-eye concealer and some powder blush in Madly, her favorite shade. By the time she had finished painstakingly blow-drying and straightening every square inch of her hair, Will had emerged from the bathroom with a towel around his waist, the steam escaping and threatening the results of her twenty minutes with the flatiron.

"Hmmm. You look *so* good," he said, grabbing her around the waist and grinding into her from behind, his towel falling to the floor. "Are you trying to excite me before I go to court today? Throw off my concentration?" He lifted her long, perfectly smooth hair and kissed the back of her neck.

She turned around to face him, pressing her naked body into his. "Hey, I just put on my makeup. But I guess I can fix it later," she said, getting down on her knees and taking him into her mouth.

"Oh, baby, that feels so good," he moaned, closing his eyes and grabbing the back of her head with both hands.

She took her time, moving her mouth around him. When she tried to tug him onto the floor next to her, he resisted. She looked up at him, surprised.

"You know I have to go," he said, staring down at her impatiently. "I have to be in court in half an hour and on my A-game. Can't you just finish up this way? Come on, baby."

Nikki sat back on her heels and grabbed a towel to cover herself. Then she thought better of it and went back to finish what she started. It probably wasn't worth making that statement right now.

"That's it, babe," Will said, his eyes closed, smiling. "Take care of your man." In only a few minutes it was over, and Nikki was left wiping off her face with the towel from the floor, removing her freshly applied makeup in the process. "Hey, babe, you know if you stopped spending your days at that salon and started spending them here, I could run home at lunch every once in a while."

She held the towel around her as she went into the bathroom and grabbed a robe.

"What do you think?" Will called, moving away from her to the walk-in closet. "Also, if you were around the house more, I bet the closet wouldn't look like this. Can you get to all of these boxes this week?"

Nikki poked her head out of the bathroom door, toothbrush in her mouth. "Huh?"

"The boxes? All your things? Can you get them organized, put away, something? It's been almost two months. I can't stand the mess." Will walked out of the closet, strikingly handsome in his navy suit and crisp white shirt. He was tying his silver-and-red-striped tie. He kissed her on the head and grabbed her ass.

"Thanks. I'll see you tonight, probably late, though. Don't wait up. I can wake you when I come in."

"What about lunch?" Nikki said, holding the toothbrush just outside her mouth. "I thought you said lunch."

"Oh, that was hypothetical. I can't make it today," Will said.

Nikki spat into the sink. "Okay," she said. "But can you please try to come home for dinner tonight? I miss you, and maybe you can help me get things organized around here. You know that you're better at that than me. Please?"

She turned around to find that he was gone.

"Bye," he called, already down the stairs and on his way out the door.

Nikki heard the door slam. She stood in front of the mirror and slipped off her robe, admiring her reflection. *I do look good, really good,* she told herself, studying her body. She was thin, but with just the right amount of curves, generous round breasts, and a teeny waist—her best feature. The pole dancing had made her strong but not muscular, and her legs looked more toned than they had when she was a teenager. She considered masturbating. There had been a moment there when she felt really turned on, but now she realized it had passed. In fact, by the time she finished the blow job, her desire was long gone.

She sighed and wandered into the walk-in closet, tripping over a brown cardboard box overflowing with jeans. She didn't know why she had been putting off the unpacking, merging their stuff. The closet had been filled with Will's clothes when she moved in: expensive suits, shirts, and ties from the fancy men's store on Chestnut Street. They were all lined up, facing the same direction, first shirts by color, then suits, then slacks, then sport jackets, with ties displayed on the rack at the far corner of the closet near the shelf of cuff links and collar stays. He had cleared the other side of the closet for her, but so far she hadn't organized a thing.

Nikki pulled out a pair of straight-legged jeans from the box and slipped them on. She didn't have to be at work until around noon, so maybe she would start to clean up today. But every time she looked at the boxes, she felt overwhelmed. *First I'll get some coffee,* she thought, *and then I'll have the energy to do it.*

She walked up Nineteenth Street and through Rittenhouse Square toward La Colombe, the best place in the city for a skinny latte. As she crossed Walnut Street, she heard a woman's voice call her name. Heading in her direction down the path was Chris's wife. Was her name Stephanie? She had brought her son to the salon a few times and had always been the friendliest of the Emerson Street clique. But she was friends with Mark—and his wife. Nikki quickly pushed the thought aside, grateful for a friendly face and the distraction.

"Hey, Nikki. How are you? We haven't seen much of you lately. Have you settled in okay?"

"Yeah, fine, I guess. Just getting organized. Our house is a total mess, and we're having the rehearsal dinner there next weekend. And don't even get me started on the wedding itself. Thank God for the planner Will insisted we hire."

"Well, you're talking to the right person. If I can help, just let me know."

"I guess, okay," Nikki said, confused. "Do you have a great cleaning person or something?"

"Oh no! I thought you knew—I have my own business. I'm a personal organizer."

"Really? I didn't know there was such a thing. What do you do, like, help me clean my house?" Nikki asked.

"Well, yes and no. What I do is help people figure out how to organize their lives by organizing their things. I'm on my way to La Colombe. I desperately need coffee. Want to walk with me?"

~

When they got back to Emerson, Nikki unlocked her front door and led Stephanie up the open staircase, glancing back at her as they climbed. "Now I don't want you to think I'm a total slob, but I want you to be prepared. It's not a pretty sight."

They turned the corner into the bedroom and stood at the opening to the walk-in closet.

"I see what you mean," Stephanie said, staring at the piles of boxes and clothes strewn across the floor. Behind them was a huge wedding dress–shaped garment bag wedged in between a bunch of other clothes.

"I just can't bring myself to do it. He's such a neat freak, and I'm the total opposite. Look at his side of the closet, for God's sake." Both women stared at Will's clothes, lined up in perfect rows on identical wooden hangers.

"All right, this is what we're going to do. We're going to start at the beginning and decide what goes and what stays. Then we'll decide the best way to set up the closet so that you can fit in as many of these awesome shoes as you want. Okay?" Stephanie said, totally up for the challenge.

"I don't know how to thank you," Nikki said.

Stephanie put her hand on Nikki's shoulder. "It's what I do. And I promise, you'll feel so much better when this is behind you. Then you can concentrate on your wedding. So tomorrow at ten, okay?"

"Yeah, I can't wait. And I do want to talk to you about that yoga class, too. I used to do gymnastics when I was a kid. And now I do pole," said Nikki, looking down.

"Pole? That's awesome. I tried it once at that studio a few blocks away," said Stephanie. "I am so not strong enough. Are you good?"

Nikki immediately relaxed. "Um, yeah, I guess I'm pretty good. Sometimes, though, I don't tell people I do pole. I just say that I dance. And if they ask what kind, I say modern."

"I've always wished I could do pole," Stephanie said without missing a beat, and Nikki relaxed even more.

"Well, maybe I can show you sometime," Nikki said. "You look strong to me. Actually, you look incredible. Is yoga how you got your body back after having a baby?"

Stephanie looked up, startled. "Are you guys thinking about kids already?"

"Oh no, not me. Kids are not in my plans," said Nikki, shaking her head slowly.

Stephanie looked at Nikki and opened her mouth to speak, then decided against it. "Well," she said finally, "kids aren't for everyone."

CHAPTER TEN

Leo tiptoed into the tiny den on the second floor of his house and slowly shut the door, stopping short of latching it. He didn't want it to make a clicking sound. He stood there for a second, listening for any movement above or below. All quiet.

He sat down on the blue plaid couch, put his feet up on the glass coffee table in front of him, and turned on the television. He went to the "On Demand" menu, scrolled down to the premium channels, then HBO, and then the specials. He took another glance toward the door, muting the television to make sure nobody was coming. At this point he could still fake it; he could pretend he was just looking for a good movie.

Leo took a deep breath, settling deeper into the couch and stretching out his crotch in front of him. In a perfect world he would be able to take his pants off, but there was no way he could do that now. Besides, he didn't want to get too excited, just turned on enough to have sex with Hope. He chose the late night selection and then went to *Real Sex*. It wasn't porn, exactly, but certain episodes could really get him in the mood. He liked the sex machine one, especially when the woman with the ponytail was suspended by some weird sort of hammock, and the mechanical penis was jutting in and out of her. There was also the one with a bunch of naked women in a big empty room full of balloons. They all ran around excitedly and squealed when a balloon popped. Tonight it was something about a strip club. He watched it, waiting.

Of all the things he had worried about when deciding to take down the walls, this was not one of them. For some reason it hadn't even occurred to him that it might be a problem. But it should have. It was hard enough sneaking around behind Hope's back, but he hadn't considered that there would now be four other adults to worry about.

The first time he did this—about a year ago—it had started innocently enough. It was one of their regular nights for sex, but he was tired. Shoshanna had been up a few nights in a row with a cough, and he was preoccupied with coordinating the wines with the new fall menu at Vega. While Hope settled Shoshanna down, Leo had been clicking through the "On Demand" menu and stumbled upon the late night section. He watched one of the shows, turned it off as soon as he heard Hope coming down the hall, and was happy to find himself more than ready for her.

He told himself there was no harm in it, that next time he would just do it, cold. Or maybe he'd invite Hope to watch it with him. But each time he was able to hide for a few minutes and watch, just to get in the mood. And now, he hated to admit it, but he sort of felt like he needed the boost.

Ah, this was better. The next segment was about sex with food, right up his alley. As he settled even deeper into the couch, spreading his legs just a bit, he felt his erection start to grow while the naked woman on the screen was being smeared with chocolate syrup. He watched for another minute while a man teased her with a banana. Then he forced himself to turn it off, took a deep breath, and went upstairs to his wife.

"Do you see the bin for the markers?" Celia asked, holding up a bunch of colorful writing utensils.

"I think it's over there," Stephanie said, pointing. She took a pile of mismatched Colorforms pieces and a stack of boxes and sat down on the stairs that led to Hope and Leo's second floor. Celia and Stephanie had insisted that Hope go upstairs with Shoshanna after dinner. She seemed tired and had taken it upon herself at the end of each day to clean up the playroom.

"Do the kids even play with these anymore?" Stephanie asked, holding up a rubbery plastic raincoat.

"Lu does," Celia said. "And Ollie might."

Stephanie nodded and carefully separated the pieces, looking at the fronts of the boxes to make sure she paired the right items with the right themes.

"All those ponies drive me crazy," Celia said when she saw the My Little Pony Colorforms box. "Somehow one ended up in my bedroom the other night. It had green hair and smelled like kiwi."

"You should have put something in the rules about all the ponies having to stay on the east side of the house," Stephanie said.

"No, it was okay," Celia said, sorry she mentioned it. "It wasn't a problem."

"For the record," Stephanie said, putting the last flat plastic pony into its box, "Ted's Power Ranger action figures were all over my bedroom floor the other day. Not that I care. You could barely see them under all the junk."

"I guess we better go ahead and get used to it," Celia said.

"I already am," Stephanie said, putting her hand on the step to push herself up. That's when she heard the sound. She sat back down, perking her left ear up the stairs and shushing Celia. She was immediately sorry. She should have ignored it.

"What?" Celia asked, moving closer. She, too, cocked her ear, and her face first took on a confused look, then her cheeks flushed red. There was the unmistakable sound of the rhythm of sex, a consistent banging of the headboard against the wall, or the bed hitting a table, or maybe it was the foot of the bed hitting the cedar chest. There were no human sounds, no words or groans, but there might as well have been.

"Oh," Celia said, looking away. She stepped back from the staircase and awkwardly placed the last of the stuffed animals in the bin. Stephanie just sat there.

"I think we're finished here," Celia finally said. "You can get up now."

Stephanie shook her head slightly. What was wrong with her? She stood and put the boxes back on the shelf. She could still hear the bang, bang, bang. She tried to suppress the tingling between her legs as the thrusting sounds got more frequent and more urgent.

"Night," Celia said, moving past Stephanie into the kitchen and finally through the living room that would lead her to her own upstairs.

"Night," Stephanie said, hesitating for one more second before turning to follow Celia out.

~

"There's a new rule," Chris said cheerfully at breakfast the next morning. Everybody but Mark was at the table. The kids were fighting over the cheddar bagels.

Celia squinted at the sheet of paper hanging below the main rule. The new rule read: "3) Please don't go up on the roof if you've been drinking—especially at night."

"I don't even know what that means," Celia said. She was in a bad mood. After hearing Hope and Leo having sex last night, she couldn't shake the thought that it had been a long time, a really long time, since she and Mark had done it. Sure, he'd been sick, but that wasn't really the reason. They hadn't been having sex for months before that. Had they since Ollie was born? She thought so, but now she couldn't think of any actual times.

"Hope, I know you'll understand it," Chris said as Hope carried a bowl of Count Chocula cereal already full of milk to the table and set it in front of Shoshanna, the only kid who preferred cereal to bagels. She turned to read the rule. Then she smiled.

"Doesn't anybody besides me and Chris read around here?" she joked. "That's taken directly from *The Cider House Rules*. One of John Irving's greatest books—well, there were many—but I loved that one."

"I'll never forget my mom reading that book and loving it, then giving it to me. It must have been when I was in high school? And an FYI for all of you, that's actually rule number three of the Cider House Rules. Get it? We have the main rule, then that other scrawled rule, which, I might add, nobody has owned up to yet. So this is rule number three for us, too. I just couldn't resist," Chris said, smiling at Hope. "I loved that book. But I also loved *Garp* and *A Prayer for Owen Meany*."

"And I loved *The Hotel New Hampshire*," Hope said, sitting down next to Chris and choosing a poppy seed bagel. "Do you remember the farting dog?"

"Of course!" Chris said. "One of the great fictional animal characters of all time."

"Well, I don't know if I would say that, but he was memorable," Hope said.

"I hate to interrupt this morning's literary discussion group, but we can't have a fake rule on our list of rules," Celia said seriously. "You're going to have to take that off. We don't even have a roof that we can get to."

"Hey, I'm just trying to lighten the mood around here," Chris said, taking the last bite of his Franken Berry before getting up and walking to the rules. He found an eraser and worked until all the words he had written were gone. As he came back to his place, he shot Hope a knowing look. She smiled back. He grabbed the cereal box and poured more into his pink milk.

"All better," he said, putting the box down. "Hope, I think I can help with the kids this afternoon. It's supposed to be really nice out. Maybe we can do some sort of art project on the street. I'll try to come up with something fun."

"Don't you have to work?" Stephanie asked. She was quiet this morning, using all her energy to fight the urge to eat a second bagel. She was so hungry, but she couldn't justify overfeeding herself to nurture a baby she wasn't even sure she was going to keep. She reached for a rye bagel, sniffed it, then put it back. She was grumpy, too. Hearing the sex noises last night had really put her in the mood. And she knew Chris would have been more than happy to oblige. But when she got upstairs, she just couldn't. What if he noticed that her body was changing? She just wasn't ready to deal with it yet.

"Of course I have to go to work today," Chris said. "We have, um, a big presentation this morning. But I think I can sneak out this afternoon. Hope's been working so hard with the kids, and I miss them. It's no big deal."

"Whatever," Stephanie said.

∼

Nobody asked Stephanie what she was doing this morning, and she was sort of disappointed. She thought Hope and Celia would get a big kick out of the fact that she was going to Nikki's house to organize. She imagined a lot of giggling when they talked about all her shoes and various requests to check out her underwear drawer or medicine cabinet for a laugh, but there just wasn't a good time to bring it up. When Mark stumbled down the stairs at the last minute, she considered telling him. But he was so distracted. He was sleeping later and later, and Stephanie worried he was either getting lazy or was a little depressed. He came down dressed, but his hair wasn't brushed, and he still looked thin and pale. He headed straight for the kitchen and poured himself a cup of coffee before going right back to the living room, flopping onto the couch, and picking up the television remote.

At 9:55 a.m., Stephanie wiped her hands on the dishcloth after putting the last of the bright plastic dishes in the dishwasher. She brushed her hands over her skirt, stopping briefly at her slightly bulging belly. She grabbed her expensive new bag, got the keys, waved to Mark, who was engrossed in the *Today* show, and walked out her front door. She looked up and down the street to see if there might be someone left outside, but it was quiet. She slowly walked the rest of the length of the block to Nikki's. Two short knocks. Then nothing. Surely Nikki hadn't forgotten. Two more knocks.

She heard the upstairs window slide open.

"One second, sorry," Nikki called from above.

"No problem," Stephanie called back. "Take your time."

She listened as the thumps of Nikki's feet got closer, then Nikki opened the door sheepishly and stepped to one side.

"Hi!" Stephanie said, reminding herself to treat Nikki like a regular new client. Now she was glad she hadn't had that conversation with Hope and Celia. She wanted this to be a professional relationship.

"Hi," Nikki said, smiling warmly. "I was just trying to get a head start upstairs, but I think I made things worse."

"Don't worry, that's why I'm here," Stephanie said, dropping her bag next to Nikki's and following her up the stairs. She stopped outside the office on the second floor—it was perfectly neat with envelopes and all different-sized papers in different slots at the back of the wooden desk. Stamps were in neat rolls, pens were all pointed down in a shiny old coffee can.

"Will's office?" Stephanie asked.

"How did you guess?" Nikki said, laughing. "He would never have to hire you."

"I guess not," Stephanie said good-naturedly. "Thank goodness for people like you, or I'd be really bored."

Nikki turned on the stairs to look at Stephanie. Then she smiled widely.

"Come on," she said, picking up her pace.

As soon as they reached the third floor, Stephanie knew what Nikki meant about making things worse. When she had been there before, the bedroom had looked okay. It was Nikki's side of the closet that was a disaster. But now boxes and shoes and T-shirts were everywhere. There was a huge plastic bin of cosmetics, and Stephanie could see that some of the bottles and tubes were leaking. A pile of socks—probably more socks than there were in Stephanie's entire house, counting all the kids' and all the adults'—had taken over the bed.

"Were you trying to sort by color?" Stephanie asked, pointing.

"At first, but then I was trying to sort by outfit," Nikki said, slumping down on the bed next to the socks. A pair rolled off and disappeared under the bed. Nikki sighed, putting her head in the middle of the pile. She wore a light pink tank top and jeans. Her feet were bare, and her toenails were painted a sparkly shade of red.

"Do you even wear socks?" Stephanie asked, realizing that of all the shoes she had seen Nikki wear—complicated sandals, fancy pumps, gold flats—none required socks.

"Not often," Nikki confessed.

"We're starting here," Stephanie said matter-of-factly, opening up a big black garbage bag that she had brought with her. "Choose seven pairs of dressy socks and seven pairs of athletic ones. We're giving the rest to a shelter."

"We are?" Nikki asked.

"We are."

Nikki quickly chose the socks, putting fourteen pairs into an empty drawer and throwing at least fifty other pairs into the black plastic bag. Nikki tossed each one into the bag, and Stephanie held it open to catch it. At first Stephanie stood in one place and Nikki threw, but then she tried to throw socks underhand or overhand, and Stephanie moved around the room ducking and reaching to catch each one. When Nikki took the last pair—black ones with tiny kittens that Stephanie would bet money she hadn't worn in years, if ever—she stood on the bed and mimed tossing it one way, then another. Stephanie laughed as she moved with Nikki's motions, finally catching it and falling backward onto a beautiful white ottoman.

"I didn't expect this to be fun," Nikki said, glancing at the now-empty bed.

"Why not?" Stephanie asked, getting up, shaking the bag to let the socks settle, and moving on to the T-shirts.

"I don't know. I guess I feel guilty. I really should be taking care of some wedding details instead of doing this, but I just don't want to. Also, growing up, my mom was always after me to clean my room," Nikki said, shaking her head. "She used to warn me that if I didn't, she would put everything that was on the floor in a bag and not give it back for a week. Anyway, it always seemed like a fight in my house."

"I don't know if that's better or worse than the way I grew up. My house was a total mess. My mom always said that life was too short to clean, so the few times a year my grandmother would visit were the only times my house was neat."

"Well, we're all grown up, I guess," Nikki said. "It's up to us now."

"You've got that right," Stephanie replied.

~

Chris didn't really have a big presentation. In fact, he had been contributing less and less to the company ever since that awful meeting with Bowman, the CEO. The strange thing was nobody seemed to notice. How could it be that he gave his all or gave next to nothing and he got the same reaction? It made no sense.

Still, he planned to go to work this morning for a little while. He walked along Chestnut Street, glancing in the windows. Inside an art supply store he saw a tie-dye display. "Bring a little color into your life," the banner over the swirly T-shirts read.

Before Chris realized what he was doing, he had pulled open the heavy door and was walking into the store. It was full of displays of paper, paints, and canvases, and had that pencil and glue smell that reminded him of art class in elementary school. He stood there in his suit and tie, feeling conspicuous, wishing he had chosen a more creative path in life. Why hadn't he ever considered teaching or writing or designing something?

"May I help you?" a perky young girl asked, startling him.

"Oh no, I was just—" he started. "Well, I was drawn in by the tie-dye display."

"That was my idea," the girl said proudly. Her name tag read "Amber." "I figured, like, people are sad that the summer is over, and, like, what says summer more than a tie-dye T-shirt?" She stood back and smiled.

"Nothing," Chris said. "Nothing says summer more than a tie-dye shirt. And I would like to make one. Is it a kit or something?"

"Follow me," she said, turning elegantly and moving deeper into the store, where the smells of creativity grew stronger. He watched her ankles bend, imagining beaded summer sandals. She led him to a shelf of kits and pulled out a bright box.

"Here," she said. "It's not much. But I wanted to, like, make something big out of something small. You'll still need to get the actual T-shirt. I think we have some in the back. How many do you want to make?"

"Well, if we do just the kids, then I'll need five," he said.

"You have five kids?" she asked, wide-eyed, taking a slight step back. "I never would have guessed."

Chris smiled. Would she like him more or less if she knew he really had only one child? He wasn't sure.

"Yeah," he said. "Five kids in my house."

"You're a nice dad," she said, moving a little closer again. "To, like, want to do a project with them."

Amber took a long time, showing Chris how to make the different patterns with the rubber bands: bull's-eyes or polka dots or spirals, single and double. She found a bunch of white T-shirts in the stock room that she was willing to sell him for five dollars each. And she recommended buying two boxes of the dye so they would have more than enough color to work with.

When Chris stepped out again into the chilly November morning, it was quickly approaching lunchtime, and he was hungry. He had sat at La Colombe for almost an hour sipping his cappuccino before even moving in the direction of work, and now he had spent more than an hour in the quiet art store watching Amber's slim fingers manipulate the rubber bands this way and that, then taking them off and starting again.

If he went all the way to work now, it would be noon by the time he arrived, and then he'd have to go right out again for lunch. But standing on Chestnut Street, the bag of tie-dye supplies heavy in his hand, Chris was suddenly eager to take control. He took his phone from his pocket and dialed Bowman's assistant.

"Kathy? Hey. This is Chris. I need to see the boss. Is he around?"

"Well, he's in the office now, but he doesn't want to be disturbed," she said.

"This can't wait," Chris said. "I'm on my way."

Hope kept Ollie out all day. They walked to Penn's Landing and back. While he slept, she got lunch at Di Bruno Bros. and ate in Rittenhouse Square. Then she rolled him into Barnes & Noble, where she read magazines. And the whole time she accepted the smiles and nods from the people admiring his fluffy blond head and chubby baby cheeks.

He was still sleeping when she left the bookstore at quarter to three and headed in the direction of Shoshanna and Harvest's school. For the twentieth time she debated putting in her iPod. She hated seeing nannies and moms tuning out their kids with music. And she never would have done that with Shoshanna. But there was this one song that kept running through her mind, and she wanted to hear it.

She glanced around to make sure she didn't see anyone she knew as she pushed the earbuds in. She was just about to call up "Shine On" by Jet when she felt a tap on her shoulder.

"I didn't know you had a younger one," said Jennifer Harrison, the mother of one of Shoshanna's friends from school, as she leaned over to get a good look at Ollie. "No wonder you've been avoiding my playdate requests."

Hope considered finishing her task of putting on the song and just walking away, but she didn't actually dislike Jennifer, she just couldn't stand to have this conversation now. She couldn't lie to someone she actually *knew*, and she wasn't thrilled about knowing what she really thought, what everybody probably thought.

"Oh, I didn't," Hope said, rolling up the wires and putting her iPod in her pocket. "Have another baby, that is. This is my neighbor's son. I'm taking care of him."

"Sorry that I assumed," Jennifer said, looking truly embarrassed. "It's just that you seem to like being with Shoshanna so much, I just always wondered why you had only one."

"Well, we've been trying," Hope blurted, surprising herself. "For a while now. But it just doesn't seem to be happening."

"Sorry," Jennifer said again. "So how about that playdate? I could bring April over to your house one afternoon. You live on that great street, Emerson, right?"

"I don't . . . well, I don't know what my schedule is like. Besides, we seem to have the stomach flu running through our house, and, well, the place is just a complete mess."

Jennifer had joined Hope as they walked in the direction of school, but now she stopped and said, "You know what, I need some Tylenol. I'm just going to run to CVS. You keep going. I don't want to make you late. But I'll call you. Or maybe we'll just stop by sometime."

Hope nodded, speechless. How could she tell Jennifer she wasn't welcome to stop by? That she wasn't, in fact, ever welcome to come over again? Jennifer had three kids; April was the middle girl, and Shoshanna liked her a lot. She was always cheery and nice, and Hope usually enjoyed talking to her when the girls played. She'd have to think of a way to get Shoshanna invited to her house.

Hope waited until Jennifer was out of sight and then took out her iPod again and got the song playing. At first the music made her feel better, but then she listened to the lyrics. Hope stopped again and went back to the menu. This time she chose Madonna's "Like a Virgin," trying not to think as she walked.

Hope was happy to see Shoshanna and Harvest standing together in the schoolyard like brother and sister. The two of them joined Hope and Ollie and walked the few blocks to their next stop, past the bright yellow gingko leaves and over the stinky smashed nuts. The minute they got there, Ted and Lu traipsed out of the school, dragging their backpacks, and joined the group. When they rounded the corner onto Emerson, Hope could see the bright orange cones blocking the end of the street, a table set up in the middle, and buckets of something lining the sidewalk. When she saw Chris come out of his door and wave, the feeling she had reminded her of the times when Shoshanna was a fussy infant who cried all day, and then Leo would come home and Hope wasn't alone anymore.

"Hey," she called, waving back and pushing Ollie faster. The kids ran ahead to see what was going on.

"I told you I'd come up with something," Chris said, smiling. "It's a tie-dye party! Oh, wait, I have to check on my cookies." Chris ran into the house. The kids milled around the buckets full of dye, each marked with a color, then started choosing T-shirts from the pile.

"Cool," Harvest said as he grabbed a bunch of rubber bands, but he dropped them quickly as the fire alarm sounded from inside the house.

Chris opened his door and poked his head out, the alarm blaring. Ollie started crying. "I've got this. Sorry!" he said as he furiously punched the buttons on the alarm keypad, to no avail.

The next thing they knew, they could hear sirens coming closer and closer, and a bright red fire engine appeared at the end of the block and stopped in front of the cones. Four firefighters jumped from the truck and jogged toward Hope and five stunned children. By now, Chris had given up trying to silence the alarm and was standing on the sidewalk looking panicked. Just as the firefighters approached, Mary's door creaked open, and she came out onto the street.

"Chris, go inside with these guys. I have the kids and Mary. Go!" Hope whisper-shouted over the sound of the alarm. "Kids, get on the sidewalk," Hope said, scooping up Ollie. With her other arm she steered Mary away from Chris's open door.

"What the hell?" Mary said. "What'd you do, set your goddamn house on fire?"

"It's okay. Just some burned cookies and a little trouble with the alarm. Come on, you should stay away. There might be smoke."

Mary craned her neck to get a good look inside, but Hope had her far enough away that she couldn't see in.

Finally the alarm stopped, and the firefighters climbed down the steps holding their axes and still wearing their helmets. Chris stood in the doorway.

"Again, we're so sorry to have troubled you," he said.

"Well, you have a nice big house in there, and you don't want it to burn down, so try to keep an eye on your toaster oven from now on," said one of the firemen. As they lumbered back down the street, Chris shut the door tightly behind him and went to take a squirming Ollie from Hope.

"Big house! Nice sense of humor those big lugs have. Hmmph," Mary said, turning to climb her steps.

"That was close," Hope said when Mary was safely inside.

"You're not kidding. Sorry about that. I guess I should leave the baking to you."

Once Chris had everyone settled with their T-shirt designs and had made a few trips into the house to get old clothes and shoes when it became clear there was no neat way to do this, he joined Hope on the stoop. She was just about to tell him that she ran into Jennifer—how conflicted she felt about wanting to have another baby and that this, right now, right here, with all the kids together and happy on the street, was the best place she could think of—when he turned to her.

"So I quit my job," he said.

❧

Leo snuck into his den. He was pretty sure Hope was ovulating, or maybe she was about to get her period; he couldn't keep track anymore. In any case, he wanted to be ready if she wanted to have sex again tonight. He took a second to listen for noises, but there were none. He turned on the television and went right to the *Real Sex* menu, hoping there would be a new one. He was happy to see there was and clicked on it, settling into the couch and putting his feet up.

This time it was about a sex class. There were a bunch of couples learning different techniques and, at times, trying them out. As the young, tattooed woman was trying a new way to give her husband oral sex, which involved a few things Leo had never even thought of, he felt his erection begin to grow. That was enough. Plenty, really. He didn't want to go too far just in case he was wrong about Hope tonight. After all, it wasn't their normal night to have sex. He reached for the remote.

"No, wait, don't turn it off yet."

Leo swung around to find Stephanie inside the door, which she had already pushed shut behind her. She was staring at the screen.

"How did you get in here?" he asked. "I, um, was just . . ."

"I called up, but nobody answered," she said calmly. "Chris is totally crashed—that tie-dye project and the visit from the fire department really took it out of him. And I saw a spider. You know how I *hate* spiders."

Leo started to get up, nodding, when the couple on the screen started to call out in joint ecstasy. Leo and Stephanie both turned to watch. Stephanie felt the blood rush down and, as she had felt only a very few times in her life, could imagine what it must feel like when a man got an erection. She closed her eyes. Those damn pregnancy hormones. She was so horny. She moved next to Leo on the couch, far enough from him so that they weren't touching. Stephanie's entrance had momentarily drained his desire, but now it was back, raging. He knew he couldn't stand up. And he didn't want to even move; he felt like it wouldn't take much for him to come.

They sat there, looking ahead, watching the couples touch and lick each other. And then Stephanie was slowly touching herself, so subtly you could almost miss it if you weren't already thinking about sex. A little faster, her breathing a little louder. And then she was moving, getting up, and Leo was going to tell her to stay. She couldn't leave *now*. But she wasn't leaving. She got up on her knees and swung one leg over the arm of the couch, which was wide and hard and soft at the same time. Leo watched as Stephanie straddled it, her back straight, her head tilted slightly back.

In less than a minute she was coming, that sharp, piercing sort of orgasm that came only when she wasn't trying too hard, when there was no pressure to have it. For one split second Leo had the thought that he should save his for Hope, but there was no saving it. He probably could have come without any physical pressure, but he couldn't help himself. Stephanie watched as he moved his hand to his erection and rubbed it through his jeans. In seconds his head was resting on the cushions behind him and he was coming. And then it was over, the muted smell of semen in the air.

The image on television had changed. Now it was a man-on-the-street segment with couples being interviewed about taking a sex class: Would they ever consider it?

"Never!" squealed a giggly blonde who kept hiding her face in her husband's shoulder. "Sex should be private, between a husband and a wife. In a bedroom. Not something you do in front of strangers, or even friends, for that matter."

CHAPTER ELEVEN

Stephanie clung to the chain-link fence with both hands and pressed her nose through one of the diamond-shaped openings.

"Bye, Harvest! Bye, Shoshanna! Have a good day," she called into the school yard, even though neither of them was looking her way.

"Harvest! Bye!" she pressed, waiting for him to turn around from his place in the line of unruly first graders about to file into the school.

Finally he turned in her direction, made a fist, and pulled it toward him, their signal that he had caught the imaginary kiss that she had thrown. Satisfied, she turned toward home.

Even though the weather was still crisp and fall-like, her mind felt like a humid August day. Between trying to convince herself that what she and Leo had done in the den was no different from guys watching porn together, completely avoiding being alone with Hope for too many reasons at this point, and trying to sort out and rationalize her feelings about her pregnancy, she could not relax.

But as she turned the corner onto Emerson Street, she started to. The leaves had mostly fallen by now, and the street was plastered with the last remnants of autumn—wet matted brown and a smattering of red, yellow, and green. Every time she turned this corner she loved it more—the warm feeling that she was home. She unlocked her front door and went straight upstairs to her office, where she opened her laptop and then her browser.

She typed "Planned Parenthood" and "Philadelphia" into Google, took a deep breath, picked up the phone, and dialed the number.

"Good morning, Planned Parenthood," said a friendly voice.

"Um, hi. I've never been there before, but I wanted to make an appointment to discuss, uh, a pregnancy-related issue?"

"Are you pregnant, ma'am?"

"Yes, I am, but I worry that, I mean, I think I would like to . . . um . . . you know . . . discuss my options?" Stephanie whispered into the phone even though she was pretty sure nobody was home.

"When would you like to come in for a consultation? I have openings on Monday at ten or one."

"I'll take the appointment at one, please." Stephanie gave the woman her name and cell phone number, then put the phone in its cradle and leaned back in her chair. She imagined that she already felt relieved just knowing that there would be someone to talk to, someone to help her know what to do, someone who wouldn't judge her.

Her cell phone vibrated on her desk. She picked it up and saw that she had a text message waiting—from Leo.

r u ok?

She hesitated, then typed.

yes, r u?

She gripped the phone in her hand, waiting for his reply. In an instant, it was there.

```
4give me wife #2
```

She smiled and relaxed in her chair.

```
If u 4give me 2, she typed.
```

```
No need ☺, he replied.
```

~

When Chris left for work that morning, he was dressed in his usual shirt and tie, dark blue suit, and Italian lace-ups, even though, technically, he had nowhere to go. He had grabbed his briefcase and walked down Emerson confidently in the direction of his office, waving good-bye to the kids who had gathered outside on their way to school. He didn't stop walking until he reached La Colombe, where he stood in line for a cappuccino and tried to decide what to do with the long day ahead of him.

He added a spoonful of raw sugar to his drink and stirred slowly, then took a seat by the window, knowing that he couldn't stay long. He couldn't risk running into anyone, especially, God forbid, Stephanie, before he had a chance to tell her the truth. He picked up a brochure from the window ledge with a photograph of an astronaut—it was promoting the latest exhibit at the Pennsylvania Academy of the Fine Arts. He had wanted to go back since his last visit in August. The day he was there, he'd wanted to check out *The Gross Clinic*, Thomas Eakins's controversial masterpiece that the museum had recently acquired, but Stephanie and Harvest had been in a hurry to get home.

He grabbed his briefcase and coffee and headed north on Nineteenth Street to Market, then east to Broad Street. When he arrived at the imposing Victorian Gothic building designed by Frank Furness, he climbed the stairs and entered the quiet galleries on the second floor. He walked through each gallery, quickly glancing at the

American landscapes and portraits, determined to get to his destination at the rear of the building. He entered the last gallery on the right and turned toward the back of the room, where the painting was positioned by itself in the center of the wall. He put down his briefcase—they had confiscated his coffee at the front desk—and sat on a low bench.

He stayed for a long time looking at the painting and thinking about how Eakins had taken a risk with his bloody and brutal depiction of a surgery in such detail—and that doing so had caused him some criticism and pain at the time, but had paid off in the end. He thought about his own father, who had left the house promptly at 7:00 a.m. every morning and came home at 6:30 p.m. every night to dinner on the table; how he had worked at the same company for more than forty years without a complaint. And when Chris felt his cell phone vibrate, he was surprised to see that it was nearly lunchtime. He looked at the display and saw that it was Stephanie calling. He hit the "ignore" button and put the phone back in his suit jacket pocket.

When he finally got up and headed out into the noonday sun, the first thing he did was call Hope.

"Hello?" She was breathing heavily, and he could hear the sound of cars whizzing by.

"Hope, it's me. What are you doing?"

"I should be the one asking you that. I assume you haven't told her."

He paused. "Not yet," he admitted.

"Don't you think you should?"

"I'm just not ready. I'll do it soon, though, I promise. I hate that you have to keep this secret for me," Chris said, waiting for her to say that she didn't mind. When she didn't respond, he continued. "So you didn't answer. What are you doing?"

"I'm taking a walk with Ollie. We're going to stop for lunch, and then I was going to get him home for a nap. Why?"

"Well, we both have to eat lunch. I'm over near city hall. Want to meet me at the Marathon Grill?"

Hope hesitated. The more she saw Chris, the worse she felt about Stephanie's not knowing what was going on. But then again, things were not so great between her and Stephanie anyway right now. Hope was still mad at her for stealing that pregnancy test and not telling her what was going on, so she had been avoiding her, which was rather difficult considering their living arrangements. Although now that she thought about it, it really hadn't been that difficult. Was Stephanie avoiding her, too?

"Okay," she said finally. "I'll see you there in a few minutes. Get a table in the back."

On Monday, the morning of her Planned Parenthood appointment, Stephanie woke up rested and feeling more like herself than she had in weeks. She hadn't even been nauseated the night before. That had been the worst part of her pregnancy with Harvest.

Despite the tension between her and Hope, it had been a surprisingly great weekend, with them barely leaving the house except to go out front to play and run to Whole Foods for groceries. On Sunday night they ordered Indian food from their favorite place in Northern Liberties, where men wearing ties delivered the perfectly spiced dishes that they craved again immediately after everything was gone. All the kids looked forward to a short week of school because of Thanksgiving, and they were all, with the exception of Stephanie and Chris, preparing for trips to see their families right after dismissal on Wednesday.

By 9:00 a.m., everyone was off to work and school, and Stephanie went upstairs to her third floor. She knew she either had to tell Chris now or postpone the appointment, but she still wasn't sure which to do. She figured she would shower and then decide. She took off her pajamas and turned the water on all the way to its hottest setting to give it time to warm up. She reached for a hair clip, and that's when she saw the blood.

It was only a little—a dark brown stain in the underwear she had left in the middle of the floor. Not like a period, really, but the sight of it startled her. When she was pregnant with Harvest, she had spotted all the time, and it had never turned out to be anything. Now she studied it to see if it looked the same as it had then. She wasn't sure.

Stephanie twisted up her long hair in a knot and secured it with the clip—no time to wash it today—and took a quick shower. She pressed a panty liner into her clean underwear before getting dressed and heading downstairs and over to Nikki's.

Nikki answered on the first knock.

"Hey, come in! I got us some chocolate croissants and a half-caf Americano for you. That's what you get, right?"

"You're the best," Stephanie said, stepping into the house and kicking off her leopard Danskos, revealing bare feet with toes painted the darkest red. "I am so excited about our project today. The shoes!"

They sat across the café table from each other in the spotless eat-in kitchen area at the back of the house, breaking off pieces of flaky croissant oozing with melted chocolate and sipping their coffee while debating whether or not you could ever have too many shoes. Still on her spending binge, Stephanie had just bought three pairs in the basement sale at Anthropologie, so she didn't have much room to talk, even though she was adamant that Nikki weed through the more than forty pairs that she had accumulated over the years.

When they finished eating and stood to go upstairs, Stephanie felt a sudden familiar cramp in her abdomen. She had completely forgotten about the blood this morning, and now she leaned against the table, surprised by the pain.

"Stephanie, what's wrong?"

Stephanie's face had lost its color. "I'm okay, I think. I have a cramp," she said, closing her eyes and trying to straighten up.

"Do you need anything? Do you want to lie down?"

As the feeling began to wane, Stephanie straightened unsteadily. "Let me use your bathroom. Maybe I ate something that disagreed with me." She climbed up the stairs to the second-floor landing, shut the door behind her, and locked it. She pulled down her pants and sat on the toilet. More blood, this time dark red.

She reached over to the cabinet under the sink and opened the doors. Thankfully there was a pack of Stayfrees. She pulled one out and secured it in her pants, first removing the almost soaked panty liner that she was wearing. She washed her hands and went back down the stairs where Nikki was waiting for her on the sofa.

"Are you sure you're okay? You don't look so great," said Nikki.

By the time Stephanie got to the bottom landing, she had to sit down. The cramps were back full force.

"This has happened before," she said. "I'm pretty sure I'm having a miscarriage."

The truth was that Stephanie had had two previous miscarriages, both of them after Harvest was born. Nobody knew. Literally nobody. The first time Harvest was a little older than two, and she was about five weeks pregnant. She had been so sure it was a girl that instead of telling Chris they were going to have a baby, she had planned to simply say, "It's a girl." But the night she was going to tell him, after she'd put Harvest to sleep, she saw the first signs of blood. At the time she thought it would be okay, but she had decided to wait to tell Chris the next day, after she saw the doctor. She didn't want to give him something he might not be able to keep.

The second time she didn't even get that far. Three days after taking the pregnancy test, she started to spot, then bleed heavily. She'd tried not to think about what the sex of the baby was that time. Whenever she thought about telling Chris, she had decided there was no point. Clearly those babies were not meant to be theirs. Clearly her body was taking care of things naturally.

Now she didn't want another baby, and she hadn't for a long time, she knew that. But for a minute she wondered if she wanted to lose it less than she didn't want it. She closed her eyes and shook her head. No. She had been right. This baby wasn't meant to be either. Only Harvest was meant to be.

Stephanie wondered if she should just go home and lie down and pretend she was sick. That way nobody would have to find out. But this hurt way more than she remembered the other times. And Mark was home, and she had already told him about the pregnancy. There was no way she could keep this one a secret. Maybe she didn't really want to anyway.

"I really don't feel well. Can you try to flag me a cab? Maybe I should go to the hospital," Stephanie said to a dumbstruck Nikki.

"Okay. Hold on, I'll be right back," Nikki said, sprinting out the door toward Eighteenth Street, where she was able to get a taxi almost immediately. The driver followed her to the end of the block and stopped in front of her house. Stephanie was sitting on Nikki's front steps looking paler by the minute.

"I'm coming with you," Nikki said, locking her door and helping Stephanie into the cab.

Once they were inside a small curtained room in the emergency department at Pennsylvania Hospital, nurses and interns filed in and out for hours. The radiologist came in and performed a transvaginal ultrasound, asking Stephanie to put her feet in the stirrups while they probed her and stared at the monitor on the cart. They moved around her, trying to figure things out, things that she already knew.

Nikki moved a blue plastic chair near Stephanie's head and sat down. She dialed Chris's cell number again with Stephanie's phone, and for the fourth time in a row all she got was his voice mail.

"I don't understand why they won't just sit down and talk to you," Nikki said, frustrated. "By the way, your cell phone has been vibrating like crazy—do you want me to call anyone else? Your friend Hope called three times."

"That reminds me," Stephanie said weakly. "Please don't ever mention what I said about this happening before. I've never told anyone. Do you promise?"

"I promise," Nikki said seriously, crossing her heart for effect.

"Okay, thanks. Now just give me a few minutes to rest, and then I'll call Hope," Stephanie said, closing her eyes. "I was supposed to help her this afternoon. I have to tell her I can't."

❧

Hope kept looking down the street, expecting Stephanie to turn the corner at any minute. She was supposed to take over with the kids this afternoon so Hope could play tennis.

She let the kids run around, hoping Stephanie would just step in and she could leave. She was already dressed in her tennis clothes and couldn't wait to get out on the court. While she waited, she pretended to be holding her racquet and made the motion of a forehand, then a backhand. Her arms felt rusty, and she was glad she'd have a chance to loosen up a little and get some practice today. She was holding her imaginary racquet over her head ready to slam the pretend ball when a woman and a young girl about Shoshanna's age turned onto the street. At first Hope was disappointed it wasn't Stephanie, and then she was horrified. It was Jennifer Harrison and her daughter April.

Hope dropped her arm and looked around at the kids, wondering if she could get them all inside really fast. But there was no way. So she took a deep breath and waved.

"Hi," Hope said as they approached. Shoshanna spotted April and swooped in like an owl, pulling her into her game with Lu.

"Hi yourself," Jennifer said. "We were at the bookstore on Walnut, and I thought I'd take a chance and see if you were around. We have an hour before we have to be at the Y for April's swim team practice."

"Huh, an hour, well, I'm leaving any minute, actually. I have a date with a tennis court," Hope said, smiling. "My, um, neighbor is going to be here soon to take over with the kids."

"I was wondering who all these kids were," Jennifer said, taking a seat on Hope's stoop. The door was slightly ajar, and Hope reached around her and pulled it shut.

"Oh, yeah, they're my neighbors' kids," Hope said casually.

"Do they all belong to one person?" Jennifer asked, looking around.

"No, they belong to two different families," Hope said. "They live there, and there."

"It's nice of you to watch them," Jennifer said.

Hope looked down the street again. Where the heck was Stephanie?

"Mommy, Mommy," April was calling. "I have to go to the potty."

"Sure, honey," Jennifer said, standing up. "Can we use your bathroom, please?"

Hope was speechless. She had no idea what to do. And this was a mother from school! By tomorrow there would be word all over the yard that Shoshanna lived in a commune. No way.

"Oh my God," Hope said, patting her front pockets and hoping Jennifer didn't look too closely at the bulge in her back pocket. "I locked us out."

For effect, Hope climbed around Jennifer to the top of the stoop and tried the door.

"Shoot, I think my keys are inside," Hope said.

"What about one of the other kids' houses?" Jennifer said, getting up and going to Stephanie's door, which Hope was pretty sure was unlocked.

"No!" Hope called, then tried to sound less alarmed. "They have a huge sewage problem in there. You do not want to go in there. Honestly, don't even open the door, the smell is atrocious."

Jennifer looked at her like she was out of her mind, but nodded and walked down to the sidewalk.

"Mommy, I have to go right now," April whined, hopping around while holding her crotch. "I think it's coming out."

"What about the other house?" Jennifer asked, clearly aware that they were running out of time. "Can we go into their house?"

"No, sorry," Hope said, actually feeling sorry for both of them, but there was no going back now. "They have huge dogs, so I don't even have that key. The parents have to be here to handle the dogs."

There was the clear sound of liquid hitting the concrete, and both women turned to look at April, her pants and sneakers soaked, a puddle forming in the corner of one of the sidewalk squares.

"Sorry, Mommy," April said. At least she didn't cry.

Jennifer looked from Hope to April and then back to Hope.

"I'm really sorry," Hope said.

Jennifer picked up her purse and took April's hand.

"I'll call before we come next time," she said huffily. Then Hope heard her say to April, "We'll rinse you off at the pool."

As soon as they turned the corner, Hope took out her phone again and called Stephanie. This time she answered.

"What the hell? I know that things aren't exactly great between us, but you told me you could stay with the kids today. I so rarely get to do anything on my own, and the one day I set up an hour with the tennis pro, you can't even make it home in time. It doesn't matter now. I've already missed it, so I might as well just stay here. Unbelievable!"

Stephanie sat silently, holding the phone a few inches away from her ear until Hope stopped her ranting to take a breath. "Are you finished?"

"Yes!"

"I'm at the hospital," Stephanie said quietly. "I'm sorry that I didn't call. Can you come? I can't get Chris. He's not answering his phone."

"Oh my God," Hope answered. "I'm on my way."

"Hand me your phone. I'll try him again," Hope said to Stephanie, who was still propped in the hospital bed waiting for the doctor to come back in. Hope had called Mark and asked him to come home and take over with the kids. But when Hope got there, Stephanie was sitting with Nikki, the hairdresser from down the street. When had they gotten so chummy? After Stephanie explained that Nikki was a client and had been there when Stephanie started to feel bad, Hope eased up a little on her skeptical looks and one-word responses to Nikki's questions. Nikki had been there for Stephanie all day, and that must say something about her, even though Hope still got a strange vibe from her.

Hope crossed paths with a young female doctor on her way into the hallway with Stephanie's phone in her hand. When she got outside the curtain, she took her own phone from her pocket and dialed Chris. He picked up on the first ring.

"Hey, you," he answered.

"Chris, we need you. Stephanie's in the hospital, and she's been trying to call you."

"Is she okay?" he asked. "What's wrong? What happened?"

"She's okay. But I'll let her tell you what happened. Just get over here."

"No way, you can't do that to me. I need to know what's going on."

"I shouldn't . . ." Hope said, wavering. But she knew how hard it would be to get this kind of phone call and not know what was happening.

"You need to. Now, please."

"She's had a miscarriage, but please, let her be the one to tell you," Hope whispered into the phone.

"A what? She's pregnant? Was pregnant? Did you know?"

"I didn't know. I suspected, though. Well, I knew there was a chance, but I didn't believe it. It doesn't matter. Please get over here and let her tell you. And don't forget, you haven't been completely honest with her lately either."

"I'll come right now," Chris said. "Pennsylvania Hospital? Right?"

"Right," Hope said. She went back through the curtain just as the young doctor was leaving Stephanie's room.

"I got him. He's coming," Hope said to Stephanie.

Hope sat on the edge of the bed and leaned in so their faces were inches apart. Stephanie tried hard to look straight ahead, avoiding Hope's eyes. "I'm so sorry, Stephanie," Hope whispered. Then she didn't know what else to say because everything seemed wrong to say out loud right now. She wanted to say that she was sorry she had been so accusatory when really Stephanie had every right in the world to be pregnant. She wanted to thank her because sitting here in the hospital made her finally feel sure that she no longer wanted to have another baby more than anything. She couldn't even conjure up the excitement she used to feel when she considered the possibility. But she couldn't say any of that, of course. "Please tell me what the doctor said."

Stephanie turned to Hope. "I lost it. The baby. Are you happy now?"

"Oh, Stephanie, you must know that I never—"

"It doesn't matter now, Hope. It's over. There's nothing left to say."

They waited in silence—Hope, Stephanie, and Nikki—in the small makeshift room for the doctor to return with the discharge paperwork. She had told Stephanie that she would have to come back tomorrow for a D & C but that she'd be back to normal, at least physically, before she knew it. Stephanie dressed slowly while Hope and Nikki stood quietly outside in the hall. As they were gathering their things to leave, Chris finally arrived.

Stephanie crossed the room to hug him, putting her head on his shoulder.

"Stephanie, it's okay," he said. "I'm here now. What happened?"

She lifted her head and looked up at him, her deep brown eyes rimmed with red. "I was pregnant," she said slowly, waiting for his reaction. "But it's gone, Chris. The baby's gone."

"We can't go now," Celia whispered to Mark. They were in the kitchen preparing dinner for everyone. Mark was making his nana's famous meatballs and gravy.

"But we have our airline tickets. They're expecting us at home," Mark said, dropping another reddish-pink meatball into the hot frying pan. The gravy was simmering on the stove. He added a bay leaf to the pot and put the lid back on.

"We'll see them after Christmas. We need to be here now. Don't you remember how everyone was here for us when you were sick?"

Mark stirred the gravy with a wooden spoon. "You're right. I'll try to change the tickets to New Year's," he said.

Hope walked into the kitchen and opened the refrigerator, grabbing a small container of yogurt for Ollie. "What are you guys whispering about?"

"We decided not to go to Kansas for Thanksgiving. It's better that we're here right now," Celia said as Hope fished through the utensil drawer for Ollie's favorite green plastic spoon.

"Well, if you're not going to Kansas, we're not going to Westchester. My mom will be with my brother anyway. And Leo doesn't have to worry about his parents. They'll be in Key West. He's going to be so excited. He never gets to cook Thanksgiving—and that's like the Super Bowl of cooking," Hope rambled, catching herself thinking out loud. "And of course we need to stay. Stephanie and Chris need us."

"What did you say about us not going to Westchester?" said Leo, peeking around the corner. "I've been hoping the day would come when you'd say we can stay here. I'm already planning the menu. Something special . . . not the traditional Thanksgiving. I've been dying to do something with a Mexican twist. Besides, if I had to see that can-shaped cranberry sauce one more year, Thanksgiving might have been ruined for me forever."

"I'll go tell them. Maybe it will make her feel better," Celia said. "Hello, I'm coming up!" she called as she headed up the twisty staircase at the back of the kitchen.

When Celia got to the third floor, she found Stephanie in her bed under the covers, dark circles under her eyes and her face blotchy from tears. Chris was sitting on the edge of the bed next to her. When he turned to face Celia, she noticed that he looked as if he had been crying, too.

She wished she had waited until they came down for dinner to tell them, but now she was stuck. "Sorry to interrupt, but I just wanted to let you guys know that dinner is almost ready. And we've all decided to cancel our Thanksgiving trips home. We think we should all be together. I hope that's okay with you."

"Thanks," Chris said quietly to Celia. "That sounds really great. You guys are the best."

"We'll be down in a few minutes," Stephanie said, tension in her voice.

Celia backed down the steps slowly. "Okay, sorry again to interrupt."

"I can't believe you quit your job without telling me," Stephanie said to Chris when Celia had gone. "And hid it for how long? A week? And how are we going to live now? My business can't support both of us."

"What about you? Don't you think you should have told me that we were pregnant? When were you planning to tell me, anyway?" Chris asked.

"I don't know. I was trying to figure things out," Stephanie said honestly.

"Hon, I just don't know what's going on with us, hiding things from each other that are so important," Chris said.

Stephanie looked down. "I know you want lots of kids. That's partly why I wanted to take down the walls, so there could be lots of kids around. I thought that might be enough if it turned out Harvest is our only child."

Chris nodded. There would be plenty of time to talk about trying again later for another baby. He wanted to give her time to be sad about this one that they lost.

"I better go down," he said. "Mark's cooking, and he might need help. Do you want me to bring food up on a tray for you?"

"No, I want to be with everyone," Stephanie said, getting up.

He reached out his hand to her, and she grabbed it.

"Thank God for this family," she said.

"I would like to thank God for giving us video games," said Harvest, as if he were acting in the school play. They were going around the table, which had been beautifully set by Hope and Celia with their combined collection of good china and silver, saying what they were thankful for. The kids had made place cards for everyone decorated with turkeys and Indian corn and jalapeño peppers and sombreros, and there was a banner that stretched across the living room that read "*Feliz Día de Acción de Gracias*"—"Happy Thanksgiving" in Spanish. At each place there was a sheet of paper with an orange and brown border that listed the menu:

First Course

Spinach salad with prickly pear cactus

Hand-pressed tortillas served with roasted corn, smoked pork, and green Chiles

Roasted yam soup with Mexican cinnamon

Second Course

Slow-roasted turkey, served with mole sauce

Cornbread stuffing with chipotle peppers

Candied pumpkin

Cranberry jalapeño salsa

Dessert

Pumpkin flan

Mexican chocolate pie

Leo had shopped all day Wednesday at the Reading Terminal Market and stayed up well into the night preparing the meal. He had given each person a job at some point in the laborious process—chopping, sautéing, plating—to arrive at this moment.

"Well, *I'm* thankful that there are *no* video games on Thanksgiving," Stephanie continued. "But I'm also thankful for my sweet baby, Harvest, the light of my life, Chris—my partner in good times and bad—and for all of you, for this house full of love, and for many more Thanksgivings together as one big happy family."

Leo raised his glass. "Hear, hear! And I am thankful for being right here on Emerson Street today—the best street in the world—and for this magnificent food, if I do say . . ." The sound of Stephanie and Chris's doorbell interrupted what promised to be just the beginning of Leo's eloquent speech. Everyone fell silent and stared at each other, paralyzed.

"What should we do?" Hope asked, panic in her voice.

"Well, someone has to answer it, and I suggest Stephanie or Chris since it is their door," Leo said sarcastically. "Besides, it's not like this is the first time someone has come to the door, right?"

"Well, yeah, it kind of is . . ." Hope said. Everyone nodded.

"Who would come to someone's door on Thanksgiving anyway?" Celia said, perturbed by the interruption. "This is exactly why we have to have a plan in place, so we aren't caught off guard at times like these."

Chris and Stephanie stared at each other. "You get it," Stephanie urged.

"Me?" Chris asked.

"Oh, what the hell, you guys are all so paranoid. I'll get it," Stephanie said, rising slowly and walking to her front door. She peered through the peephole and saw Nikki, carrying a tray of aluminum foil–wrapped dishes. Stephanie turned to the five adults staring in her direction. "It's Nikki," she mouthed.

"Her *new friend*," Hope said, rolling her eyes.

Stephanie threw Hope a piercing look. She turned the dead bolt and opened the door just a crack, slipping her body through the small opening and shutting the door quickly behind her.

"Hey, Nikki, Happy Thanksgiving," she said, her hand still on the doorknob and her back flat against the outside of the door.

"Yeah, um, Happy Thanksgiving," Nikki said, leaning to look over Stephanie's shoulder. The shades were drawn, as usual, so she couldn't see in the window. "Am I interrupting something?"

"No, no, not at all," Stephanie lied. "We were just having dinner, and, well, the place is a total mess."

"Oh my God, who cares? Do you remember who you're talking to?"

"Yeah, but it's especially bad today. Embarrassing, really."

Nikki stared at Stephanie for a moment, then remembered the tray in her hand. "Anyway, you said that you and Chris would be alone for Thanksgiving, so I brought you half of our dinner. It's not much, since I didn't cook a thing myself. But tomorrow's the rehearsal dinner, and the wedding is Saturday, so I guess I have an excuse. Besides, Di Bruno's makes really great prepared foods. So here you go." Nikki pushed the tray toward Stephanie and slowly backed down the sidewalk.

"That is so totally thoughtful of you. I can't tell you how much this means to me," Stephanie said as Nikki inched away. "And I want to thank you again for the other day."

"Yeah, sure, anytime. I mean, well, you know what I mean," Nikki said.

Stephanie stood on her stoop, tray in hand, and watched until she saw Nikki walk up her steps and close the door behind her.

CHAPTER TWELVE

Celia squatted in front of the refrigerator looking for the source of the smell. She moved the Aquapod water bottles, the Go-Gurt box, the tub of Total yogurt that Leo insisted on. There, in the back, she found the culprit—the old turkey carcass. She reached in and pulled out the plate with the meat, a messy piece of aluminum foil loosely covering it. She stood up, holding the plate away from her, walked to the garbage can, and dumped it in.

"That's the last of it," she called to Mark, who was sitting on the couch in the next room with all the big kids reading *Tales of a Fourth Grade Nothing*. Ollie was already asleep. "Thanksgiving is officially over."

"What do you mean?" Mark yelled back. "Wasn't it over a week ago?"

"No, silly, you know what my mother always said," Celia said, walking into the living room. "It's over when you throw away the last of the turkey."

"Oh yeah, that does sound familiar," Mark said, going back to the book. Fudge had just ingested the pet turtle, and the kids were dying to know what happened next.

"Don't read for too long," Celia said quietly as she headed back to the kitchen. "It isn't every night that we have the house to ourselves."

Mark looked up to see her face, but she was already back at the refrigerator, trying to find a place for tonight's cooling leftovers. She took a minute to organize—there were usually so many hands putting things in and taking things out that there was no time to think about the order of it all. She found five jars of pickles—all kosher dills—and put them in one corner. She placed all the different salad dressings on the door shelf. She piled the three boxes of eggs on top of each other. Then she opened the freezer. It was messier than the refrigerator. She moved all the frozen peas, corn, and lima beans to the door. She was just about to put the frozen dinners in a more orderly pile when she noticed the vodka way in the back.

Celia glanced toward the other room. All was quiet except Mark's excited voice reading about rushing Fudge down in the elevator to the waiting ambulance. The kids were mesmerized. Celia looked around for a cup but saw only a faded plastic Bratz one. She grabbed it, turned her back toward the den, pulled out the cold bottle, quietly untwisted the top, and poured a good inch of the clear alcohol. She put her cup on the counter, put the bottle back in, and lifted the cup to her nose.

She could hear Mark getting louder and more animated as he read. A sudden roar of laughter from the other room almost made Celia drop her cup. She held it tightly for a minute, then drank the icy vodka in one gulp. She stood still, letting the warmth spread from her chest to her belly and the lightness creep to her head. She smiled to herself. "I think I'm ready," she said under her breath.

∽

Hope and Leo and Stephanie and Chris were all at back-to-school night and planned to go out to dinner afterward, so it would probably be a pretty late evening. After Mark finished the page, they started to take the kids to their usual bedrooms before realizing they would need an extra adult to do that, unless they wanted to keep someone up later and make him or her wait until the others were settled. But they were all so tired, and Celia had plans of her own.

"Let's let them all sleep in Harvest's room tonight," she suggested, and Mark knew immediately that he had not misinterpreted her earlier comment. "That way they can all be together."

"Yes, yes, yes," Ted said, punching his fist in the air. The kids jumped around, picking up the yes cheer. Before Mark had a chance to say anything against that plan—like the fact that it was a school night and the other adults might not be thrilled—the kids were all in a frenzy, shouting, "Yes, yes, yes," so loudly that Mark had no choice but to give in. He quickly ushered them into the kitchen and shepherded them up the twisty staircase to Harvest's cozy room.

Celia went up her own stairs, letting Mark handle the kids himself. She debated taking a shower, but thought that would be too obvious, maybe even pathetic. She decided a little touch of her favorite perfume would be plenty of freshening up. She brushed her teeth, put on some lipstick, then blotted it off so she would look nice but it wouldn't get all over when they kissed. She wondered about cute pajamas or even the silky negligee she had buried in her drawer, but decided that being naked was the best route to take. That way there would be no question about her intentions. She pulled off her jeans and underwear, brushed her silky blond hair, and slipped into bed. Then she waited.

❧

Mark was in no rush. In fact, when Lu begged him to continue reading, arguing that she wouldn't be able to sleep until she found out what happened to Fudge, he settled onto the bottom of Harvest's bed and continued the story. There were only five pages left in the whole book, and the end came way too fast.

As he neared the final page, when Fudge is fine and Peter is given a dog instead of another turtle, he read as slowly as he could.

"More, more, more," they chanted to the tune of their yes chant.

"That's the end," Mark said. "The end of the book. Hey, Harvest, do you have *Superfudge*? I think that one comes next. I could read the first chapter?"

"No," Harvest said. "That's the only one we have."

"Okay then, it's sleep time," Mark said. "I'll sit outside for a few minutes."

He pulled the door almost shut and sat on the wooden stairs. Why was he being so weird about this? It was no big deal; he'd go to his room and have sex with his wife. But even as that thought moved through his mind, he felt nothing—no arousal, no desire. He just felt tired. But he'd been gone way too long, and the kids didn't need him anymore. He could hear them all breathing deeply. Someone was snoring—it was probably Lu, whose nose had been stuffy all day.

Mark pushed himself up to standing and headed downstairs, through the kitchen, and into the living room. It was there that the image of Nikki came into his mind, as it so often did. He sat on the couch for a minute, remembering their kiss. Then he thought about how she had been right outside the front door on Thanksgiving, so close he could almost touch her. She had been married for about a week now. He wondered what her new married sex life was like, tried to picture them together—her straddling Will with her head thrown back, her smooth dark hair spilling down to her waist. He let the image remain in his mind for a minute, just enough for his erection to start to grow, and then he jogged upstairs to his waiting wife.

∽

"Hey," Celia said. She was sitting up in bed reading. The covers were pushed down to her waist so her breasts were exposed. They looked soft and inviting. He had always liked her breasts, and they were still surprisingly perky, even after breastfeeding three kids.

"Hey," he said back, moving toward her. He was glad she had clued him in earlier and was relieved to be ready. Otherwise it would have been like all the other times lately—and he would have to make up one excuse after another. He went around to her side of the bed and undid his jeans, letting them drop to the floor. Then he unbuttoned his dark blue shirt and let that drop. Celia pulled back the comforter to invite him in, and although his erection was gone for now, he moved on top of her, kissing her. The hard bridge of her nose was suddenly in the way. Was it always that hard? With the skin so tight across the top of it? It bugged him. He moved his head to one side.

Celia licked her fingers and started to touch his soft penis. She did all the things she used to do, but he just couldn't feel it. The more he thought about it, the worse it got. But now he was in too deep to get out. It would be too big a deal. He could pretend he wasn't feeling well—but how many times could he use that excuse? He pushed her hand away gently and moved down to kiss her, lower and lower. This would give him some time. She lay back and closed her eyes, making tiny sounds of pleasure.

"Mama! Mama!" Ollie cried over the monitor. "Mama!"

Mark sat back on his heels, his penis still soft.

"Shit," he said.

"I really thought he was in a deep sleep," Celia said. "Should I ignore him?"

"No," Mark said, leaning over to kiss her on her forehead. "Go get him. Maybe he'll go back to sleep."

Once Celia was out the door and on her way to Ollie, Mark couldn't shake the phrase that kept running through his mind: *that was close.*

Mark tried to wait until 10:00 a.m. People usually weren't so eager for a haircut that they called before then. But at 9:46 he couldn't stand it anymore, and he dialed the number.

"Modern Man, this is Nikki, may I help you?"

"Hey, Nikki, it's Mark, from Emerson Street, the one with the Dago fro," he said without thinking. He might as well have said *the idiot you kissed that time*. He had to get a grip.

"Mark, hi," she said, making it easy for him. "I was wondering about that Dago fro of yours. Is it time for a cut?"

"Yes, suddenly I'm desperate," he said. "For a cut," he added quickly.

"I'm completely booked, but if you can come in at noon, I won't take a lunch," she said.

"I'll bring you something," he said.

Mark spent the next two hours trying to decide what to take to Nikki. He didn't want to bring a romantic picnic, but a slice of pizza seemed way too ordinary. He thought about a hoagie, but decided that the onions and peppers wouldn't be a good idea. In the end he settled on a cheesesteak, hold the onions. He knew Leo would cringe at the thought, but Nikki probably wouldn't care.

At 11:55 a.m. he walked into Modern Man and took a deep breath. Then, without checking in with the girl at the desk, he sat down, filling the room with the steak smell that was seeping through the bag.

Nikki watched him. She had seen him the minute he walked into view through the big window facing Nineteenth Street. She had gone over this scenario so many times during the last few weeks—the time when Mark would call to set up his next haircut. And every time, during her imagined conversations, she told him that she thought it would be best if he went somewhere else: *Sure, we'll run into each other on the block, but, just to be safe, we probably shouldn't spend any time alone together.* Never in any of her imagined conversations had she pictured him coming in with lunch for her. But when she heard his voice, deep but a little shaky, she just couldn't help herself. And just one week after her wedding! That could be blamed on Will, really. At least that's what she told herself. If he hadn't been so caught up in his big case, they would be on a honeymoon right now, far away from Mark and Philadelphia and Emerson Street.

Nikki took a little extra time to brush off her chair before she went to Mark. It was covered with red hair from her last appointment. Boy, that strange guy had really been flirting with her, reaching out his freckly arm from under the cape to touch her wrist every now and then. But he had been easy to resist. He was no problem.

"Mark?" Nikki called as she came to the waiting area. She sounded a little like a nurse calling a child back to a doctor's appointment. Mark smiled and held up the brown paper bag.

"Come on back," she said, holding her formal tone. She led him through the main part of the salon, past the two waxing rooms, and through a door. She was relieved to find the staff table empty.

"Is this okay?" she asked, softening a little. "I'd say we could go sit in Rittenhouse Square, but if you really want your hair cut . . ."

"I do," Mark said quickly, flashing her a nervous smile. "You can't let me walk around with this big hair, can you?" He ran his free hand through his hair, puffing it up a little.

He could barely stand it—all the sexual tension that was so clearly missing during his encounter last night with Celia was right here. He was going to burst, and all he wanted to do was touch Nikki. What was wrong with him? When had he turned into someone who would think things like that? He sat down quickly and pulled out the two foil-wrapped sandwiches, holding one up to Nikki. She took it, sitting down across from him.

"Thanks, that smells great," she said, immediately starting to unroll the foil. "I got married, you know."

"Oh yeah, I know. I was going to ask you about that. How are things? How's marriage?" he asked, trying not to look at her. Suddenly he wasn't very hungry. Maybe he never was.

"The same," she said, taking a big bite of the steak and licking the juices from her lips. "Totally the same."

"How was the wedding?"

"Nice, it was a nice party," she said, swallowing. He was fascinated by her total lack of self-consciousness while she was eating. Celia would be taking tiny bites, talking with her hand in front of her mouth to block any view of chewed-up food. "But afterward we just went home. To Emerson Street," Nikki continued.

Mark took a small bite and worked hard to swallow it. Then he wrapped up the rest. Nikki put the last of her first half into her mouth and chewed as she rolled up the other half.

"I'll save this for later," she said. "Will's working late."

Mark leaned back in his chair and took her in—her dark eyes and full lips. "How does he do it?"

"Do what?" she asked.

"Resist you," he said, shaking his head and letting out a long sigh. "It just doesn't seem humanly possible."

"You're too much," Nikki said, lowering her eyes. "You know, I was going to say that maybe I shouldn't cut your hair anymore. Maybe this is too hard."

At that moment the door opened and a petite Asian woman walked in.

"Hi, Nikki," she said, not even glancing at Mark.

"Hi, Ronnie," Nikki said, getting up. Mark followed her lead. They walked out through the door into the back hall toward Nikki's chair. But at the entrance to one of the open waxing rooms Mark stopped and pulled her in, taking an awkward moment to figure out how to shut the door. He had a desperate feeling that this was going to be his only chance.

"Watch out!" Nikki said just before Mark almost collided with a vat of hot wax.

"Whoa!" he said, turning toward her. It didn't take much to be face to face in the tiny room.

"Does the door lock?" Mark asked.

"Yes," Nikki said. But before she had a chance to turn around, they were kissing. Kissing like Mark hadn't kissed Celia in what seemed like years. Kissing like Nikki imagined she would kiss Will on their honeymoon but never did. And then Nikki was easing down onto the narrow table behind her. She carefully moved her foot around the vat of wax. As Mark climbed on top of her and pulled up her skirt, she fumbled to undo the button fly on his jeans.

There was a knock at the door.

"We'll be out in a minute," Nikki called, managing to sound fairly normal. "I could get fired for this," she whispered to Mark, sitting up and straightening herself out. "Plus, I've barely been married a week."

"Will you meet me at my client's house tomorrow at noon?" Mark asked, already wondering how he was going to face Celia when he got home, and how he would make it another twenty-four hours before he would see Nikki again. "He isn't living there during the renovations, and it's an amazing house. He's at Eighteenth and Delancey. Just a few blocks away."

"But tomorrow's Saturday," Nikki said. "Won't that be hard?"

"No," Mark said. "I always go to clients' houses during the weekend."

"Fine," Nikki said. "Tomorrow. Noon. What about your hair?"

"Forget about my hair."

"As you walk out, rub your back, like it's sore because you just had it waxed."

"Are you kidding?" Mark asked. "I don't have a hairy back."

"No, I'm not kidding. If you don't want people to be suspicious, rub your back!"

"If only it were that simple," Mark said, opening the door and twisting his right arm behind him, rubbing and moaning dramatically. Nikki giggled.

"I need some Band-Aids! Does anyone have any Band-Aids?" he half-shouted.

Nikki put her hand over his mouth and tried to shush him, trying desperately to hold back her own laughter. She gave him a little shove from behind, and he walked down the hall and out the door, perfectly composed.

"He's cute," Ronnie said as Nikki stood leaning on the reception desk. "Funny, too."

"Don't get any ideas. He's married," Nikki said, turning to go back down the hall.

She went to the staff room and dismantled her sandwich. She wrapped the meat up in a Ziploc and put it in the refrigerator. She stored the roll in a bag on the counter. At 5:00 p.m. sharp, Nikki retrieved her food and headed home. She took her time, wandering through Rittenhouse Square, taking a detour to Wawa for ice cream. Her plan was to heat up the meat in the microwave and toast the bun. That would be her dinner. But when she pushed open her door, the smell of baking fish and oregano reached her nose. The table was set with their wedding china and a replica of one of the centerpieces from their wedding. There were candles everywhere.

"Happy one-week anniversary, babe," Will said, coming toward her. "You didn't think I'd forget, did you?"

"No," she said, letting herself be taken into his arms. "I just thought you had to work."

"Not tonight," he said, kissing her. She wished she had had a chance to brush her teeth. She could still taste Mark and the cheesesteak. "Tonight I'm all yours."

⁓

"Can I come?" Chris asked the next morning after Mark told him he was going to a client's house in a little while. "Maybe I could learn something—maybe about architecture or cabinetry or, I don't know, plumbing."

"*I* don't even know anything about plumbing," Mark said. "And no, it isn't a good time for you to tag along. It's an important meeting, and the client has to make some big financial decisions."

"Didn't you just say he wasn't going to be there?" Chris asked suspiciously. "I could have sworn you just said he was in Barbados for a preholiday vacation."

"Did I say that?" Mark asked, trying to recover. He was actually a little surprised that Chris had been listening so closely. He had seemed to be reading the paper while Mark talked. Still, Mark knew better than to lie like that. "Oh no, I meant that he's leaving today. After our meeting."

Mark glanced at his watch. He still had an hour to go, and he was already showered and dressed. He'd finished reading the paper. He didn't want to walk around and get windblown and dirty. But he could barely stand to sit here with Chris—who knew what he might say next? He and Chris were the only ones at home. The women had taken all the kids to the playground, and Leo was at a fancy breakfast meeting with some important wine guy from Italy.

"What's your plan for the day?" Mark asked, trying to have a normal conversation.

"Tennis? Watching football? What else is there to do?" Chris said.

Mark had the urge to be mean. The words *look for a job* ran through his mind, but he held back. It was Saturday, after all. But Chris seemed to treat every day like a vacation day ever since he'd been found out.

"Oh, and I was thinking about getting a haircut later," Chris said, running his fingers through his thick blond hair. "Maybe I could go see NikKAY. Do you want to come? You look like you could use a cut."

"No, no, I can't today," Mark said, stopping short of saying she wouldn't be there. "But tell her I say hi if you go."

"Sure," Chris said. "I hope she can fit me in for a little afternoon delight."

"Uh-huh," Mark said, getting up from the table.

"You know I'm just messing around, right?" Chris said seriously. "You have a strange look on your face."

"Oh, sorry, I guess I'm just thinking ahead to my meeting," Mark said. "But I know what you mean. She is really something."

"Mark, can I ask you something, seriously?"

Mark froze, his coat half on and half off.

"Sure," Mark said, trying to sound casual. "What's up?"

"Well, you know how I'm out of work, obviously," Chris said, shifting in his seat. "So I was thinking, instead of getting another full-time job right away, what would you think if I worked here? At home?"

"That sounds great!" Mark said out of sheer relief. He had no idea what Chris was talking about, but he didn't really care.

"Good, good," Chris said, cupping his hand over his chin and rubbing his two-day-old stubble. "I could be our cook, maybe, be responsible for all the meals. That would take the burden off everyone. I could be the one who plans the meals, shops, cooks."

"You mean, work here and not get paid?" Mark asked. "Don't you need money?"

"Well, yeah, but I cashed in some stock options that will keep us going for a while. And think of what Hope contributes by being with the kids. I could contribute by budgeting the meals better, cooking ahead so we don't have to order out."

"But your idea of cooking *is* ordering out," Mark said, coming toward the table again. "Besides, if anyone is going to be our chef, I vote for Leo."

"No, really, I think this is something we should talk about," Chris said seriously. "And I could be our official maintenance person, too. We could save money that way, not having to call a plumber or whoever. Which leads me back to wanting to come with you today."

"Speaking of which," Mark said, walking into the living room and toward his own front door. "I'll see you later."

Mark got to the house first. He used his key and then left the door the slightest bit ajar, so nobody from the street would notice but Nikki could just push it open. He wandered into the kitchen first, wondering what he could take. A bottle of wine? A shot of whiskey? It was completely against his usual policy, but so was sneaking around with someone who wasn't his wife. He couldn't believe how good it felt, at least right now. Once he started on the slope down, the sky was the limit. Or maybe the opposite of the sky was the limit—the bottom of the valley was the limit. How low could he go? He glanced at his watch. *Just five more minutes.*

He planned to walk her through the house, showing her the sconces he had found at their favorite store in Old City. And, as luck would have it, the ones he was proudest of, the ones with the intricate metal design and frosted glass that he found unexpectedly in a store in Fishtown, were on the second floor, right outside the guest room. He wondered if there were even sheets on that bed. He hopped up the steps, two at a time, and glided along the warm brown runner toward the stark white room. Yes, as far as he could tell, the bed was made up. But maybe they wouldn't go near that, maybe this nice brown carpet would be soft enough. He checked his watch—she was five minutes late.

Mark walked back down the stairs and sat on the third one from the bottom. Here he would see the door push open, but he'd have enough time to get up and look busy.

An hour and a half later, he was still waiting.

Stephanie and Celia watched as Hope took Shoshanna's hand and walked toward Chestnut Street. They were on their way to get Shoshanna's hair cut. Hope turned once and smiled and waved, and they waved back. Then the two women continued to head east on Lombard with Ollie in the stroller and the other kids running ahead.

"She seemed totally happy just then," Stephanie said. "Did you notice that?"

"Well, I guess she's excited about Shoshanna's haircut," Celia said innocently.

"I think she's just excited to be alone with Shoshanna," Stephanie said.

"There's nothing wrong with that," Celia said. "I wanted to talk to you about something anyway."

"Okay, sounds serious. What is it?"

"Sex," Celia said.

"Really? What about it?"

"Well, the other night, when you guys were all out at the school meeting, we, well, I tried to, you know, rekindle the fire between us," Celia said.

"Celia, you are such a dork. Do all the people in Kansas talk like that?"

"Come on, Stephanie, I'm serious."

"Okay, okay, the fire. Tell me all about it," Stephanie said, trying not to laugh.

"So we put the kids to bed, and I, you know, took my clothes off," Celia said.

"That seems like a good place to start," Stephanie joked. "Sounds hot—get it, fire . . ."

Celia rolled her eyes. "Anyway, we were *about* to do it when Ollie started in on his screeching. Well, to make a long story short, when I had Ollie all quieted down and I got back, Mark was asleep. And we haven't mentioned it since."

Stephanie shrugged. "I think it happens to everyone once in a while. It goes in waves, you know? Sometimes you're totally into it, and sometimes you just have other things going on. Why don't you try it again tonight, see if it was just a fluke? I'll keep the kids out of your hair. We can do another sleepover in Harvest's room if you want. And I can take Ollie."

"No, thank you, but I should be able to have sex with my husband without shifting the whole house around. I'm being ridiculous. You're right—I'll just try again. I have to remember that he did just go through a lot, being sick and all."

"Taking your clothes off is a good first step, but if you want it to be a sure thing, you should do my naked yoga trick," Stephanie said.

"Ugh, that sounds too weird," said Celia, wrinkling her nose.

"It may be weird, but when he walks in on you in a downward facing dog in the buff, sparks will fly and the fire will ignite. Believe me."

Stephanie felt her phone vibrate in the back pocket of her jeans. She stopped for a second and let Celia move forward to catch up with the kids, who were doing an obstacle course in and out of a bike rack. She saw that she had a text. It was from Leo.

```
Den, 2night?
```

CHAPTER THIRTEEN

"Goddamn it! Open the goddamn door," Mary howled. "I know you're in there!" The knocker squeaked loudly as Mary picked it up then banged it—hard—against Stephanie and Chris's front door.

Stephanie stood paralyzed on the other side, feeling the vibrations against her back, hoping that Mary would get tired soon and just walk away. There had been surprisingly few incidents since the one with Nikki on Thanksgiving. It was then that they had decided it would be too risky to open the door for anyone. Celia had suggested that they immediately institute a no-exceptions policy on all visitors, which Leo named Code Turkey. They had all laughed, but agreed unanimously to abide by the newest house rule, which Celia quickly added to the list.

The knocking continued for another tense minute, until Mary seemed to give up and started muttering to herself. "Never there when you need them, goddamn kids," she said. Stephanie relaxed a little and tiptoed away from the front door.

She hopped up the narrow steps as quickly as she could when she heard the *Law & Order* theme song, her latest ringtone. She grabbed her phone and glanced at the display.

"Nikki, hey," she panted. "I'm so sorry, I owe you a phone call. I know we need to set up another appointment." Stephanie could still hear Mary complaining about her from outside—was the window open? On a day this cold? Then she realized that Mary's voice was coming through the phone.

"No, Stephanie," said Nikki, "I'm standing out front with our neighbor, and she wanted me to try and call you. I thought that I saw you go in a few minutes ago. She's been knocking on your door for a while. She says—"

Mary's voice exploded in Stephanie's ear. "Yeah, Stephanie! This is Mary! I've been knocking on your goddamn door all morning. I need your husband to change a light bulb in my bathroom for me."

"Sorry, Mary, he's out right now. Can I tell him to stop by later?"

"What the hell am I going to do all day? I can't sit on the toilet in the dark."

Stephanie sighed and relented.

"Okay, let me take a look at it for you. I'm out right now, but I'll be home soon," Stephanie said, trying to lie her way out.

But Mary had already handed the phone back to Nikki before Stephanie could finish her sentence. "Stephanie, I'm sorry. I thought you were home. And Mary insisted I try to call you. Where are you, with a client?"

Stephanie hesitated. "I'm . . . I'm not far. I'll be there in a few minutes. Just tell her to go back inside and I'll come by. It's too cold for her to be out there," she added, padding the lie.

"Okay, call me, and we can pick up where we left off last week," Nikki said. They had finally finished the shoes, and now they were moving on to the cosmetics—drawers full of untouched lipsticks from Clinique and Estée Lauder specials and eye shadows and shampoo samples that had made the trip to Nikki's new home in a big white plastic bag.

Stephanie put the phone in her back pocket and grabbed her pale blue down coat and matching mittens from the downstairs closet. After bundling herself up, she slipped out the back door, deciding it would be best for her to sneak out and pretend to come back. She couldn't walk toward Nineteenth Street—Nikki might be near one of her back windows—so she walked through the parking lot behind the houses, staying close to the back wall, toward Eighteenth and then over to South Street, positioning herself behind the row of trees that lined the sidewalk. She kept her head down just in case and turned the corner, safely out of sight.

She walked to the end of the block and dawdled a little before heading back toward Emerson Street. The season's first snow was falling, and even though it looked like Christmas now, with only a week and a half to go, it was inevitable that it would turn warmer and the snow would be gone by the time they all wanted it for the holiday. Everyone had gone to school and work today—except for Chris, of course, who was out playing tennis at the university—but with the way things were progressing, they would probably all be home early.

When Stephanie turned the corner, Nikki was still standing in the middle of the street with Mary, politely nodding her head as Mary ranted about something—most likely the proposed property tax increase or the fact that the newly elected mayor would be just as bad as the last one. Stephanie hurried up to them and let out a big sigh for good measure.

"I came as soon as I could. Let me see what's going on in there, Mary," Stephanie said. "Thanks, Nikki, I can take it from here."

Nikki shot Stephanie a grateful look and hurried away. "Thanks," she called. "I've got to get to work. I'm already running late. Talk to you later!"

"I saw you go in this morning, and I tried to call after you, but you must not have heard me," Mary said.

Stephanie waved her off. "I'm here now. Let's go change that light bulb. Can't have you going to the bathroom in the dark, can we?"

By lunchtime, there were four inches of snow blanketing the street, and there were no signs that the tiny swirling flakes would relent anytime soon. The sky was gray and heavy, and it was cold—but not too cold—and the air was still and quiet. School was being dismissed at one o'clock, and Stephanie and Hope were in the middle of the dining room trying to wrangle Ollie back into his snowsuit. Each time Hope shoved one of his little arms into a sleeve and began to work on the other, he would pull out the first one and laugh.

"Ollie!" Hope said firmly. "Cooperate!"

"Why don't I just get the car and pick them all up? That way you can stay here with Ollie and dig out all of their snow gear. You know they'll want to play outside as soon as they get home," Stephanie said.

Hope sat back, letting Ollie wriggle out of her grip and run screeching into the playroom. "That would be great. I've already had him in and out of this stupid thing twice today, and I don't think I have the energy to do it again right now."

Stephanie grabbed the keys to Mark and Celia's old Mercedes station wagon from the hook inside the door. They had all chipped in to install a third row of seats in the back since none of their cars had been big enough to transport all five kids. It had been expensive, but worth it, especially for Hope, who, in bad weather or on days when she had to take one of them to the doctor, could now get them all where they needed to be at one time.

"See you soon," Stephanie said to Hope and trudged down Emerson toward the snow-covered car. She hated to lose the prime parking spot at the corner of Eighteenth Street, especially with the snow continuing to fall, but by now she was running late, and to get to both schools on foot in a reasonable amount of time would have been nearly impossible. She quickly brushed the snow off the front windshield with her arm—no time to find the scraper—and decided to get Lu and Ted first since they were the farthest away, if only by a few blocks.

When she finally pulled back onto Emerson nearly an hour later, Hope was standing between her screen door and the wooden one behind it, holding it open a few inches, and glancing nervously up and down the street. The trip had been harrowing, even for Stephanie. First she couldn't find a parking spot near Lu and Ted's school because someone had driven their car into the schoolyard fence. Then, by the time she got over to Shoshanna and Harvest's school, they had been moved inside since they were the last kids left in the snowy yard. Stephanie had to park again, this time dragging Ted and Lu inside with her, and then she had to strap four kids back into the car, which, by the time she was finished, was covered with snow.

"Oh my God. I was so worried. Is everyone okay?" Hope asked as she opened the car doors and unstrapped the kids. "Ollie's taking a nap upstairs, and I have all of the snow stuff out, and I made hot cocoa and those Toll House break and bakes. I was waiting and waiting."

"We're fine. It's just such a pain to get around this city in the snow I went as fast as I could, and I forgot to grab my phone," Stephanie said, getting back into the driver's seat. "I need to go park the car. Get on the sidewalk, kids!"

The kids had already started picking up and throwing the snow, which was so light and fluffy that it never made it into snowball form. They scattered to the houses on either side of the street and waited for the car to slowly pass. When Stephanie looked into her rearview mirror, she saw Hope shepherding them into the house.

By the time Stephanie trudged back up Emerson after circling the neighborhood for more than half an hour, they were back outside, dressed in snow pants and hats and mismatched mittens that had been pulled from three plastic bins of winter clothing extracted from three basements. Celia had come home early from work and was helping to shovel the snow into a big pile in the middle of the street so that the kids could take turns riding the plastic snowboard down the man-made hill.

"Remember that thing we talked about—you know, with Mark and me?" Celia said to Stephanie after she'd passed the snow pile-making responsibility on to Hope for a while.

"Um hmm," Stephanie said, sipping Swiss Miss with mini marshmallows from her Starbucks mug. "How'd it go? Did the yoga thing work out for you?"

"I guess you could say that," Celia said, lowering her voice to a whisper. "He walked in as I was doing the downward facing dog." Stephanie could see that Celia was starting to blush, even though her cheeks were already pink from the cold. "I timed it just right. But . . ."

"But what?"

"When it was over—I don't know—he just seemed distracted. Not that he wasn't, you know, *satisfied*, but maybe it's just my imagination. Anyway, it was good that we did it, it definitely lightened the mood a little. I think it will get better if I keep on making an effort to ease him back into it. He's been through so much this year."

Stephanie was trying her best to concentrate on what Celia was saying, but imagining her doing yoga naked and what must have happened after Mark walked in made her mind wander to the den and Leo, and that was exactly where she didn't want it to go. She could blame the first time on the pregnancy hormones and her incredible horniness, not to mention her fear of Chris catching on to the pregnancy. But what excuse did she have for the times they'd done it since?

"What are you guys talking about so seriously over here?" Hope interrupted, resting the snow shovel against the house. The kids had just finished taking turns climbing to the top of the snow pile, standing on the snowboard, and trying to ride it down.

"Stephanie gave me a little bedroom advice, and it worked like a charm," Celia said.

Hope's eyes widened. "Are you guys having problems? Because I have to say that we have been, too. For the last few weeks, Leo's been, well, let's say *overly* enthusiastic. Frankly, he's wearing me out."

"Really?" Stephanie mumbled, avoiding Hope's eyes and the desperate urge to walk away.

"Well, darn, I wouldn't consider *that* a problem," Celia said. "For a man, that is."

"Yeah, I guess it's not that big a deal. It's just that we have, you know, a regular schedule. Right now it's Tuesdays and Fridays," Hope said.

Stephanie and Celia looked at each other.

"Did you say Tuesdays and Fridays? Like you have a regular sex schedule?" Stephanie said.

"Yeah, don't you guys?"

"Maybe we should," Celia said, running over to the snow pile to break up an argument about who was more like the Flying Tomato, Harvest or Ted.

"Sex shouldn't be so complicated," Stephanie said as they watched Celia help the kids decide on their own snowboarder names.

"But that's exactly why I insisted on a schedule, so both of us always know what to expect," Hope said. "Even if I don't feel like doing it, I know that I need to gear up for it. You know, get myself ready. But when he wants it all the time, not to mention," she said, lowering her voice, "he can keep it going for much longer lately, if you know what I mean, it gets a little—"

"You know what?" Stephanie said brightly, turning toward the house and climbing her steps. "We haven't even talked about dinner." She was more than ready to change the subject. "How do you feel about chili?"

∾

The basement of the museum store was packed with holiday shoppers fingering the hundreds of colorful Christmas ornaments—angels made of glass or paper or feather boa, tiny instruments covered with silver glitter, and miniature Santas posed in every possible scenario, from stirring a pot of soup to knitting a sweater. It was the place to go in the city for the hippest, must unusual urban gifts. Mark was searching for the perfect present to leave his Delancey Street client, who was scheduled to move back into the house this weekend, just one week before Christmas. The living room with floor-to-ceiling windows looking out into the beautifully landscaped yard was the ideal place for an extravagant twelve-foot Christmas tree. He finally decided on a box of shiny MOMA glass ball ornaments in pop art colors—creamy mint green, Pepto-Bismol pink, scarlet, and butterscotch.

He waited for the box to be gift wrapped in matte black paper and topped with a shocking green bow, then wandered down the city sidewalks covered with yesterday's snow, no longer white and clean, across Rittenhouse Square toward the town house on one of the most beautiful streets in the city. He had been in the Delancey Street house many times since the day he had waited for Nikki, and every time he felt the same twinge of embarrassment. But this would be the last time, and he was glad. He needed to be done with her, with the feeling that something had been left unresolved. He decided that today he would call her, let her know that it had all been a big mistake.

He unlocked the door and stepped inside, taking a seat on the entryway sofa without taking off his coat. He stared at his phone, willing himself to dial.

"Modern Man, may I help you?"

Mark hesitated. "Does . . . Nikki happen to be working today?"

"Yes, she does, and she is on her way out the door as we speak. May I ask who's calling?"

"Tell her it's Mark, please."

Mark fought the desperate urge to hang up the phone, but he had come this far, and there was no turning back.

"Mark," she said, her voice soft and warm and a little raspy, just like he remembered.

"Nikki. How are you?"

"I'm just about to walk out the door, but I do want to talk to you. Can you meet me somewhere?"

"Yes, that would be great. I'm at 1818 Delancey, if you want to meet me here," he said, not believing his own words. Wasn't this the opposite of what he had set out to achieve by calling her? No, it was good; they could talk in person. "I don't know if you remember. It's my client's house."

"I'll be there in ten minutes. Please wait for me."

The next ten minutes crawled as Mark rehearsed what he would say to Nikki. He needed to be able to say it first, to preserve his last shred of dignity. *I completely understand. This is wrong. You were right not to come. What were we thinking? You're newly married—you need to concentrate on that, and I'm sorry if I assumed . . .*

He paced through the spacious first floor, from the back of the house to the front door, without getting too close to the entrance. He didn't want to appear eager when she rang the bell. But when she did, right on time, he stopped in his tracks in the kitchen between the stainless steel refrigerator and black granite-topped island, suddenly forgetting all the lines he'd rehearsed. He forced himself to walk slowly to the door, and when he opened it, he couldn't help but smile. She was bundled in a white knee-length down parka and wearing her big black sunglasses. Her hair wasn't pulled back as usual, but hung down her back in a dark brown silky sheet. She had both hands jammed into her pockets, and her face was flushed from the cold.

Fuck dignity, he thought.

"Take your coat off. Stay a while," he said, opening the door for her.

"Wow, this place looks finished. Sure no one's home?" she said, stepping past him into the entryway.

He looked at his watch. "Not yet, but in about seventy-two hours, I guarantee it will be a mess. God, I hate it when it looks so perfect, and in a matter of days, hours sometimes, they mess it up with all of their junk."

"So you're a minimalist? You'd hate living with me then."

"I wouldn't go that far."

Nikki smiled and shook her head slowly. "Can we sit down?"

Mark led her into the living room. It was his favorite room in the house, with clean white walls except for the one behind the sofa, which was a deep shade of pumpkin. The original pine floors had been beautifully restored and were a pale caramel with the kinds of flaws that made them perfect. The snow from the backyard brightened the room, even though the day was gray. They sat together on the low leather sectional, and Mark couldn't help but feel guilty, but not for being here with Nikki. When she hadn't shown up that day, he had thrown himself into it with Celia, which was made easier by her little yoga stunt. But now he couldn't shake the very strange thought that he had cheated on Nikki with his own wife.

"Thanks for meeting me. I know what that must have looked like, you know, when I didn't show last time. I felt so horrible about it that I couldn't even bear to call you to explain," Nikki said. Mark noticed that her hands were shaking.

"Nikki, no, please. No explanation necessary. You're married. I'm married. I crossed a line I shouldn't have, and you were right to stop it before it went any further. I've never been one to rock the boat, but something's changed in me lately. I'm doing things I would never have done before."

"Don't give me too much credit. I *was* going to come. But when I got home that day, Will had planned a surprise weekend trip to celebrate our wedding. A kind of mini honeymoon. And when he did that,

I thought I just needed to try a little harder with him. I know this isn't fair to him or you, but I have to say it."

She took a deep breath and continued. "Over the last few weeks, even while we were away, all I could think of was you, not him, and that just seems wrong, but I don't know how to stop those thoughts from coming."

Once again Mark thought, *Fuck dignity. Fuck everything.* He stood up and held his hand out to her. She took it and stood in front of him, then accepted his kiss, first barely responding, then reciprocating, reaching hungrily for his lips and tongue.

"You know," he said softly, "the upstairs of this house is even better than the downstairs."

"Show me," she said.

"I thought we needed a change of scenery, that's why," said Hope as she craned her neck to look up at Leo, who stood on the open elevator at the restaurant, reaching for a bottle of Chateau de Beaucastel.

"This is a great Châteauneuf-du-Pape," he said as he pushed the lever and slowly descended to the ground. "But this isn't a change of scenery for me. I practically live here. Let's plan a nice dinner out somewhere next week. Maybe the new Italian place on North Broad," Leo said once he was face to face with Hope but still standing in the funny little elevator, which always reminded her of the kind of crane that window washers used.

"But I got Stephanie and Celia to watch all the kids. I know you're busy, but I just wanted us to have a chance to talk, you know, alone?"

"Okay, sweetie, just let me get a few things settled in the kitchen. Sam!" Leo called to the elegant blonde standing near the podium. "Would you mind taking my lovely wife to the private dining room? She's surprised me for dinner tonight."

Samantha waddled over to Hope. If she hadn't been eight months pregnant, Hope might have been jealous about the fact that Leo spent most of his waking hours with her. When Hope saw them together, they almost seemed like girlfriends—gossiping about the chef at the new bistro on the corner or complaining about an annoying guest. Even big and pregnant, Sam was glamorous with her shoulder-length blond hair and Barbie doll features. Not too long ago the big pregnant belly would have induced its own intense jealousy.

Samantha looked at Leo and raised her eyebrows. "Are we celebrating?" she asked, like she knew something Hope didn't.

Hope glanced from Samantha to Leo and could have sworn she saw him give Samantha a panicked look.

"Oh, Samantha, every day with my wife is a celebration," Leo said one beat too late. He gave Hope's shoulder a squeeze.

Samantha led Hope to the back of the restaurant, where there was a cozy room for small private parties, and directed her to sit at the end of the long table lined down the middle with tea lights.

"Enjoy your meal, Hope. So nice to see you again," Samantha said, making a quick exit.

What the hell is going on? Hope wondered. *Is he having an affair with Sam?* She really didn't think so, but something just didn't seem right. When Leo returned with two elegant glasses and started to open the wine that he'd left on the table, Hope decided she was being ridiculous.

"I miss being alone with you," Hope said, trying to come off as romantic but sounding whiny instead. She cleared her throat. "I mean, I think it's time we started to focus more on us again." What she wanted to say was that she was ready to put the idea of having another baby behind her so they could just *be*, instead of always wanting more.

Leo slid his chair next to Hope and gently ran his hand over her silky dark hair. He leaned in and looked directly into her eyes.

"Hope, sweetie, what's going on? I have never stopped focusing on us. You are always my top priority. And there is something I want to tell you. I didn't mention it sooner since I know how private you are, but I think this is going to make you very happy. I've been talking with Sam about our problem."

Hope started to panic. What had he done? Talked to this stranger about their sex life, about what happened behind closed doors in their bedroom?

". . . Sam has this great doctor—a fertility specialist. Did I mention that she's having twins? Anyway, it's impossible to get an appointment with him—he's the best in the city. But she's pulled some strings and set up a meeting for us. I know having another baby is very important to you. I wanted to show you that I'm in it, too. This is my contribution!"

Hope stared at Leo, who looked like he had just told her he won the lottery and that their lives would be changed forever. It took a minute, but what he was saying finally registered.

"I . . . what? I don't understand . . . when did you do this?"

"Just this week. It seems like you've been agonizing about it for so long and that you don't want to talk to anyone about it, even me. And that if I just took the initiative, maybe we could be pregnant soon. It only took Samantha three months after years of trying," Leo said.

One of the new servers interrupted them with a plate of fragrant goat cheese ravioli with brown butter and pine nuts.

"Shall I pour some wine?" the server asked.

"Yes, please," Leo said, taking Hope's hands in his. "Are you angry?"

Hope shook her head. "No, no, I'm not angry. I love that you did this for me. I love that you want to make me happy and that you did this all on your own. But, I, well, forget it. Never mind. Thank you, thanks for setting that up."

"Sweetie, I would do anything for you. Don't you know that? Don't you know how much I adore you?"

Hope looked at Leo and nodded, but she couldn't help feeling disappointed that they were in such different places. It reminded her of the O. Henry story where the woman sells her hair to buy a chain for her husband's beloved watch, but the husband sells his watch to buy his wife a beautiful comb for her hair. In the end, both gifts are useless. Hope couldn't remember what happened to the couple at the end of the story. She would have to go back and read it.

❧

Nikki snatched her pink bikini underwear from the bedpost, suddenly embarrassed by her nakedness and the memory of using that same pole as a prop when she first took her clothes off not long before. Mark had stared at her when she held on to the post, bending forward and back. At first she thought she had blown it. What was she thinking? But she'd quickly realized she hadn't. He had loved it. She could see that loud and clear when she looked at his naked body. She still couldn't figure out what had made her do it.

Now Mark was in the bathroom off the client's master bedroom with the water running, and she could hear him whistling. The bed was messed up a little, but still covered with the white duvet that had been so neatly stretched across it when they got to the second floor. When Mark led her into the room and over to the bed, he had eased her down gently, his urgent kisses still somehow seeming tender, careful, kind. He took his time, undressing her slowly, and she had relished the attention. And then she had stood up and done her moves with the pole. After that, it was a frenzy of trying to get as close as they possibly could to each other.

"You're dressed," Mark said, emerging from the bathroom. "And I'm not," he said, looking down at himself then back at Nikki. He slid over to the bed and slowly twirled around. "What the hell, I don't care. I just committed adultery and loved every minute of it. I'm going to enjoy it as much as I can."

Goddamn, he was so cute. Something was so free and playful about him; there was a spark she loved. It made her feel close to him. It made her feel like she could actually be herself.

"We better get out of here," Nikki said, standing up to look for the rest of her clothes.

Mark pushed her gently back onto the bed and climbed on top of her. "No! Don't leave me! I was just getting warmed up."

"You're pretty energetic for a forty-year-old," she teased.

He rolled off her onto his back and threw his arms over his head. "Oh man, that was harsh. But I'll forgive you if you will give me the pleasure of another one of your dances."

She turned away, wishing she hadn't done that. But he moved closer and gave her a hug from behind. A real hug. When was the last time Will had done that?

"Sorry, did I say something wrong?" Mark asked gently. "It's just that it was so amazing, so unexpected."

Nikki relaxed a little.

"It's just a hobby, you know," she said, trying not to sound too defensive. "For fun and exercise. I'm not, you know, a stripper or anything."

"I never thought you were," he said. "But for my purposes, that hobby is a pretty good one."

She smiled and turned so that they were face to face.

"How about one last kiss?" he finally said.

Nikki leaned in and gave him a long, slow, deep kiss.

"Ah, that one will last me a long time," he said, closing his eyes and smiling wide.

∽

It was starting to get dark outside when they finally made it to the front door after procrastinating as long as they could. Nikki slipped on her coat and grabbed her bag from inside the door.

"What will we do?" she asked, turning to face him.

"I have absolutely no idea," he said. "But for right now, we'll have to leave separately, I imagine. We shouldn't take any chances."

"I hate walking home alone," Nikki said, more to herself than to him. "I feel like I'm always walking alone."

"You're not going to be alone—at least not with me around," he said. She nodded and opened the door, then started the short walk down Delancey to Eighteenth Street.

She heard the door close, but she didn't need to turn around. She could hear Mark's footsteps behind her as she walked, and somehow she knew that he would be there as long as she needed him.

CHAPTER FOURTEEN

"It was a *miracle*, it was a *miracle*, it was," Hope sang under her breath as she turned the corner onto Emerson, moving the heavy plastic grocery bag from one hand to the other. She couldn't remember the rest of the words, so she tried another. "Dreidel, dreidel, dreidel, I made it out of clay . . ."

Hope thought she heard other people singing, too, but she wasn't sure where it was coming from. As she got closer to her door she clearly made out the tune to "Happy Birthday." Was it someone's birthday? Had she been so distracted that she forgot? No. She couldn't have missed a birthday. As she walked up the stoop, she went through everyone's dates in her head—she was sure there wasn't a single one in December.

She transferred the bag back to her other hand and fished for her key. She pushed it into the lock, turned, and shoved open the door.

"Happy birthday, dear Jesus, happy birthday to you!" The song reached its climax just as Hope stepped inside. She put the bag down and looked around to find a full-blown nativity scene with Shoshanna dressed as Mary and Harvest dressed as Joseph. Lu, Ted, and Stephanie were wise men, wearing gold and purple robes of different lengths and holding gold sparkly boxes out in front of them. A big star hung over a wooden structure that was decorated with straw. Stuffed animals filled out the scene with Shoshanna's stuffed Donkey from *Shrek*, Lu's sheep, and a camel that Hope had never seen before. And there in the center of the playroom, which used to be her living room, was Ollie lying in the middle of a hay nest, wrapped in what Hope guessed were swaddling clothes.

"Wait, I have a cake," Stephanie said suddenly, moving away from the other wise men and running into the kitchen. She emerged with a small round cake iced with bright yellow frosting and flecked with gold sparkles. Small stars adorned the sides. Stephanie held it up. In purple writing it said, "Happy Birthday Jesus."

"I should have brought it out before we sang," Stephanie said. "Oh well, does anyone want any? Hope, you got here just in time. Do you want to be the angel? I have a really great angel costume with wings and everything."

Hope hadn't moved since she walked in the door, but now she tried to smile at everyone.

"Uh, I don't think so," she said. "I want to put this stuff away before it defrosts."

She took her bag into the kitchen, glad to get away from the biblical scene. It was the first night of Hanukkah, and even though Leo, who made the best potato pancakes, had to work tonight, Hope still wanted to celebrate. She had bought frozen latkes, sour cream, applesauce, and Dunkin' Donuts. The donuts had been an afterthought, but definitely in the spirit because donuts were, after all, sweets fried in oil. She thought the kids would love that.

She pulled the boxes of frozen latkes out of the bag and put them in the freezer, put the sour cream and applesauce in the fridge and the donuts on the counter. Would the kids even want them now that they were stuffing themselves with cake? Hope took a deep breath and forced herself to go back into the playroom.

"Do you want a piece of cake?" Stephanie asked. She had the baby Jesus in her lap now and was feeding him bites of cake. Hope wanted to tell her that there was no part of the story where a wise man fed the baby Jesus cake, but she held back.

"No thanks," she said, going over to Shoshanna and giving her a hug.

"I hope you don't mind the mess," Stephanie said. "But one of my clients was cleaning out. I guess she used to do all the costumes for her church nativity play, and she didn't want these anymore. I couldn't resist."

"No, I don't mind," Hope said, trying to relax. "It's the first night of Hanukkah, you know."

"Oh my God," Stephanie said, getting up and taking off her purple scarf. "I had no idea. Is this bad? Like totally sacrilegious or something?"

"No, no," Hope said. "It's fine. Really. I was just surprised, that's all."

"Great! So do you want to give the baby Jesus his first gift?" Stephanie asked, holding up one of the gold boxes. "I couldn't remember what Jesus's real gifts were, so I put some Silly Putty in there."

Hope paused, shaking her head. "To tell you the truth, I guess I was planning on celebrating Hanukkah; you know, light the menorah, play dreidel, eat potato pancakes."

"It's Hanukkah tonight?" Shoshanna asked excitedly. "Do we get presents?"

"Maybe," Hope said. That was something she hadn't quite figured out—presents. In years past they had all spent one night of Hanukkah together, and Hope had loved it. She would decorate the house in blue and white, put out all their menorahs, lead everyone in singing the songs. She would buy each child one nice present. After that, the three of them would spend the rest of the holiday either alone at home or going to various parties. This year she had declined the invitations to the two parties they were invited to, though she worried about single-handedly keeping up the festive environment for eight nights in a row.

Shoshanna was used to getting a present every night, and so far Hope had eight for her but just one for each of the other kids.

"Presents, presents, presents," the kids chanted.

"On second thought, let's clean this up," Stephanie said, pulling Ollie out of his burlap swaddling. She released him to run free in his diaper. "Come on, kids, put on your regular clothes."

"No, that's okay," Hope said. "You don't have to stop the play. Really."

"We were practically finished anyway," Stephanie said, pulling the star down and folding up the manger. Some of the straw fell onto the carpet, and she stooped to pick it up before she stashed the manger next to one of the bookshelves. "Do you have Hanukkah decorations? Let's get them up."

Hope had a bag upstairs full of white and blue lights, all the menorahs, tons of dreidels. Last week she had bought a carton's worth of Hanukkah gelt. But suddenly she didn't feel like it. She just wanted to be alone.

"You know what? I'm going to take a shower. I didn't have a chance this morning. I'll be down in a little while. Do you mind?" Hope said.

"No, go, take your time," Stephanie said.

"Thanks," Hope said, turning toward her stairs. As she reached the third step she heard Shoshanna sing, "Happy birthday to Jesus, happy birthday to you."

~

Stephanie and Nikki sat on Nikki's bedroom floor going through her underwear. The cosmetics had been sorted easily and quickly. They threw out all the items that had frost in them, the corals and fuchsias, and organized the rest in the vanity outside the bathroom that was empty except for whatever Nikki had fished out of one of her bins that morning. So now it was on to underwear. Clients were always so squeamish about underwear, and yet it was often one of the places they needed the most help. But Nikki didn't seem to mind.

"It's all clean," was all she said as she dumped out three full drawers' worth of cotton bikinis, lacey thongs, bras of all colors and sizes, and slips that Stephanie was sure Nikki probably never wore. And one by one they went through each item.

"When's the last time you wore this?" Stephanie asked, holding up a beige slip.

"Middle school, I think," Nikki said, laughing.

"Out," Stephanie said, placing it into the big black trash bag. "These?"

Stephanie was holding up a pair of pink bikini panties.

For the first time since Nikki and Stephanie got together that day, Nikki blushed and looked away. Stephanie glanced from the seemingly innocent panties to Nikki and then back to the panties. Of all the things they had gone through—the lacey push-up bra, the crotchless underwear, the lime-green teddy—this seemed to be the least interesting.

"What?" Stephanie asked, dangling the pink underwear from one finger. "Did you wear these on your wedding night or something?"

"No, nothing like that," Nikki said quietly, still not looking at Stephanie.

"So I assume you want to keep these?" Stephanie said, smiling.

"Definitely," Nikki said, smiling back. "Do you . . . oh, forget it."

Stephanie waited, pretending to be looking through a small pile of sachet pillows. She picked up the light purple one and held it to her nose. It smelled like lavender, of course. Stephanie put it down and looked at Nikki, who had grabbed the pink panties and was holding them tight in her fist.

"Can I tell you something and you won't tell anyone in the world? Not even Chris?" Nikki asked. She couldn't believe she was going to do it.

"Sure," Stephanie said. "What is it?"

"I think I might be in love."

"Well, obviously," Stephanie said.

"What?" Nikki asked, sounding alarmed.

"You just got married, I would imagine that you're in love," Stephanie said.

"Oh yeah, I know, that's what makes this even more difficult," Nikki said. "I think I'm falling in love with someone who isn't my husband. He's another man. A married man."

A few months ago Stephanie wouldn't have let the conversation get this far. It was hard to avoid learning about her clients' personal lives; they were so often sifting through very intimate items that raised so many emotions and memories. But when it came to confessions, Stephanie was pretty good at stopping them before they were offered. She would have, for example, stood up and aggressively gone through a bunch of underwear instead of waiting and opening herself up the way she did. Or she would have excused herself to go to the bathroom, and, more often than not, the client would lose his or her nerve by the time she returned. But things had been different with Nikki from the beginning. And things were different with Stephanie lately, too. It was almost like ever since she and Leo had been "running into each other" in his den, she wanted to know what other people did that they shouldn't.

"Huh," Stephanie said. "Is this someone you're admiring from afar?"

"Not exactly," Nikki said.

"You mean you're having an actual affair?"

Nikki took a deep breath. Her relief over the ability to talk to someone about this overwhelmed the nagging feeling that maybe she should have kept it to herself.

"Yeah, I guess you could call it that," Nikki said.

"I assume it was going on before you got married?" Stephanie asked as gently as she could. She had no idea this morning was going to get so interesting.

"Why do you assume that?" Nikki asked seriously.

"You've been married for how long? A month? What are the chances of meeting someone in the last month and starting an affair?"

"Well, no, our relationship changed after I got married," Nikki admitted. "I knew him before, but . . ."

"Do you think Will suspects anything?" Stephanie asked.

"No, Will has no clue. He's barely here anyway, and he's so focused on his job that I feel like I could switch souls with someone, and as long as my body was here to have sex with and to say good morning to every once in a while, he wouldn't even notice I was gone," Nikki said.

"Switch souls?" Stephanie teased. "Is that something you do often? Is that why you have so much disorganized stuff? You keep switching souls and changing your mind about what you like?"

"Ha ha, very funny. No, of course not," Nikki said, shifting her position and stretching her trim legs out in front of her. Her bare toes touched Stephanie's knee and she let them. "Didn't you ever see that movie *Prelude to a Kiss*? With Meg Ryan and Alec Baldwin?"

Stephanie shook her head.

"Well, Meg Ryan, the bride, somehow ends up kissing this really sick old man on her wedding day, and they switch souls. So the bride and groom go on their honeymoon, to Jamaica, I think, and the bride looks normal with her beautiful body, but she isn't there. She's stuck back in Chicago in this miserable man's body living with his worried daughter. Anyway, it takes Alec—I can't remember his character's name—a little while to figure it out, but he does, and he misses her desperately, even though her body is right in front of him. I don't think Will would notice if I kissed an old man and switched souls and he was here instead of me. As long as I looked like this, that is."

"Wow, that sounds really lonely. I had no idea it was that bad," Stephanie said. She couldn't help thinking that Chris would definitely notice if she switched souls with someone. He might be a little lost and have a bunch of faults, but he would notice that.

"Yeah, it is lonely," Nikki said quietly.

"So tell me about him," Stephanie asked. "Who is he?"

"Oh, well, it's all so new, and I didn't even mean to say this much, really," Nikki said, getting up. Then she sank back down in a knee bend in front of Stephanie. "I don't think it really matters who he is. I mean, it matters to me, but I don't want to say that out loud yet, maybe ever. But I am so glad that I could tell you."

"Oh, come on, tell me more," Stephanie said, surprised by her own demand.

"This is so cliché, but when we're together, it's like nothing else matters, like we're the only ones in the universe," Nikki said. "We close the door, and for that half hour or however long we have, I don't even think about Will. It's like the whole world out here doesn't even exist."

"Wow. That sounds so romantic. What are you going to do?"

"Do?" Nikki asked, startled. Hadn't she asked Mark the same exact question? "I don't know, honestly. I do know that when I'm with him I feel better taken care of than I've ever felt with Will, or any man, for that matter. But I just got married. And no matter how hard I try to imagine a happy ending, I can't figure out what that would look like with either one of them. So I don't try."

"That's so sad," Stephanie said. "Sad to keep it going, sad for it to end. Just sad."

"No, don't you get it? I'm not sad, I'm happy," Nikki said. "I'm not thinking about what might happen or where it might lead. I just know that in this moment in time, I'm happier than I've ever been in my whole life. Do you know what I mean?"

"Yeah," Stephanie said. "I do. I know exactly what you mean." Stephanie might have left it there, but felt she had to ask, "So do you feel bad about the wife?"

"The wife?"

"You said he was married, right?" Stephanie asked. "Do you feel bad about the wife?"

"I try not to think about her," Nikki said honestly. "Otherwise I think I would feel bad. It's better to imagine that she's not real, I guess."

Stephanie nodded and stretched out her legs. "Hey, are you hungry?"

"Actually, yes, I'm starving," Nikki said, pushing herself up and putting the rest of the underwear pile back in the drawer. "What do you want to eat?"

"There's a crepe place on Bainbridge. I can drive. Come on, we'll finish this later," Stephanie said, heading down the stairs. Nikki grabbed her coat and purse and followed Stephanie out the door. But as soon as they were outside, Stephanie realized that she needed to go inside her house to get the car keys. If only she'd thought of it before, she could have left Nikki at home and come right back. But now Nikki was out, and her door was locked.

"It's freezing out here. Where's the car?" Nikki asked.

"You know what, why don't we just go to that new coffee shop around the corner on South Street? We can walk there. It's easier," Stephanie said.

"No way, crepes sound good," Nikki said. "Which way?"

"I have to go home first to get the keys," Stephanie said. "Do you want to wait here?"

"I'll come with you," Nikki said. "It's really windy out here. Besides, isn't it crazy that we're neighbors and I've never even been in your house?"

"Yeah, I guess," Stephanie muttered, stalling. But there was no use. "Nikki, I have to tell you something—a huge secret. I guess this is going to be a day of confessions."

Nikki's eyes lit up, and she picked up her pace. Stephanie's heart was beating fast. She didn't think anybody was home, but what if someone was there? Hope and Ollie were at a music class, and Chris was at the university helping with a tennis clinic, but either one of them could have changed their plans. Nikki was a step ahead of her as they approached the stoop. Stephanie stood at the bottom, taking her time getting the house key out of her pocket, but Nikki was already on the top step, trying to look in the windows.

"What's the deal with this?" she asked. "Your blinds are always down. I can never see in."

"Uh-huh," Stephanie said as she joined Nikki.

Nikki was shivering and bouncing up and down. "Come on already. Open up."

Stephanie finally turned her attention to the lock and opened the door. Nikki walked right in, first looking ahead, then at the playroom on the left and the common living room on the right. She looked at Stephanie, stuck her head out of the door to make sure she was properly oriented, and moved back inside.

"Wow," she said. "What is this?"

"Let me get my keys, and I'll explain it in the car. I don't want anyone to come home and find us. We have a rule that we never let anyone in," Stephanie said. "Absolutely no one."

"But I want to see the rest," Nikki begged.

"Actually, this is it. Each staircase leads to our own floors, which look pretty much the same as every other house on the street. We just took down the walls on the first floor," Stephanie explained, grabbing the keys from the hook by the door. "Let's go."

"No, wait a minute," Nikki said, moving deeper into the house. She studied the playroom, noting how it looked like a toy store with the bright colors and packed bookshelves. She moved toward Mark's house and tried to remember how it looked that day she went inside. Just being this close to the spot where they first kissed almost took her breath away.

"Hey, come on, we really need to go," Stephanie said urgently.

Nikki took one last look before following her out and to the car on Eighteenth Street without saying a word, not even processing the fact that Stephanie and Mark lived together.

"So spill," Nikki said once they were driving along Bainbridge Street. "That is a crazy secret. I can't believe no one's found out! Tell me everything, absolutely everything!"

"It's really pretty simple," Stephanie said. "We spend all our time together, and we love each other. We take care of each other's kids. It just made sense for us."

"Wow, everyone thought you guys were making porn movies in there with the blinds down all the time."

"What?" Stephanie asked, taking her eyes off the road for a second. "That's so funny! We're, like, the most boring people I know."

"Well, actually, not everyone. It was really Mary's idea," Nikki said. "I told her she was crazy. But a commune? That's so cool. That's like the opposite of lonely. I've never been a part of anything like that, really. It must be nice to come home at night and know someone will be there. Is that nice?"

"Yeah," Stephanie said. "It's nice. It's really nice."

The next morning Mark felt as light as the first snowfall. He had managed to fit in a half hour with Nikki by making an appointment to have his back waxed. He stuffed a soft, clean pillow into the bottom of his architect's tote to put at the top of the waxing table, told Miles he was off to shop for appliances with a client, and hurried to the salon and Nikki, who was waiting eagerly for him at the front desk. The only glitch was that they couldn't make any noise at all, but in the end he realized that it just added to their pleasure.

Now he walked along Nineteenth Street, smelling the woodsmoke escaping from fireplaces, and entered Rittenhouse Square. The huge tree was bright with white lights, and as he got to the center of the Square, he saw a small crowd of people wearing red Santa hats.

"Ho ho ho," a festively dressed woman said to Mark, and instead of walking by like he usually would, he stopped.

"Ho ho ho to you, too," Mark said, smiling. "Are you guys selling something?"

"We are, and for a good cause, too," the woman said, sweeping her arms toward a stack of trees. "We're selling trees to raise money for the Square. Can I interest you in one?"

Mark hesitated. There were two more nights of Hanukkah, and they had decided to wait until Christmas Eve to buy and trim the tree. Hope had been so strange about the holiday, not her usual enthusiastic self. That first night she had brought out the lights and the dreidels, they lit the menorah, she'd given each child a very thoughtful present, and they had a good time eating frozen potato pancakes. When Leo got home later that night, after the kids were asleep, he made real ones, grating the potatoes and onions and frying up perfect crispy fritters, which they had been eating all week. But except for that, they hadn't done much more to celebrate. So why not get the tree now? They looked big and robust, and Mark was as much in the Christmas spirit as he had ever been.

"I'll take one," he said, pointing. "That big one on the end."

Hope hadn't said much when Mark carried in the tree two nights ago. She had clearly given up on celebrating Hanukkah, throwing the rest of the potato pancakes into the garbage. But now that Hanukkah had officially given way to Christmas Eve, Mark was relieved to see her sitting on the floor with everyone else, humming "God Rest Ye Merry, Gentlemen" and putting the finishing touches on the massive tree that sat just perfectly in the front of the dining room. The kids had begged to make popcorn strings, and even though Celia usually said no because she didn't want to tempt any mice, this time she said okay, figuring that if a mouse should find its way in, there would be someone around to get it.

Mark waltzed past the table to Celia, who was standing at the microwave monitoring the pops to make sure it didn't burn. He came up behind her, slipping one hand around her back and placing the other on her hip. He pulled her toward him, continuing to waltz.

"Hey, wait a minute," Celia said, giggling. "This is gonna burn."

"Burn, shmurn," Mark said, twirling Celia. "It's still popping a mile a minute. Hey, Leo, do you have any of that good bubbly? Something you might have stashed for New Year's Eve? And some Chambord? I want to make my wife here a Kir Royale. What do you say?"

"Sure," Leo said, getting up from the couch where he sat trying to mend old Christmas ornaments. He had already fixed the noseless Pinocchio and the headless angel and was now trying to rebuild a taxicab with a big red bow on it. "But let's do it right and use the crème de cassis—there's some in the cabinet over the refrigerator. And I have so much champagne that we're never going to be able to drink, especially with you guys out of town." He ducked into the refrigerator and moved things around. "This is a good one. Do you want me to make them?"

"Does Santa have a sleigh?" Mark asked, releasing Celia back to the microwave just in time and waltzing over to Leo, who already had the crème de cassis on the counter with six champagne glasses lined up. He was eyeing the amount of black currant liquor that he was pouring into the bottom of each glass.

"The trick to a perfect Kir Royale is to not put too much of the liquor in," Leo said seriously. "Watch and learn, my friends. Watch and learn."

Everyone was quiet while Leo finished pouring and handed the drinks around.

"A toast, to Christmas Eve," Leo said, purposefully not catching Hope's eyes.

"Hear! hear!" they called.

"When are we going to put these kids to bed?" Hope said without taking a sip.

"Oh, I guess we better do that," Stephanie said. "I'm thinking they should all sleep together tonight. That way Santa will be better able to keep his eye out for stray children. What do you think?"

"I think that's a great idea," Celia said. "What do you think? Harvest's room?"

"Yeah!" the kids cried in unison, moving toward the stairs.

"I have this," Stephanie said. "But I'm skipping the baths. Santa might care if they're naughty or nice, but he never said anything about being clean."

"What about the rest of the popcorn?" Celia asked quietly so the kids wouldn't hear.

"I'll have some," Hope said, trying her best to be in the spirit. "And I'll help do the last string."

"Okay, thanks. And I wanted to tell you that I have a few extra presents that we can give to Shoshanna. I know we said that we would just go ahead and do our own families, but I had this list, and I wanted to make sure I allocated the same amount of gifts to each child. I guess I just didn't want anyone to feel slighted," Celia said, lifting her glass of light purple liquid and taking a long sip. "I hope that's okay."

"Thanks for doing that, but I decided last week to save Shoshanna's Hanukkah gifts for Christmas. It made the most sense, and to tell you the truth, after that first night, she never asked for another, so we have plenty," Hope said.

"Oh good, it'll be a toy bonanza," Celia said.

"Speaking of which," Mark said. "Who is going to help me assemble all those Playmobils? It could take hours."

"Why can't you just wrap the boxes and leave it at that?" Leo asked, already on his second drink.

"No, we can't do that," Mark said. "Santa brings presents that are ready to be played with. Believe me, you'll thank me in the morning."

∼

Three hours and two bottles of champagne later, Mark and Leo sat on the hard dining room floor trying to put together the Playmobil zoo. They had already assembled the knight castle and the pirate ship. Leo's hands were cramped and tired from handling the tiny pieces, and his eyes were blurry from reading so many intricate directions. Mark, on the other hand, wasn't complaining one bit. He went on to each new page like it was his first.

"Okay, what is going on with you?" Leo finally asked, putting down the instruction book he'd been studying. "You're the one who usually plays the recurring role of Ebenezer Scrooge around here. Why are you so happy?"

"Let's just say that there are times in a man's life when everything changes, when life takes a surprising turn," Mark said.

"Do you mean your being sick?" Leo asked.

"I guess that was the beginning of the change for me," Mark said. "But there's so much more. Let me ask you this: Isn't there something you've done the same way forever and then did it a different way, and, voilà, it's like you found your old self again? You've experienced something like that, right?"

Leo was stunned. Did Mark know about what he and Stephanie had been doing? Maybe he had come across them at the exact moment when they were tuning everything else out, and this ruse of acting happy was just his way to get Leo to admit to it.

"Um, no, I haven't, um, experienced anything like that," Leo said just as Chris made his way down the stairs.

"Sorry about that," Chris said, walking directly to the tree and placing a small red box under it. "I wanted to wrap something for Stephanie, and I had to wait until she fell asleep. I really hope she likes it. How's this going?"

"Good, good," Leo said quickly, getting up and handing Chris his instruction booklet. "You can take over for me. My fingers need a rest. I'll see you guys tomorrow. Merry Christmas."

"Merry Christmas," Mark and Chris said in unison.

CHAPTER FIFTEEN

Ten more minutes to go, Mark thought as he folded up the stroller and lifted it into the back of the station wagon. He had everything planned out perfectly. He would finish packing the car, tell Celia that he was running out for coffee, and be back in time for Chris to drive them to the airport.

"Here you go," Chris said, handing Mark the white canvas tote bag full of coloring books, DVDs, juice boxes, and fruit snacks.

"Thanks. Anything else in there?" Mark asked, his hand on the hatch, ready to slam it shut.

"Nope, I think that's it. You want me to start loading kids in?"

"Not yet. I want to run out for a cup of coffee first. I think I have about half an hour, right? The flight leaves at eleven twenty, so if we leave here by nine, we should be good."

Mark had already rehearsed the timeline in his head more times than he could count since he and Nikki made the plan the last time they were together. He hated lying to Chris, but he had no choice. He needed to see her before their trip home to Kansas for New Year's—just one last time.

"I just made a fresh pot of coffee. You don't need to go out. And I just got some of those Styrofoam to-go cups. But don't tell Stephanie. She thinks they're bad for the planet," Chris said, leaning against the side of the car.

"Thanks, but I think I need to take a quick walk. You know, clear my head before the long flight with the kids." Mark couldn't believe how easily the lies came, but then again, he couldn't believe half the things he had done during the last few weeks. "Will you tell Celia I'll be back soon?"

Mark was getting antsy. He and Nikki had planned to meet at 8:30 a.m. at Metropolitan Bakery, just a few blocks away from Emerson Street. It was relatively risky, but they had decided that if anyone saw them, they could act like they had just run into each other. Besides, without an empty house to go to, they couldn't have arranged any real time together. This would have to be good enough.

"I'm going now. I'll see you soon," Mark said, inching away from the car.

"Okay, but hurry back. Celia will take it out on me if you're not here in time. I bet she has everything planned out to the minute. I can pick up your slack, but not for too long," Chris warned. He turned to go inside, but stopped when he heard a door slam at the end of the block. "Hey, there's Nikki."

Mark turned around. He waved casually, but inside his heart was pounding. He watched as she paused on her top step. He knew she was trying to decide what to do next. Finally she walked down the stoop and came toward them.

"Hey, guys. Merry Christmas," she said when she got to Mark's door.

Damn, she looked so great. Every time he saw her, he hoped the feeling would pass and that the reality of what he was doing would take over and the old Mark would come roaring back, but every time he was more drawn to her than the last. Standing here in front of Chris, unable to touch her, was torture. Mark braced himself against the side of the car next to Chris.

"What brings you out so early in the morning the day after Christmas?" Mark said to Nikki, trying hard not to look her in the eyes.

"Oh, just running out for a cup of coffee. You?"

"Just packing for the family trip back to Kansas. Always an adventure," said Mark, rolling his eyes and shoving his hands deep in his pockets. "And I, too, need caffeine to make it through this day. I'll walk with you," he said, suddenly not caring what it looked like or what Chris would think. But Chris didn't seem to think anything of it as he hopped up his steps.

"See you, Nikki. I'll give you a call this week. My hair looks terrible. Do you think you'll be able to fit me in?" Chris asked.

"I am so wide open this week, it's not even funny," Nikki said.

～

They walked a foot apart down Emerson, hands in their respective pockets, not looking at each other or saying anything until they safely turned the corner.

"I have something for you," Mark said, looking straight ahead.

"Do you really have to go?" she whispered.

"Yeah, I do. My parents are expecting us, and we missed our Thanksgiving trip. And Celia . . ."

"Right," Nikki said.

"I guess we'll need to get some coffee," Mark said, crossing the street and heading for the bakery on the corner of a small alley, just a block from the park. He held the door open for Nikki, and the smell of buttery croissants and strong coffee overwhelmed them. They stood in line behind two elderly women accompanied by a nurse. They waited while the women debated whether they should get a baguette or a ficelle and which one would be harder to chew. Mark and Nikki didn't mind. It gave them more time together. When it was finally their turn, Mark ordered two black coffees, but as soon as they got outside, he seemed surprised by the warm cup in his hand, as if he had sleepwalked through the last few minutes. As the door shut behind Nikki, he grabbed her by the hand and pulled her into the narrow alley beside the bakery, leading her past a tall Dumpster. He took her cup and put them both onto the ground beside him.

"I'm really going to miss this," he said, pulling her to him.

She nuzzled her face in his neck. She could smell his laundry detergent. It always seemed so silly every time she thought it, but she loved the smell of his clothes. What she tried not to let herself think about was the fact that that probably had a lot more to do with his wife than with Mark.

"This sucks," she said.

Mark moved away from her and reached into his coat pocket. He pulled out a small square bronze box. "I got this for you," he said, handing it to her. "Go ahead, open it. I wanted you to have it before I left."

Nikki lifted the lid. Inside was a delicate gold chain with a tiny dragon charm hanging from a bronze card. The card read, "FEARLESS."

"Oh my God, I love it," she said, lifting the card from the box and removing the dainty necklace.

"No, you have to read the whole card. I wanted to make sure that you're okay when we're not together."

Nikki looked at the card and read out loud, "Make a wish to be fearless each time you put on your necklace. You hold the power to make anything you desire happen. Trust your inner strength and your fearless spirit."

"When I saw this, I thought of us right away. Do you like it?"

"It's perfect. Nothing could be more perfect," she said, looking down. "But I have nothing to give you," Nikki said.

"Not true," Mark said. "Not true at all."

"Now this one is all the rage," Leo said, untwisting the wire ring on the champagne bottle. "Rosés are hot right now, and this is one of my favorites. It's a Veuve Clicquot."

They sat around the big table, just the four of them—Leo, Hope, Chris, and Stephanie—indulging Leo in his annual New Year's Eve champagne tasting. This year he had gone all out, complementing the champagne with caviar he had gotten through his purveyor to the restaurant.

"This one tastes just like the last one," Hope said, taking a long gulp of her drink. "I just don't get it."

"No, hon. That's impossible. You have to try it with the caviar. Let me show you," Leo said, letting out a dramatic sigh. He picked up one of the blini that he had made from scratch and slathered it with crème fraiche. "You'll see. They are all very different in their composition, especially when enjoyed with fine caviar."

"Ewww. No thanks. I do not do fish eggs. I don't care how fancy or expensive they are," Hope said, wrinkling her nose. "You know that."

"Yeah, man, I'm not so into the little slimy things either. I like the finer things as much as the next guy, but I think I'll take a pass," Chris agreed.

"Come on, guys, step out of your comfort zone once in a while. You don't know what you're missing," Leo said, putting the blini down on the square white ceramic plate and taking a gulp from his champagne flute. "Stephanie's with me, right, Stephanie? You like adventure."

"Absolutely. You know what they say about me. I'll try anything once," Stephanie joked, hitting Chris on the bicep.

"That's my girl, always open to new things," Chris said, craning his neck to get a look at the clock in the kitchen. "Ten more minutes till midnight, so we should start wrapping it up. You know our tradition."

Stephanie rolled her eyes. "You are such a creature of habit," she said, turning to Hope. "Why does he have to do this every year? Leave the party right after the clock strikes midnight—sheesh! What a party pooper."

"What? So what if I want to be alone with my wife to ring in the New Year?" Chris said.

"Aww, that's so romantic," Hope said, turning to Leo. "Why don't we have a tradition like that?"

"Because you always want to be the first to leave a party or go home whenever we go out, so what would be the point?" Leo asked.

"I guess you're right," Hope admitted.

Leo scooped a generous dollop of caviar on top of the blini with a dainty mother-of-pearl spoon. He rolled it up like a cigar, slowly and carefully, and took a bite.

He groaned with pleasure. "That is amazing. Absolutely incredible," he said, holding the remaining bite out to Stephanie, who was sitting directly across the table from him. "You need to try this."

She put both hands on the edge of the table and leaned forward out of her chair, opening her mouth and closing her eyes while Leo fed her the other half of the blini filled with caviar. "Oh my God, that is unbelievable," she gushed, sitting back in her chair.

"Thanks for your enthusiasm, Stephanie, but you don't have to indulge him. You can be honest, you know," Hope said.

"No, I really love it. Honestly," Stephanie said, looking innocently from Hope to Chris.

"Oh my God! I forgot. I saved the best for last and didn't even bring it up from downstairs," Leo said, jumping from his chair and bounding down his basement steps toward his private wine refrigerator. He returned just in time for the countdown.

"Five, four, three, two, one . . . Happy New Year!" they said in unison, raising their glasses. Chris grabbed Stephanie around the waist and tilted her backward to give her a big Hollywood kiss, while Hope and Leo shared their first kiss of the year, too. Then they switched.

"Chris," Hope said, giving him a peck on the lips and a warm hug. "Happy New Year. And it will be, now that the job offer came in," she whispered, smiling.

"Thanks, Hope," Chris whispered back. "Tonight's the night . . . I'm going to tell her the good news."

Leo moved around the opposite side of the table toward Stephanie, but as he grabbed her around the waist, he could feel himself immediately getting aroused. She looked into his eyes, and he began to blush. "Happy New Year, Stephanie," he said and kissed her awkwardly on the side of her mouth.

"You too," she said, patting him on the back. "Now let's get to opening that special bottle."

"Oh yes, you're really going to love this," he said, snapping even deeper into sommelier mode. "It's a 1995 Bollinger Grande Annee. I've been saving it for a really special occasion."

Leo tore away the black foil from the top of the bottle while Stephanie went to the kitchen for clean glasses.

"Whoa there, guys," Chris said, tapping his watch with his index finger. "It's about that time. Two minutes after midnight."

"Oh, Chris, do you mind? Can't we postpone for just a few minutes? Leo's been talking about this bottle for weeks, and I really want to try it," Stephanie said, pouting.

"I guess, okay, that's fine," Chris said. "But I'm going to go up now anyway. Happy New Year, guys. And Stephanie, I'll be waiting."

"Good night!" Hope said, waving. "See you tomorrow!"

Chris slowly climbed up the two flights to the bedroom, intent on getting ready for their New Year's tradition. He brushed his teeth, dabbed on a tiny drop of cologne, undressed, lit the tea light candles on the dressers, slid between their flannel sheets, and waited. He could hear voices rising through the heating vent next to his bed.

Almost an hour later, Chris was still waiting, still listening to the laughter and conversation coming from downstairs. He got out of bed and blew out the candles, and when he finally heard Stephanie tiptoeing up the stairs, he turned out the light on his nightstand, rolled over, and pretended to be asleep.

~

"Hey, Lu! Hey, Ted! Missed you, Ollie! How was Kansas?" Stephanie gushed as she watched them come down the escalator toward baggage claim. She was waving both arms over her head frantically even though it was impossible to miss her.

When they got to the bottom, Stephanie grabbed Ollie from Mark and snuggled her nose in his neck. He giggled uncontrollably and threw his head back.

"We really missed you guys. New Year's wasn't the same without you. The kids are dying to see all of the gifts from your nana and hear all about your trip," Stephanie said, leading them through baggage claim as they looked for the right carousel. "So? Was it fun?"

"It gave us the opportunity to see my sisters and brothers and their kids. Not all of us made it home, but it sure was a rowdy crowd," Celia said, grabbing for Ted's and Lu's hands as they tried to touch the moving belts.

"How about you, Mark? Did you have a nice week?" asked Stephanie, looking over her shoulder. "I'm sure your mom and dad were glad to see these little kiddies," she added, rumpling Lu's spiky blond curls.

"Let's just say I am happy to see the City of Brotherly Love again," Mark said.

"Aww, you party pooper," Celia chided. "He always complains when we go home—too many people, too many presents, too much running around. Bah humbug!" Celia said to Stephanie.

"Okay, Ebenezer, how about Celia and I take the kids out to the car while you wait for the luggage?"

"That sounds like a plan," Mark said, pulling Ollie's blankie from his back pocket and handing it to Stephanie.

Stephanie led Celia and the kids through the sliding doors and out to the sidewalk between the terminal and the short-term parking lot under the cement canopy. When they got in the car, Stephanie blasted the heat. It was the worst kind of Philadelphia day—wet, with a freezing cold wind that chilled you to the bone, and the sidewalks full of dirty, melting snow.

"Brrrr," Stephanie said, leaning over to talk to Celia through the open passenger door. "Welcome back to Philly and one of the crappiest weather days of the year."

Celia climbed in next to Stephanie, slammed the door shut, and turned to face her.

"Is Mark acting strange to you?" Celia whispered, keeping her voice low so that Ted and Lu didn't hear.

"You married him. You tell me," Stephanie said. "I've never known how to read him. He's an enigma."

Stephanie pulled out of the parking spot and drove through the gate, letting in a cold blast of air as she rolled down her window to pay the cashier bundled up in the small booth.

"He seemed so down for a while. But right around Christmastime he was, I don't know, really happy, his old self again. But the entire time we were away, he was totally distracted. I couldn't get him to engage. I mean, I know he always hates the trip home, but this time he really didn't make any effort. There was a three-day stretch when he didn't even change out of his pajamas. I had to make one excuse after another to my family," Celia said. "I just worry."

"About what?" asked Stephanie, pulling up to the sidewalk in front of the baggage claim and putting on the flashers. She could see Mark inside standing by the conveyor belt, still waiting for the luggage. What was he smiling at?

"Remember back when he was sick? They told us that he might not be himself, that he could have personality changes? I've tried to talk with him about it, mentioned that he should go back to the doctor and get checked, but he insists that he's fine. Do you think there could be something really wrong?" Celia asked.

"I don't know, Celia. Didn't they say he was okay? That all his tests came back normal? What did they call it—a miraculous recovery?" Stephanie said, keeping her eyes on Mark, who was still in the terminal.

"Yeah, I guess you're right. They did say all his tests were perfect. That we shouldn't worry. But, I don't know, he's just so moody, and that's never been him. He was always, you know, the guy you could count on to be consistent. I never really noticed how bad it was until recently. Have you noticed anything different about him?"

Stephanie saw that Mark had found the bags and was walking toward the glass doors, whistling to himself. "I wish I could say, but the truth is I think all the guys are in some sort of midlife crisis. Look at Chris. He just up and quit his job," Stephanie said. "Shhh. Here he comes."

Mark knocked on the back of the station wagon for Stephanie to unlock the hatch. He loaded the bags and the stroller in and climbed into the rear-facing seat. "Okay, let's do it," he said, slamming the door.

As Stephanie pulled into the line of cabs, cars, and shuttle buses, she could hear Mark singing along to "Every Little Thing She Does Is Magic" playing on the radio.

～

"That was rough," Stephanie said to Hope as they walked away from the now deserted yard of Shoshanna and Harvest's school on the first day back after the holiday. "I always forget how hard it is to get back in the swing of things after a vacation."

After a morning of tantrums, the last straw had been when Chris, dressed in his tennis whites, had grabbed his racquet-shaped bag and left Hope and Stephanie to deal with the kids. He couldn't help it, he said. He had regular court time now every Monday at eight. It wasn't his fault that the first day back to school fell on a Monday this year.

"Where are you going now?" Stephanie asked, pulling her scarf up over her nose and mouth and wrapping her coat tighter.

"Home. I refuse to walk all the way down to playgroup in this weather. It's inhuman," Hope said, picking up the pace. "You want to stop at Café Lutecia for a cup of coffee? We could warm up for a few minutes."

"Okay, but only if we don't stay too long. I need to do some work stuff. I wonder what time Chris will be home," Stephanie said, thinking out loud.

"Probably about nine thirty, unless they want him to hang around for a meeting," Hope said.

"Really? Why would he be going to meetings? Did they offer him the job?" Stephanie asked. She opened the door of the small corner café for Hope so that she could maneuver Ollie's stroller inside. The mustard-yellow walls decorated with empty wooden brie wheels and vintage French posters and the dark wood counter filled with fresh pastries made them feel warm and welcome even on this cold day.

Hope hesitated. "Uh, yeah. You didn't know? They offered it to him last week—all he needs to do is get his background checks and clearances, and he can start officially. They want him to run all of the camps and clinics," Hope said. "I'm so sorry, I should have let him tell you himself. He said that he was going to—on New Year's Eve, I think."

Hope turned to the owner of the café, a kind, balding man with a shy smile who was standing behind the counter waiting patiently for them to stop talking and order. "May I please have a black coffee?"

"Now that I'm here, I'm suddenly famished," Stephanie said, unwrapping her scarf. "I'll have a toasted baguette with butter and jam and a cappuccino, please."

Stephanie waited for Hope to offer more information, but she was too busy taking off Ollie's hat and mittens.

"So what else did he tell you?" Stephanie asked.

"Nothing much. He's really excited about it, though. Isn't it his dream—to work with kids, do something athletic?"

"Yeah, I guess so. I just wish he had told me. I thought we were past keeping secrets."

"I doubt he's keeping it from you on purpose. He's probably waiting for a special time to tell you, and it hasn't come up. I'm just around all the time, and so is he," Hope said, worried that she had gone a little bit too far.

"Yeah, I guess you're right," Stephanie said, twirling her hair around her finger as she looked out the wall of windows next to her. The ledge between the table and the window was covered with piles of old French magazines, including *Paris Match* and *Vogue*. Two women in down parkas were standing on the corner outside waiting for the bus. "Thanks for helping him through this. I know he appreciates it."

"I'm just glad I can be there," Hope said. "You know, when you can't."

"So what should I say to him, do you think?" Stephanie said.

"Speak of the devil," Hope said, kicking Stephanie under the table and nodding toward the door behind her.

"Hello, my lovely wife," Chris said, lowering his voice. "Or should I say wives?"

"That joke is getting so old," Hope said, even though she couldn't help but smile.

Chris bent down and kissed Stephanie on the head, then rumpled Ollie's curls. "And my little Ollie! We missed this little guy, didn't we?"

"Can you stay? Do you want to sit down?" Stephanie asked, clearing the coats and hats from the chair next to her.

"Absolutely," he said, taking a seat. "I'm so glad you're both here. I have some news."

"You do?" Stephanie asked.

Chris mimed a drum roll with his hands on the table. "I just got the news this morning. Feast your eyes on the new program director of tennis activities at the University of Pennsylvania."

There was a brief moment of hesitation, and Hope didn't dare look at either of them.

"Yay! I'm so happy for you," Stephanie finally said, hugging him tightly and glancing at Hope over his shoulder.

"Me too," Hope said, staring into her coffee cup. "That's great news."

~

When they got back to the house, Chris lit a fire in the grown-up living room, and Stephanie wrapped herself in a blanket on the couch and settled in with her laptop. Hope began crocheting a sweater for Ollie, her hands a blur of navy and white yarn and shiny needle. Now that his time at home had suddenly become limited, Chris felt motivated to fix things around the house. He mounted extra hooks inside the coat closet, cleaned out one of the junk drawers, and rearranged the pantry. Before they knew it, it was almost three o'clock.

"Chris, Hope and I need to go and pick up the kids," Stephanie yelled down the basement steps. He was in the back taking out all the things he wanted to put on eBay—the two extra microwaves, Ikea tables that were still around from their college days, and some old lamps that didn't work with their new modern décor.

"Okay," he yelled back. "Is Ollie staying here?"

"Yep," Hope said. "The monitor is at the top of the steps. I turned the volume way up."

"I'll go get Lu and Ted, and you can get Shoshanna and Harvest, okay?" Stephanie offered. She knew how much Hope liked to pick up Shoshanna, who was always so excited to see her.

"Sounds good," Hope said, closing the door behind her. They had gotten a little sloppy, leaving from the middle door together, although Hope figured it was possible that they could both be hanging out in Stephanie's house. She reminded herself to have Celia put it on the agenda for the next house meeting. "Do you have your key?" Hope asked. "I don't have mine, and I want to lock the dead bolt. Chris will probably forget."

Stephanie nodded, and as she fished in her purse for the key, she saw Nikki walking toward them. *Shit, I hope she won't let anything slip,* Stephanie thought. *Please, not in front of Hope.*

Nikki was wearing her chocolate-brown cashmere hat and was snapping shut her bright white down coat as she walked toward Stephanie and Hope.

"Hey, Nikki. On your way to work?" Stephanie asked.

"Yeah, I hate going in at four. But I have some time to kill, so I'll probably stop at La Colombe. Do you want to come?"

"No thanks. We're on our way to get the kids. But I'm going in that direction. I'll walk you over to Spruce," Stephanie said.

Just as Nikki was about to snap the last snap at the top of her coat, Stephanie caught a glimpse of a shiny gold necklace she didn't recognize. It was funny how she knew everything in a client's house. She always made a game of it—each time she saw a client, she would mentally go through their closets and drawers and decide if anything they were wearing was new.

She and Nikki had gone through all the jewelry already and sorted the earrings into trays that looked like egg cartons and hung the necklaces on hooks inside the walk-in closet. Stephanie was sure she would have remembered this one. It was just like the necklace Chris had bought for her fortieth birthday, but with a different charm.

"What's that? A Christmas present?" Stephanie asked, fingering the delicate dragon charm hanging from the thin gold chain at Nikki's throat. "Is it from Dogeared? Look, it's just like mine." Stephanie held up her necklace for Nikki to see, a tiny gold circle hanging from the same delicate chain.

"Yep, isn't it so great?"

Hope was tapping her foot, eager to get moving. She hated to be late for pickup. She wanted to be standing by the double doors when Shoshanna and Harvest came out. And besides, what was Stephanie's fascination with this girl anyway?

"Yeah, I totally love it. My charm means karma. I forget what the dragon stands for . . ."

"Fearless," Nikki said.

"Nice," Hope said, suddenly aware of how much Nikki and Stephanie seemed to actually like each other. "Your husband must be romantic."

"Not really," Nikki said, glancing at Stephanie. "I got this from a friend."

"That's so funny you both have them," Hope said. "Maybe you have the same friend."

Nikki stared at Hope, suddenly silent. She snapped the top snap of her coat. "I—I have to go," she said and hurried off down Emerson without saying good-bye.

"Bye, Nikki!" Stephanie called, but Nikki kept going.

"Strange girl," Hope said, watching Nikki turn the corner.

"No, she's okay. Just a little lonely, I think."

"Whatever. Aren't we all sometimes?" Hope asked.

"Not really, not us."

CHAPTER SIXTEEN

Ollie giggled as Shoshanna retched into the bright blue plastic bowl. When Shoshanna was finished, she let her body fall backward onto the carpeted floor, exhausted. Ollie giggled again.

"Oh, Ollie, it isn't funny," Hope said gently. "Shoshanna isn't feeling well."

Hope put the half-full bowl on the floor and leaned over Shoshanna, feeling her forehead. Her cheeks were flushed, and she hadn't been able to keep anything down all day. How much longer could she stand this?

"Uh-oh," Ollie said staccato, and Hope turned to find Ollie sitting in Shoshanna's vomit, the bowl overturned.

"Oh no," Hope said, jumping up. She ran to the kitchen for paper towels, trying to keep her eyes on the kids. "Don't move, Ollie. I'll be right back." Thinking better of it, she jogged back to the playroom and scooped Ollie off the floor, holding his hands away from him as she walked to the sink.

"Mommee," Shoshanna called weakly. "It smells."

"I know, sweetie," Hope called from the kitchen, putting Ollie down and quickly drying his hands. "Can you move over a little? Try to scootch away from the mess, okay?"

"I can't," Shoshanna said quietly.

"I'm sorry about this, Ollie, but I have no choice," Hope said as she wheeled the stroller over to him and forced him in, making sure the clips were secure. She rolled him back to the playroom, maneuvering the wheels over the slight step down that separated the houses.

Hope lifted Shoshanna off the floor and put her on the couch as far away from the puddle as she could. She cleaned it up, running back and forth to the kitchen for paper towels and sponges. By the time she was finished, she had almost filled the entire garbage can, Shoshanna was fast asleep, and Ollie was whining. She eased him out of the stroller and placed a puzzle on the floor. She took a deep breath, stretched her neck in an attempt to relax and refocus, and was about to show Ollie how the lion peg fit over the lion picture when the phone rang. She ran to it, not wanting the sound to wake Shoshanna.

"Hello?"

"Hi, this is Jane from Sutherfield School. Ted is sick and needs to be picked up," the woman said matter-of-factly. "He'll be waiting in the nurse's office."

"Um," Hope said, wanting to tell Jane that she had a sick child who had thrown up all day finally sleeping on the couch and a fussy toddler who had just stopped whining happily doing a puzzle. How was she going to manage it?

"Thanks," Jane said before Hope had a chance to say anything else. Hope held the phone to her ear longer than she should have after Jane hung up.

"Okay, we can do this," Hope said, more to herself than to Ollie. She considered getting the car, but it was parked three blocks away. Shoshanna certainly couldn't walk. She settled on calling a cab, which came right to her door, and somehow she was able to carry Shoshanna and hold Ollie's hand. She offered the driver a double fare if he waited, managed to get them both in the school, forced a pale, lethargic Ted to walk himself to the cab, and got everybody back to Emerson in one piece. Ted wasn't in the door for five minutes before he threw up.

⌒

"Hope, are you awake?" Celia called through the half-open bedroom door. "Hope?"

"What time is it?" Leo asked, rolling over. Shoshanna was in bed with them. She hadn't thrown up in about five hours, which was a good sign, but she certainly wasn't going to school today. Leo reached over Shoshanna and pushed Hope. She sat right up.

"Hope?" Celia called again, this time a little louder.

"Hi, come in," Hope said.

Celia walked in slowly, trying not to look directly at them. She was fully dressed in a black suit with a red blouse and pearls perfectly situated underneath.

"Ted still isn't feeling well," Celia said. "And now I think Lu has it."

"Oh no," said Hope. "I'm so sorry."

"I just hate to ask, but Mark's boss is in New York for the week, so he has to be in the office for back-to-back client meetings. And I would offer to stay home today, but it is the worst possible day. I have an interview with our president, and if I pass this one, I'm a finalist for the VP spot—I'll go on to New York to meet with the board."

"It's okay," Hope said, not letting her finish. "I think Shoshanna is on the upswing. I can't promise you a stimulating day for Ollie. I'm sure we'll watch a ton of TV, but we'll be okay."

"Thanks," Celia said. "I don't know what I'd do without you."

"Good luck," Hope said, getting out of bed. "And don't worry, we'll be fine."

But two hours later she wasn't so sure. Shoshanna had slept for about an hour longer, but now she was awake and wanted only to sit on Hope's lap. Lu and Ted were both as sick as Shoshanna had been the day before, and now Hope had given up on getting to them with the plastic bowl in time and instead set them up on Mark's couch with plastic Target bags. She had to move them away from Shoshanna, who kept saying she couldn't stand the sound, and who could blame her?

Ollie, unfortunately, was feeling fine. He took every opportunity when Hope's attention was on something else to lick the shoes piled by Stephanie and Chris's door or pull out all the plastic bags he could find and try to put them over his head. Hope hadn't sat down, eaten anything, or brushed her teeth. She had abandoned her careful hand washing because she knew a few minutes later she'd probably be cleaning up more vomit. And she lived in constant fear the phone would ring and Harvest would be the next to fall.

At 11:00 a.m. she couldn't stand it anymore. She called Stephanie.

"How are they?" Stephanie asked instead of saying hello.

"Bad," Hope said. "Lu and Ted are totally sick, throwing up one after another, Shoshanna is whining, and Ollie is trying to kill himself. Can you come home, please?"

Stephanie didn't say anything. Hope could hear some noise in the background, so she knew she hadn't hung up.

"Oh, come on," Hope said. "I know how much you hate throwing up, but these are the kids! You have to help me."

"I can't," Stephanie said quietly.

"Yes, you can. You have to," Hope said.

"Hope, remember that time before we took down the walls when you were all over, and we were playing cards, and all the kids were in the basement, and Harvest ran up and said his stomach hurt, and he threw up? Remember? He threw up all over the place. Do you remember what I did?"

"Fine," Hope said harshly, remembering how Stephanie had jumped up from the table and hid in the kitchen while Hope took Harvest into her arms and Celia cleaned up the mess. "I'll find someone else."

She tried Leo next.

"Hi, it's me," Hope said.

"Hey, what's up?" Leo asked like it was just a usual day.

"Well, Shoshanna is freaking out because she wants me to herself and can't have me, every five minutes either Ted or Lu throws up, and Ollie is licking everyone's shoes. Oh, and I think I might lose my mind."

"Come on, Hope, it can't be that bad," Leo said. "Can't you just put in a movie or something?"

"No, I can't," Hope said, trying to sound rational. "I need you to come home. I need you to be in one room with the sick kids while I'm in the other. Or I'll be with the sick kids and you be with Shoshanna and Ollie. I need to take a shower, and I want you to bring me something to eat."

"I can't, Hope. I wish I could," Leo said. "That guy just got here from North Jersey to do the espresso and cappuccino maker demonstration—you know we're looking for a few new machines. And the lunch rush is about to start, we have a big party coming in, and Sam's out. But I can try to come home early. Okay?"

"Forget it," Hope said. "We'll be fine."

"Of course you will," Leo said, and Hope wished she could strangle him through the phone or throw a hot cup of espresso at him. "See you later, sweetie."

Hope sat for a minute and stared at her phone. Then she heard Ted moan again, and she knew she had to do something. She called Chris. He was really her last hope.

"Hey, you," Chris said after the first ring. "I'm between games."

"Chris, I can't do this. Everyone is sick, and I thought I could, but I can't," Hope said, starting to cry. "I can't take good care of everybody. I need you."

Chris was quiet for a minute.

"Tell you what, I'm going to talk to the assistant pro and see if he can take over for me," Chris said. "I'll, um, I'll just tell him my kid is sick. What's more important than that, right? I'll be there within the hour."

At five minutes to noon Chris walked in the kitchen door carrying three white plastic bags with smiley faces on them, and Hope knew he had stopped at the good Chinese place near the university, the one she loved but Leo refused to go to because he thought it was mediocre. For the first time all day, Hope smiled.

"Sit," Chris said as he put the bags down on the big table. "How is everyone?"

"A little better," Hope admitted. "I put Ollie down for a nap, Shoshanna finally fell asleep in there, and the other two haven't thrown up in about thirty minutes. They're watching TV."

"Oh my God, you let the throwing up kids sit on Mark's good couch?" Chris asked, laughing. "He would kill you if he knew."

"Too bad," Hope said. "They're his kids. And Shoshanna couldn't stand listening to them. But we've been careful. Nothing's gotten on it so far."

"Okay," Chris said, pulling a huge bottle of hand sanitizer out of a CVS bag that was hidden behind the others. He twisted the pump top open and placed it in the middle of the table. "We need to remember to use this—we have to do our best to avoid getting sick. But be careful of Ollie. I just heard a news report about kids actually getting drunk from this stuff, it's so full of alcohol. And with the way Ollie licks things, you never know."

Hope smiled for the second time.

"So I brought wonton soup for Shoshanna. Hopefully she'll want some when she wakes up. I asked for plain broth for the sickies. I brought dumplings for Ollie. And for you, madam, I brought your absolute favorite moo shu chicken with extra pancakes and extra plum sauce. Do you want some now?"

"Yes, please," Hope said, taking a seat at the table and watching as Chris did everything, from setting the table to laying out the dishes. He pulled out a big cold Coke, Hope's favorite indulgence, from one of the bags and placed it in front of her.

"Can I have some?" Shoshanna asked sleepily as she came around the corner.

"You bet," Chris said, putting his arm around her shoulders and guiding her to the table. "Some soup to begin?"

"Yes, please, thanks, Daddy Chris," Shoshanna said sweetly.

Things went so smoothly after Chris's arrival that Hope felt like she'd been a bit of a wimp. Lu and Ted seemed to be over the worst, and Shoshanna was happy watching SpongeBob. But when Ollie woke up from his nap throwing up and Harvest's teacher called to say he was lying on the floor not playing or talking, Hope wasn't happy, exactly, but at least she didn't feel like she'd made Chris come home for no reason. Not that he was complaining.

"Hey, why don't you go get Harvest?" Chris offered. "You haven't been out of the house much in two days. His teacher didn't sound too alarmed. You should walk there, get a cup of coffee, and take a cab home if he's really tired. I'll hold down the fort here."

"Thanks, Chris," Hope said, leaning her head against his chest. He was much taller than Leo, so her head landed at a completely different part of his body.

"Anything for our family, Hope."

❧

Hope stood at the top of the stoop holding Ollie's hand. She watched as the older kids ran and spun and jumped in the middle of the street in front of the house. For days, no one had been well enough to play, and it had been bitter cold before that. Hope couldn't remember the last time they had all been out on the street.

"Come on, Ollie," Hope urged. "Let's get down there. I want to put the cone out."

Ollie looked up at her but didn't budge.

"What's wrong, baby?" Hope asked, sticking her free hand into his belly and tickling. "We've been inside for a long time, I know, but I think you'll remember how to play outside, right?"

Ollie giggled, nodding his blond head. He followed Hope down the steps and stood on the sidewalk.

Hope picked the cone up and walked it to the bottom of Emerson, officially closing their one-way street to traffic. She took a seat on the concrete bench outside Mary's house. She had a good view of all the bigger kids, who were sitting in the middle of the street drawing with sidewalk chalk.

She took a deep breath of the unusually warm January air and looked over at Ollie, who was just standing and watching them.

"Do you want me to play with you, little man?" Hope asked, getting up from the bench. "We can chase each other."

Hope leaned over so her face was at Ollie's level and ran to him. He threw his head back and let out a huge belly laugh.

"Hey, Ollie, look at the puppy," Hope said. "It's one of those Lab poodles. What do they call them? Labradoodles?" Hope pointed across Eighteenth Street. She was considering taking the kids over to pet the fluffy black animal when she heard a loud motor behind her, coming from the opposite end of the street. She turned to see a white cab moving fast toward them the wrong way down Emerson. It had to be going at least thirty miles per hour, and it wasn't slowing down at all.

"Car!" Hope screamed frantically. "Car! Move!"

She turned away from Ollie and ran to Shoshanna, who was still drawing on the pavement.

"Car!" she screamed again, scooping Shoshanna up seconds before the car reached them. She ran across the sidewalk to the wall of the nearest house, as far away from the street as possible. And then the car was through, slowing down at the cone before it drove onto the sidewalk and around it toward the intersection. Hope was breathing hard as she looked frantically for the rest of the kids, afraid of what she might find.

She saw Lu leaning against the wall of a house across the street while Ted and Harvest were sitting on Harvest's stoop, the ball in Ted's lap. And Ollie, little Ollie, was teetering on the edge of the sidewalk about four inches away from the street. If the cab had gone slightly off course, or if Ollie had taken even one step . . . Hope put Shoshanna down and ran to the corner, where the cab was stopped, and banged hard on the trunk.

"Hey!" she screamed at the driver. "This is a one-way street! We play out here. There are kids. What were you thinking?"

She looked at the driver, waiting for an apology, but all he did was shrug. Then he drove across Eighteenth Street and continued the wrong way down the next block of Emerson.

"Come on, we're going in," Hope said, speaking almost as harshly to the kids as she had spoken to the wayward driver.

"No, Mommy, we just got out here," Shoshanna said, returning to her street drawing.

"No, Mommy Hope, we haven't played in a really long time," Harvest said. "And we were good. We moved when the car came."

"Now! We're going in," Hope said, picking up the cone and putting it back in its place beside Stephanie's stoop. "Now!"

She took Ollie's hand and led him into the house. She stood there as each child walked reluctantly up the stairs. Once everyone was in, she closed and locked the door.

"Sit," she told them, pointing to the playroom. "Shoshanna, let Ollie sit on your lap for a minute. Don't let him go anywhere." She turned on the television and punched in the numbers for the Disney Channel, not waiting to see what was on. She walked into the dining room, sat at the far end of the table where the kids couldn't see her, and let herself cry.

Leo leaned over to Hope's side of the bed and nuzzled her cheek. Oh no, was he after sex again tonight? She turned reluctantly and kissed him, putting down her book.

"Hi," she said.

"Hi," he said, sliding his hands under the blankets.

"This has been the hardest week," Hope said, leaning into him. Maybe she could muster up the energy for sex tonight. Maybe that was just what she needed.

"You did a good job," Leo said, "taking care of everyone."

"Well, Chris helped," she said gently, not wanting to start a fight. "So that was good. And I'm not really sure I did such a good job."

Hope put her hand on Leo's chest and rubbed gently. She rested her head on his shoulder and moved her hand down a little, toward the opening in his boxers.

"Are you excited about tomorrow?" Leo asked.

"What's tomorrow?" Hope asked quietly.

"Our appointment!" Leo said, sitting up a little. "With the fertility specialist! What do you mean, what's tomorrow? Haven't you been counting the weeks or whatever you do when you can't wait to go somewhere?"

Hope stopped moving her hand and let it rest on Leo's hip. She couldn't think of anything to say. She knew Leo had made an appointment, of course, but it was the last thing she wanted now. She just wanted to be alone with Shoshanna. After the awful week with everyone sick—when all she wanted to do was sit with Shoshanna and read to her or make up stories the way Shoshanna liked—and with what had happened today out on the street, clearly she had been right to let go of her thoughts of a second baby. Clearly she was meant to be a mother to just one child.

"I don't want to go," Hope said.

"What?" Leo asked, pushing himself up now, moving away from Hope.

"Leo, come on, we haven't even talked about getting pregnant in months. Haven't you noticed? And the more I learn about myself as a mother, the more I realize we should just let things be."

"Where is this coming from?" Leo asked, his voice tight. "The last I heard, you felt your life wouldn't be complete unless you had a second baby. You were willing to do anything to have one."

"That was a long time ago," Hope said. "That was before."

They sat silently, each moving to their own side of the bed. Hope wished Shoshanna were here, a buffer in the middle, someone they could hide behind.

"Before what?" Leo asked harshly.

"Before I got tired of trying, of having sex whether I wanted to or not. Before I started dreading the time each month when my period inevitably arrived. Before I stopped getting that tiny feeling of excitement, that *maybe this will be the month*. Before I learned how incredibly hard it is to take care of a bunch of kids, especially when sometimes you just want to be with only one of them. And it was before I left the other kids on the street to be run over while I saved Shoshanna."

"I don't know what you're talking about," Leo said. "Why didn't you tell me you didn't want this appointment? Samantha went to a lot of trouble to get this for us. He's supposed to be the best."

"Is that all you care about? The stupid appointment and Samantha? Did you not hear what I said? That I changed my mind about a major life choice? Isn't that the takeaway from this discussion? I told you when I came to the restaurant for dinner that I want to just be happy instead of thinking we need something more to make that happen. I'm tired of that. And did you not hear me say that I left the kids to die today— really? It was just luck that no one was hurt."

"What happened?" Leo asked.

For a minute Hope thought about just telling him to forget it, that nothing happened. But she had to tell him. She had to tell someone.

She couldn't stop thinking about it, and she knew she couldn't tell any of the others. So she told him the story from beginning to end, staring straight ahead the whole time. When she was finished, she kept her eyes focused on a painting Shoshanna had made in preschool of Hope wearing a striped shirt and huge brown shoes.

"Oh my God," Leo said. "I can't believe you did that."

"Well, I—I didn't want to do that," Hope said, crying now. "I mean, if anything bad had happened to Ollie or to any of them . . . I love all of them. But I'm not sure I'm able to be a mother to so many kids. Not in a crisis. So why in the world would I want another baby now?"

"I guess you wouldn't," Leo said.

"Why are you being so mean?" Hope yelled, angry now. "It was a mistake! People make mistakes! What would you have done?"

"I would have stood in the middle of the street and waved my arms over my head until the cab stopped," Leo said. "I would have let the cab hit me before I took a chance with any of the kids."

"But, Leo, I didn't have a second to think! Shoshanna was sitting in the street," Hope said, getting up. "I'm going to sleep in Shoshanna's room tonight. And please, cancel that appointment."

"Consider it done," Leo said, settling back onto his pillow and picking up his book. Hope watched him for a minute. She wanted him to come after her. That was her usual way of handling this sort of thing. But she had a feeling he wouldn't come. She had a feeling that what she'd done was inexcusable. If she had a choice, she wouldn't want to sleep with herself either.

～

It was still light out, a perfect night for a walk, but as Nikki approached her house, she decided she would just go inside, close the blinds, and put on her pajamas. More often than not lately she would push open the door hoping Will wasn't there, and tonight that hope was stronger than ever. She had her key out when she heard hard footsteps behind her. She looked toward Nineteenth Street and saw a little boy—was that Mark's kid?—sprinting toward her, red-faced and angry. She thought about slipping inside quickly, but then she heard a woman's voice yell, "Stop! Ted, you stop right now!"

It was Celia.

"Grab him!" Celia yelled. "Please!"

Without much thought, Nikki jogged down her steps just in time to intercept him as he ran by, hitting her in the stomach full force with his head as she stopped him. He was sweaty, and once she had him, she didn't know what to do with him. She had never touched one of Mark's kids before. Really, she hadn't touched many kids at all. He seemed sticky.

"Thank you!" Celia said, coming up quickly. She was red-faced and angry, too. "Thank you so much. I didn't know if he was going to stop at home or keep going. He ran clean across Nineteenth Street without even looking. He could have been . . ."

Celia turned her back, and Nikki knew she was crying. Her shoulders were moving that way, and she was wiping her face so hard it looked like she was hitting herself.

The boy, who had been struggling, finally slumped, and Nikki eased him to the ground. She watched as Celia took an especially deep breath and turned back toward them. Her face was still red, but she looked much more in control.

"I don't even know what happened," Celia said quietly. "One minute we were walking home from the park talking about dinner and the next he was freaking out and running. It's not like him. It took me off guard. I don't usually say this, but sometimes I feel like I need to put them on a leash or something."

Celia smiled a smile that told Nikki she was sharing a deep, dark thought with her. All Nikki could think was that Celia wouldn't want to know her deep, dark thoughts. And why did Celia have to be so nice—and vulnerable? Nikki had managed to avoid her completely since she'd helped her with her keys when Mark was still sick, and she had done her best since then to think of her as a robot, not a person feeling real things. She never even thought of her by her name—she was always Mark's wife when the thoughts crept in—but now that Celia was right in front of her, she couldn't help it.

"Well, he's going to be punished," Celia said, not seeming to notice that Nikki hadn't said a word. "No screen time for two weeks, mister. Maybe longer. And if this ever happens again, you will never get any screen time again—As. Long. As. You. Live."

Nikki wondered how the boy would react. Would he make a run for it again? No, he just sat there, head down, making a small hole in his jeans bigger.

"Well, thanks again," Celia said. "You saved him. And me."

Nikki nodded and watched as Celia grabbed Ted's hand roughly and pulled him up, then marched him down the street to their house. Nikki turned back toward her door, still not knowing if Will was inside or not. She pulled the key out of the lock and turned back around. There was a pole class at 7:15 p.m. she was pretty sure Kat would go to. Sitting around in her pajamas no longer sounded comforting. She needed to keep moving.

~

Leo tiptoed into the den. The week had started out awful. With the kids being sick, his fight with Hope, and his having to tell Sam that he canceled the appointment with the fertility doctor that she had pulled so many strings to get for them, he had been pretty miserable.

But now things seemed to be getting back to normal. Hope was finally sleeping in bed with him again, and he was sorry that he had been so harsh when she told him about what had happened outside. He knew without a doubt that she would never want anything bad to happen to any of the kids. He knew that as sure as he knew how much she loved Shoshanna.

Hope was fast asleep now. Ever since the incident on the street, she had been taking a little Xanax, and that always made her sleep like a rock.

Leo picked up the clicker and scrolled through the "On Demand" menu. He was glad to see there was a new *Real Sex* listed—he was tired of the old ones. He clicked on it, waiting. He had texted Stephanie after he was sure Hope was asleep, but she hadn't texted him back, which wasn't unusual. Ten, fifteen minutes went by, and he was getting ready to start without her. When he finally heard footsteps, he panicked at first, thinking they were coming down from upstairs and that he must have been wrong about Hope. But when the door opened and Stephanie slipped in, Leo breathed a sigh of relief.

She walked silently past him and moved to the other side of the couch, *her side* as Leo had come to think of it. She didn't even glance at him; she looked straight ahead at the screen, waiting. Leo hesitated.

"Hi," he whispered.

"Shhh," Stephanie said, still looking ahead.

"I've been thinking about you since New Year's," Leo tried again.

"Shhh," Stephanie said a little louder.

"You know, since midnight," Leo said.

This time Stephanie laughed.

"You've been thinking about me since midnight on New Year's Eve?" Stephanie said, giggling. "But that was weeks ago. And I've seen you every day since."

"Well," Leo said, clearing his throat. "I've been thinking about this since then."

"Speaking of which, no talking," Stephanie said, looking back at the screen. "Come on, turn it on."

But Leo didn't want to. He didn't care about the weird sex segment in this episode. It was supposed to be about a strange fantasy business where someone comes and says he wants to have sex with a farm girl, and he pays a lot of money, and they dress someone up in braids with a bandanna and a cowboy hat. Not so different from hiring a prostitute, he guessed. Stephanie moved her hand in the air, telling him to get on with it. He looked at her smooth, bare legs—she had taken off the thick brown tights she had on earlier—and thought that all she had to do was pull her denim skirt up a tiny bit higher and he'd be able to see her underwear. He could feel his penis begin to respond, so he turned back to the television and pressed "play." As the opening song began its catchy melody, Stephanie settled into the couch and pulled her skirt up, just as Leo had imagined a second before. Her underwear was a pale blue. When she noticed Leo looking at her, she pointed back to the television.

The first part of the show was about how to handle a man's penis and give the most possible pleasure. A bunch of women sat around someone's suburban home, each with a model of a penis in front of her. They were able to choose size and skin color. As they touched the penises, moaning a little, Stephanie watched intently and then, almost like she was deciding she didn't have time for the show, leaned back and closed her eyes. Leo took the chance to watch her, and that's when his erection grew strong and stiff. He was careful to move his eyes back to the television image when she opened hers for a second. He watched as she came, enjoying every last shudder and whispered moan. But when she opened her eyes and smiled, she looked surprised to see that he wasn't touching himself at all.

She raised her eyebrows at him, asking him what he was waiting for.

"It's just—" he began, but Stephanie put a finger to her mouth, telling him to be quiet. Suddenly she was on her feet, moving out of the room.

Leo quickly turned off the television, wondering what had happened, what had come over him tonight. He could hear Stephanie move down his stairs. He pictured her going through the playroom, into the kitchen, and heading up her own twisty stairs, her long skirt in her hand, her bare, beautiful legs taking her to Chris.

CHAPTER SEVENTEEN

Nikki shivered and inched her arm out from under the fluffy down comforter. She snatched the TV remote from the table beside her bed and hit "mute," then traded it for her phone and dialed Will's number.

"Hey! This is a surprise. I thought you'd still be asleep on your day off," Will said. Nikki could hear the rumble of the train in the background. *Thank God*, she thought. *Now I can relax.*

"It's nearly ten thirty. I'm not *that* lazy," she said.

"So what's up, or did you just call to say you missed me?"

"Just wanted to say have a good day in New York," she said.

"Thanks. I'll see you tonight, late. We're going out for drinks after the deposition."

"Okay, bye. Have fun," Nikki said.

"Love you, babe," Will said.

Nikki ended the call and unmuted the TV. It was so cold out today, and all she wanted to do was pass the time until the clock read 11:00. She pulled the blankets up around her chin, snuggled deeper under the covers, and turned her attention to the DVR'd *Today* show and Brad and Angelina. She watched them look at each other lovingly and wondered what it was like—to be such a perfect couple with everything you could ever want. *I wonder if they're really in love,* she thought. Just as Matt Lauer went to commercial and she started to fast forward through it, Nikki heard a sharp knock at the door.

She looked over at the clock on the nightstand. It was probably Mary again—she had knocked yesterday around the same time. Lately Mary had latched onto her whenever Stephanie was too busy. She was harmless enough and actually seemed like she might be a nice person under the gruff exterior, but sometimes it was just too tiring having to keep up her end of the conversation.

Nikki climbed from under the covers and trudged downstairs. She lifted up one slat of the off-white wood blinds and saw Stephanie standing on the top step in her yoga clothes and no coat. She turned the dead bolt and opened the door.

"Hey, you look terrible. What's up?" Nikki said, sticking her head out though the opening.

"Thanks for the friendly greeting," Stephanie said. "I need to talk to you. Do you have a minute?"

Nikki pulled her head back in and glanced at the clock behind her on the kitchen wall. She had only twenty minutes. "Sure . . . come in," she said, opening the door wide enough for Stephanie to pass, trying desperately to think of an excuse to get her out of there quickly.

Stephanie sized up Nikki in her pale pink satin pajama shorts and matching tank top with lace edging around the thighs and neckline. "Well, aren't you the lady of leisure. I've never seen this one before. Is it new?" Stephanie asked.

Nikki blushed. How the hell did Stephanie remember everything she had in her drawers?

"As a matter of fact, yeah. I got it over at that place off Walnut," Nikki said, expecting Stephanie to make a snide remark, but instead Stephanie flopped heavily onto the couch and threw her head back.

"So what's going on?" Nikki said, purposely standing so that Stephanie wouldn't get too comfortable.

Stephanie took a deep breath. "I haven't slept for days, and I'm totally exhausted. I tried taking that all-natural stuff to help me sleep, but it just made me have these totally crazy dreams that freaked me out even more. Anyway, I need to ask you something, and I need your honest opinion."

Nikki waited while Stephanie closed her eyes and rubbed her face with her hands.

"So there's this totally innocent thing. A sexual thing, but not a big deal, no touching, nothing like that. Just this crazy fun. Everything is fine, but the other person involved in this thing started to act different, like he started *talking* about things, looking at me in a different way, and I just have no idea what the hell he's thinking. Did he really think I wanted to . . . ? Anyway, I need to know, am I absolutely nuts in thinking that it was all innocent?"

Nikki couldn't believe it. Stephanie? Cheat?

"Whoa, it sounds like you have officially entered the world of eternal sin with me. Let me see . . . now which commandment was the adultery one?" Nikki asked.

"Come on, Nikki! This is serious!"

"Okay, you're right. Sorry. Go on."

"Maybe I was totally stupid, but in some way, it seemed like if we didn't touch each other it wasn't sex. I mean, it's like we were each in our own worlds, but in the same room. I don't know, maybe I'm just making excuses, but, really, it didn't seem much different from guys watching porn together."

"Okay, I don't even want to know what you're doing with this guy. It sounds pretty twisted. All I can say is that if it looks like a duck, and it quacks like a duck . . . you know how the rest of the saying goes. Take it from me, with my guy, it was sex even before it was sex."

"Oh my God. What the hell have I done? I need to fix this," Stephanie said, closing her eyes and leaning her head in her hands.

Nikki inched forward and stole a peek at the clock on the wall in the kitchen. Ten fifty-five. When she turned back, Stephanie was staring at her.

"Okay, what's going on? The outfit, the looking at the clock. Am I interrupting something?" Stephanie said, narrowing her eyes.

Right on cue, there was an urgent tapping on the glass door at the back of the house.

Stephanie sat up straight. "Oh my God. Is that him?"

Nikki looked out the glass door and shook her head desperately. She turned to Stephanie. "No, it's not what you think. I mean, I can't . . . oh shit."

Stephanie stood up and looked through the pass-through between the kitchen and living room. Outside the door, staring back at her, was Mark.

❧

By the time Stephanie looked at Nikki and then back at Mark, he was gone.

"What the hell?" she asked, walking over to Nikki, standing close enough to make her uncomfortable. Then she pictured herself in the den with Leo, and she took a step back. Nikki just stood there shaking her head, her face so red that if this had been a few minutes ago, Stephanie would have worried if she was okay. Now, well, she didn't know about now.

"I can't believe this," she said as she walked toward the back door. But she knew he was probably long gone, either far away from here or at home trying to act normal and trusting that Stephanie wouldn't make a scene. So she reversed her course. With Nikki still standing there, red-faced but silent, she went to the front door. As soon as she touched the doorknob, Nikki was there.

"Please," Nikki said. She didn't sound right. She sounded off, like it was an effort to get the words out. "Please don't tell anyone. I never meant to . . ."

"You never meant to what?" Stephanie said, spit, really. But was she talking just about Nikki here, or was she talking about herself, too? She never meant to what? And then Nikki said it, for both of them.

"I never meant to mess anything up. I never meant to hurt anyone."

Stephanie was out the door and down the street before she knew where she wanted to go. Then she knew where Mark would be. She was so sure of it that she wasn't at all surprised when she opened the door to Dante's and saw him sitting at the far end of the empty bar, an almost finished drink in front of him. What was she going to say to him? That he'd done something bad? He knew that already. That he'd messed everything up? He knew that, too. He hadn't seen her yet, so she stood for a few seconds, half in and half out. Before he looked up, she let the door close quietly in front of her.

~

"So what are we going to do?" Stephanie asked.

"How can you even ask that question? It's our responsibility as her friends. Wouldn't you want to know?" Hope demanded, angrily unloading the dishwasher, the plates and silverware clinking loudly against each other.

Stephanie sipped her Vitaminwater. "I don't know. Is it really our responsibility? Isn't that something *he* should do?"

"But he knows you know, and he clearly hasn't told Celia. I knew she was trouble, that girl. I just knew it from the minute I saw her. My God, how long did it take her to get her hooks into him?" Hope spat. "And him! He's not just doing it to Celia. He's doing it to all of us. We took care of him, his kids, picked up the slack for him, and this is what we get? He betrays us all?"

Hope scrubbed the counter furiously with the scratchy side of a sponge. Stephanie wished once again that she had talked to Mark yesterday when she had a chance. She felt now it might have been a mistake to include Hope. Why had that been her instinct? Now it was too late.

"Well?" Hope asked, turning to Stephanie, who was leaning on the counter across from her, staring out the back window. "Don't you agree with me?"

Stephanie hesitated. "Yeah, I know what he did is wrong. But as close as we are to both Celia and Mark, who knows what goes on in their relationship? I'm just afraid that it's not our business," she said. "What if . . . what if we talk to him? Let him know how we feel, and tell him that he needs to fix it."

"And what if he disagrees? What if he tells us to mind our own business, and he just keeps on sticking it to Miss Slutty down the street? What then?"

"Then we decide. But first we give him a chance. And for the record, and I'm not saying she did the right thing, but you could take it a little easier on Nikki, too. People do make mistakes. Sometimes there are extenuating circumstances," Stephanie said.

"Not in my book," Hope said. "A betrayal is a betrayal."

⁓

"Mark, we need to talk," Stephanie whispered, stepping out in front of him as he came down the stairs into the living room. Celia was in the kitchen packing her lunch, the usual—a peanut butter and jelly sandwich, a banana, and a premade yogurt smoothie.

"Whoa, Stephanie, can't do it right now. Besides, as you can imagine, this is a little awkward," Mark said, avoiding her eyes and trying to get past her. She moved left and right to block him.

"I told Hope."

Mark sucked in his breath. "Fuck."

"Nice language," Stephanie said.

"You can understand my concern, though. She's probably out for blood. Am I right?"

"You're not wrong."

"Okay, let's talk. But please, let's wait until Celia's not around. Can you give me that?" Mark asked, this time looking Stephanie square in the eyes.

"Can you go in a little late today? I think we should do this now."

Mark nodded and slipped past Stephanie into the dining room. "Hey, kids. Hey, Ceil. What can I do to help?"

Celia had to drive to New York for her final interview with the board, so she was dropping all the kids off at school before she left.

"Lunches are already made, sweets. Books are packed. You can get the coats and shoes. I've got to go get the car," Celia said, kissing Mark as she walked to the front door.

Hope stole a glance at Mark, who was leaning over the shelves next to the door that held all of the kids' shoes.

"I'll have the kids ready when you get back," Hope said to Celia, still staring at Mark, who finally lowered his eyes.

"Come on, kids. Let's get moving," Hope said as she shuffled them to their respective doors, stuffing arms into sleeves and handing out backpacks. "Mommy Celia will be back in a minute with the car."

When Celia and the kids were safely gone, Hope turned to Mark. "You're staying, right?"

"I told Stephanie that I would. But take it easy. Ollie's here."

"There is nothing I could do to that child that could be worse than what you've done," Hope hissed.

She got Ollie situated in the playroom in front of the TV and joined Stephanie and Mark around the dining room table. Mark stirred his coffee slowly and deliberately, his spoon clinking against the sides of the photo mug of him and the guys on the beach on Father's Day last year. Stephanie had her head down on the table, her chin propped on her arms. She lifted her head when Hope sat down.

"Mark, Hope and I thought it would be best if we talked," Stephanie said. "We feel . . . some obligation to Celia to make sure that, well . . . I'm sure you know what I'm trying to say."

"No, Stephanie, maybe he doesn't," Hope said, turning to Mark. "What she's trying to say is that you need to come clean with your wife, or we will."

Mark stared at Hope, then sat back in his chair.

"Let me begin by saying thank you very much for all of your understanding, Hope," Mark said. "Despite what you think of me, you have never been in my shoes, and I resent your judgment. And Hope, my dear, I don't remember that you were standing on the altar with us when Celia and I got married. I can't help but wonder why you think I have to answer to you."

"Well, sorry if our concern for Celia seems like an intrusion to you, but correct me if I'm wrong—aren't we a family here? What you've done is inexcusable—to Celia, your children, to everyone in this house. When you did what you did, you did it to all of us," Hope said. "Don't you get that?"

"Do you feel that way, too, Stephanie?" Mark asked.

"I don't know how I feel," said Stephanie. "I'm not saying I don't agree that what you did is horrible. It is. But I guess I do think that it's not our place to tell Celia. It's yours. And that's why we're coming to you to ask you to please, please stop what you're doing and fix this."

"And you think that telling Celia is the best thing?" Mark said, looking only at Stephanie. "For her, I mean."

"I don't know. I've been over this in my mind a thousand times, and I just can't decide if I would want to know. That is, of course, assuming you wouldn't do it again—this thing you're doing," Stephanie said, realizing that there was something she hadn't considered. "You don't *love* Nikki, do you?"

Mark shook his head slowly. "Not in the way I love Celia," he said quietly.

Hope snorted. "Love? You're in love?"

"That's not what I said exactly, Hope. I know you can't understand any of this, and there's nothing I can say to make this better in your mind, so I think we just have to agree that the last thing any of us wants right now is for Celia to get hurt. I give you my word that I'll do the right thing for me and Celia, whatever that is," Mark said.

"So you'll tell her? Because I for one would want to know," Hope said. "Then at least I would be able to make an informed decision."

"But do we know for sure that Celia would?" Stephanie asked. "And he hasn't even said for sure that it's over between him and Nikki, right?" Stephanie looked at Mark, her eyes rimmed with tears.

"Just fix it," Hope said, pushing her chair away from the table and getting up to attend to Ollie's shrieks from the playroom.

Mark looked at Stephanie and shrugged. For the briefest second she thought she saw his face spasm like he might start to cry, but he didn't. Instead, he put his head down on the table and whispered, "I'm sorry."

"I know you are," Stephanie said gently. Then she leaned forward across the table and added, "But please, for all our sakes, just do something."

"Can you be out of there in thirty minutes?" Mark asked Leo.

"Well, I don't know about this. Is Chris with you?" Leo said, wavering, sizing up the dinner crowd.

"Chris?" Mark said, handing the phone over.

"Of course I'm here. Do you think you'd be allowed out if you couldn't bill this as a guys' night out? Stephanie already gave me the green light, and Celia doesn't seem to have a problem with it. It's all you, man. Come on, you can do it. Make that call," Chris shouted into the cell phone.

"Well, okay, but I can't promise it'll be pretty. The Borgata? Couldn't you have picked a tamer place for a guys' night out than an Atlantic City casino?" Leo asked, already dreading hearing Hope's voice on the other end of the phone.

Mark was back. "Just make the damn call. We're on our way over there, and we won't take no for an answer."

Leo stood holding the phone, even though Mark had already hung up. Reluctantly he dialed Hope's cell.

"I suppose you want to go to the Borgata?" demanded Hope, who picked up after the first ring. "How do you think you're going to get out of work? I mean, you couldn't get out of work when I needed you when all the kids were sick."

"Sweetie, now listen. I've been here all day, and I'm scheduled to be done at eight tonight anyway. I'd only be leaving a few minutes early. Besides, everyone's going. It would be nice to go out once in a while," Leo reasoned.

"But we were going to do a family outing tomorrow—just you, me, and Shoshanna—don't you remember? To Longwood Gardens? I don't want you to be tired and grumpy all day. We never get to spend any time alone together anymore. Do you really want to ruin our morning for a few hours at a stupid casino?"

"Of course I don't want to ruin our day together. But I haven't gone out with the guys in a long time, and I promise I won't drink too much. I'll offer to be the driver, and I'll make sure we don't stay out too late. And I'll use two of my free passes for this one night. Okay? Don't you trust me?"

Hope softened a little. "Of course I do, but I worry. I don't want you to lose our money—how much are you going to gamble?"

"Come on, Hope. You know I won't gamble a lot. I don't want to lose money either. Just a little bit of fun. I promise I won't go overboard,"

Leo said, looking at his watch. The guys would be here in a few minutes, and he hadn't even arranged to get out of there early. "Look, sweetie, I've got to go. Is this okay? Are we okay?"

"Fine, yes, we're okay," Hope said. "But I'll wait up for you."

"Love you," Leo said. "Bye!" He ended the call and let out a deep breath. *Not so bad.*

Five minutes later, coat in hand, everything settled in the kitchen, Leo headed for the front door and the station wagon waiting outside.

"You're going to pay for this," Chris teased as Leo climbed into the back seat.

"Dearly," Leo said, shutting the door and bracing himself for the ride.

Stephanie and Celia stared at Hope as she hung up the phone.

"Don't you think you're a little hard on him sometimes?" Celia asked, sliding the pan of chicken nuggets out of the oven. She looked tired, and her voice sounded drained.

Hope stared back at her friends. "I don't know," she mumbled. Why didn't they care what their husbands did? Hope couldn't believe what those guys got away with. And my God, look where it got Celia—a cheating husband, right under her nose!

"You know what I say, good riddance," Stephanie said, filling a small stainless-steel pitcher with water. "I just want to cozy up to a good chick flick. It's nice to have some time to myself. The night is young, ladies, and I think we have the makings of margaritas and some ultimate nachos. I say we get these kiddies in bed early and have a little party of our own."

"Fine," Hope said, relenting. "We can watch old episodes of *Sex and the City*. Leo never wants to do that," she said, setting out the plastic Ikea plates for the kids and squirting ketchup on every plate but Lu's. "Kids! Dinner!"

Ted, Lu, Harvest, and Shoshanna were arguing noisily when Stephanie finally went into the playroom to extract them. "Your chicken nuggets are getting cold! Let's move it!" she urged, taking Harvest by the hand.

"But Ted is hogging the controller. I never get a turn!" Harvest argued.

"Yes, you do!" Shoshanna shouted. "I'm the one who never gets a turn!"

"Okay, come on, kids, no more video games tonight. Dinner, then bath, then bed for all of you! The mommies have big plans," Stephanie said, helping them into their chairs and filling their plastic Harry Potter cups with water.

"What's the bedtime plan, guys?" Celia asked from the kitchen after a few minutes of welcomed silence.

"Let's just get them in their own beds tonight. Shoshanna's a mess. She needs some sleep," Hope said. "I want to be out of here early in the morning to get to Longwood Gardens."

"Sounds good to me. I could use a little alone time with the kids. I'm going to bring Ollie up now, and I'll be back down for the other two. Okay?" Celia asked, scooping him out of his high chair. She couldn't wait to get away from the group and was trying to figure out how to get out of the evening's festivities entirely.

"No problem," Stephanie called as she gathered up plates from the abandoned table. The kids had inhaled their dinner and were already back in the playroom. No matter how much time they spent together, they couldn't seem to get enough.

"I cannot believe the nerve," Hope said as Stephanie loaded the dishwasher. "After our conversation this morning, he up and organizes a trip to Atlantic City?"

"He probably just needs some time to figure things out," Stephanie said. "At least we know where he's not."

"True. But do you think he's going to tell her it's over?"

"Tell who it's over?" Stephanie asked.

"Nikki, of course," Hope whispered. "What the hell are you thinking?"

They cleaned the kitchen in silence, except for the running water and rambunctious shouts of the kids from the playroom, sliding past each other to open the dishwasher door and put things away in the freezer. Hope and Stephanie had disagreed on things before, but never like this, never to this extent. *How can Stephanie be so sympathetic to Mark and Nikki? Isn't she supposed to be Celia's friend?* Hope wondered. *Maybe I don't know her as well as I thought I did.*

"Well, Ollie's down. Now for the other two," Celia said, who had changed into her gray sweats and oversized Jayhawks T-shirt. "Come on, Ted. You too, Lu. Time for a bath."

Hope and Stephanie collected their kids, and each family headed up its separate steps, agreeing to meet downstairs in thirty minutes flat. Hope was the first one down. Shoshanna had been exhausted and had fallen asleep after a few pages of *Wonder*. Auggie had just left for his camping trip with school. It was a really good part, but when Hope looked over, Shoshanna was sleeping like an angel. Hope was disappointed for a second; *she* wanted to know what happened with Auggie. But she decided it was a good thing, and she'd have a lot of time to read to her tomorrow. She pulled the flowered comforter over Shoshanna's shoulders, kissed her on the cheek, and turned off the small yellow ceramic lamp on her bedside table before she tiptoed downstairs to get dinner ready for the second time tonight.

Hope was grating a big block of orange cheese onto a green plate when Celia joined her in the kitchen.

"You know what, I'm pooped," Celia said when she saw all the makings of the party she had no desire to be a part of tonight. "I might just go ahead and go to sleep myself. It's been a long week."

"No!" Hope cried. "We have to have as good a time as the men do."

"Fine," Celia said, not wanting to be asked what was wrong. She wasn't ready for that. "What can I do?"

"We have some of those hot peppers in the fridge. Can you grab them?"

"Sure," Celia said, scanning the shelves of the packed refrigerator before finally handing over the tall jar of yellow peppers. "I'll get started on the margaritas." Celia ran downstairs to what used to be Hope and Leo's kitchen in their basement. She grabbed a gallon jug of margarita mix and a bottle of Patrón from the cabinet. Alcohol would help.

By the time Stephanie joined them in the living room, there was a pitcher of margaritas on the rocks and a gooey plate of nachos on the glass-topped coffee table that Mark had picked up at an auction. It was a 1950s piece that reminded Hope of her grandmother's house in Westchester.

"Girls' night in!" Stephanie announced, finding the show on the "On Demand" menu. "My favorite kind of night. Is season three okay?"

"Which one is that? I've been falling asleep on my saved *Sex and the Cities* lately," Celia said, taking a long sip of her margarita.

"Let me see," Stephanie said, reading the description on the screen and munching loudly on a nacho. "Oh yeah, it's the one where Big marries Natasha, and Carrie is with Aidan until . . ."

". . . Carrie cheats on him and gets caught!" Hope said. "Remember that scene when she tells Aidan that she slept with Mr. Big right before Charlotte's wedding? I can't believe he didn't know. I felt so bad for him."

Stephanie turned and stared at Hope. Celia caught their visual exchange. She put down her drink, trying to ignore the awful feeling of salt around her mouth.

"How could he have known?" Celia asked Hope pointedly.

"Let's just watch the show," Stephanie said quickly, pointing the remote at the TV. "Ready?"

Celia kept her eyes on Hope while she poured herself another margarita. Hope shifted her eyes and stared silently at the TV. "Go ahead and start watching," Celia said finally, picking up her drink and standing up. "I need to go upstairs for a few minutes."

Celia walked past them and up her steps.

"You could have been a little more subtle," Stephanie whispered. "What is your problem?"

"I didn't really mean to say anything," Hope whispered back to Stephanie. "Maybe he told her."

"He couldn't have. They didn't even see each other today."

"Well, I was just talking about the show," Hope said, turning her attention to the opening sequence where Carrie gets splashed by a bus with her own picture on it.

"Please, Hope, just don't say anything more. You promised," Stephanie pleaded.

"I'll try," Hope said. "I can't help it if I care about our friend."

Halfway through the first episode, Celia came back downstairs. Her eyes were bloodshot, her face was pale, and her glass was empty.

"What did I miss?" she asked in the most normal voice she could manage.

~

The three women stayed up late into the night, watching episode after episode, pretending they couldn't stand to leave any of the storylines hanging. But the truth was they were avoiding having to talk to each other.

At some point Hope gave up staring at the door and the clock waiting for Leo to come home and eventually fell asleep on the couch with her feet touching Stephanie's under the polka dot fleece blanket. Celia was stretched out on the woven chaise, eyes slightly swollen and barely open, halfway through episode eight when she heard the key turn in the lock. She picked up the remote and turned off the TV as the guys tiptoed in the middle door—first Chris, then Leo, then Mark behind them—trying to avoid the floorboards that creaked the loudest.

Celia sat up as Mark entered the living room and headed toward the steps at the back of their house.

"Hey," she said.

Chris and Leo stopped in their tracks when they heard Celia's voice and exchanged a panicked glance.

"Well, come on over and get your wives. They've been snoring all night long," Celia said. "I've had just about enough."

Within a minute, they roused Stephanie and Hope, who followed their husbands upstairs, glancing back at Celia but avoiding Mark's gaze.

Mark watched them go, then turned back to face Celia.

"Hey," he said.

"How was guys' night out?"

"Uneventful. And your night?" he asked.

"Oh, you know, drinkin', smokin', wild orgies. The usual."

"That's my girl," Mark said, smiling. "Still crazy after all these years."

Celia had to work to not smile back.

Mark sat down on the arm of Celia's chair, and they both stared at the blank TV screen. Celia was the first one to speak.

"Is there something you need to tell me?" she asked, turning to face Mark.

He sighed. "You got me. I lost five hundred bucks on the craps table."

"You know that's not what I meant."

"Right," he said.

"I know, Mark. I know there's someone else."

He let out a long breath and looked away. "Did Hope tell you?"

"Hope? No, not really," Celia said. "No one needed to tell me."

"So I guess I just did."

Celia nodded. "For a while I wanted to believe that you were sick again, as crazy as that sounds. But you seemed healthy, so I decided that wasn't it. Then, well, it started to become clear. When you took off tonight, I knew for sure. You might not remember, but that's exactly what you did in New York after you kissed that annoying girl, Kristin, during that study group our first month living together—you went to Atlantic City. Somehow I think this time the damages are going to be much greater."

"Celia, I'm . . . I don't know what to say," he said.

"Do you love her?"

"I love you," he said.

Celia nodded. She didn't have any more tears left. She had spent the last few weeks dealing with the possibility of it on her own, alone, and now that she knew for sure, she just felt numb.

"What do you need me to do?" Mark asked.

"I don't know yet," Celia said, hugging her knees to her chest. "I have so many questions, but I still can't decide if I want them answered."

Mark nodded. They sat for a minute, both staring at the spot where Stephanie and Hope had been sleeping on the sofa.

"I think I'll just stay down here tonight."

"Whatever you need to do," he said.

CHAPTER EIGHTEEN

Celia kept her eyes focused on the green lamp in the lobby. She crossed and uncrossed her legs, leaning down to run her finger over the tiny run in her stockings. For one brief second she had a moment of panic, wishing she could go back to her office and change her stockings, and then she remembered why she was there.

"Celia," the board chair said, appearing out of nowhere. She had imagined this moment so many times.

"Ellen," Celia said, getting up, trying to smile.

"Please, come in," Ellen said, leading Celia into the empty conference room. There was a pitcher of water and two glasses on the table.

Ellen took her time walking around the huge conference table, flanked by floor-to-ceiling windows on two sides. She took a seat at the head of the table and poured herself a glass of water, then held up the pitcher, offering one to Celia, who was too distracted to notice.

Celia took a seat, crossed her legs, and waited. Ellen had been her champion for many years, mentoring her and guiding her toward a leadership position. She had been the CEO until she retired a few years ago and accepted the position of board chair. She was feared and admired by most everyone at the company except Celia, who only had admiration for her.

"Celia, I'm sure you know why I invited you here today," Ellen said, smiling widely.

"I guess I do," Celia said.

"I am very happy to say that we want to offer you the job," Ellen said. "Let me be the first to congratulate our newest vice president."

Celia had the urge to lean over and make the run in her stockings bigger. She wanted to stick her finger into the fibers and rip. She wanted to rip until they tore into shreds. She wanted to throw the shreds on the floor and walk away.

"Ellen, thank you," Celia said. It felt like she was listening to her own voice from someplace across the room. "This has been my aspiration for a long time now. But I'm going to have to decline."

"I'm sorry," Ellen said. "Did you say decline?"

"Some things have happened at home recently, and I'm afraid that the increased responsibility will present too much of a challenge. I'm sorry, Ellen, I appreciate the chance you've given me. And I'm sorry to have wasted any of your or the rest of the board members' time," Celia said. "But I'm going to need to stay where I am."

Celia had the urge to run, to be anywhere but that bright, still conference room, making the choice that she had just made.

"Celia, I've known you for a long time, and I'm hesitant to pry, but I must ask. After all of your hard work to get to this place in your career . . ." Ellen stopped, then began again. "Why do you do this work?"

Celia took a deep breath and relaxed her shoulders. She owed this to Ellen. "I guess it's because it's who I am. I've always worked hard and achieved. I like the impact I'm making here, and I like the way I feel about myself when I accomplish something important," she said.

"I've observed that you thrive on responsibility, that you perform best—and seem happiest—when expectations are high," said Ellen, meeting Celia's gaze. "So why do you feel that the responsibility of the leadership position would be a challenge instead of an opportunity?"

"Well, maybe being responsible for so many things has made me irresponsible," said Celia, looking away.

"Perhaps I can give you a bit of unsolicited advice from someone who has spent her life managing career and family. I urge you to consider the fact that you might not be responsible for everyone and everything. That you would be well served to be responsible for only the things that are within your control," said Ellen.

Celia's head was swimming again. She had thought she knew exactly what she needed to do after everything that had happened over the weekend, but now she wondered if she had been looking at it all wrong.

"Would you take some time to reconsider?"

Celia nodded slowly. "I think I will take a few days to think about it," she said, rising and extending her hand to Ellen, who stood to accept it, placing her other hand over Celia's and giving it a gentle squeeze.

⌒

Just as Hope was about to turn left out of the school gate with Shoshanna, Harvest, and Ollie to go get Lu and Ted, Stephanie ran up from behind.

"Hi!" she said, pushing her purple scarf back over her shoulder and giving Harvest a quick hug.

"Hi," Hope said.

"Where are you going now?" Stephanie asked, taking Shoshanna's hand and falling into step with the group.

"What are you doing here?" Hope asked, her voice a little less than nice.

"Oh, well, the truth is I was supposed to meet with Nikki this afternoon, but she canceled, so I thought I'd find you guys," Stephanie said as lightly as she could.

"I assume you would have canceled if she hadn't, right?" Hope demanded.

Stephanie chewed on her bottom lip. "I don't know. Probably," she finally said.

"I'm fine with them," Hope said, gesturing toward the kids.

"Oh, I know that," Stephanie said, a little taken aback. "It's just that after everything, I just sort of wanted to be with you. I don't want you to be mad at me, and I was hoping to talk a little about the whole thing. Where are you going now, by the way?"

They came up to a stop sign at Pine and Twenty-Fifth. Hope felt so tired that she was suddenly grateful to have Stephanie there, being the one to walk out into the street to make sure the traffic stopped. Now she could just push the stroller and not be 100 percent on guard.

"I thought I'd get Ted and I in early since these guys had a half day. There's no sense in waiting around. Don't you think? I thought we could go to the Franklin Institute or something," Hope said.

"That sounds good," Stephanie said. "I can come. If that's okay."

"Yeah, that would be okay," Hope said. Harvest and Shoshanna ran ahead along the iron fence that ringed Fitler Square. Every now and then one or the other would try to climb it.

"Harvest! Shoshanna! Stop at the end of the fence," Stephanie called. "So what was your take on yesterday?"

"I was farther away than you were," Hope said. "I tried to stay on our side of the house as much as I could. But I know something wasn't right, and I guess I imagined that someone was packing. Mark, probably. Celia would never leave the kids. I guess she could take them with her, though."

"Oh, I didn't even think of that. I—" Stephanie stopped when her phone rang. She fumbled in her pocket.

"Who is it?" Hope asked.

"It's Celia," Stephanie said quickly. "Hi!"

They turned left at Twenty-Second Street while Stephanie listened to what Celia was saying.

"Where are you now?" she asked her. "Oh, good, we're just going to pick up Lu and Ted early and take them to the Franklin Institute." She listened again. "Probably the sports room. They always want to go there first. Okay. See you there."

"How did she know you were with the kids?" Hope asked.

"She called earlier, but I couldn't talk," Stephanie said. "I told her I planned to find you."

"Huh, I wonder why she didn't call me," Hope said.

"No reason, I'm sure. Anyway, she said she left early, she couldn't stand to be there, and she wants to talk," Stephanie said.

"Okay," Hope said.

Thirty minutes later they were settled on a bench in the big, bright sports exhibit at the Franklin Institute, watching the kids fight over the surfboard. Luckily the room was empty, so there was no competition beyond the Emerson Street kids. Hope sat back with Ollie on her lap. She knew they could be here for a long time. It was the kids' favorite spot in the museum.

Celia came in and looked around. She was wearing her black suit with a gray shirt underneath. No jewelry, very little makeup. She looked like she just came from a funeral, except for the tennis shoes.

"Over here," Stephanie called, even though Celia was walking directly toward them and there wasn't anyone else in the room.

"Hi," Celia said, reaching for Ollie. There was that brief, awkward moment when Ollie hesitated, almost as if he might prefer to stay with Hope, but he went to Celia, nuzzling her shoulder. Celia took a seat on the other side of Stephanie.

"Hi," Hope and Stephanie said at the same time.

"Okay, so I don't want to have a long discussion about this, but obviously I need to download," Celia said quietly. "I know you know. And I know you knew before I did."

Celia didn't look at them while she spoke but instead watched the kids push each other off the moving surfboard. Ted pushed Harvest so hard he fell, grazing his cheek on the hard board. None of the grown-ups moved. Harvest crumpled dramatically to the floor, crying, but clearly not seriously injured. Eventually Shoshanna put her arm around him and eased him up.

Ollie fussed. Celia cooed in his ear, trying to comfort him, but he just got louder. Finally she sighed, stood up, walked to Hope, handed Ollie to her, and sat back down. Both Hope and Stephanie waited for Celia to keep talking.

"I want you to know we talked a lot this weekend, Mark and I," Celia continued, still staring straight ahead. "And I think we've reached an agreement we can live with. I'm not saying it's going to be easy, but I do want to say that it takes two to mess up a marriage, and I don't think I've been perfect. I don't think I saw the signs . . ."

"Oh my God, Celia," Hope said. "You're not blaming yourself for this, are you? I mean, you can't possibly think this has something to do with anything you've done. You are the perfect wife, taking care of the family, taking care of the kids, taking care of your husband, giving him some space, for God's sake, which we are not all so good at, not to mention bringing in at least half of your family's income."

"That's not the point," Celia said. She hesitated for a second, and Hope could tell she was trying not to cry. "I mean, sure, in my mind I thought I was keeping things together. I thought I had the loose ends covered, but I don't think I've given Mark what he needs, what he really needs, to be happy."

"Did Mark tell you that?" Hope asked angrily. "I completely disagree. Isn't it Mark's responsibility to tell you what he needs to be happy?

And even if you didn't give it to him, he should have told you instead of doing what he did. Stephanie, you must have something to say here."

Stephanie shifted on the hard bench, rearranging her dark green skirt over her chestnut UGGS.

"Look, Hope, we've been over this before. No matter how close we are, I don't think we can know exactly what's going on in someone else's marriage. Who knows why people do the things they do?" Stephanie said.

"Are you kidding me? That's all you have to say?" Hope said even louder, making Ollie turn his head to see if she was yelling at him. She tried to smile at him, but it was a weak attempt. Was everyone going crazy here? "Did Mark really, on top of everything else he did, make you feel like you did something wrong?"

"No!" Celia said, turning to look at them for the first time. "No, he did not. He completely blames himself and nobody else. I believe he regrets what he did."

"Do you even know exactly what he did?" Hope interrupted her. "The details, I mean. Did he share all of that with you? Because if Leo . . ."

"Hope, I want to make this clear. I do not want to know the details. And that's completely my choice. That's how it has to be for me to be able to continue," Celia said. "Really, I don't want this to be a big, long discussion. I just want you to know where we stand. We are, after all, living in the same house. Mark offered to tell me everything, or any particular part of what happened, but I feel that I know enough. I don't need to know the when and where of it, or even the who. I know it happened, and I know it won't happen anymore."

"How do you know that?" Hope pleaded. "How do you really know that?"

"Hope, come on," Stephanie said, sticking her finger into Ollie's tummy. He stared back but didn't laugh. They all knew they shouldn't be talking like this in front of him. No matter how little he was, he must know there was something bad going on. "Please, give Celia a break. She didn't do anything to you. And she's suffering, obviously."

"Yeah, why are you so mad at me?" Celia asked Hope.

Hope took a deep breath, feeling a bit of the anger drain away.

"I don't know," she said quietly. "I just don't know."

"Well, don't be anymore," Celia said. "I need you."

"Okay, I'll try," Hope said. "So what are you going to do?"

Celia was quiet, and Hope worried she was going to tell them she would be taking the kids back to Kansas.

"Who's going to move out?" Hope prompted as gently as she could.

"Move out?" Celia said, shocked. "Nobody is moving out. He's my husband, and people make mistakes. We all make mistakes. And he almost died last fall. That can't happen without making a person a little crazy. When I thought he was having aftereffects from that, and then it turned out to be this, the real truth is, and I was surprised myself, but the real truth is that I was glad. We can fix this, but if his brain isn't right, how are we going to fix that?"

"I'm not sure his brain is so right," Hope mumbled under her breath.

"I think I'm going to go," Celia said, getting up. "Somehow I thought you'd be more supportive, relieved even, that things might not have to change so much. I'll go back to work. It's easier there."

Hope and Stephanie watched as she walked out of the exhibit room without saying good-bye to any of the kids.

"Okay," Stephanie said, trying to make sense of it. "So everything is going to be okay. She's forgiven him, and we should forgive him and continue on like nothing happened."

"I don't know if I can do that," Hope said, bumping Ollie up and down on her knee. "How am I supposed to do that?"

"You are so hard on everyone," Stephanie said. "So black and white. Don't you think that in the course of a, say, fifty-year marriage, and that's if you're really lucky, that there's going to be a lot of gray? That things are going to happen that you didn't expect, that you never factored in? Things that you are just going to have to accept, somehow, and get past?"

"I hope not," Hope said.

~

Mark knew Nikki was outside. He could see her from his desk, walking up the tiny tree-lined street where his office was, pausing at the corner and rooting around in her purse before heading the other way back down the street and doing it all over again. She must have been at it for about fifteen minutes already. At least she had the good sense to not come inside.

"Hey, Miles, I'm going to get a cup of coffee, clear my head a little so I can think about the Spruce Street project—I'm blocked. Can I get you anything?" Mark asked as he stood up, slowly wrapped his scarf around his neck, and pulled on his black coat.

"No thanks. On second thought, I could use a latte," Miles said, not even looking up from his computer.

"No problem," Mark said, watching Nikki walk by his office door again. He wanted to time it so she would be at the far end of the street when he walked out. He had no idea what state she was in. He hadn't seen her since that terrible morning when Stephanie learned everything. He could still feel the shock of that moment whenever he let his mind wander, which he tried not to do too much these days.

When Mark was pretty sure Nikki would be at the other corner, he opened the office door and stepped out into the sunny February day. For a minute he thought she had gone, that he'd missed her, but then he saw her coming back around the corner, walking as casually as if this was her first time here. He walked quickly toward her.

"Hey," he said as he approached her, his hands in his pockets.

"Hey, I was hoping I'd see you," she said. Her coat was as white as ever, and her hair was straight down her back. He wished she had worn it up; that was easier to resist. "Can we go somewhere?"

"Oh, Nikki, I don't think so. That's what got us into trouble in the first place, right?" Mark said, moving a little faster toward Pine Street, closing his eyes for a split second to take in her warmth next to him. "I was on my way to get some coffee, though. Do you want to come?"

"I don't mean like that," Nikki said, brushing her long hair over her shoulder and gently punching his arm. They stopped walking for a minute, looking right at each other and grinning.

"I mean to talk. I have something to tell you," Nikki said.

"Okay," Mark said. "I'm just going to that new place on the corner."

"Can we sit down there?" Nikki asked. "I just need a few minutes."

"I think I can arrange that," Mark said.

Nikki didn't say anything as Mark entered the store, holding the narrow door for her and not moving out of the way when she brushed hard against him to get in. She stood back while he ordered.

"Can I get you something?" he asked after he ordered a latte and a black coffee.

"No thanks," Nikki said. She waited while Mark paid before pointing toward the back.

Mark nodded, following Nikki through the small door into the dark room. There were four tables, and they were all empty. Nikki sat down at the only one that looked dirty—butter streaks and bread crumbs. Mark thought about suggesting a different table but decided it didn't matter. He knew he couldn't stay with her for too long.

"So I'm leaving," she said as soon as she sat down. "I'm leaving Will."

"Nikki, don't," Mark said, forgetting about the dirty table and putting his left elbow down, just missing some jam. "Please don't leave him for me. I'm going to, well, Celia is going to let me stay. She knows some of what happened. She didn't want any details, really, but she's not kicking me out. So I can't do this anymore. I can't see you again."

"I'm not leaving him for you!" she said. "I'm leaving him for me. You know I haven't been happy with him pretty much from the beginning—certainly since long before we were married. He doesn't seem all that happy either. He's barely going to notice I'm gone, at least as long as this trial continues. And I'm sure there's another trial around the corner. He comes home for a few hours here, a few hours there. Truth is, I think he'll be relieved."

"Have you told him?" Mark asked.

"Yes, of course, and he said all the right things, that we're just starting out, that of course there will be bumps in the road. That we should give it some more time."

"No, I mean, did you tell him about us?" Mark asked.

"Oh no, not directly," Nikki said, looking at the table and picking someone else's crumbs up with her thumb and forefinger. Mark watched as she moved them around between her fingers before dropping them to the floor. "I think he knows. He might be absent, but he's a smart guy. He didn't seem to want to know, or at least he didn't ask me to confirm it. I don't even care. It's like all the rest of our marriage—just move forward, don't look around. Ugh."

Mark looked at the coffee cups on the table and picked them up.

"I have to go," he said. "I have to get this to my boss before it gets cold."

"Please, just give me a few more minutes. I'll buy you another cup to take back to him," Nikki said.

Mark put the cups down and leaned back in his chair.

"I didn't want to talk to you about Will," Nikki said. "It's just that I didn't want to disappear. I wanted you to know where I am. I've taken a leave of absence from the salon. Right now I'm saying a month, but I have to see how things go, and I'm going to New York to live with my aunt. I thought about just going to my mom's in South Jersey. I even had a moment when I thought about actually pole dancing, taking my friends up on their longtime offers of a gig, but that didn't seem right. So anyway, I leave on Thursday."

Mark sat for a minute. Images of Times Square and speeding trains ran through his mind, followed by the image of Nikki dancing around the bedpost in the Delancey Street house. He stood up.

"Hey, will you tell Stephanie I'll e-mail her when I get settled?" Nikki asked.

"Sure," Mark said, trying to force himself to move toward the door. "This coffee is still hot." He looked around, making sure the room was empty. He walked to Nikki's side of the table. He stopped short of offering her his hand and stood there waiting for her to get up on her own. When she did, he took a small step back.

"I wish you happiness, Nikki," Mark said, not daring to look in her face. "I wish you true happiness."

"And to be fearless?" she asked quietly.

Mark smiled. "Yes, and to be fearless."

He didn't look back as he walked through the tiny door into the main part of the café. He tried not to think as he walked along Pine and turned toward his office. But as he walked up the charming street, lined with gingko trees that were now free of leaves and nuts, and approached the town house with his office on the first floor, he was overcome with relief.

～

Chris tried a few of the smaller stores in Chinatown, but they didn't even know what he was talking about. So he went right to the source: their favorite Friday night restaurant, Lee How Fook.

"Table for one?" he was asked when he walked in.

"Not today, thank you. Actually I have sort of a strange question. Do you sell those lazy Susans?" Chris pointed to one at a big corner table. Every time they came here, they all said how helpful it would be to use one to pass food on their own big wooden table. And now, more than ever, Chris felt they needed something to make things easier, something that would remind them of happier times.

"No, we don't, but Mr. Chang does. His store is at Tenth and Race," the man said.

"Thanks."

It was more expensive than Chris expected, and of course heavier, so he had to take a cab home. He put the huge wooden circle on his stoop while he opened the door. He came in to find a scene that could be classified as the opposite of their boisterous Friday night Chinese dinners. The kids were in front of the TV in the playroom. They were so lethargic and quiet that Chris wondered if they were sick again.

He looked at the table where the grown-ups were sitting quietly. Hope had obviously been crying. Stephanie had that shocked look on her face. Leo was at the far end, nursing some alcoholic beverage even though it was just barely lunchtime on a Sunday. And Celia and Mark sat next to each other, looking like they were leading the meeting.

"Hey," Chris said when nobody spoke. "What's up?"

Hope turned to him. Her eyes were red and swollen.

"Well, guys, looks like you need a pick-me-up," Chris said, taking the brown paper off the new lazy Susan, moving a few glasses and bottles out of the way so he could place it smack in the middle of the table. "Perfect." Chris got to work putting the sugar, ketchup, salt and pepper, and Leo's various hard-to-find hot sauces on it. Chris took a seat and looked expectantly at everyone.

"We're not going to need that anymore," Hope said finally, her voice cracking.

"What?" Chris asked. "What do you mean?"

Hope wanted to explain, but knew she wouldn't be able to. She rubbed her eyes. Over the last few months she had certainly thought about this, wondered if it would make things any easier, if they'd made a mistake in the first place.

"Can someone please fill me in?" Chris asked.

"We've been talking," Celia began in her professional mediation voice. "And, based on the events of the last few weeks, well, months really, and considering that Mark and I are going to need to concentrate on our relationship, and obviously that's going to take some work, we've decided that the best thing for all of us is to go our separate ways, to close up the walls."

Chris felt like he'd been punched. Sure, he knew things had been sticky lately for so many reasons, but closing up the walls had never occurred to him as a possibility. He just figured they'd push through and help each other like they always did. He looked over at Leo.

"Can I have some of that?" he asked, pointing to the caramel-colored liquid in front of Leo.

"Sure. It's single malt, is that okay?" Leo asked, getting up.

"The stronger the better," Chris said.

"I'd like some, too," Hope said.

"Me too," Stephanie said.

Leo got out the rest of the glasses and poured the drinks, and without even asking Celia and Mark, he put one in front of each of them, too. Celia shook her head, but Mark put the glass right to his mouth. Leo stood there while he drank, and when his glass was empty, he poured some more.

"Thanks, man," Mark said, patting Leo on the back.

"Where is this coming from?" Chris asked.

"Chris, come on, things haven't been easy," Celia said. "I think we would all agree that we've sacrificed parts of our immediate families for the bigger group. I'm not saying that was completely wrong, but in light of what's happened between Mark and me, I, we've, decided that we have to focus on us."

"Come on, Celia," Hope said. "I know we've given up small things here and there, but I can help you now more than ever. I can pick up most of the slack with the kids while you focus on each other. I've been upset, too, but we don't have to give up our family and our home. Please, just give me some time to get used to the whole thing."

"Hope, I don't have any time," Celia said. "It's hard enough being two adults in a marriage—I'm beginning to think six adults is four too many."

"I don't think it's such a bad idea," Leo said. Hope snapped her head toward him and stared. "Mark and Celia have a lot to deal with, and I do think some things have fallen to the wayside. Hope, you've said more than once lately that you miss your time alone with Shoshanna. Oh, and remember the holidays? How hard it was for you to navigate the different traditions? Remember how you told me that you didn't really enjoy either Hanukkah or Christmas this year?"

"No. I mean yes, but I didn't mean I wanted to close up the walls," Hope said, crying openly now. "You know me. I always need something to complain about. I need time to get used to things."

"I sort of agree with Celia and Leo," Stephanie said. You know how much I love being with all of you, but if we're not all on the same wavelength, if it doesn't feel right, then maybe it isn't. Maybe we need to move on." She couldn't, of course, mention her real reason for wanting the walls back up, that closing the walls would put the necessary distance between her and Leo. "Maybe we all just need to put more energy into our own families for a little while."

"You can do that with the walls down," Hope pleaded. "What if we write more rules and factor in some time alone with our immediate families? We could try that first."

"Hope, we can't force them to stay," Chris said. "I don't think we have a choice."

"He's right," Stephanie said. "If we're not all in this anymore, there's no way it's going to work. It's all or nothing."

"Mark," Hope said, addressing him for the first time in a long time. He looked at her. "Do you have anything to say about this?"

Mark looked around the table. He looked through to the playroom and back over his shoulder to his own house and the grown-up living room that they had really managed to keep just that. Finally he looked back at Hope.

"I'll call Yogi tomorrow," Mark said. "He'll know how to put the walls back up."

CHAPTER NINETEEN

"Everybody ready?" Mark asked, standing inside his front door, snow shovel in hand. He looked at Chris, who stood at his own door to Mark's right, and Leo, beyond Chris on the opposite side of the house, the walls between them still down.

"Let's do it," Chris said, zipping his ski jacket to his chin and pulling his black wool cap over his uncombed blond hair. He turned the latch on his dead bolt and reached for his doorknob.

"I'll bring out the salt," Leo said, lifting a heavy brown and white bag in one arm while he opened his door with the other.

Three doors opened and shut almost simultaneously, and Mark, Chris, and Leo found themselves in the middle of a good old-fashioned March snowstorm. They knew that this would probably be the last of it. There always seemed to be one more storm just when the fickle Philadelphia winter was supposed to have ended, and it was always the best one. Lots of accumulation, not heavy or icy. Just the perfect nor'easter to give them one last excuse to spend the whole day at Dante's drinking Belgian beer and eating hot wings.

"Well hello there, Chris," Leo said, turning to his left and giving him a wave from his stoop. "Fancy meeting you here. And Mark! Nice to see you, too. Looks like we all have the same idea. Can I interest you in some salt for your steps?"

"Why thank you, my friend. Nice to see you both. It's been way too long. How about a beer after we've finished our snow removal duties?" Mark asked, trudging down the steps and pushing the snow off the sidewalk and into the unplowed street. Emerson Street was so narrow that the city hadn't been able to get a plow down it in years. Each year there was a rumor that the city would invest in a small plow, but each year when the snow came, the street remained covered until the temperature rose.

"I'd like that very much," Chris said. "How about we meet back here in, say, exactly thirty minutes?"

"I'm getting mighty thirsty," Leo said. "We may have to speed up this little project."

The street was scattered with people shoveling, some neighbors and a few industrious strangers looking to make some money on a snowy day. All was quiet except for the sound of metal sliding through snow, shovels sometimes hitting the pavement beneath. Even the sounds of traffic from the busier street behind Emerson were absent since everyone seemed to be playing hooky from work today and all the city's schools were closed. The door to Mary's house creaked open.

"Mark! Woo hoo! Mark! Are you gonna shovel my sidewalk or what?" Mary screeched, the sound of her voice startling everyone on the street. She peeked out from inside her door, wearing a green T-shirt that skimmed the tops of her thighs and what Mark hoped was underwear underneath, but from his vantage point, it looked like she was naked except for the shirt.

"Get back inside, Mary. It's cold out here. I'll take care of your sidewalk as soon as I'm finished," Mark said, waving her away and trying hard not to look in her direction.

"Wait a minute. Let me get dressed and bring you some biscotti. I got it at the bakery yesterday. Hold on," Mary said, closing her storm door and slamming the wooden door behind it.

"Oh my God. Did you see that?" Chris asked. "Has she lost her marbles?"

"Did I see it?" Mark said, shaking his head. "A better question might be, can I unsee it?"

Leo, who had almost finished his portion of the sidewalk, climbed his steps and pushed open his door. "Hope! We have a big pile. You can come out now!"

Mark's door slammed open, and Ted and Lu bounded down the steps bundled like snowmen in their bright red fleece hats and scarves. Harvest and Shoshanna came out of Leo's door together with Hope chasing after them with their mittens in her hands.

"Shoshanna! Get back here right now! You are going to turn into a Popsicle!" Hope scolded.

"I'm not cold!" Shoshanna shouted, stomping her foot on the top step and nearly sliding off.

"Me either, Mommy Hope," Harvest said. "It's warm out here."

Hope came out coatless and grabbed both kids by the arms, pulling them just inside the door. "You will put on these mittens right now or you will come inside," she said, one by one covering each of the four little hands with dark blue fleece mittens. "Watch them a second while I get my coat?"

"No problem, sweetie," Leo said. "Not much to watch for, though. No car is getting down this street for quite a long time."

"What's *that* supposed to mean?" accused Hope.

"You are so sensitive," Leo mumbled under his breath. "Kids! Stay close until Mommy Hope comes out."

"Here's your cookies!" Mary shouted, holding tightly onto her black wrought-iron railing. This time she was bundled in a full-length black mink coat.

"Mary, my dear," Mark said, crossing the street and taking a cookie from the Tupperware container in her outstretched hand. "So nice to see you fully clothed. Now let me get to work on that sidewalk."

"Goddamn right," she said, smiling. "How long am I gonna have to wait? Until I slip and break my neck? Damn snow. I shoulda moved to Florida with my sister when I had the chance."

Mark adjusted his gloves and started in on Mary's sidewalk.

"Here, kids, take a cookie," Mary said, shoving the Tupperware in the direction of Ted and Lu, who had the bottom two parts of a snowman already completed. The kids gathered around Mary while Hope ran toward them in her slim-fitted royal blue ski parka and snow boots.

"No, kids, no more cookies! You've been eating junk all day."

"Oh come on, don't be such a stingy bitch. Let the kids have some cookies," Mary bellowed.

Ted, who was reaching into the Tupperware, froze, his hand in midair, and stared from one woman to the other. Finally he dropped the cookie back into the pile.

Hope put her hands on her hips and glared at Mary.

"Mary, I don't care how mean you are to me, but you need to watch your language around the kids. And *I* get to determine whether or not they have cookies, not you," Hope said, one hand still on her hip and the other pointing in Mary's face, just a few inches from her nose.

"Well, who died and made you queen?" Mary asked, relishing Hope's challenge. "Just come from one of your dirty movie-making sessions inside that closed-up house of yours? What the hell is going on in there anyway? Shades always drawn, doors never open."

"Not that it is any of your business," Hope yelled, the pitch of her voice rising, "but we happen to be a family in there. There is nothing going on at all—just three families living together in one house and taking care of each other like they should."

Mark, Leo, and Chris had stopped shoveling and stood speechless, unable to take their eyes off Mary and Hope standing in the middle of the street, a container of cookies between them.

"And it's people like you who make everything a mess, who ruin what we have—people who don't mind their own damn business and stick their nose in ours," shouted Hope, tears in her eyes.

"Don't get your panties in a bunch, Hope," Mary said, her voice now softer and quieter. "I was just teasing you. I didn't know you'd get so upset. Really, I'm sorry."

"Well, okay then," Hope said, turning to walk toward her door, but changing her mind and instead walking toward Mark's. "Mark, I'm going inside our house for a few minutes," she announced. "Keep an eye on all of our kids for me."

⁓

"You sure you want to do this?" Yogi asked. He was standing in the space between Mark's and Chris's and staring up at the framed opening in the ceiling. "Not only lots of work, but sometimes putting walls between you is not so good."

"Thanks for coming so quickly and bringing the guys," Mark said, looking past the dining room into the playroom at the two handsome olive-skinned young men sitting on the low futon, watching cartoons on TV. Every few minutes they laughed heartily and talked to each other in Hebrew.

"No problem, eh? I come to help. You got any coffee?" Yogi asked.

"Sure, I'll make some. I guess they can get started whenever they're ready," said Mark, again glancing over his shoulder into the playroom as he headed toward the kitchen.

"Hey! Yaakov! Yefet!" Yogi shouted in his high-pitched voice. "Get out of there. Do your work!"

"Yah, yah. We're coming," said the taller one, standing up and grabbing a pile of paint-stained blue plastic tarps from the floor next to him.

Satisfied, Mark opened the navy blue bag of coffee and measured out five scoops. He pulled the nozzle from the faucet and turned on the water to fill the coffeemaker. He took out two mugs, one for himself and one for Yogi. Mark paused in front of the personalized Father's Day photo mug but reached behind it for the Starbucks mug instead.

When Mark came out of the kitchen, Yogi was sitting at the table he had given them as a gift the last time he had been at the house, and the two younger men were standing on ladders securing a tarp to the ceiling between the dining room and living room with screws that they threaded through grommets at the top. Mark suddenly felt strangely uncomfortable in what used to be Chris's living room as his own house disappeared from view.

"So I thought that if you hung the tarps and helped me pack up the table so Chris could have this room back, we'd be good to go until you can get back next week to start on the walls," Mark said, taking a long sip from his mug as he tried to avoid looking behind him at the quickly materializing wall of blue plastic.

"Yah, yah, we come back next week," Yogi said. "So you don't like living with your friends?"

"It's a bit more complicated than that," Mark said.

"What? What's complicated? You got a big beautiful house. Nice big family. You know, in my house we always have lot of people living there. Just like back in Israel, in Pardes Hanna."

"I guess we just need some time to ourselves, that's all."

"Bah. You Americans. Everyone for himself, no? What kind of life is that? Let me tell you something. It's not easy starting over."

Mark shifted in his chair. He didn't need Yogi's advice. What he did need was to have these walls closed up so things could go back to normal and he wouldn't have two extra women judging him. Why had he ever thought that would be a good idea? But Yogi wasn't going anywhere for a while, and long stories about his life back in Israel were his specialty. The guys moved the ladders to the other side of the room and went to work on the space between Chris's and Leo's. This time Mark couldn't avoid watching the walls close in on him.

"Back in Pardes Hanna, I lived in a village with a courtyard in the middle. I was surrounded by family and friends. We eat together, take care of kids together. Like you think of a kibbutz, but not official. My mother and father. My brothers, their wives and kids, our friends. We were all there living together. But I'm the youngest, and I want to come to America because I think my life will be so good. I leave my wife and baby in the village so I can make it in America."

Mark nodded politely and watched as the playroom disappeared from view. He had forgotten just how narrow a fifteen-foot-wide house could be, especially when filled with a table that seated eleven.

"I miss it, but I need to make it here. After a few years I could bring my wife here and raise my children in this place. America has been good to me, but it will never be home. I help these boys," Yogi said, nodding toward the guys as they finished hanging the second tarp. "And they become my family for a while, but then they go, and the house is quiet all over again." Yogi shook his head. Both men sat quietly for a minute.

Mark felt suddenly big in the small room, trapped in someone else's house that wasn't quite home anymore. "So I guess this is it. The table's next. Can you take it for me?"

"Yah, yah, I can take it and store it for you, in case you change your mind . . ."

"We won't," Mark said.

"When you have family around you—whether they're blood or not—you're a lucky man," Yogi said.

"Just because we're not living together doesn't mean we can't be family," said Mark.

"True, true, but remember, once you put walls between you, you can never go back. Something always missing. Trust me, I know. An ocean, a wall—it's all the same."

~

Hope could hear Chris moving around right next to her, only the tarp separating them. It seemed so stupid, as if that piece of fabric was supposed to mean they couldn't talk to each other. She listened as he sang a familiar song while she desperately tried to tackle the mess that was the playroom. She could really use his help. Screw the tarp.

"Hey, what's that song?" she called into the other room. "I can't place it."

Instead of answering he sang louder, which made her smile, and then she knew. It was "I Can See It" from *The Fantasticks*, her favorite off-Broadway show ever. And Chris knew that. He was *trying* to get her attention.

"It really is a pretty little world," Hope said half to herself. Chris poked his head through to the former playroom. He smiled. He clearly didn't want to be alone any more than she did.

"I was hoping you would hear me," he said. "Got to love *The Fantasticks*. I was thinking about it today—that's why that song is stuck in my head. When you think about it, we were living it."

Hope was sitting on the floor surrounded by toys and three huge cardboard boxes. "Oh my God, you are so right. The walls are up, they come down, and then they go up again. What happened in the end?"

"I think it has a happy ending—or at least I hope it does now."

"I wish they wouldn't do this," Hope sighed.

Chris nodded and surveyed the piles of junk on the floor. "I would be happy to give you a hand," he said.

"I don't think there's anyone who can sort out this mess," she said, looking around her. "I can barely remember what belongs to which kid anymore." She picked up a yellow Power Ranger missing a leg and tossed it back into a colorful pile of plastic action figures. "You know, no matter how many times the kids try to explain it to me—Mystic Force, Dino Thunder, SPD—I still have no clue which Power Ranger is which. Doesn't Harvest like the SPDs?"

"Don't look at me. That's not the kind of help I was talking about. I have something much better to cheer you up," Chris said, reaching out his hand to her.

"Don't tell me there's a Dumpster outside and I can throw all of this out and start again. Now *that* would be good news," Hope said, taking his hand and standing up.

"No such luck, but I did reserve a court tonight at Penn. Want to join me?"

"Oh my God, Chris. I haven't played tennis since, since, wow, since we moved in together. Could that be true? It seems unbelievable," Hope said.

"I know. I've noticed. And now that you have me on the inside, I can get you a court whenever you want. Maybe it's time you take advantage of that and do something for yourself once in a while," he said.

"Just let me run upstairs and tell Leo. Maybe he can try to sort through some of this junk for me," she said, bounding up the stairs. "I'll change and be right down."

She was so obviously excited about getting out on the court again when she went upstairs that Leo even agreed to work on cleaning up the playroom while she was gone.

Twenty minutes later Chris and Hope pulled up to the tennis pavilion on the edge of the Penn campus. He parked right in front in the nearly deserted parking lot.

"Hey, Andy," Chris said to the white-haired man behind the front desk. "I reserved a court for nine o'clock. Which one's open?"

"Go ahead in the back, Chris," Andy said, staring at Hope and waiting for an introduction. "I've seen you around here before, right, madam?"

"Oh, this is my neighbor, Hope," Chris said.

"Hi! So nice to meet you!" she said, holding out her hand to him. He stood up to shake it. "I haven't been here for a while, even though I used to come all the time. But I'm back, thanks to Chris!"

"Come on, Hope," Chris said, leading her through the narrow space between two heavy vinyl curtains at the back of the courts to the right of the front door. After they got to a small opening on the other side with a water fountain and piles of equipment, they went through yet another curtain toward the far back court.

They dropped their coats and bags on the bench at the side of the net.

Hope pulled her dark hair into a short, low ponytail. "Now you're going to need to take it easy on me," she said, doing a few hamstring stretches.

"No way. You are not getting any mercy from me," Chris said. "Don't you remember that you're the one who used to give me a run for my money back in the day?"

Hope stretched her arms above her head before picking up her racquet and jogging onto the court to warm up.

From her first serve, she could tell that Chris wasn't playing his hardest like he used to. But she didn't care. She had missed this immensely—the chance to clear her head and challenge herself physically. It all came right back to her—that adrenaline rush, the control of her movements, her determination to win.

After a few sets, the hour was suddenly gone. Hope was sweating for the first time in months, and it took her a few minutes to catch her breath. They sat together on the narrow bench drinking from their water bottles and staring at the empty court in front of them.

"Thank you," Hope breathed. "I know you already know this, but I needed that so much. The problem is that I didn't know it."

Chris nodded. "I know all of this has been hard. Ever since we took down the walls, so much of the responsibility for the kids and the house has fallen on you—it seems like most of it, really. Maybe it will be a good thing for you when the walls go back up. You'll get your life back."

"Back?" she said. "I could never go back. You know that. This is my life now."

"Yeah, I know," he said. "Even with all that's happened, we're better off together than we are apart, right? I never would have quit my job, spent all this time with the kids."

Hope turned to Chris, her face still flushed. "Everything I wanted before, suddenly that's all changed. It's all become much clearer to me since we've been living together. I'm not saying that everything I've done is right or that I have it all figured out, but what I do know is who I am now, what I want. Does that sound silly?"

"Not at all, Hope. Not at all," Chris said.

"I guess our little commune did it to both of us. Or maybe we're just getting older. But what I'm saying is that I've learned too much, and I'm not willing to stop now. Even though," Hope said seriously, "I'm not perfect."

Chris turned to her, grinning.

"And I know I never will be," they both sang at the same time. It was a song that Shoshanna and Harvest sang at school. Hope cleared her throat, her laughter gone.

"I always want to control things so much, and I was so afraid of losing what I had that I held on too tightly. I've been working on that, letting go a little more," she said.

"No one's perfect, Hope."

She nodded and turned to face Chris again, the kids' song ringing in her ears. "I have to tell you something," she said.

"Okay," Chris said gently.

Hope took a deep breath and exhaled slowly. "One day when I was outside with all of the kids, a car came speeding down the street going the wrong way," Hope said.

Chris waited for her to continue.

"And my instinct, I mean, what I actually did, was grab only Shoshanna. I just left them, Chris, all of them. Even Ollie."

Chris shook his head.

"You wouldn't have let anything happen to them, Hope."

"But I just got lucky that nothing *did* happen. At first I thought it meant that I shouldn't be with all of them, that I cared more about Shoshanna. But now, now I realize that there's nothing more important to me than to be with the kids. All of them. I just don't know what I'll do or who I'll be without them," Hope said.

Stephanie was at the computer trying to find *Jurassic Park* party supplies for Harvest's birthday when her phone vibrated in her pocket.

She grabbed it and hit the center button and saw that she had a text.

Meet me . . .

She stared at her phone. Could he be serious? Her phone vibrated again with another message.

. . . in the playroom!

Stephanie smiled, put the phone on her desk, and headed downstairs. She walked to the front of the house and poked her head through the tarp. "You texted?"

Leo looked up and smiled. "I knew that would get you," he said.

"Leo, I . . ."

"Oh, Stephanie, I was just kidding. I thought you could help me sort through all these toys and we could talk. You know, since our spouses are out on a date?"

Stephanie sat down cross-legged on the floor across from Leo and sorted through a huge pile of teeny *Star Wars* Legos that were once the *Millennium Falcon*.

"So you want to talk?" Stephanie asked. "Let's talk."

"What can I say? I'm an idiot. I don't know what got into me, but I know that I shouldn't have done anything. I feel like I crossed the very fine line between us, and I'm sorry," Leo said, looking at Stephanie. He was holding an orange My Little Pony in his hand.

"I know. I'm responsible, too. I let it happen. Somehow I convinced myself that what we were doing was okay," Stephanie admitted. "As long as there was, you know, no cross-touching."

"It *was* fun, though," Leo said.

"Well, duh, of course it was fun," Stephanie said. "But maybe not fun enough to hurt the people we love. What would Chris and Hope do if they knew?"

"Yeah, I have wondered about that many times," Leo said, tossing the plastic pony into the box on the right labeled "Shoshanna" in thick black marker. "More than I can say."

"So we need to stop," Stephanie said.

"That would be the right thing to do, I guess," Leo said, "but you can't deny that our spouses have their own connection that we're not part of, just like we do."

"You're not saying that you think . . ." Stephanie said.

"Chris and Hope? Come on, they might be out talking about books or dissecting the grammar in the day's newspaper, but I never in a million years think either of them would step over the line, as thin as that line might be," Leo said.

"Yeah, you're right," Stephanie said. "Leo, do you think this is what marriage is supposed to be like?"

"What the hell do I know? This is the only marriage I've ever been in," Leo said. "I'm just muddling through as I go along. With some help from my very good friends. Isn't that the only thing we can do?"

Stephanie nodded slowly. "But did you ever think you'd get here? This place where we are in our lives, in our marriages?"

"No. I mean, when Hope and I got married, I didn't specifically think our lives would lead us here, to this street and this house—these houses. But that's what makes life interesting. You never know what the future is going to throw at you or how you'll respond."

"I guess I'm doing a lot of things I never thought I would," Stephanie said.

Leo picked up a plastic pizza and tossed it in the Ollie/Ted/Lu bin. "Life is just like a good menu. There are appetizers, main courses . . ." he said.

"And desserts," Stephanie said, grinning. "Don't forget the desserts."

"There are small plates that are meant to simply whet your appetite," Leo continued, smiling pointedly at Stephanie. "There are the bigger dishes that are supposed to sustain you through the day or night. You try some new things, you stick with some old favorites, and you keep what works and lose what doesn't. And most people, it seems, keep going until they figure out the combination of what most satisfies them."

"And sometimes we're hungrier than other times," Stephanie said, looking him straight in the eyes. "And we overdo it."

"So true," he said.

"So what do we do now?"

"I don't think there's anything to do. Once Yogi comes and our walls are back up, the problem will solve itself."

CHAPTER TWENTY

Celia stood at the sink letting the warm water run over the crustless white bread in her hands. She used her elbow to push the faucet and stop the flow, clenching her teeth as she squeezed the water out of the bread. She turned to the huge mound of meat next to her in the large stainless steel bowl and dropped the bread into it.

"Okay, let me think: meat, egg, salt, pepper, oregano, soaked bread, cheese, what am I missing?" Celia asked. Mark looked up from the newspaper he had spread out on the table.

"What?" he asked.

"For the meatballs, am I missing anything?"

"Oh," he said, going back to the paper. "No."

Celia hesitated with her hands hovering over the bowl. She didn't want to dig in and mix until she was sure she had everything.

"Look at this huge amount of food," Celia said, taking a step back so Mark could see if he wanted to. "It's like I'm still cooking for eleven."

"What?" Mark asked again, this time not even bothering to look up.

"I was just saying—nutmeg!" Celia said.

Mark looked up. "Nutmeg?" he asked.

"That's the ingredient I forgot. Nutmeg, where is it?" Celia asked. "Can you find it for me? My hands are all wet from the bread, and it's about to get pretty messy here."

Celia watched as Mark slowly closed the newspaper section and pushed himself up. He walked over and stood in front of Celia for a minute, as though he were trying to remember what he was doing there. He opened the cabinet where they used to keep their spices before. Now it was stocked with glasses for the wet bar and lots of Tylenol, Advil, and vitamins. No spices in sight.

"Nutmeg, nutmeg," Mark said to himself as he looked at the bottles. "What does it look like, exactly? It doesn't seem to be here."

"It's like a nut, inside a metal grater. You know," Celia said.

"I do?" Mark said, continuing to look.

"Oh, skunks," Celia said, wiping her hands on her mustard-yellow apron. "We don't have any nutmeg. We never had any nutmeg. It's Leo's nutmeg."

"Forget the nutmeg," Mark said, shutting the cabinet door and heading back to the table.

"No, I can't," Celia said, picking up her phone. "They don't taste the same without it—now that I'm used to it, that is."

Mark shook his head and went back to reading. Celia stood still and listened. She could clearly hear the television blaring through the tarp in Stephanie and Chris's house. When they lived together, they had decided early on not to watch television while they ate. Chris had protested at the time, saying he enjoyed morning television, but once they'd decided, it never came up again. She guessed Chris was taking advantage of his freedom now, or else it was too quiet in their house, too. She felt silly doing it when she could just shout through the two tarps, but she dialed Hope's number anyway.

"Hey," Hope said after the first ring. "Do you want your kids back?"

"Soon," Celia said. "Are they driving you crazy?"

"No, not at all," Hope said. "We're playing Clue, and Ollie is on my team."

"I'm making meatballs. If you want some, I can bring them on over," Celia said. "And I was wondering if I could borrow your nutmeg."

"No thanks to the meatballs. Leo is making some slow-cooked brisket or something, but yes to the nutmeg," Hope said. "Do you want me to bring it over when I walk the kids home?"

"No, I'll come get it now, if that's okay," Celia said.

"Sure," Hope said.

Celia hung up and looked at the tarp. Then she put on her coat and headed out the door.

"I'll be right back," she called over her shoulder.

At Hope's door she knocked three quick times. She could hear the kids laughing, and it took Hope a minute to answer. When she did, Celia couldn't believe the progress they'd made with their first floor. Their usual furniture was back, and Shoshanna's toys were in two neat bins—one of which looked to be filled completely with My Little Ponies. The kids were sitting around the old table that used to be there, the game board spread out in front of them. Hope must have put Ollie down on her chair when she got up because he looked adorable peering over the table at her.

"It looks great in here," Celia said. "We haven't done much yet."

"I'm having a hard time sitting still these days," Hope admitted. "I needed a project. Here, stay with the kids for a second and I'll get the nutmeg."

Celia went over to the table and walked clockwise around, kissing each child on the top of his or her head. When she got to Ollie, she stooped down and kissed his belly. He threw his head back and laughed.

"We're having meatballs tonight, little guy," she said to him. "Your favorite."

"Nooo," wailed Lu. "I hate meatballs. What are they having here? Can I stay?"

"No," Celia said firmly. Hope emerged from the basement kitchen with the grater in hand. She passed it to Celia.

"The nutmeg is inside," she said.

"Oh yeah, I know, thanks," Celia said. "Do you want me to take them now?"

"No, no, let us finish the game. We have to figure out who did it! We have it narrowed down to Colonel Mustard and Mrs. White. I'll walk them down in time for dinner, I promise," Hope said. "Your dinner, that is. Our dinner is going to be late, Leo just said. He's down there paying way more attention to his wine bottles than he is to the meat. I think the thing that bothers him most about putting the walls back up is that he's losing his wine cellar because we have to turn it back into a kitchen."

"Well, if you change your mind about the meatballs, just let me know," Celia said. "I'm making enough for all of us. Oh! And Hope, I just want to let you know that I should have a nanny within the week. I've narrowed it down to two people. I can't thank you enough for being so patient about it."

"Celia, I've told you a million times, you don't have to get a nanny I'm happy to continue to take care of all of them," Hope said. "In fact, I would prefer it."

"I know, and I appreciate that," Celia said. "But if we are really going to do this—separate, I mean—we have to make some changes. I don't know what else to do. And it will be good for you, too. You can run again, play more tennis. You'll be able to get your life back."

"Everyone keeps saying that. Celia, how can you not understand that this is my life?" Hope said, remembering her conversation with Chris.

Celia looked at the floor and didn't say anything. She was so clearly trying not to cry that Hope immediately felt sorry for pushing her about this once again.

"Okay, okay," Hope said. "Let us finish the game. It shouldn't take long."

"Thanks," Celia said, moving toward the door. She pulled her coat around her as she walked back home. When she pushed open the door, Mark wasn't at the table anymore. She had hoped he'd join her in the meatball making like he usually did, each on one side of the big bowl, squishing the meat through their hands. She thought about searching the house for him, but decided that if she didn't get started they'd be eating as late as Hope and Leo.

Celia grated some nutmeg into the pile, quickly washed her hands, and mixed, slowly, one hand moving over the other. She pulled down a frying pan and put it on the hot plate they were using until they got their kitchen back together. She formed two patties of meat to test, just to make sure the seasoning was right before she committed to it. She slowly pressed the patties with a spatula, hoping Mark would reemerge. When he didn't, she put the patties on a plate and put on her coat with the intention of heading back to Hope and Leo's. But before she touched the doorknob she stopped. This was getting ridiculous. She took a small bite and moved it around in her mouth, realizing she had no appetite at all, then removed her coat and went back to form the meatballs alone.

∼

It occurred to Celia on her way to work that she'd forgotten to freeze the meatballs—and they had been in the refrigerator for three days already. It wasn't her fault, really. She kept forgetting to take them down to the bigger freezer in the basement since they were still using the mini fridge that went with the wet bar. The meatballs wouldn't begin to fit in that tiny freezer meant only for ice. Now she wondered, would they still be any good? All that work, and nobody had eaten any. Mark had had a headache; the kids had wanted hot dogs. Even Ollie had refused them. She thought about calling Stephanie to ask her to throw them in the freezer, but she was trying so hard to get out of those habits.

As soon as her late-morning meeting let out, she decided to go home for lunch. She had been thinking about Ellen's advice since that awful day when she had felt so unclear, full of hurt and self-doubt and shame that left her numb and raw at the same time. But earlier today, standing in front of a room full of colleagues, she knew for sure that she would accept the promotion. She had left the meeting feeling surprisingly relieved, even a little bit elated.

As she got closer to Emerson, she kept repeating *meatballs, meatballs* in her head so she would remember to go right to the kitchen and take care of them. When she walked by Hope's door, she wondered who was inside and what they were doing. She still hadn't picked a nanny; none of them seemed quite right. And, really, if she held Hope up as her model, she was never going to pick anyone. But the girl with the bushy brown hair would probably be okay, she thought. She had to stop optimizing and move on.

She slowly got her keys out of her bag, hoping she'd run into Hope and Ollie. When nobody appeared, she pushed open her door. It took her only a second to realize something was missing. What was it? The room had been reconfigured so many times this last week. Oh, she realized, the couch.

Without even closing the door behind her, she walked to the place where the couch had been and sat on the floor. *Of course it had to go this way,* she thought to herself. *What other way could it have gone?* She crossed her legs and covered her face with her hands.

"What are you doing home?" Mark's voice came from behind her. She swung around to find him standing just inside the open front door. "I thought you had an important meeting."

"I did," Celia said slowly. "But I forgot to freeze the meatballs, and I thought I'd come home quick. Where's the couch?"

Mark hesitated for a split second. "Miles helped me carry it to the office. You just missed him. I, well, I want it to be with me."

"Where are you going to be?" Celia asked, looking at her hands.

Mark closed the door and came to sit next to Celia on the floor. All was quiet on the other side of the tarp, and for once Celia was glad.

"Look, Celia, I'm trying, I really am," Mark said. "But it isn't as easy as I thought it would be, or hoped it would be. And believe me, I know you're the one who should be calling the shots here. But somehow, I can't stand it. I feel like I've spent my entire life on the chairlift. You know? Letting it take me along, waiting for it to stop. And now, well, I need to make it stop. I need to get off and ski. Just for a little while."

"With her," Celia said angrily.

"No, no, not with her. I don't mean that. I mean I want to stop being in the background of my life. And I need to figure out what that means, but I can't do that without standing on my own for a little while. I'm not saying I'm leaving for good. I just want a week. Maybe two, to think, and then we can talk about it. I'll sleep at the office on the couch. We'll tell the kids I'm away on business."

"That will never work. What if you run into them?" Celia asked, narrowing her eyes.

"I won't. I'll be careful," Mark said. "I've arranged with Hope that I'll pick them up today. She's going to come get them at the office before dinner. I just want some time alone with them. I'm not going to say anything. I just want to be with them."

"Mark, please, you don't need to do this," Celia said. "We'll get past it. I thought we already were. If I can put things behind me, you certainly should be able to. I can help you."

"No, Celia, not this time. You can't," Mark said. "I need to do it on my own."

"This has got to be about her. Do you miss her?" Celia asked.

"No. But I miss who I was when I was with her. I thought that version of me would still be here, but he's not. That's what I miss," Mark said.

"How can I compete with that?" Celia said, getting up. "I can do a lot of things, but I can't make you like who you are when you're with me."

"Celia, I didn't mean it to sound like that," Mark said, reaching for her hand. She pulled it away. "Just a week, maybe two, then we'll talk."

"You seem to forget that I work in human resources. I have never, in all my years, witnessed someone walk away from something he or she thought was worth fighting for. I've seen lots of excuses and lots of sugar-coating. But I have never seen someone walk away and come back."

"I'm not walking away," Mark insisted. "I'm—"

"Well, I'm walking away now, just like I should have done when I found out," she said, putting her hand on the doorknob. She turned back quickly. "Does Hope know?"

"No, not everything," Mark said. "But I think she knows something is up."

"I can't believe this is happening," Celia said. "I thought, well, when I didn't make you leave, I thought I was being so strong. I thought I was giving you a gift."

"I think that might be part of the problem," Mark said.

As soon as Hope heard Leo turn his key in the lock, she was on her feet. The kids were playing video games, and Ollie was trying to grab the remotes out of the bigger kids' hands.

"What's up?" Leo asked as Hope met him before he was even fully in the door.

"My stomach is upset," she whispered. "I have to go to the bathroom."

"Nice to see you, too," Leo said, taking off the spring jacket he had pulled out of the storage bin that morning.

"Will you watch them?" Hope asked.

"Sure," Leo said, hanging his jacket on the hook and joining the kids in front of the television.

Hope ran up the stairs two at a time. She dug around in her drawer for the plastic bag, but then she remembered: Stephanie had stolen her last pregnancy test months ago. As she turned around, wondering if she could sneak out the back door and run to the store, she saw the shoe box in the top of her open closet. Her other hiding place, of course! The one she'd used when she was trying to get pregnant with Shoshanna so many years ago.

She slid a chair over to the closet and reached on to the shelf. Inside the box, under the satin dress shoes she wore once a year, under the tissue paper beneath them, was a box with one last pregnancy test.

She went to the bathroom and closed the door. She looked at the box and searched for a date: the test had expired well over a year ago. She unwrapped it anyway and peed on it; she didn't even hesitate, putting the stick back on the sink and waiting, hoping Leo had the kids under control. Her period was three days late, totally unusual for her, and she needed to know.

She picked up the stick and watched as the sign emerged in the center of the white window. She breathed a long sigh of relief: negative. She threw the garbage away, pulled up her pants, and skipped down the stairs.

Leo had one of the remotes in his hand and was playing Sonic Heroes against Ted, totally ignoring the other kids. Ollie was standing on the recliner. Hope reached him just as he gave it a bit too much weight and it pushed back, throwing him off balance. Hope scooped him up, about to yell at Leo, but then she remembered the test. Everything was going to be fine.

A key turned in the lock, and Hope and Leo looked at each other before looking back at the door. Celia opened it sheepishly, poking her head in ahead of her body.

"Mind if I come in?" she asked, her voice hoarse.

"Of course, come in, come in," Hope said, carrying Ollie over to her. As soon as she got closer, Hope could see that Celia's eyes were so swollen that they were almost shut. "Are you sick? Are you having an allergic reaction?"

Celia didn't answer. She accepted Ollie from Hope and walked to an empty chair and sat. Leo had already gone back to the game.

"What's going on?" Hope prompted. "Do you need Benadryl or something?"

Celia put Ollie down and motioned for Hope to follow her to the small table.

"Mark's gone," she said.

"You know, when he wanted to see the kids today and had me pick them up at his office, I wondered if there was something going on," Hope said, standing close to Celia and leaning on the table. "So you couldn't forgive him, and you asked him to leave. I don't blame you one bit. In fact, I wasn't sure how you could stand—"

"No, Hope, you don't get it," Celia said, tears squeezing out of her swollen eyes. "I wanted him to stay. He left. He left me."

"What? Are you sure? How can that be?" Hope asked.

"Well, he claims he just needs a little time," Celia said dismissively. "He claims he's been on the chairlift too long, and now he wants to ski. He said that he needs to do it on his own."

"Maybe he means all of that," Hope said, suddenly worried that Celia's eyes were going to get so swollen that she wouldn't be able to open them at all. She wanted to rush down to the kitchen to get a cold compress, but she didn't want to leave her. "He must feel guilty about what happened. Maybe he just needs to process it. How could he leave all of you?"

"Are you okay?" Leo asked, coming up to the table. Hope glanced at the kids. Shoshanna was trying to teach Ollie how to work the remote while she played against Ted.

"Mark's gone," Hope said.

"What?" Leo asked.

"The worst part is that he took the couch with him," Celia said.

"Oh," Hope and Leo said at the same time.

The tarp rustled. Hope walked to the back of the house and peered around it into Stephanie's house. Stephanie was right there. Hope smiled, looking behind her to the room itself. It was a mess, nearly unrecognizable, and yet so familiar at the same time.

"Come on over," Hope said quietly. "We have a crisis."

Stephanie raised her eyebrows as if to ask if she could come through the tarp. Hope held it back to make room for her. Chris looked up from the evening news and slid in behind Stephanie.

"I was just about to come get Harvest," Stephanie said.

"Sure you were," Hope said, smiling.

"Oh my God, are you okay?" Stephanie asked as soon as she saw Celia. She sprinted back through the tarp and ran water over a paper towel. When she came back, she pressed it gently to Celia's eyes, just like she would do for Harvest. Celia let her.

While Celia rehashed the story for everyone, Hope walked the length of the tarp, listening. She could see that all she'd have to do was tug a little to loosen it.

"Can I have dinner with you guys tonight?" Celia said to no one in particular. "I can't stand to be in that house alone right now."

Hope reached up and tugged, and a corner of the tarp fell away.

"Yes, absolutely," Stephanie said. "We were just going to order pizza, I think. You can eat with us."

Hope moved down the line, closer to the table where everyone was standing, tugging and loosening, tugging and loosening, and soon the tarp was attached by only the last eight feet or so. Nobody said anything. Nobody seemed to notice. Or at least they pretended not to notice.

"Or you can eat here," Leo said. "I have a great Italian red I want to try. I was thinking we'd have some ravioli or something. Tomato sauce will be perfect with the wine."

Hope pulled down the last of the tarp, letting it drop to the floor. Suddenly the room seemed so big and open. So full. Hope waited for someone to say something. Chris walked right over the imaginary line to reach the drawer in his kitchen where he kept the menus, found the one for the little Italian place around the corner, and brought it back without a word.

"Here, we can order from this place," Chris said, handing the menu to Leo. "The kids can have pizza, and we can order ravioli and maybe some spaghetti and meatballs."

Hope was already halfway through pulling the tarp down between Celia's and Stephanie and Chris's.

"Meatballs!" Celia said. "We can have meatballs. I have a ton from the other night."

She turned and walked through Stephanie and Chris's to where Hope was standing, half expecting someone to yell at her. Celia smiled and kept walking. She walked right through the now open space into her own house, bent down at the small refrigerator, and pulled out two plastic containers full of meatballs and sauce. Chris was already at his stove putting two big pots of water on to boil. Leo came up from his kitchen with three boxes of fancy spaghetti and two bottles of red wine.

"We're going to need those old card tables we use outside," Chris said. "Where are they? Does anyone know?"

"I think they're in my basement," Celia said. "In the back left corner near the freezer."

Chris sprinted over and down and was back in a minute with a card table under each arm. He opened the first, setting it up next to his own smaller table. He did the same with the other, putting it next to the first one. Stephanie was right there with the tablecloth they had used for the big table. It fit well enough.

"Seven, eight, nine, ten, el—" Stephanie started counting to make sure they had enough places.

"Ten," Celia said firmly, getting the plates from her cabinet and putting them around the table.

Leo heated the meatballs, Stephanie threw together some garlic bread, Chris made a salad.

"Hey, I have brownies for dessert," Hope announced. "I made them today. From scratch."

"No way," Stephanie said. "I didn't think you knew how to do that."

"The kids helped me," Hope said proudly.

"Are we living together again?" Ted asked as he came to the table and took the chair that best corresponded to where he used to sit around the big table. All the other kids did the same. Hope lifted Ollie into his high chair and strapped him in.

Nobody answered Ted's question as they placed the steaming food on the table in huge bowls with plenty of serving spoons. Hope went around the table giving each child just what he or she wanted without having to ask.

They had been eating for only a few minutes when the doorbell rang. All movement and noise came to a halt as everyone looked up, trying to figure out which bell it was. It rang again. It was coming from Hope and Leo's door. Chris imagined it must be Mark, thinking better of his decision. How could he leave his family like that? How could he leave all of them? Celia, Stephanie, and Leo were all sure it was Mary.

She'd been more attached to Hope these last few days, and she probably needed someone to open her tea canister for her or figure out why her flashlight wasn't working. Hope didn't even think about who it might be as she jumped up from her chair.

"No, wait," Celia called.

But it was too late. Hope was already there, pulling her door wide open.

ACKNOWLEDGMENTS

This book wouldn't exist without my friend, neighbor, and brilliantly creative writing partner Melissa DePino, who turned to me one day years ago and asked, "Do you want to write a novel together?" I am so glad I said yes. Some of my absolute favorite moments were getting the book back after she wrote a chapter to see how she had moved the story forward. I can't wait to collaborate with her again.

I want to thank our amazing agent, Uwe Stender, who, even after working with me for over ten years, continues to surprise and delight me with his insights and greatness. Thank you to everyone else at TriadaUS including Brent Taylor, Laura Crockett, and Mallory Brown.

Thank you to our wonderful editor, Jodi Warshaw at Lake Union, for wanting to publish *Pretty Little World* and embark on a second adventure with me. I am so grateful.

Thank you to the Lake Union team including our smart and thoughtful developmental editor, Jenna Free; our meticulous copyeditor, Renee Johnson; our careful proofreader, Nick Allison; and our fabulous cover designer, Emily Mahon. Thank you to Kathleen Carter Zrelak, Dennelle Catlett, and Jeff Umbro, who have worked so closely with me this last year to help get the word out about *The Restaurant Critic's Wife*. They are the absolute best.

Jennifer Weiner has continued to cheer me on, and I tell her all the time I won't ever be able to thank her enough but I keep trying—so, thank you! Thank you also to everyone who has supported me along the way including Ivy Gilbert, Simona Gross, Melissa Jensen, Nika Haase, Doug Cooper, Mary McManus, Joanna Pulcini-Ascaso, Meghan Burnett, Amy Einhorn, Kathleen Woodberry, Maureen Fitzgerald, Andrea Cipriani Mecchi, Petula Dvorak, Leah Kellar, Lisa Kozleski, Dawn Davenport, Jennifer Mansfield, Michelle and Ofer Shlomo, Jane Greer, Sarah Pekkanen, Elin Hilderbrand, and Elisabeth Egan. Thank you to all my Philadelphia neighbors both past and present. And thank you to my family—my incredibly supportive husband, Craig LaBan; my generous and loving kids, Alice and Arthur; my extremely encouraging in-laws Joyce and Myron LaBan; my brothers- and sisters-in-law Patty Rich and Terry LaBan, and Amy LaBan and Eric Meyers; my cousins Stacey Picket Cunitz and Lauren Kozloff Sinrod; and my Aunt Fran Whitehall. Thank you also to the most supportive and loving parents I ever could have asked for, Barbara and Arthur Trostler, who I wish could be here to read this book.

—E.L.

~

When we started this book many years ago as friends and neighbors, I couldn't imagine the day when it would actually be in print. But here it is, and the person I want to give the most thanks to is my talented, kind friend and coauthor, Elizabeth LaBan. You gave me so much: the confidence to write, the amazing experience of collaborating so effectively that I no longer know who wrote what, and the fun and excitement of never knowing what you would come up with next. This was a true team effort, and I am so very grateful to be on your team.

I am also grateful to our persistent agent, Uwe Stender at TriadaUS, who always believed in the story of Emerson Street, and didn't give up until it found its way into print. Thank you, Jodi Warshaw at Lake Union Publishing, our talented editor. I am afraid that you have spoiled me forever to other editors. You knew exactly what needed to be adjusted to make the story richer and more full of life. Thank you to our developmental editor, Jenna Free; our meticulous copyeditor, Renee Johnson; our proofreader, Nick Allison; and Emily Mahon, our cover designer.

To my life, my loves, my children, Drew and Luke. You are always my inspiration. To Doug Cooper, who is both a great father to them— the best I could ever ask for—and friend to me.

Thank you to my writing muses: my mother, Catherine, and my sister Lauren. I can only hope to be able to continue to put as much passion into my writing as you both do.

To my father, Andrew, my sister Shayna, and my other "sister" Theresa for always believing that I could do it. To my grandmother, who I wish could be here to see my name in print.

To my everyday muses: Annemarie Boyan, Kathy Martin, Nancy McDonald, Nyeema Watson, Sharon Ravitch, Amy Brueck, Jane Shore, Molly Weingart, Jenny Raphael, Liz Trasmundi, and Betsy Lau. The next one is for you.

Thank you, Jane Abrams, from the bottom of my heart.

And to all the neighbors with whom I spent many years after my children were born. Those were some of the best years of my life. They were beautiful and messy and sometimes heartbreaking, but always real and alive, and I will always cherish them.

—M.D.

ABOUT THE AUTHORS

Photos © 2016 Andrea Cipriani Mecchi

Elizabeth LaBan is the author of *The Restaurant Critic's Wife*; *The Tragedy Paper*, which has been translated into eleven languages; and *The Grandparents Handbook*, which has been translated into seven languages. She lives in Philadelphia with her restaurant-critic husband and two children.

Melissa DePino is a former high school English teacher and founding partner, principal, and editorial director of Leapfrog Group, a branding and marketing firm for nonprofits. She grew up in the suburbs of Philadelphia and earned degrees at both Villanova and Temple Universities. She lives in Center City, Philadelphia, with her two sons. *Pretty Little World* is her first novel.